P9-EIG-178

⁶/¹⁴

THE ANARCHIST

THE ANARCHIST

JOANNA HIGGINS

The Permanent Press
Sag Harbor, NY 11963

This is a work of fiction based upon historical events. Although these events, as depicted, are true to history in so far as I have been able to make them, the historical figures are imaginatively portrayed. In some instances names have been changed.

For information, address:
    The Permanent Press
    4170 Noyac Road
    Sag Harbor, NY 11963
    www.thepermanentpress.com

Library of Congress Cataloging-in-Publication Data

Higgins, Joanna—
    The anarchist / Joanna Higgins.
        pages cm
    ISBN 978-1-57962-356-2
        1. Anarchism—Fiction. 2. United States—Social
    conditions—1865–1918—Fiction. 3. United States—
    Politics and government—1901–1953—Fiction. I. Title.

PS3558.I3574A53 2014
813'.54—dc23   2013048496

Printed in the United States of America

For my mother
in memoriam
And for Jerry, as always

"Will the Czolgosz tragedy haunt me to the end of my days?" I kept asking myself.

—EMMA GOLDMAN, *Living My Life*, Vol. I

An·arch·ism (an'er-kiz'm), *n*. [<anarchy + *-ism*]. 1. the theory that all forms of government interfere unjustly with individual liberty and are therefore undesirable. 2. resistance, sometimes by terrorism, to organized government.

—*Webster's New World Dictionary
of the English Language*,
College Edition

1872

MARUSHA

I do not want to go. There are plum blossoms in the village and the air is soft. Who can leave such blossoms? But Misiak comes for us in his pony cart and we climb in, with our bundles. In the fields others are planting potatoes. They straighten to wave hats and kerchiefs. Another one leaving for America! My two boys are so proud. They wave back and shout farewell. I tell myself to be like that. Look to future. What is here for my boys but the kaiser's army? So I call good-bye! God be with you! May we meet in heaven!

Misiak's pony trots on, and in time we come to Zwiebodzin. This village is larger than our own, but Misiak guides his pony with confidence. Soon we are at the railway depot. It is a pity, Misiak tells me, that he is so old or he would come along too. I laugh and blush, but I know he means the words decorously. In my heart I wish he could come with us. I am frightened now. There is much noise from carts and station people and travelers. Misiak takes us inside the depot and I buy tickets for myself and my two boys. These tickets will allow us to go to Hamburg. But Misiak tells me we must change trains in Berlin first. I fear I will not be able to do this and begin to cry in front of my children. "Madam," he says, "your husband and eldest son await you in America. All will be well, God willing."

As our train leaves the depot, Misiak stands next to his cart with his cap over his heart. I do not wish to cry again so I open our basket and find bread and raspberry jam.

Jacek and Adam sit close as we watch our homeland pass. The fields are large. The earth is almost black. There are windbreaks of poplars and every so often a sugar factory for the sugar beets. Soon Jacek and Adam sleep. I do not.

There are many houses in Berlin, and my breath comes fast. Jacek begins to cry. "Hush!" I say roughly. This is not my way and I ask forgiveness. When an official passes in the corridor, I do as our priest told me. I reach and grip the sleeve of his uniform and show him the note written in Polish and German by our priest. The official tells me in Polish to wait in our seat. My heart beats so. Everyone else leaves the train, but there we sit. He will not return! The train will go on with us on it! I hold my boys' hands so hard. At last the official does return—a good omen! He himself takes us to another train and waits while we climb into a carriage. I turn to thank him, but he is no longer there. Like angel, I think. As before, we find a bench and sit close to one another. My hands tremble for a long while.

In Hamburg I must find a boarding house for one day and one night's stay. I take another note from the pocket sewn inside my jacket and show it to a man who has a horse and carriage. Only then I see that both horse and carriage are too fine. He points to a poor-looking carriage and we walk there. Mother of Mary, do not let this one rob us! I show the driver my note and we climb inside. There is dirt on the floor. From another pocket I take out a German coin and hold it.

The boarding house he brings us to is not a good place. I see this at once. Three men standing outside it do not lift their hats, but they laugh and say something in German. My husband warned me about such places, so we walk quickly away. And then, by the grace of God and the help of His Mother Mary, I find a good place for us. There is a flowerpot holding red and white flowers. The door is green. Boldly I ring the bell. Inside, I smell the kind of soap we use at home. My children and I sleep through the day, as we never have before.

The next morning, again with Our Lady's help, we find our way to the harbor. The ships! They are like big buildings! In the right shed I show my money for a second-cabin ticket. The clerk points to a German word on a chart. "You want instead?" he says in Polish. I know this word. It means the bottom of the ship. "No!" I say. "Second cabin!" This is what my husband advised. In the bottom of the ship, he wrote, you lie like pigs in waste. The clerk holds German money in the air. "I give you," he says, "if you go steerage." I refuse. He is angered with me. A man and a woman and a young boy stand waiting nearby. They are watching us. The woman comes up to me. "Please," she says in Polish, "our son is ill." I look at the boy, a child of perhaps eight. He does not look ill, but illness can deceive. I turn to the clerk and nod. The family rushes forward as the clerk gives me the German marks. I put this money in my hidden pocket as well as the money I just saved. Perhaps my husband will not be angry with me. Then I lead my boys to a long line. The ones for cabins are shorter. The family with the ill boy stands in one. The boy plays with a ball on a string. What is twenty-nine days, I think.

What is twenty-nine days? Time enough in which to die. By the third day I fear for the child in my womb. I am sick. The thin cabbage soup that sloshes from its vat onto the floor sickens me further. There is vomit as well on the floor and excrement from diarrhea. There must be three hundred of us here, but only two water closets, so naturally people cannot help themselves. Jacek and Adam are sick. I beg for a doctor but one does not come. Our large room tips back and forth and we with it. At first I count days. One, then three, then seven—a week! After that I no longer count. It becomes a single night without end. I beg Our Lady, and one day sunlight enters our large room. The room no longer tilts. Soup no longer sloshes. My two boys are still alive. The child in my womb moves. By the grace of God we live. Someone plays a harmonica. Someone else, an accordion. Coins drop down upon us from the open hatch. Also sweets. Above us, passengers look down as if from the white clouds of heaven. I imagine I see the family with the ill boy, but perhaps I am mistaken for my eyes are used to dimness, not light. But I do see how people hold handkerchiefs to their faces at the stench of us. Someone closes the hatch and it is dark once more. Again the room tilts and bucks. We stumble to our cot and remain there. But that light has given me hope that we will live to enter America.

And so we do, on the twenty-eighth day of June, 1872, in the year of Our Lord.

In the place called Castle Garden, I sit for a moment on a small barrel, but an old woman scolds me in Polish. "Get up! Get up! If they see you are weak, they send you back. Up! Keep moving! You see? They mark the coats of those they want to send back to the kaiser."

We walk on. There is much noise and confusion and we are so dirty. This is shameful, to enter America this way. But so many are like us that I soon forget the shame. There is something worse—my fear that the officials will find us unworthy of America. They shout at us in Russian and German and Polish and in languages I do not know. We stand a long time in a line only to learn that it is the wrong one. Jacek and Adam look so small and pale. I pray that they will not be sick here. My basket is empty of food, and they are hungry. But they do not cry now, my boys, and I am proud of them even though I know that pride is a terrible sin. It is a small pride, I explain to Our Lady. It is because they are so little and already becoming wise. A long while later, we reach the desk of three officials. One looks into our eyes, another into our mouths. There is a piece of chalk on the table such as a tailor might use. At the next table an old man is weeping as he shows one official a handful of coins. This must not be enough, for another official marks the back of the old man's coat. I am asked in Polish who will care for us in America. My hand shakes as I show the letter I have carried near my heart. "My husband! My husband and son in Detroit, Michigan!" "Is he here to meet you?" "No, no, I must travel some more!" I show the American money from my husband. I tell them he has work in America. He works for the city of Detroit!

Someone directs us to the railway line, and we pass a mesh pen where people wait. What for, I do not know until I see the chalk mark on one's back. I walk faster, Jacek and Adam trotting like Misiak's pony alongside me. From a woman selling near the train, I buy a loaf of American bread and a piece of cheese. A boy appears and asks to help us find a room. My husband wrote that these boys only wish to rob you. "No!" I say in Polish. "Leave us!" I am shouting, but no one appears to care.

In the train carriage there is a bench for us. There is American air to breathe. I am overcome with joy and cannot help tears. Later when I think of heaven, I see this train carriage with its benches and open windows.

Leon, our fourth son, is born in a brick house in a new settlement just outside the city of Detroit. Our house is one of only two brick houses in our parish. We live on the first floor, another family on the second, and our land-lady and her daughter on the third floor. I hang laundry in the backyard, and when I see our travel clothes and smell their clean smell, I remember to thank God, Our Lady, and the Saints. Four sons! A husband with a job! Yes, he works in the sewers, and each day I must wash filth from his clothes, but he has work. I am strong and take in washing and so add to our savings. When my boys are ill, I know how to make them well. For Easter and Christmas we have ham and sausages, raisins and fruits. My boy Leon, at three years of age, speaks many English words. So, all is a miracle. This I know.

But then my husband wishes to work in light and air. He fears cave-ins or being drowned because of some drunkard's stupidity. This I understand, for when he talks to me about the darkness and foulness, I remember the belly of the ship that brought us to America. We will journey north, he says. There is work in the forests and lumberyards. They call for men even in Prussia.

I say farewell to people at church and shake like a poplar in wind as I pack food and clothing. From our train window, we look out at settlements little more than shacks built on heaps of sawdust in small clearings. My husband sits with one hand on each knee. His fingers are knobbed and swollen. How can he work, with those hands? And in such woods! In the Detroit railway carriage, I say my rosary. To the right of the train is a lake like the ocean. To the left is forest. At times, the forest comes right up to the tracks. So the train squeezes between woods and lake.

In the settlement of Rogers City, my husband works for a German named Molitor who owns much land. But he pays only in scrip and is without shame. No woman in the settlement, young or old, is safe. He races his stallions along the roads. He wears a blue German uniform with sash and sword and tells everyone he is a son of the kaiser. We come so far only to find, here, the kaiser again? How can this be? That winter, when the snakes are all asleep, my husband works with a gang cutting down trees. In the summer, he builds log roads. In our house I keep our door barred day and night. I think often of the brick house in Detroit.

One day Molitor and his clerk are found shot in the back of Molitor's store. Conspirators, it is said, did this. Soon after, my husband says we are going south, to the town of Alpena, on the big lake. So we go, and he finds work stripping logs. His fingers swell even more.

In Alpena there is a fine church and also a good school taught by nuns. My Leon is so smart, the nuns give him stars on his work. But I am tired and it is not so easy to work. Still, I take in laundry, though not so much as before. When my husband tells me he wants to move again, I say no. I don't feel so good. Also, here, the nuns will teach our children.

But he wants to go. He wants to farm, with those hands of his. Stripping logs, he says, is no good. I remind him of the story of the *baba* who had it so good she went out and bought a pig and then this pig makes dirt everywhere. But my husband does not listen. He gives notice at the lumber mill and we travel north again, to the village of Posen. This is how the Germans call it. We call it by our name, Poznan, like in the old country. On our farm there is too much for me to do. I always thought I could work forever. Now I am tired all the time. I think I am dying but I say nothing to my husband. I do not want him to worry. In my heart there is fear for our children and another baby I will soon have, God willing. Eight, now! How will he care for them? And my Leon needs books and learning or he will not be happy. I pray to Our Lady, but the day comes when I cannot pray much. There is fog around me and I want to sleep. Sometimes I hear angels singing. Is it possible they come for me? Let it be so! With my last strength I give birth once more and tell my children to study and be learned. Then they are there, my angels, and I go.

1886

CARTER "THE EAGLE" HARRISON

So far it ain't much. Fifty, sixty people gathered in a corner of Haymarket Square, which can hold a couple thousand. I suppose the damn agitators were expecting a lot more. Well, I might get home early tonight, after all. There's a whippy wind blowing in. There's a big storm cloud, looks painted on there, over the warehouses to the west, with sunset light spiking up out of the top. That'll do the job on 'em, probably. All to the good. But I don't blame the hands for wanting better. They have it damn hard, working fourteen hours straight or more. But hell, for agitators to cause all kind of ruckus ain't right, either. Take what happened out at the McCormick Works yesterday. A damn mess. A strike going on out there, and scabs hired, so there's bound to be trouble, it being May Day and the reds out in force. This Spies fellow talking right now was out there, standing atop a flatbed car in front of a planing mill and factory, not far from McCormick's. In my opinion there's nothing wrong with a speech if it's not the inflaming kind. What the hell, it lets off steam, and we're supposed to be able to *talk* in this country, right?

Also, I have to agree with a lot of their demands, like the eight-hour day. But Spies got a little wild, as he is wont to do, and then somebody in the crowd heaved a rock at a window, and the crowd turned into a mob smashing up the lumber place with rocks and bricks. Someone from the Lumber Shovers' union came out and told them to calm down. The company already agreed to *pay* ten hours' wages for eight hours' work. But then an agitator threw a brick at him. Some in the crowd grabbed the hooligan, and things settled until McCormick's started letting out, and there's August Spies, up on that freight car, waving his slouch hat in firebrand fashion. And so the merriment starts up again. *Get the scabs! Kill the scabs!* There's more brick throwing and craziness and then shooting, them or us, it's not sorted out yet, but people died, some women, too, and little ones, and now we got tonight to get through.

The thing I'd like to say to Mr. Spies right now is, "Sir, this is *my* city—not yours—and it ain't going to be destroyed on my watch. This I vow." Oh hell, the strangeness of this time we're in. Spies, I learned through my own spies, comes from good family back in Germany. His father was some official, and wealthy relatives sent him here to learn the furniture business. But then what? Working as a hand at some job in New York, he gets sick and quits. After that, it's the Socialist Labor Party for him. Then for some reason he comes out here and sticks in Chicago, starts up a newspaper, prints pamphlets, and makes my life miserable. This is exactly why I'm for reform. To take away their reasons for complaint and this damn agitation all the time.

People tell me I resemble Bobby E. Lee, which is a compliment, but I'm not about to be losing any war. Funny thing—*his* name is Spies, but tonight my boys and I are the spies, and dressed exactly like them, slouch hats and all. Ha ha, because here's another thing that's not exactly funny, though is, in a way. People tell me I'm too soft on the reds so maybe I'm one of them after all.

Sure am, tonight. Keeping an eagle eye on it all.

One of my boys leans in close and says, "That's German for *revenge,* Mayor."

It's the word they're shouting now, people in the crowd in front of the wagon. Then somebody yells, "Hang him!" Meaning who?—McCormick? A little boy repeats the words *hang him*, and people laugh. And now, more people are entering from Randolph Street and Desplains and Halstead. Spies is spieling in German and English, and who knows what all he's saying in German, a bellicose language if ever I heard one. See, that's the thing that riles me. These people, these anarchists and communists and who knows what all, have their own newspapers and militias and languages just like separate countries. My boy Otto here, he translated a notice about tonight's meeting in their *Arbeiter-Zeitung*. A lot of fancy puffed words that end with, *To arms we call you, to arms!*

More bellicosity! *To arms.* Now, they'll tell you that their outfit's a peaceable one, but when you've got words like that being slung around, what's a man to think? Right now, for instance, Spies is rushing into a charge so pleasing to him, probably, he can't, or won't, halt the damn words—in English, as if for my very own benefit. "At McCormick's, police again shooting down and clubbing workingmen! Why? Because the police are the *hirelings,* the *blood*hounds of the masters, and the masters do not want you to ask for anything, do not want you to organize or have any power. You are only *hands* to them, not men, and as such you have *no* rights. No right to think for yourselves, to work decent hours that will allow you time for yourselves. Time to think, to read, to rest. Friends! The eight-hour workday is only the *tip* of the iceberg!"

Apart from the raucous fellows right near the wagon, though, most of the folks listening look a little like people in church who've heard the same message all too often. Either that or they're dead tired. If I'm a lucky man, Spies is going to lose his voice, folks'll be in bed soon, and I'll be home, enjoying a cigar.

I was right. It is going to storm. Fine needles of rain are blowing in on us now, and folks are leaving. Good. Spies is losing them, and he knows it. Oh hell, now he's calling someone else up to speak, hoping, I suppose, to whet curiosity and draw folks back.

"Who's that, Otto?"

"Albert Parsons, sir. Supposedly he can trace his ancestry back to the Mayflower."

Leave it to my own little bloodhound. Otto knows everything about everything where these folks are concerned. He should. He told me he was in their camp up until a year ago or so. It's possible he's a spy for their side as well. But what can I do? I need him.

So—Mr. Parsons. Good-looking fellow. No slouch hat. Nice head of hair. Nice curve to the eyebrows, from what I can see. Looks like a banker type. Where do they get these fellows? More to the point—who's lining their pockets?

And quite the scholarly one. . . . *Passion needs to be checked by rationality. Force is barbaric, a violation of every natural right. Only reason can save us* . . . Still, it's dead dull stuff, serving only to drive more folks away. All to the good! Keep talking! Even my boys look ready to drop.

"So, Otto, if reason can save us from boredom, I say it's reasonable to be heading home about now. What say you?"

Otto laughs and passes along the wit.

Ah, be done with it, man! I need my cigar.

Mr. Parsons finally jumps down from the wagon, hurrah, boys, but hell's bells, if there's not *another* one climbing up, and it's raining harder now.

"Who's *that* undernourished fellow?"

Otto gives his pursy smile. "Big Sam Fielden, sir. Englishman. Runs his own stone yard."

"Voice a stone splitter, too."

So. A businessman. Body like two barrels roped together. But the words pure preacher larding on the *light* and *darkness* and *redemption*. My boys are hunched up in this rain. Should do them a good turn and let 'em go, for tonight.

So I say, "We'll be going, boys, but first I want to stop at Bonfield's station house."

We do that, and I tell Captain Bonfield that it seems like we worried for naught. Bonfield gives me a look I can't read and tells me to head home. He didn't know I was even out there, he says. "What if you was recognized, Mr. Mayor?"

"What if!"

"You're too trusting. You know what those damn anarchists want, right? Mayhem and revolution! You go on home now, Mr. Harrison. I got my boys keeping an eye out."

Outside, I have second thoughts. My boys tag after me as I head back to the square. A watched pot don't boil, it's said. The cigar can wait.

Ah! Thunder now. "Just a few more words!" Big Sam pleads, trying to draw back the deserters. They're leaving by the score. ". . . You know how the capitalist papers always charge socialists with cowardice, saying we never stay around for real danger, well, here you are, despite all those threats yesterday. Despite the storm. Here you are and here you'll remain until ready to leave on your own . . . Better to die a hero than be starved on sixty cents a day as a wage slave!"

"Don't exactly look starved to me."

My boys don't laugh. "All right, boys. All right." I start walking toward Desplains. Folks are running past us, soaked to the skin.

But then—What the hell?

Police. A whole phalanx of them entering the square from Randolph Street. My boys and I swing around to watch them marching in, all silent. They've got clubs in hand. Who the hell ordered it? Bonfield? One of them commands Big Sam to get down off the wagon and then yells at folks to disperse.

Well, hell, they already were, weren't they?

Fielden says something before jumping off the wagon.

Then some snaky thing comes flying down from a warehouse above Crane's Alley. It's burning like the fuse of a rocket and sputtering, and it lands right amid the police. An explosion shakes buildings all around us, and we drop to the ground. Broken glass flails us, and there's nothing but screaming. My boys pull me up, wanting to get the hell out of there, but I head toward the stricken column, now just a heap. My boys gang atop me as the night turns into a grid of red streaks coming from all sides. Then we're crawling over fallen bodies strewn along Desplains. I pull back, there's a wounded child—"It's his leg," I yell—but my boys are too much for me. They got me in some hard grip and are dragging me along like some damn sack, and there's a sickness in my gut, and I'm screaming, *Damn it all to hell!* but can't even hear my own damn words.

EMMA

On our Shabbat table are *cotellets* of chopped beef with rice, *vareniki* stuffed with sweetmeats, cabbage in butter sauce, and three kinds of bread, but I have no appetite. My father is enjoying this meal. So is our guest, Mrs. Lindorf. But the back of my head is aching again with its ghost pains. This happens sometimes when I look at my father. It is as if the bone there remembers. He has struck me only twice, here in America. In Saint Petersburg, it was often, once even for studying a French grammar. *Girls should not waste time on such foolishness! Learn to make gefilte fish and cut noodles. Learn to take care of babies. That is all you need to know.* My sister Helena he loves. Well, everyone loves Lenka. She is beautiful and kind and pleasing in every way. I am . . . I don't know what I am. *Maybe from the pig woman in the market. You are no child of mine!*

"Eat," he tells me now in Russian. "What is wrong with you? The food is not good enough?"

I take one of the *vareniki* Mother and I made yesterday. She has taught me well. The dough is thin and tender, not heavy like some. The filling of sweetmeats is not overly sweet.

"She quits her job at Garson and Mayer's!" Speaking to our guest Mrs. Lindorf, he has switched to German. "Can you imagine? She quits because of some hand there who faints. *Acht!* What a reason!"

Hand. We are hands now. It's true. The heavy ulster fabric slipping under the needle and framed by my hands was all I could see when I closed my eyes at night. But to the foreman at Garson and Mayer's we were something more than merely *hands*. I blush to remember. To get a machine near a window, one needed to find certain favor in the foreman's eyes. Do I tell my father this? No, because he will not believe it. Or else he will blame me for something I never would do.

"She thinks that in this America jobs grow like weeds everywhere!"

No, though I did find another job right away, a better paying one at Rubinstein's, and there met Jacob Kershner. And now Jacob, my Yakov, staying with us! A boarder. This still astonishes me. To have him so near! Does Father really not see what is before his eyes? In Saint Petersburg, he missed nothing. In Saint Petersburg, he managed a dry goods shop. Here, in Rochester, he wears carpet slippers and plays cards, often with Yakov. It is my sister Helena and I who support him now. I cannot understand why he is still so wrathful to me. Does it become habit? Does a person *need* to be wrathful?

And somehow he must equate my small uprising at Garson and Mayer's with what happened at the Haymarket. "You don't kill the goose that lays the golden egg, yes?" he is saying to Mrs. Lindorf. "Those men were fools."

"I agree," Mrs. Lindorf says. "They should be convicted."

He slips back into Russian, addressing me. "Now don't you take their side. You know nothing about it."

We have been through this before, of course. And I know that neutrality has always come hard for him. Also, the Haymarket defendants have been shaming our German community these past months, the newspapers filled with their names and backgrounds, and there it is, another excuse for my father's self-righteous rage. I have kept quiet on this topic at other Shabbat meals, not wanting to ruin them with argument, but something about Mrs. Lindorf rubs me wrong. She is a widow, younger than my mother, and she has inherited money and so can afford to dress in Italian velvet. But that's not it. I don't care what people put on their backs if there is some . . . worthiness. Some goodness of heart. Mother has that. Certainly Helena. Mrs. Lindorf's heart isn't a heart at all, I suspect, but one of those puff mushrooms filled with black spores. And her mind, well, that's a cheese full of holes.

So I hear myself saying, "Responsible people"—I stress the word *responsible* for Mrs. Lindorf's benefit—"are saying that the housepainter Gilmer was in the pay of the police, so naturally he'll say whatever they want him to say."

"And the papers *you* read are in the pay of crackpots," Father says, unloosing the rage.

"There is no proof of that! It's not clear at all who threw the bomb in Chicago. It might have been a Pinkerton or a provocateur."

"They drill with weapons, those secret societies! They are giving us all a bad name. Soon, pogroms here, wait and see!"

That is his greatest fear—that the persecutions will follow us from Russia. "They drill with weapons," I say, "because they need to protect themselves."

"And throw bombs at the police. What kind of protection is that?"

"Your father is right, Emma," Mrs. Lindorf says. "They are murderers. They deserve to be hanged." Mother and Helena remain silent, as always, during such so-called discussions.

"True!" Father adds. "And then all that stupidity may end for good."

"You're wrong," I say. "Then it will just begin." I look at Yakov, pale, narrow-faced Yakov, blue eyelids all but trembling. To him as much as to Father and Mrs. Lindorf, I say, "Neebe was at a picnic, not even at the Haymarket. Parsons was at a saloon called Zepf's, with his wife and another friend when the bomb was thrown. And Spies as well, I think. And one man—Schwab—he was at another meeting altogether. Fielden, Sam Fielden was shot twice, far from where the bomb was thrown. And Engel, where was he? He was at home, playing cards! Just as you like to do, Father."

"They lied. Or else, they could have hired someone to throw that bomb. The papers you read lie. Lie and inflame and—"

"But why would they choose to undermine all their work here? To drive people away? Make everyone afraid to go to a meeting anywhere?"

"To start a *revolution!* Don't you know anything?"

Mrs. Lindorf laughs and then, *then,* she pours herself more wine. I look to Yakov. "What do you think, Yakov?"

His long fingers hold the edge of our cloth-covered table. He says he doesn't know. He says a trial might bring it all out. This is America. Maybe truth will come out.

"It already has!" Father all but shouts.

"You are absolutely right, Abraham," Mrs. Lindorf says. "I salute you!" She raises her glass to him.

I am my father's child after all—and not from the pig woman in the market. I become pure motion devoid of everything but anger. Without the least sense of it, I am out of my chair and knocking away her wine glass, then pushing her backward. She falls to the floor, chair and all, and my hands frame her throat. I squeeze until my father pulls me away with terrible force, and then my head is banging against the floor and filling with the sound of waves smashing against rocks. Surely, it will break this time. Surely this time I will die.

But Mother and Helena finally get me away from him. Upstairs, my sister holds me while rocking back and forth, humming, as if I were an infant.

"You are brave," I tell her.

"And you, foolish."

"But, Lenka—"

"Ssh, we will talk tomorrow."

"I have to leave here tomorrow."

"Emma, please don't think, now. Rest, please."

But already a thought, followed by the disquiet that comes when you recall how someone you love and respect tells you what you do not want to hear.

You don't like him very much, do you, Lenka?

No.

Why not?

I don't know. It's just something.

But what*? He's a good man. He reads Dostoyevsky and Turgenev and we talk about books. He speaks very good Russian. He's a skilled cutter making a good wage. And he loves me.*

Emma, don't marry him. You've asked me before, and I must tell you again. I don't think you should.

I love my sister but hate that word *no.*

LEON

Four men hanged yesterday in Chicago. Here at the Natrona bottle factory, we do not talk about it so much anymore. Done is done. Those men were said to throw a bomb that killed policemen in a place called Haymarket Square during some speeches last May. I am thinking of my brother's words, that the police themselves, or someone they hired, threw that bomb. They wish to discredit reds and anarchists, Waldeck tells me. Today he wears a black band on his upper right arm as we all did when our mother died. As for me, I try to keep my nose to the work. There are often strikes and lockouts somewhere in the country, or a train disrupted, and then soldiers come. Always something, never nothing, as my mother used to say. Only, she meant work on the farm. She did not want me to work on a farm, and I do not want to either. I am fourteen years old and hope to save enough to go to a school one year soon. By eight o'clock tonight I will have another seventy-five cents if I do not ruin any bottles. Often it happens through no fault of my own. A bottle sags out of shape from some stress you can't see and there goes five cents. But if I daydream, I might accidentally bump a hot bottle against another in the kiln, ruining both, and lose another ten cents. Waldeck says we need a union. A Bulgarian here argues with him. Waldeck tells the Bulgarian that he is a skilled worker, and Theo, the Bulgarian, says, "Skill? What is skill? This is skill!" He pounds his big arm or slaps his *posladek*. Meaning, ass. "Everybody got skill!"

Waldeck was drunk last night and this morning walked to work like an old man. I said to stay home, you will break too many bottles, but he said he better not because at home he just might kill our devil of a stepmother. Or she him. It is true. She will not let him rest. There will be the evil eye or the prodding with the broom. She cannot stomach having anyone home on a workday. Well, no. I am wrong. Her own two sons she treats well, considering that she is a *wiedzma,* meaning witch.

Ah! There! I've just ruined a green bottle by nicking it against the kiln door, and sure enough, the foreman marks it.

"Whatsamatter, Red?" Theo is calling to Waldeck. "You got a sore arm? Girlfriend bite you?"

"Shut up, Theo," Waldeck yells back.

There is snow outside but inside all is heat and steam. Our shirts stick to us, and our pants droop down. Since starting here last December, I lose much weight. Also, the *wiedzma* does not feed us well. When she is mad about something, there is only bread and maybe a little milk. The rest she locks up somewhere.

Soon we are doing a batch of red bottles, and I worry. Sure enough, Theo starts up again. "Hey, Red! We do your batch! Hey, Red, look at me!"

Waldeck holds off, but men all around are laughing. I glance at Theo, then tell Waldeck *no*! But I am too late. Waldeck finally turns and sees Theo making fun of Louis Lingg, the Haymarket defendant who blew himself apart with a blasting cap of mercury fulminate rather than hang. What Lingg got was a drawn-out death a hundred times worse than hanging. Now there is Theo, pretending to swallow something, and then bulging out his eyes and making a face.

Waldeck throws a mold. Theo steps aside in time. Waldeck draws his knife from his boot and charges, battering into him. All work stops. Men are yelling and urging on one or the other. I throw down my long fork and run to them just as Waldeck swings his knife, grazing my face. I fear for my eye, but when it clears of blood, what I see is Theo dangling Waldeck over a vat of molten glass. Waldeck's face and arms are red.

Today I earn only twenty-three cents after fines for breakage and lost time. Theo is also fined. But Waldeck is fired. They don't want any reds, the foreman tells him. "You be warned, Leon. Don't go getting ideas like your brother."

Our stepmother pounds on our bedroom door with her fists. "Jake just tells me! Fighting! And for what? So no job now? I'll give you, no job!" She kicks at the door and it springs back, hitting the wall. Fists raised, she goes after Waldeck.

He stands to meet this advance and then grabs her arms.

"Don't you disrespect me in my own house! I'll tell your pa, and he'll whip you, grown man or no."

Waldeck gets her out the door and leans against it so it can't fly open again.

She pounds on it. "I want you out, Waldeck! Go find someplace else to live. You can't stay here no more. I can't have fighters and drunks and troublemakers. Go find someplace else to lay drunk in. I don't cook for you no more. You have to go, I'm telling you!"

He looks at me. "I think she means it this time. You want to come with me?"

I do and I don't. There's our little sister Victoria and Jake and Michael. I worry what she might do to them.

"Maybe later I'll come live with you, but where will you go?"

"For now, to get a drink."

She is on a rampage downstairs in the kitchen, banging everything.

"Use the front stairs. Don't fight with her."

"I'll send word where you can find me." He pushes clothing into an old valise and then is gone.

In a drawer I find my own black armband and slip it on. Courage fails me and I take it off before going downstairs for a poor supper. The next day I keep it in my pocket. At the bottle factory, Theo gives me a look before we start but stays quiet the whole day, and so do I.

It is a sixty-eight-cent day.

EMMA

With my warm hand, I gather up the soft mass, but it refuses to become anything else and soon he is asleep. This is how it is every night. Tonight I think he is merely tired, after his fifteen hours. So I lie here, thinking, as usual. My mind is its own factory! Because I am no longer working—Yakov does not wish me to work—I am never tired. I can sleep as long as I wish after he leaves in the morning, then all I have to do is clean our small house, go to the shops on East Main, come home, prepare food, nibble, and wait. I look out the kitchen window at a sapling. It is a black stick, against the snow. Sometimes I smoke a forbidden Kimball's cigarette out on the back porch, where no neighbor can see me.

So he is tired, but I am not. He is even tired on Sundays. He wants to play cards on that day. It relaxes him, he says, and I say, "Exactly the problem!"

Cards! We do not go to the park. He no longer reads books, so we don't discuss anything of importance. We go to my parents' house for Shabbat, and there I remain silent, and so does he. Lenka regards me with pity. She, too, is married now but so happy.

Ah, sister. You were right.

She does not tell me that things might soon be better. She tells me to consult a doctor. This I do. First to discuss Yakov, and then to discuss my own condition, diagnosed in Saint Petersburg as an inverted uterus. That can be corrected surgically, the physician tells me, but I am afraid of surgery, not of the pain, but that they will botch it, and it will only be worse. As for poor Yakov, I must build him up with meats and fruits and walks in fresh air.

This, too, is a failure. Not that he does not eat. He eats, oh yes, like a barbarian. I spend hours making the *vareniki*, and he eats them all in two minutes. The beef broth soups disappear in a day, the breads, the fish, he eats with both hands. With head bowed. With groaning sounds!—then he naps. His face is widening. His stomach is mounding up.

And that is all.

A year ago, I was attending lectures at the Germania Club, where Johanna Greie spoke. What a night that was. Such an elegant woman, but in mourning. Her face pallid, her bearing halting, her speech halting, too. I sat there, rapt, as she talked about the Haymarket Massacre. Through her words, I saw it all so clearly. The dark cobbled square surrounded by warehouses. Wind coming up, then rain blowing in, and the crowd dispersing. The final speaker jumping down from a wagon bed after telling a police officer they all would go peaceably. But then the bomb, sputtering and arcing down onto the column of policemen. After that, a pandemonium of small arms fire—police firing into the fleeing crowd! And some in the crowd of course shooting back.

After the lecture, Johanna Greie came down to where I was still sitting and sat alongside me to ask if I knew any of the defendants personally.

"No," I said, "although I feel I do, now."

She looked at me very keenly for a long while and then she took my hand. "I have a feeling you will come to know their ideal as well and make it your own."

That night I woke Lenka, already prudently asleep, for the next day we needed to be up before dawn. I told her everything.

"Oh, Emma, you're not becoming an *anarchist,* are you?"

"I don't even know what that is!"

Soon after, at a newsstand on East Main, I bought an issue of *Die Freiheit* devoted exclusively to the Haymarket affair. Of course I had to hide it at home. I still keep it hidden now from Yakov.

Anarchism! A new world!

I cannot even resurrect poor Yakov.

LEON

I come to these meetings at the Natrona Library first to get away from our stepmother but also to learn more English. Tonight's speaker, though, she loses me. The advertisement says she will talk about H. D. Thoreau, a great American thinker and writer. So far I understand only a few words and feel most unlearned. I would like to leave except that I do not wish to stand and make interruption. All the chairs in the room are taken, and the way out is across the room. The advertisement says the speaker, Mrs. Clara Heuvel, is a teacher from Pittsburgh. She looks like a teacher. Her eyeglasses hang from a long black ribbon. She wears a suit patterned with feathers, or birds—I cannot quite see from where I sit. She is very happy and pleased with herself. Imagine being a teacher who knows much. You can go anywhere and talk to anyone. You can read any book without having to struggle. People ask you questions and you know the answers. You would not hesitate, reading difficult words, as she does not. *"What is man but a mass of thawing clay? The ball of the human finger is but a drop congealed. . . ."*

What is *congealed*? She does not pause to explain. It was a mistake to come tonight. Now she is on about vegetable leaves and in the next minute she says we should hold one hand before our eyes and look at it. Everyone does, so I do, too.

"Mr. Thoreau is asking us to imagine a river there, do you see it? Now, a leaf, a maple leaf. Now a star. Now river, leaf, and star all in one. Do you see, ladies and gentlemen? It is nothing less than a miracle."

I stare at my hand. It is clean for I scrubbed it hard before coming tonight. I see lines you might imagine are rivers. I do not see a star—yes, I do, and yes, a maple leaf, the way the fingers fan out. But why is this a miracle? The Bible tells of miracles—Our Lord changing water into wine. Our Lord driving out demons. Our Lord curing the blind man, the leper, and raising Lazarus from the dead and then rising Himself after His crucifixion. Those are miracles. I do not understand Mr. Thoreau's miracle but am afraid to ask a question.

Is it possible to find that book and study it?

". . . Remember, ladies and gentlemen, the whole universe is within you! Never be discouraged. Never allow discouragement a place in your heart."

Never allow. But how do you stop it when it is just there, taking up all the space inside you like the chairs in this room. And here is something else. If I am a miracle, then is our stepmother also? Is the hangman who put the nooses around the necks of the Haymarket men a miracle, too?

What kind of miracle is that?

My head hurts. Maybe it is just fatigue. Maybe, thirst. I am always thirsty, so when the talk finally ends, I go with everyone else to the refreshment table. My turn comes, and I pour lemonade into a cup. One hand holds the ladle, the other the cup. Where is the miracle in this?

"May I," someone is saying in slow English, "if you now finish?"

I turn quickly to ask pardon. A young woman stands there. Her hair is pulled back, making a heart of her face. She wears thick eyeglasses in round silver frames. They blur her eyes, but from what I can tell, the eyes are large, and blue. Her hair is dark. I give her the ladle and step aside.

"You think about the lecture?" she goes on in English as she pours her own cup. "She is good, no? The speaker?"

"You know what she said?"

"Only . . . some. And you?"

I move away from the table to give others room. She walks with me. This seems very bold of her. If not for the eyeglasses, I might have other thoughts about her. In Polish I say, "Your ears are like red cabbage leaves."

She smiles at this—so she speaks Polish! I go on, "Your nose is a pink carrot. Mine is a white turnip."

Now she laughs and tells me in Polish that my hair is a wheat field.

"Your cheeks," I tell her, "are lakes at sunset. Your eyes are two large potatoes—blue! Your neck, a white tree, imagine!"

What demon has gotten into me, teasing her as if she were my little sister! She scolds me in Polish, saying I am a donkey, a crazy thing, an *idiota*. What do they have in that punch, vodka?

I ask to escort her home, and she allows this. On the streetcar she tells me in Polish that she lives in a white house across from a grocery store. The store belongs to her uncle, and she works there every weekday, helping to make sausages, stock the shelves, put up orders, change the sawdust on the floor, and doing whatever else needs to be done. On Saturdays, she cleans for her aunt and cooks and bakes for Sunday. She came to America ten months ago but is still a greenhorn because she does not go out much, except for these Sunday evenings put on by the German Society. At Castle Garden, in New York, they almost sent her back because of her poor eyesight— nearly blind!—but she managed to explain to the immigration officer, through an interpreter, that her uncle was a rich storekeeper, and she was going to work in his store. She considers this the bravest thing she ever did in her life, besides leaving her family to come to America.

"I was so proud. I thought, this is how you do, in America. You are brave. You fight. So then I think it must be in the air, here. Whatever it is that helps one do this."

"Excuse me," I say. "What is your name?"

"Oh! Lucenia! Lucenia Dragewicz." Before I can give her mine, she is saying, "Let me tell you how it was when I could *see* for the first time, with my new eyeglasses. Mrs. Heuvel talked much about *seeing* tonight. Let me tell you how it was for me!"

And so she tells me, in Polish. "Stones! Leaves! Beehives! Blades of grass! Barrels of soda crackers and pickled herring, links of sausage, shelves of tinned goods—everything so clear in outline and detail and color it often made me laugh aloud. I had no idea the world was like that, that things weren't supposed to be hazy and far away. I found myself staring at the coins people gave me. Or else staring at the white string that went, from its roll on a bracket, all the way up to a hook attached to the tin ceiling, where there are squares showing flowers and garlands, and then all the way back down to the scratched oak counter. I found myself staring, even, at the bloody meat in the trays, the rainbows sometimes there. Or at people's faces. The old *babas* with their million wrinkles, each one a little hill. And the babies, the *babekas,* like flower petals. I sometimes still do this, and Uncle often hollers at me when he notices. My aunt does, too. Also, she does not want me to read so much at night. She says I will ruin my eyes some more and then even these eyeglasses won't help. I pray that this does not happen because I cannot stop reading! I must read! A neighbor gave me some simple English books and told me about these meetings and even brought me to the library, the first time. And now I smile because I meet another American who wishes to learn."

When we come to her stop, I get off in order to help her down, then hop back up and the car is moving. *Idiota!*

I might have walked to her house with her. I might have told her my name. My heart takes a long while to slow. It seems to me that each gaslight is a small moon, and each water drop on the window holds another moon. I look at my hand and try to remember the feeling of holding hers. It strikes me as almost a miracle—how each of us goes around encased in heat, like the sun. And then sometimes, like tonight, the two globes of heat come together like these drops on the glass.

Is this what Mr. Thoreau means by *miracle*?

Lucenia. It is a name that might be from the Latin word for light.

EMMA

He earns fifteen dollars a week so I do not need to worry much about expenses. I can buy eggs and cream and good cuts of meat and also the oranges he loves. I bone chickens for meat-stuffed crepes. I fill cabbage rolls with beef I grind myself, the grinder fastened to the enamel table and meat spilling out like red and white noodles. I fry chicken livers with onions and serve them with kasha. I make *cotellets* of chopped beef with rice. Once a week I make Napoleons and eclairs and Baba au Rhum. Eating, he is a happy man.

Some days I go to the Dime Museum for its afternoon vaudeville show, Emma Kershner attending alone! It is nearly a scandal, but let them talk. It means nothing to me. I return to our house and begin preparing the evening meal. While the potato soup simmers and the bread bakes, I sometimes go to the trunk in the empty bedroom upstairs, remove layers of winter clothing and find, under everything, that issue of *Die Freiheit* about the Haymarket defendants. The print, the stories, even the smell of that paper transport me bodily, it seems, back to that time, and at first, rage and empathy breathe life into me. Yet soon after comes a crushing weight of sorrow for the loss of it all—theirs and, yes, my own.

Alive? Dead? What am I? Have all the beatings affected my brain? Is this new life, this so-called life, some *punishment* without end?

Mounds of snow in the yard remind me of his stomach.

Mounds of snow in the yard remind me of graves.

One day I see in an issue of *Die Freiheit* that a dress-making class is about to start, here in Rochester. Dress-making! I know how to make gloves and how to attach arms and collars to overcoats, but I have never made a dress. It is possible I could learn this skill and work at home. Ladies could come here to be fitted and choose a style. I might even design new patterns and create something very different and beautiful—instead of merely shopping and cooking all day.

I let a week pass, then two. Each time I look in the paper, there it is, the notice. *Learn dressmaking. Improve your skills. Earn more money!*

At night I dream of my hands framing fabric again. But there is joy in the dream, not the despair of drudgery. One afternoon, the snow brilliant in the yard, the sun warm, I go to East Main to shop, but instead of later attending the vaudeville performance, I search out the address. Soon after, I am learning to make dresses, mornings. And not long after that, with money saved from the housekeeping account, I buy my own machine, which I hide, each afternoon after practicing. My plan is to first learn and then tell Yakov after I have made my first dress. I do not even tell Helena, for fear of her censure or, possibly worse, her disappointment in me should I fail.

Summer comes, with its hot winds and heavy heat filling the house, especially the upstairs rooms. Yakov still sleeps alongside me in the lap-dog way he prefers, his face tucked under my right arm. He is losing at cards now and says even less than before. I am tired all the time because I cannot sleep in this heat, with him breathing alongside me. His skin sticks to mine, and we lie there like rolls of soggy dough.

One early morning soon after he leaves for work, the air still holding something of the night's coolness and moisture, I take my machine and valise and go to St. Paul

Street, then take a northbound streetcar, which passes the shop where he must be cutting out his fourth suit jacket of the day. At the New York Central depot, I buy a one-way ticket to New Haven.

Why New Haven?

Why one way?

Why anything! I wished to go. I had a name, found in *Die Freiheit*, of a labor organizer there. The body knows what it knows, and so does the heart.

Helena writes to me that I must think about returning. It is not good to be so alone in the world. What if I become ill?

Our rabbi writes to me that I must return for the good of Yakov, who is despondent.

Yakov himself writes that he will kill himself if I do not return, and his death will be on my head and I shall one day burn in the flames of Gehenna.

Father does not write but I know what he would say if he did: *You are no child of mine. You must be from the pig woman at the market.*

As it happens, I become ill with catarrh and a terrible cough that will not abate. The foreman at the corset factory does not seem the least disturbed when I give him notice. In my rented room I cough and attempt to sleep. In fever dreams I burn in Gehenna. Mornings, I check my handkerchiefs for blood. It comes to me that dying alone is no good. In my fevered state, this seems wisdom.

My brief rebellion lasted a mere four months. After that I am on East Main again, aware of ladies whispering as I pass. *Look how pale! Her hair so thin now! What happened to her? Well, he said he was going to swallow rat poison, so she came back, the headstrong, ungrateful thing. Let her suffer now and see how she likes it.*

In time I am sewing again, afternoons, when I am not too tired. Much of the time, though, I nap. One day I awake well after the hour I'd planned. Rushing to prepare dinner,

I hide my machine in the pantry, but neglect to gather the pieces of pattern. After dinner Yakov finds them in the sitting room, still on the sofa, and pinned together.

"Emma?" He comes into the kitchen, the tissue-thin pattern in hand. Of course he recognizes it for what it is but says, as if testing me, "What is this?"

"A dressmaker's pattern, Yakov, as you well know."

"Who left it in our sitting room?"

What shall I say—the neighbor? Helena? I say, "I did, Yakov."

"You are making dresses? Why do you not tell me you are making dresses?"

"I am only learning how."

"But you do not tell me?"

"I wished . . . to surprise you . . . with my skill."

"Why do you need this skill? There is no need."

"I thought to make dresses for myself and, possibly, others."

"You do not need to make! There is enough money for you to buy. Do you go somewhere to learn this?"

Again, I might lie, but instead I tell him about the advertisement and the shop off East Main.

"Is your teacher a man?"

"A man, Yakov? My teacher is a woman Mother's age."

"Are men there also, learning?"

"Yes. Two brothers."

"Then you must not go anymore. I forbid it."

"Yakov—"

"I forbid it, Emma!"

"You *forbid?*"

"Yes. Do not go there again. You are my wife and must obey. Do you sew by hand or do you have a machine?"

"By hand. At the school, we use machines."

"If you wish to sew here, that is your decision. I tell you it is a waste of time, but if you can manage all your other work and not overexert yourself, you may sew here, at home, but you cannot go to the school."

That night I do not even try to resurrect him. He does not know this now, but I will never try again.

THE MAJOR

How many days have we been at it now? A month, at least. You'd think it such a simple matter to understand—that we *must* protect American economic interests. But if my opponents, the Democrats, pass their bill, tariffs will be reduced and a great number of commodities—farm machinery to tablecloths—will be put on the free trade list. So then, our own manufacturers, large and small, will be forced to compete with any and all manufacturers in Europe and elsewhere. How sensible is that? The thing my colleagues on the other side of the aisle apparently fail to understand is that passing the Mills Bill will be one sure way to cause even more discontent in the secret lodges, more labor disturbances, more incidents such as the unfortunate Haymarket affair two years ago. Well, today I hope to speak to this matter *if* the former colonels and captains still waging their old battles will finally lay down their arms against one another, stop the fracas about who is to speak next and for how long, and who is yielding to whom and whether or not this yielding follows the proper order. It's a terrible squandering of time, but I trust that the Divine Being who guided us through the awful bloodshed of the war will guide us through all this nattering as well. And soon, I do hope.

Ah. Mr. Albert Anderson, the gentleman from Iowa, finally has the floor—we're on the tracks, again, boys, hurrah. "What do tariffs do?" Mr. Anderson asks. "Why, they place colossal fortunes in the hands of the few at the expense of many. When you eliminate honest competition, you bring on demoralization. Should undue advantage be the rule? When the smoke clears from all this, everyone will be able to see that a trust is a trust, a pool, a pool, and protection is protection. And unrestrained protection is—*monopoly!*"

There's the usual rain of applause and booing and hissing, which takes a while to abate. Someone on my side of the aisle is shouting that the party of free trade was also the party of human slavery. "Remember, too," someone else shouts, "that the people haven't asked for free trade. Who has? The *Democrats* and *England!*"

The Speaker admonishes us, and then there's another hour of words before it's my turn. When I stand alongside my desk, the chamber grows perfectly quiet, in deference, maybe, to my expertise, though I do not mean to boast by saying so. It is true that I am somewhat an expert, but I have become so more by chance than design. It was President Garfield, some years ago, who turned me in that direction. "Take on the tariff question, young man!" he said. "Become an expert on that. Lord knows we need an expert." He also recommended me for the Ways and Means Committee. I must acknowledge that it made for exceedingly dull work, studying every known commodity from pin lace to pig iron, castile soap to marmalade. It has gotten so that everything I use in a day, be it my shaving razor and cake of shaving soap or the blankets I turn back at night—*everything*—has numbers attached to it. It's like knowing a secret language. Of course, few other congressmen were interested in hearing me spout until our current president, President Cleveland, a Democrat, made the tariff question a national issue. So now, this respectful silence, which I must say is somewhat humbling, yet superbly gratifying.

So I begin simply—I don't know how to do it any other way—by defining terms. "A revenue tariff, which the

Democrats want," I say, "will *not* tax imports which are also produced at home. A protective tariff, on the other hand, *will* tax imports the like of which are also produced at home, or capable of being produced here. So a protective tariff protects and encourages our own industries. A revenue tariff, in contrast, places *high* taxes on raw materials but low taxes on imported finished products. Therefore, there will be a high tax on steel billets, but low taxes on nails and wires. With that kind of encouragement, gentlemen of the House, we might as well shut down our factories altogether and buy everything from foreign countries."

There's more, much more—a full three hours' worth. Mainly I take issue with the Democrats' desire to kowtow to foreign countries in this crucial matter. "We are one country, one language, one allegiance, one standard of citizenship, one flag, one Constitution, one nation, one destiny. It is otherwise with foreign nations, each a separate organism, a distinct and independent political society organized for its own, to protect its own, and work out its own destiny. We deny to those foreign nations free trade with us upon equal terms with our own producers. The foreign producer has no right or claim to equality with our own. He is not amenable to our laws. There are resting upon him none of the obligations of citizenship. He pays no taxes. He performs no civil duties; he is subject to no demands for military service. He is exempt from state, county, and municipal obligations. He contributes *nothing* to the support, the progress, and glory of the nation. Why should he enjoy unrestrained equal privileges and profits in our markets with our producers, our labor, and our taxpayers? We put a burden on *his* productions, we discriminate against *his* merchandise because he is alien to us and our interests, and we do it to protect our own, defend our own, preserve our own, who are always with us in adversity and prosperity, in sympathy and purpose, and, if necessary, in sacrifice. That is the principle which governs us. I submit it is a patriotic and righteous one. . . ."

There's a volley of gratifying applause, and from both sides, it seems. I continue and at one point open up a bundle containing a suit of clothes from a Boston store owned by a member of the House, a Democrat. Holding it aloft, along with a bill of sale, I show that the suit hadn't gone up in price as a result of protectionism. There's much laughter and applause then, and when I finally end my speech, there's a great hue and cry: *Vote! Vote!*

But of course we can't. Colonel William C. P. Breckinridge of Kentucky has yet to speak, among others. It's his words that stick with me afterward, despite all the congratulatory praise and slaps on the back I get, later. Whereas my argument was based on fact, statistics, and logic, the gentleman from Kentucky nonetheless won the day, at least in my opinion, by conjuring a vision of some glorious future brought about by free trade and untrammeled commerce, with all burdens to progress thrown aside. "The children of exiles and emigrants welcomed here, willing hands finding work and a livelihood! The silence of rivers turned into the sweet hum of progress, the secret lodges of the discontented, the operatives, becoming open assemblies of happy families! The shadow of want leaving their hearthstones, giving way to the mild radiance of permanent comfort! We must look to the rising sun and an east of new hopes and set our steps in that direction!" In the end the speech seems more like some prayer. The applause for Colonel Breckinridge lasts for several minutes, it seems.

It confounds me that a person can say so much, so many *fine* words, I'll grant you, with nary a fact in support, and have those words come out as supremely *valid*, supremely weighty, besting all facts and making careful logic seem like some form of petty chicanery. It certainly takes the starch out of one. I gave my speech all the passion and eloquence I'm capable of, but evidently it wasn't enough.

Outside on Pennsylvania Avenue there's a breeze spinning dust, and the light actually hurts my eyes. So many hours spent in the dim House chamber swathed around in velvet makes us rather like cave dwellers incapable of bearing light. As I walk toward the Ebbitt House, I can't seem to get Breckinridge's mellifluous phrases out of my head. I'll admit I was stung to the point of tears myself, at moments, no matter that any reasoning was largely absent from his words—in contrast to my own. I am thinking it's what it is to be second-rate. You can't even congratulate yourself on a job well done because it's simply not good *enough*. Still, I did give them my best.

The lobby of the Ebbitt House is loud with bonhomie—and shouted *Congratulations, Major McKinley!* I nod and smile and sidestep colleagues and quickly climb stairs to my rented suite, where it's as stuffy and hot as our chamber on the Hill. The windows are all closed and the drapes drawn, but at least my dear Ida is up and not in her bed. She's polishing her jewelry again, which is something she much enjoys. Her polishing gloves are blackened at the fingers, and she looks up at me with an abstracted expression as she removes them. So she has taken her medicine. Good. I lean to her and kiss the top of her head, the cropped hair, once so gloriously long and full. When she wore it up, she often complained of the heaviness. Like a crown, I always joked. Ah, Ida. Such a beauty, still!

"My dear," I say, "how has your day been?"

Her hand trembles in my own. Her eyes are so dark, now, the pupils eclipsing the irises. Each eye seems a black pool of water, an image I never welcome but one that always comes.

"Has anyone been to see you? Have you played euchre?"

She shakes her head and focuses once more on the brooches and necklaces, the rings and bracelets on the cloth—all anniversary gifts. It astonishes me that I have been able to give her all these on such a small annual salary. The array of gifts there on the table, coupled with that shake of her head, cause my eyes to fill—for the second time today. No one has come to visit her again. What do other ladies do all day? Go for carriage rides? Shop? Have tea? Could they not ask her to accompany them, upon occasion? Perhaps once a week? Or at least every two weeks? Some small thing? Is it too much to ask? To hope for?

Perhaps so. The women are afraid. They have seen me cover her face with a handkerchief when a fit comes upon her, and so, I suppose, no one wishes to be alone with her. I understand that, I do. But where is their Christianity? If she were the Ida of eighteen years ago—

Anger dies back, becoming the old pain of memory. I feel it all again, like an old wound come to life. Our baby, Ida's namesake, dying, the wee frail thing unable to live beyond five months, and then three years later, our beloved five-year-old Katie also lost to death. And now my dearest suffering from some brain injury her doctors can neither fully understand nor cure. They think that Ida's extreme grief when her mother died may have triggered the convulsions that led to the brain injury and perhaps even to our little Ida's difficult birth. Theories, though, seldom comfort. Only one's faith in Providence can. Still, it's a mercy when the awareness of it all sinks somewhere deep, during the course of a demanding day on the Hill. In my wife's presence, though, there's no forgetting. I have only to look at those drug-enlarged pupils, the abstracted expression—and hear of no visitors again.

Now I take both her hands and hold them within my own until they warm nicely.

"Look," she whispers, pointing to a pair of candleholders I hadn't noticed.

"Are they new?" I ask. "Did you order them, my dear?"

My Ida was raised in a well-to-do household, and her tastes remain extravagant, but how can I deny her anything even though her spendthrift practices often alarm me. She shows me a card from the owner of the Washington shop where I buy most of her presents. *An American-made gift in appreciation of Major William McKinley's efforts on behalf of American industry.* The candleholders are of flawless glass and exceedingly heavy, each with a handsome octagonal base. *Steuben Crystal Made in New York State.* I know, within a few pennies, the cost of these, and the sum causes my heartbeat to skip. "My dear, they are beautiful indeed, but we cannot accept them."

"But I want them!"

"Don't we already have several fine candleholders?"

"Not as fine as these."

"You know how I cannot accept . . . gifts from any industry."

"But these . . . the box was addressed to me. I'll show you. There's the wrapping. The maid hasn't yet taken it away."

"I understand. It was sent to you. I—" Her head is trembling now. "Ida. Ida, Ida, my dear, listen. Are you listening, my dear? I will buy them for you. I will go to Mr. Gill's shop tomorrow and buy them. Don't cry, my dear. Please don't upset yourself. Would you like to play a hand of euchre? Or better, let's take a carriage ride. Tonight I must return to the Hill, but we have three hours yet. Come. The afternoon is quite fine. You'll see many flowers."

After our outing and while she dresses for our small dinner, I step across the hall into my office and there find a number of buff-colored telegraph envelopes. More congratulations—from railroad men with connections to Standard Oil and Carnegie Steel; from James Duke's American Tobacco Company; and from other magnates whose names I don't immediately recognize. While I glance through these, another gift arrives for Ida, this time with no card—a vase of roses, the variety known as American Beauty and wildly popular in the highest circles. These are particularly large and splendidly red—a dollar fifty each, at least.

I remove them from the vase and place them facedown in my wastebasket, along with the torn-up telegrams. Minutes later, I retrieve them and take them into our small dining room where she waits, in a brilliant yellow gown, one of the newly polished diamond pendants gracing her bosom.

"*Another* admirer!" I say. "What on earth am I going to do?"

I'm rewarded with her smile. A moment like this seems to assuage, somewhat, the pain of our losses; indeed, we should not feel such moments as deeply were it not for those losses.

The next morning there's a nasty editorial in a Democratic newspaper, the first of many more to come, I fear. *They have him in their deep pockets, just as they have much of the Republican Party sewn up! Why is it that we as Americans, who are so opposed to anarchism in politics, hardly hesitate to embrace its practice in the business world, where trusts place themselves above, outside, and beyond the law every day of the week including Sunday?* An accompanying cartoon shows a baby with my likeness for a face peeking out of some massive black coat pocket. Tiny hands grasp the pocket's edge. An idiot's smile festoons its overly pronounced jowls.

This newspaper goes into my wastebasket though it is not as easy to rid myself of resurging anger and, yes, fear at the course this is taking. I have to circle my desk several times before I feel calm enough to draft a reply. It's so simple finally! Why can't people see it? Necessities, luxuries, foodstuffs, tools, goods of every type are not only things, nor merely numbers, but *people*. Laborers, farmers, ranchers, shepherds, shopkeepers—and if they are happy, if they are secure, if they are unthreatened and prospering, then so too is the entire corpus. And the way to achieve this is likewise simple. Control the numbers!

No, I am *not* working for the plutocrats. That is an erroneous assumption. I am working for the *people*.

Is this so difficult to understand?

EMMA

I walk down Broadway, switching my valise from hand to hand at times. There's wind but not the cool lake wind as in Rochester. Here, it is hot and odorous, some odors good—fry cakes! coffee! roasting meat!—emanating from shops and lunchrooms. But others—from the urine and rotting garbage in alleyways, even piles of bloody offal outside butcher shops and rotting fish outside fish mongers' shops—nauseate me. Broadway is a befouled, cacophonous flow of omnibuses and wagons and carriages and horses dashing, where they can. The sidewalk, a lesser stream but no less crowded with humanity. At first it was exhilarating, leaving the depot on Forty-Second Street and launching out into the wind and this tide of everything, but now my head hurts, and my legs are throbbing. So far I have walked twenty-seven blocks south and long to sit in shade. My face feels very hot, and I know my hair has come undone in the wind. I can imagine it—a wildness of small curls. What will my aunt think? It worries me now. I should have written despite my fear that she might tell Father. Now there will be a surprise. *Tante! It is Emma! From Rochester!* This is a scene I have imagined for many weeks. What we imagine we must be able to create, no?

At last I compare a number on a door with one on a slip of paper I have taken from my handbag. They are the same. The house is made of dark stone and is connected to others on either side. Its door is painted black and needs to be scraped and repainted. The window on its first floor is closed and curtained, unlike others I passed where curtains blow out into the day. I walk up five stone steps and at the door raise and lower a tarnished brass knocker. Steam seems to lift off my clothing, and I am light-headed from hunger but also joyous. When the door opens somewhat, I smile because now the scene will begin.

"Tante! It is Emma! From Rochester!"

"Who?" A triangle of lines forms between her brows.

"Emma Goldman," I say, raising my voice. "From Rochester." Still I smile but she does not open the door any farther. "Your *niece*," I add.

"Emma Goldman? From Rochester? Is he with you, your husband?" The ripples of flesh between my aunt's eyebrows do not ease as she looks beyond me to the sidewalk.

"He is in Rochester, Tante. I came by myself."

"By yourself! All that way? Why, by yourself?"

"May I enter, Tante, and I will tell you why."

Staring at me all the while, she opens the door wider and steps to one side of the entryway. I feel so disheveled and unkempt. When she closes the heavy door, all sound from the street is muted to nearly nothing. I am at once conscious of the quiet and of the chill, at first most welcome. "It is early!" she says. "Did you already have breakfast?"

I explain about the trip, the ferry, the walk from Forty-Second Street. "No breakfast yet, Tante! I'm starved." But as I sit alone at the dark dining room table while she makes tea in the kitchen, I'm afraid it will take more than the ritual of offering food to melt the frost here. Silently, she places a glass of hot tea before me and a dish of sugar lumps. Silently, she returns to the kitchen and reemerges later with plates of rye bread, butter, and slices of smoked fish on a tray. She leaves again, and I hear her calling Uncle down from somewhere upstairs. Soon the two are sitting opposite me at the table, watching me eat. After a while she says, "So tell us, now, Emma, why do you come all this way? Did you run away again from your husband?"

I should have written them. I want to lean back, but my clothing is too sweaty. I sit very straight and try, again, for a charming smile.

"Run away? No, Tante. I have talked to Yakov. We have agreed to . . . separate."

Her right hand rises to cover her mouth a moment, then she turns to Uncle and nearly shouts, "They have separated, Emma and her husband."

Uncle is my mother's brother and has always been meek, like Mother. His hair has become gray, and his skin appears lifeless. His monocle obscures his left eye as he holds it there to gaze at me. "Ah," he says finally. "It is Emma Goldman."

"Yes, Emma!" his wife says. "She comes here without her husband. They separate, she says. What do you mean, Emma, *separate*? Does the rabbi allow? Talk loud so he can hear you."

"I did not ask the rabbi, Tante," I say, raising my voice. "And *separate* means that Yakov and I have agreed to part."

"Your husband agreed to this?"

"Yes," I lie. "We both have agreed. Now I wish to begin a new life. Here, in New York." To me it sounds as if I'm also shouting.

Tante's hand goes to her chest, her fingers spread outward. "Emma, it is not so easy here in New York. How will you live, on your own? *Where* will you live?"

"I am hoping that you and Uncle might let me stay with you. In one room," I add quickly, for the words cause her to join her hands together, the large knuckles yellow. "Just a bedroom and just for a short while until I can find work and lodging. I will pay you and Uncle for everything, Tante."

My aunt turns to Uncle. "She wants to stay here now! With us!" To me, she says, "Have you told your father this?"

"No, Tante," I finally say.

"And why not, child?"

"I . . . think that he would have forbidden it. He would never agree to anything giving me happiness. He would have refused just to spite me."

"You have to talk louder for him," she says, and repeats my words for Uncle before saying, "I don't know if we can allow it either, Emma. It might cause trouble between our families." She stands and takes my tea glass to the kitchen, to refill it, I think.

"Uncle?" I say, but sense it is futile. He is sitting there in a kind of daze of sweetness and incomprehension. Tante appears to be the strong one here, the decider.

"Maybe she can stay a little while," my aunt says, returning without the tea glass and leaning close to Uncle, "but I think she should go back after she thinks things over for a day or two, yes?"

Uncle nods several times. "Suit cutters make a good wage, no? He is a good man, your Jacob. Forget your little quarrel, Emma. It is merely a youthful quarrel, and now it is time to be reasonable. Go home and ask forgiveness. He will give it because he will be happy to have you back, my girl."

"*Ja*," Tante says. "Words of wisdom! Don't let your pride mislead you. You will regret it for the rest of your life. Go home and ask forgiveness, like a good wife."

A good wife.

Impossible, I see, to stay here in this cold cave.

"Do you want more tea? I forgot to bring it back. I'll get you some more if you want."

"No, thank you, Tante," I say, pushing back the heavy chair and standing. "Maybe it's best if I stay with a friend tonight and not impose on you and Uncle." My voice shakes and tears are rising.

They are both quick to stand as well. Tante, giving directions for taking the elevated railway back to the depot, leads me to the hall door. "Go back, Emma! It is for the best!" In the next minute I am outside again, in the furnace heat.

It feels good. I raise my face to the sun and know, with all my being, that I made the right choice. How quick she was to close that door! The relief in their faces—when I said I wouldn't stay there, with them! Tears blur the scene before me, and I nearly step on a man sleeping on a pile of discarded drapery and stripped away wallpaper. Sleeping or dead? I stop. His mouth is open, and flies crawl about it, rising when he snorts but soon alighting again. I look around for someone to help him but see only three children, two of them astride a banister, the third drawing something on the pavement with a stone.

"Go get someone to take him inside," I tell one of the children.

The boy looks up from his drawing. "Aw, he's just drunk. He lays there every day."

"Where is his family?"

"Him? Don't got one."

"Where does he live?"

"Don't know. He'll wake up and go off somewhere for a while and then come back here. Nobody cares."

Words I interpret differently than the boy intended.

"You a greenhorn, hey?" he says.

Noticing that the boy's gaze is flicking downward every so often to my valise, I walk away quickly and turn into the first lunchroom I see. At a table near a wall, I study the bill of fare and, realizing that I'm still hungry, order blueberry pie and coffee, an expense, which will leave me with four dollars and eighty-five cents. Also, it is an expense that makes me feel guilty when I think of that man on the pile of rags. Why does no one take him in?

But then I think of my Tante and Uncle.

Those figures become Yakov, arms open, eyes glazed and reddened and melancholy with need. *Come back, Emma.*

Relishing the intense sweetness of the pie, I think of nothing for a blissful minute until it occurs to me that I could make a better crust. And better coffee, too. It further occurs to me that if necessary I can find work in such an establishment.

These thoughts give me the courage to open my handbag and take out the two other addresses I'd stowed there. As I do so, the haunting image of Yakov fades to nearly nothing.

"Have another sandwich," Solotaroff shouts over the din of voices at Sach's café on Suffolk Street. "And more coffee!"

His was the second address on my list, Hillel Solotaroff, the labor organizer I'd met while working at the corset factory in New Haven. When I'd asked for reading materials after one of his speeches, he'd also given me his address in New York. With this address in hand, I left the Bowery lunchroom and began searching through a tangle of streets. At last I found his residence—but Solotaroff no longer lived there with his family, a janitor told me. It was growing dark with an impending storm. The air felt thick. Wind blew scraps of paper everywhere, and in the streets, horses shied from these scraps while thunder marched in closer. Children, screaming themselves crazed, raced one another into houses. The janitor must have sensed my rising panic, must have noticed the tears I'd been trying to restrain. He gave me the name of the family's street but not their number. That he didn't know, he said, and turned to go inside.

Wet and trembling with fatigue and fear, I went from house to house and up and down flights of stairs, making inquiries. Had I been anywhere near the train depot, there would not be this *now*:

This being *taken in*. This being *a part of*.

At a nearby table a young man eats alone. He has ordered a steak and eats it like a wolf. When he ordered it, in Russian, his voice was as demanding as any aristocrat's. He looks like a worker, in cap and shapeless jacket, but it surprises me that he is here, for he does not act like an ordinary worker. "Who is that?" I ask Solotaroff. "Do you know him?"

"Where? Oh, that's Berkman. Alexander Berkman. I'll introduce you." Raising his voice over the din, he calls the young man over.

My face warms even more. "Is he wealthy?" I ask quickly.

Solotaroff laughs. "Not any more so than I am. He must have just got his pay."

Then Alexander Berkman is standing before us and asking if we want to go with him and hear Hannes Most speak that night. Saying this, he looks directly at me.

Hannes Most. Johannes Most, editor and publisher of *Die Freiheit*, and his, the third address in my handbag.

Berkman is everything Yakov is not, his skin brick-hued, his neck large, the shoulders wide and thick with a workman's muscle, his gaze not dreamy but intent. My face aches, now, with heat. This Berkman is not just trying to place me, remember me from somewhere. It is more than that. He is attracted but also sizing me up; this I know. In New Haven there were women who attached themselves to the organizers not out of any love for ideals but rather for the institution of marriage. It must be that way here, too, for Berkman apparently wishes to know which one I am.

Well, I will show him. "Yes," I say in Russian. "Above all I wish to hear Johannes Most." For Berkman's benefit I delicately emphasize the *all*.

"You speak Russian!"

"And German."

"Good. We will go."

The hall, a long room adjoining a saloon not far from the café, is filled to capacity. We stand, Solotaroff, Berkman, and I, shoved closely against one another, and I am too conscious of Berkman's presence alongside me. The air is gray with smoke and loud and dense with talk until Most steps onto a low platform several feet in front of us. He appears gaunt and not very tall despite being up on the platform. And there is something odd about his face. He wears his beard swept to either side from the center of his chin, but on one side it bulges outward quite a bit. I cannot deny my disappointment. I'd expected so much more than this gnomish figure.

But then he begins to speak.

In a voice sonorous and deep and worthy of the finest stage, he opens with a serious analysis of the Haymarket affair, his words grounded in logic and reason. Several in the crowd utter their approval at times while Most strides back and forth on the platform, using his arms singly or together for emphasis. I have read these same arguments in his newspaper, but how he brings them to life, on that platform. *Yes*, I am saying to myself. *Of course. Of course.* It must be very late, but I have no real sense of time or fatigue, just of rightness. It brings chills, though not the kind I felt that afternoon in my aunt's house in the Bowery.

That afternoon?—years ago, it seems now.

But then Most is shouting that "Murder is the killing of a human being, and a policeman is not a human being!" Words causing laughter and applause but in my heart sudden fear. *Not a human being? What, then?* On the conspiratorial union of industrialists and politicians against the eight-hour day, he says, "Strangle them all with the guts of clerics!" There is much laughing now and stamping of feet. On either side of me, Berkman and Solotaroff are motionless and silent, their eyes following Most's every gesture and move. I cannot gauge their feelings, but my own earlier joy has eroded. *Is the man speaking metaphorically?* "How is a toilet like the Stock Exchange?" Most is now asking. No one responds. "Well, I will tell you, comrades. On Wall Street, first the paper falls and then comes the crash. In a toilet, the crash comes first." Solotaroff smiles. Berkman's mouth crimps a little. There's shouting now, and *hoo-hooing.*

". . . History will be rewritten with blood and iron. The question is not *will* there be a revolution, but *when* it will break out. People need only be shown that the enemy is rotten with corruption, tottering and ready to be smashed. Storm the bastille of capitalism! Strike the match! Hurl the bomb! Stab through the heart . . ."

The room becomes one long howl of approval, and I understand, or at least partially. Most is saying what others here wish they could. He is giving voice to their impotent rage and excruciating need and temerity. When he is finally finished, many in the crowd return to the saloon, while others press forward to speak with him. Solotaroff guides me to one side, away from the surge, and Berkman comes, too. When we don't leave the room, I know they are waiting for the crowd to disperse and then, yes, we are approaching the man who is still breathing with effort. As we near, I see what causes the lack of symmetry. The right side of his face, under the beard and rising a distance above it, appears to be all twisted and exposed knobs of bone. It looks raw and painful. It looks like a botched model of a face. I am nearly physically sickened. In the next minute Most is saying, his voice now low and penetrating, "But I do not always play the demagogue, do I, Berkman? Bring her to the paper tomorrow, and she will see." He turns from us to greet others.

That night, lying on a sofa at Solotaroff's, I'm deeply disturbed by the demagoguery as well as by the memory of that twisted, protruding bone. A stepmother in Germany,

Solotaroff said, had locked him in an unheated bedroom. His face froze and quacks later got at it. He had wanted to be an actor. Here in America, while he was in prison on Blackwell's Island, guards compounded the damage.

Come back, Emma, Yakov again implores me. *Come home.*

Bring her to the paper tomorrow, Most counters, *and she will see.*

What I see now are the lampoons of "Jack" Most in the Rochester and Buffalo papers—Jack Most, a skinny, bristly man in black, wearing a dagger-studded belt and holding lighted dynamite bombs in each hand, with smoke coming from ears and nostrils. *Satan's Little Helper.*

As tired as I am, I cannot sleep, or perhaps I do—but it is more like wandering endlessly through some hall of images. Finally the room brightens and Solotaroff's little boy and girl are there, giggling and whispering, and I smell coffee brewing. Then I remember. Alexander Berkman is calling for me at ten.

I will not be going back to Rochester. At least not today.

HANNES MOST

I have only to be in a theater for it to begin. The theater might be large or small, opulent or dingy, no matter, it begins with chills, and my mouth shaking, and even my teeth banging, and then I am shaking all over with joy— and life. I am *most* myself, I think, in a theater! Oh, a poor joke, but undeniable. Now, looking at the blood-red curtain of the Metropolitan Opera House's stage, I can hardly control the shaking. Does the girl notice? We are standing against a back wall in the second balcony—an indignity!— because we arrived, having walked thirty blocks up from the Lower East Side, well after the house had sold out this performance of Bizet's *Carmen*. Ahead of us, in row after row, are the bourgeoisie, the pampered and tiara-ed, the rotten-to-the-core and soon-to-plop-from-the-trees rich, but never mind. Below us is that jewel, the stage and its infinities.

The curtain sways open just as the orchestra begins the galloping charge of the first overture, and I gasp, a small sound in the din of music and applause for the stage setting, a square in Seville, gushing fountain, brilliant flowers, Spanish buildings, and everything, setting, soldiers, and people smoldering in the golden haze of some perfect Mediterranean light. I have read this opera several times in German, and then, nearly knowing it from memory, read it in French. On the walk up Broadway from the girl's flat on Suffolk Street, I told her the story of the doomed Carmen and Jose, but what is telling to this? Now I glance at her, standing on my right side, my good side. Her mouth is open a little, her eyes unblinking.

The tragedy unfolds. Micaela, the charming village girl enters, looking for her love, Jose. She leaves. Street boys sing their bugle march and exit. The cigarette girls from the factory enter, singing sweetly of smoke that goes to the head and fills the soul with joy. *The sweet talk of lovers, that is smoke . . .* Then comes the tumultuous appearance of the gypsy Carmen, one of the cigarette factory girls, and music veers from the ethereal, down, down into the tempestuous. Young men encircle her. *Be nice, Carmen! Tell us when you'll love us! When?* she asks, looking at Jose, beyond them. *When? Maybe never! Love is a rebel bird no one can tame. A gypsy child! It has never known a law. L'amour, L'amour, L'amour!* The young men ring her around, but she escapes, singing of the rebel bird Love, the gypsy child, Love.

We applaud madly after this aria. Emotion chokes me, and I want to weep. After a while, I remember the girl at my side and again glance at her. Her eyelashes glitter in reflected stage light, her face is pinched with emotion. This delights me, she being so moved, someone so young, pretty, and intelligent.

Carmen throws the acacia flower at Jose, who jumps up in anger at this witch's gift. The cigarette girls return to work, and Micaela enters again, finding Jose. The music ascends, becoming hymnlike. Micaela brings a letter from Jose's mother, who forgives him, and also sends, via the chaste Micaela, a matronly kiss. Jose believes himself saved, but by the end of the first act he belongs to Carmen, who sings mockingly of defiance when she addresses the captain, Zuninga. *I defy everything—fire, steel, and heaven itself!* Because she takes such a tone, he tries to imprison her, but with Jose's help she escapes. This I understand, this defiance! This passion to defy!

When the lights come up after the second act, I see that the girl has been weeping. "It's not even over yet," I tell her. "There's far worse to come."

"It's my feet. I wore new shoes tonight, and we walked so far."

"Then take them off!" This, more a growl than speech. *New shoes!* What stupid vanity! Bah. I turn away from her.

Jose and Carmen are in the mountains, where the gypsies sing of pressing on, heedless of danger and difficulties, storms, torrents, and soldiers. I must close my eyes at those words, which have become *my* words: *Sans souci du torrent, sans souci de l'orage! Sans souci du soldat qui la-bas nous attend . . .* When I open my eyes, I see the girl hunched over, unfastening a shoe. *Shoes!* I cannot imagine Carmen worrying about such a thing! Is there a Carmen in the real world? No, probably not!

The real world drops away again, as Carmen draws a card to read her fate. But it is spades: the death card. Again and again she draws. *In vain, hoping to avoid bitter answers, in vain you will shuffle . . .*

Yes, yes, spades, and again spades. Sentence after sentence, the Tombs, Blackwell's, death by hanging or, more simply, rotting in prison. The shovel card! My fate as surely as Carmen's and Jose's. And how the libretto unifies dramatic image and theme! Jose, the enraged bull who kills both Carmen and himself.

The girl limps alongside me as we leave the theater, but I am still deep in the opera and hardly notice. If elemental passion is stronger than bonds of family convention and chaste love; stronger than duty to country, but not, finally, stronger than fate, stronger than destiny, what does this mean for the autonomy of the individual? And defiance—what is defiance, in the face of destiny? And what are my own miserable words—just so much passed gas? And the cause, our sacred cause, our so-called movement—what of that?

Maybe just a grand movement of the bowels.

I enter a café and fall into a chair at a table. There is the girl—still. I had forgotten about her! Blondkopf. Pretty. I order a bottle of liebfraumilch, and when it arrives, I say, "Milk of woman's love! But it is not so sweet, I think, woman's love! *Prosit!*"

"I believe it can be, though," she says.

We drink to woman's love, and the wine courses through me, unfastening the rage as the girl unfastened the offending shoe.

"I did not think you would be so vain," I say. "Little blondkopf. New shoes! Too tight!"

She blushes the color of a deep pink rose. A childish color, not Carmen's scarlet.

"So. A little vanity. But never mind. How did you like the opera?"

"I was in rapture, especially after I removed my shoe."

The roar of laughter surprises me, and then she is laughing as well, and there we are, the two of us, drawing all eyes in the place as we yowl like idiots over our wine glasses. Soon she is telling me about the first opera she'd seen, when she was a young student in Konigsberg, a favorite female teacher taking her. *Il Trovatore.* Her eyes flash with the memory. Her small hands take flight. Her skin blooms again as she tells of her great anticipation, then the journey to the theater, the dim house, the magnificent chandelier, and the audience entering, in their silks and jewels, and the orchestra tuning, and finally the tragedy of the troubadour and Leonora unspooling on the stage, and she, the young girl, inside it all, every nerve taut and seared. And mine too, for she has transported me to that Konigsberg theater, and I see it with her eyes. In fact, I have begun shivering again, and my jaw shakes.

"To this day," she says, "I don't understand the . . . possession. How it could be—can be!—so real."

Carmen may have her castanets and gypsy dance, but this girl . . . this little blondkopf . . . has her voice, her dance of words.

"Do you know something, blondkopf? I have forgotten your name."

"Emma," she says. "Emma Goldman."

"Ah. That's right." I refill her glass and then raise mine. "Let us drink, Emma, to your first speech."

"Herr Most, do you make fun of me?"

"Hannes. Not Herr! Listen. I am looking into the future, like Carmen with her cards. And I see . . . *you!* On a stage, the hall filled. Do you know something else? I will make you great, Emma. You will be my protégée. And when I am gone, you will . . . take my place!"

The truth of this crashes through me like the opening chords of the prelude to *Carmen*. Yes—destiny. Yes—the death card. But I must not forget that before that there is *life*.

"*Prosit*, little blondkopf!"

"*Prosit!*"

EMMA

"He took you to the Opera? He bought *wine*?"

"Sasha—"

Berkman paces in my tiny flat. There is hardly room to move, with fabric in piles, the cutwork, and half-finished silk waists on the bed.

"Wine! He drinks too much wine! He spends money that's meant for the movement on operas and wine. What next? Meals in expensive restaurants? A new suit of clothes? A flower in the boutonniere?"

My face betrays the truth of those words. Hannes *had* worn a red carnation in his suit lapel that night. He loves flowers as much as I do.

"Sasha, he's an artist, a man of the stage. He can appreciate the . . . subtleties. And *Carmen* has great meaning. The story is about liberty, freedom—"

"So. An artist can take liberties where the common man cannot?"

"Sashenka, sit a moment. Sit down. I'll make tea."

"I do not think art has anything to do with the movement. It is beside the point, at least for now."

"But Sasha . . . the stage . . . it's a powerful tool, no? Ideas enter the mind through the heart."

"We have heads for that!"

"The heart, Sasha, is not necessary?"

"The stage, the heart, the opera—no! None of it is now *necessary*. Only the movement is necessary. Afterward, there might be time for . . . pursuits of leisure. The heart!

There's too much work to do now to worry about the heart. The money he spent we could have used to rent a hall, print circulars."

"Yes, you are right. But we are not machines. We have feelings. We must feed the soul, Sasha, as well as the body, I think."

"The soul."

"Yes. And in that way, too, help the movement."

"That is a rationalization. Until all can have equally, why should just a few have?"

I see again the poor in the Bowery, children playing in dirty puddles, alcoholics lying on piles of paper, and working men and women crowding the halls, desperate for change. "Sasha," I say, "do you really think that everyone can finally be raised to some equality?"

"Think? I believe it! I know it! It's only greed that prevents it. The corrupt system and greed and selfish notions like attending an opera rather than working for the people."

"Sashenka, the tea is ready. Sit, please."

He does but then touches the violets wilting in their small water glass. "These," he says. "Where do you find these, in November?"

"Please, Sasha, don't rage at me. You have no right."

"In some hothouse they are grown, and he buys them for you!"

"Yes. He did. And you are jealous."

"Emma, you do not know him as I do. Yes, he can give a rousing speech when he wishes, but you don't know how he regards women. His view is that they are all sexual opportunists who only hang around to find men. Then the first thing you know, they're married, and the movement is out a good comrade. But he's old, Emma. He's embittered and tired. I think he's looking for someone himself. You must stay away from him. I see how it is now, with him."

"Sasha, I left my marriage because my husband was jealous and possessive. I vowed always to remain free—in love, particularly. I refuse, I absolutely refuse, to be ordered or commanded except by my own heart. I do not believe in marriage, but I do believe in love, in following my heart."

"So are you telling me that you love *him*? So soon?"

"No! I am telling you what I have come to understand and what I intend to do. But I think you may be mistaken about him, Sasha. He's not embittered. He still believes in the movement. He has strength and conviction, and he said—"

Abruptly, Sasha stands and goes to the door.

"Sasha! *Sashenka!*"

I push myself between him and the door. "You are free to leave but only after we make up this quarrel."

"And just how do we make it up?"

He is so young, only eighteen, and now he seems even younger—a hurt child.

"You are so . . . pure, Sasha dear. Can you learn to tolerate us lesser mortals? For the good of the movement?"

I lean against him and rest my head on his chest. I encircle his broad back with my arms. On the night of the opera, Hannes told me that he has need of ardent friendship. That many idolize him but no one loves him. In retrospect, yes, he did seem something of an old man begging, though what a man. And I just a factory girl, as I told him. With Hannes there will always be the self-consciousness, the awareness of irremediable inequality—his vast learning, for instance, compared to mine. But this boy, this Sasha! We are the same. His hunger, mine. His youth, his neediness, mine.

We lie on my small cot under the window, and I give myself to him and it's painful, as always with me, but a streak of pain bringing, this time, tears of joy. A seam of cool air from the window drifts over our joined bodies.

"Sasha," I whisper. Just to say his name.

LEON

On Tuesday and Thursday evenings, when my shift permits, we meet at the library in Natrona, which is a fine house. Soon, I come to connect its church-like quiet with Lucenia's silver eyeglasses and heart-shaped face. Walking in tonight, I see Lucy, as she likes to be called now, at a table, a book in front of her, and her head lowered nearly to the page. The librarian has told us that Mrs. Heuvel's lecture was based on Henry David Thoreau's essay called "Spring." So we have started there, with its first sentence, which I have since memorized. *The opening of large tracts by the ice-cutters commonly causes a pond to break up earlier; for the water, agitated by the wind, even in cold weather, wears away the surrounding ice.*

Tracts. Agitated. Wears. Surrounding. Those were the first words we looked up in the English-Polish dictionary and wrote down in our tablets. Often, it takes us a full evening to read through one of Mr. Thoreau's pages. Then it is hard to remember the sense of it, but that doesn't matter. Sitting at our table off to the side, where the librarian allows us to whisper since we are studying, I feel holy, like in church after I go to confession. Here is another sentence I memorized. *The day is an epitome of the year. The night is the winter, the morning and evening are the spring and fall, and the noon is the summer. Epitome* means that something can stand for something else that is larger. But for me, the sentence is not so much true because even though it is night now, it does not feel like winter. It feels like spring.

"Here is another hard word, Leon," she whispers. "*Phenomena.*"

We write it down, and she turns through pages of the dictionary. I wait for her to whisper the definition, but she keeps reading. When she raises her head, her eyes appear even more watery behind the eyeglasses.

"What is wrong?" I whisper. "Is it a word we should not know?"

"I cannot understand the definition!"

I pull the book over and try to read the definition. It is impossible! Before I can think what to say, Lucy takes the book to the librarian's desk. When she comes back to our table minutes later, her face is brighter.

"It means what we experience, Leon! We look at something and observe. We touch it and feel. So it is something we experience through our senses."

"Then it is something real?"

"It can be."

The word is not clear to me, still. But I know what I observe. I know what I feel. I want to touch her white hands. Where people have knuckles, she has dimples. I want to touch each one. Are they phenomena? Dare I use the word?

No. I'm afraid it will be wrong if I say it.

"Leon? Were you listening? Here's another good word. *Cosmos.* It means everything. The universe. What God created. *Chaos* means what was before the Creation. Disorder and darkness."

She writes in her tablet so I do, too. *Cosmos. Cosmos. Cosmos.* I want to say, in Polish, your hands have little pools where fish swim, but she is studying the essay again. I only want to look at her.

"Leon! Listen to this! *A single gentle rain makes the grass many shades greener.* That is true! We have seen this for ourselves, but we probably didn't think it important, and here this man writes about it in a book!"

I smile because she is so happy. Then we come to a sentence that takes a long time to unravel. *We should be blessed if we lived in the present always and took advantage of every accident that befell us.*

After we have written the sentence in our tablets and defined for ourselves its harder words, I take her tablet and write: *Meeting you was accident. I am blessed.*

She writes in mine: *To live now is to be blessed.*

We bow our heads over each other's words. I am trying to understand what she wishes to tell me—or not. At first it seems something very good but then just the opposite. My face begins to burn because I have told her more than she wishes to tell me. Why I do what I do next is a mystery. Later I think how I am nothing but a fool. I push my tablet to the side and then slide hers toward me. *Lucy,* I write. *You know something? I love you.*

She takes back her tablet and stares at the words. Color climbs her neck and reaches her cheeks and ears. Slowly she closes the tablet and lets her hand rest on its cover.

She does not look at me. What does this mean? Yes?—or no.

Outside, there is a cold rain. We hesitate to leave the library's porch, and this causes me to do something I know I should not. I try to draw her to me, and at first she stiffens, then eases, but finally she pushes me away. I am at once very sorry for doing that and I tell her so.

"Leon," she says. "Think."

Behind her, hazy street lights look like smaller and smaller globes on a string. What is there to think? I love her but now am afraid of saying anything more.

She opens her umbrella and walks out from the shadows and toward the tram stop. The tram arrives almost at once, it seems—too fast! Sitting alongside her in the car, I say, "Lucy, marry me."

"*Now*, Leon?" She smiles and makes it seem a joke.

"Soon. Whenever you say."

"But we both need to know more, first!"

"What do we need to know?"

"Everything!"

Again she uses the same voice as when something amuses her.

All the phenomena I see tonight tell me that she does not love me, cannot feel as I feel, and might never. In my thoughts Mrs. Heuvel says I am allowing discouragement a home in my heart.

"So," I say when the conductor has gone to the front, "we better study fast if we don't want to be eighty years old when we marry!"

She laughs and it is better.

1893–1899

LEON

A bitter mist clouds the light and stings the eyes and skin. Steel rods drawn through tungsten carbide blocks whine. To me it sounds like something being changed into something else forever but not wanting this change. We stand on planks laid over a brick floor and work with rollers and vats, cisterns and cauldrons, drawing blocks and winding blocks. At every hour of the day hot metal has to be cooled and cold metal heated; dry metal lubricated and wet metal dried. Always something, never nothing. Now I lower a coiled bundle of steel rods into a vat of what we call pickling solution. The sulphuric acid boils and hisses like a witch's brew. We do this because the rods were heated to over a thousand degrees and came out scaly with chips of iron oxide all over them. These scales will ruin the tungsten carbide drawing blocks, so we must get them off. But the acid will ruin the machinery, too, so the rods must go from acid bath to water bath, and then into a lime emulsion. But that is handled by other men farther down the line.

I stay with this job because the wage is good and I know how to do the work well. I am one of the acid men, in charge of vats and of the carboys of sulphuric acid, hydrochloric acid, and nitric acid. Each day I dip five hundred coiled bundles of rods twice, once in acid and once in water. I often wonder where a particular bundle of new wire will be going. This one might make fences. That one electrical cord or a well drill or a suspension bridge, or maybe a ship hawser or lightning rod, birdcages or mousetraps, or buckles, screws, nails, springs, bolts, or even a piano. This bundle here might become bright wire, annealed wire, galvanized wire, electroplated wire, or plain old barbed wire. It might be lead-coated, aluminum-coated, enamel-coated, or finished in copper, brass, or tin. It will be a good thing, after all it has to go through, and I am proud of that. The bad thing is how it makes me feel—other men, too, I think, though nobody complains. If you complain, they give you the boot. So we say nothing, but I can feel the acid in my eyes and burning on my hands and forearms, face and neck. Also, it burns the inside of the nose and mouth and throat. They say you get used to it. I have, somewhat, but at night before sleep, I hear that whine of rods being pulled through the blocks, and it is something I cannot get used to. Often, the sound is in my dreams, and often, the first thing I hear when I wake up in the morning.

After my shift, I go to my father's saloon on Todd Street. We live in Cleveland now because my father craved a change. The saloon is crowded with off-shift men filling up on beer and the free ham sandwiches, beans, and boiled eggs that go with it. My little sister Victoria has made me a ham sandwich with sweet pickles, and she places a cup of coffee alongside it because beer no longer goes down well but burns too much. Victoria is fourteen years old and already a beauty, with gray eyes and pale curls about her forehead. The rest of her hair is in two braids she winds in circles. In the heat of the saloon, her skin is pink. I do not like that she has to work here, and I do not like the way men sometimes look at her.

Victoria also brings me today's newspaper, but as I thank her, I suddenly cannot exhale. Air is filling me but has no way to get out. I leave the saloon and in the alley behind it, I heave until I can bring up the phlegm. Then I have to stand there, waiting for my heart to slow. This happens sometimes at the factory, but in all the noise, my heaving and coughing is nothing. Other men do the same, so I think it is just the acid needing to come out.

Inside, I eat a bit to please Victoria before telling her that I will walk her home. "But it is not time yet, Leon!" she says in Polish. I go and tell Father I will take her home, she worked long enough, there all day. He says nothing because he is too busy behind the bar. He should hire somebody else, some *wiedzma* like my stepmother who could hold her own here, but then she might drive everybody away.

Outside it is cold, with wind. Victoria shivers as she tells me our parents want to move yet again, they were talking about it today. She speaks in Polish, but I answer in English. "They always want to move."

"This time a farm, Mother says."

"Say it in English."

Slowly, she does. "A farm. Mother says."

"Say the whole thing."

"Oh, Leon."

"You have to or you won't learn. You will sound uneducated." I say this in Polish so she will understand.

"I am uneducated!"

"No, your English is fairly good but needs to be better."

"Why?" she says in English and slowly explains that she will be going to live with our sister Celia when Celia marries soon.

This is news, and I think how our family is pulling apart like old cloth. Waldeck gone. Jacek in northern Michigan, Adam in North Dakota. Michael in the regular Army. Soon Celia and Victoria gone.

And Lucy, too—in Pittsburgh, with Mrs. Heuvel.

I remind Victoria how Lucy left her aunt and uncle because they wouldn't let her spend time reading and because they also refused to pay her a wage. So what does she do? She writes to Mrs. Heuvel, the teacher in

Pittsburgh, tells her how things are, and asks to come work for *her*. Mrs. Heuvel sends Lucy money for the train, and now Lucy is in school, in Pittsburgh.

"But Leon, I don't want to go to school!" Victoria says. "I want to marry, like Celia, and have my own house and family."

In these words I hear how Victoria does not want to better herself. In these words I hear how Lucy does not want to marry me now or ever. Otherwise she would not have gone to Mrs. Heuvel. Otherwise she would write to me once in a while. I don't know how to think about this. I am glad for her, but not for myself, and I understand that she does not write to me because she never cared for me in the first place.

We reach our house on Gertrude Street and go in quietly. Upstairs, I drink from a bottle of Dr. Hermann Pencz's Remarkable Miracle. The liquid is brown and comes out like sludge. The smell is of rotten fish although that might be the taste. It goes down with a burn, but that might be my throat. I lie on my bed and think how maybe I should write to that Mrs. Heuvel myself. At least she might tell me how Lucy is. Or maybe I should go to her and ask if maybe there is some work I could do there.

The thought frightens me and yet almost gives me hope. But how can I find the address and get time off from the factory? Are both even possible? And what if they fire me when I return? Or should I stay in Pittsburgh somehow? Could I even find new work there, coughing like I do? And then live how? And what would Lucy think if she did see me?

Idiota! She will see a sick man she won't want anything to do with.

I tell Victoria to try and improve herself, but my voice lacks conviction now. No wonder she doesn't listen.

EMMA

I take the strawberry-rhubarb pie from the oven and set it with others cooling on wire racks. These racks were manufactured here in Worcester, less than a mile away, farther down the Blackstone River. We bought—Sasha, Fedya, Sasha's cousin, and I—two commercial-quality racks, along with four large cast-iron skillets, the enamel-ware pans and covered pots, the large coffee pot, the cutlery, and a set of durable china. Just last month, we also purchased a new soda fountain assembly. This outlay of money brought on, in me, nervous headaches.

What madness. Revolutionaries buying soda fountains!

While making my pies and tortes, I have time to think just how mad, just how curving and unpredictable our course has been since I met my Sasha in New York five years ago. First, Most's tutelage, and he sending me out on speaking trips, one even to Rochester, where I scandalized our entire community. Then both Sasha and Most falling in love with me—*acht!* Most an old man, so disfigured, so needy. For love. For beauty. For the opera.

He's a fraud. An old fraud! Revolution? Hah. What he wants is a warm fireside and a woman to serve him.

Sasha, can we not have art and beauty and *the revolution? Personal love* and *the revolution?*

No. Love and beauty—those are for later. After the revolution.

But we are human, Sasha, no?

Yes, but we have to rise above those base needs for now.

Rising above such base needs, we make love, Sasha and I. After serving our many customers, after buying a soda fountain, after making pies and soups, we lie in the heat of our room over this lunchroom—while Fedya in the next room paints—and indulge in bourgeois pleasures that drive us both to the edge of rapture. Is *this* less base than the opera? I ask, touching his erect penis? And what of *this?*— I holding his tongue between my teeth. And how does *this* compare to a bunch of violets?—my tongue licking each of his fingers and the palms of his hands. After Most's old man's body, I revel in Sasha's, the beauty of it, the power, the perfection of it. Oh, yes, Sasha, beauty! I must have it, revolution or no. And he, of course, my revolutionist, does not refuse me. Never refuses. Thinking this makes me tremble with need for that body. I look over at him. He is pouring flour from a twenty-five pound bag—Rochester flour!—into a great mixing bowl.

Well, and what are we doing, then, in this lunchroom if we are revolutionists?

A good question. Poor Hannes is in prison—*again.* He may die there this time. As revolutionists, we could not finally get the proletariat to go beyond thinking of its own need for an eight-hour day. Beyond that, nothing matters to them. Ah, America, you are too hard, too infertile. Hannes would have sent Sasha to Russia to work for the revolution there, but American comrades did not contribute enough, finally.

So it is up to us. Our good comrade Fedya found work in Springfield, making crayon enlargements and tinting photographs. I followed and became an order clerk for the photographer, who was quite successful. It gave us ideas. *Come to Worcester with us,* I wrote to Sasha. *We'll open our own studio and soon have more than enough money for Russia.*

Imagine us three in a rented buggy, traveling the back roads around Worcester, Sasha not able to control the horse, and the buggy knocking into posts and trees and granite stones, and Yankee farm women watching with suspicion as horse and buggy meander up their lanes, and a young man calls out in heavily accented English: *Crayon enlargements! Crayon enlargements of family portraits!*

Who wants?

No one.

Sasha railed, saying that these farmers are not peasants. There is no peasant goodness in their hearts. They are capitalists—not the proletariat. Their farms are factories.

But an American capitalist, our landlord, so proud of his acumen and success, gave us an idea. *Can the young lady cook or bake? Then start a lunchroom! There's money in that. I know just the place. Fact is, it's in another building of mine.*

So we have meandered, just as we had in that rented buggy drawn by the intractable horse, here, into this gold-mine. Now we are like the storybook elves who nightly spin straw into gold. Only in this case, it is our good German and Russian food that pours the gold into our cash register each day. Soon, perhaps by summer's end, we will have enough for all three of us to go to Russia and work for the revolution there.

It is where we belong.

Well, I can say this yet still feel somewhat guilty— "Sasha, my dear, more flour here, please"—for an ugly situation has been developing at the Homestead steel mill near Pittsburgh, and I have been wondering if leaving America now, just as workers are beginning to wake up and fight, may not be both selfish and shortsighted. While Mr. Carnegie is off on another trip to Scotland, his ruthless partner and manager Henry Clay Frick has his orders: Break the union.

Could this not be just the opportunity we need? The moment that will awaken the whole of America?

"You know, Emma, they are using language as a weapon here."

"What do you mean, Sasha?"

"This morning, in the paper, they call Carnegie a capitalist. Now, tell me. What is a capitalist?—a business organizer. One who brings together companies. So, my Emma, what then is a labor organizer?"

"One who brings together workers?"

"No, Emma—a red!"

"A socialist, an agitator," Fedya calls from our small dining room, where he is finishing his wonderful mural of a Russian birch grove.

We laugh because it is amusing in a terribly dark way.

"The paper also said that Pinkertons will be brought in to restore law and order. And what are Pinkertons? Hired armed men, often criminals, but when in the service of capitalists, they are lawmen *restoring* law and order. But if you have armed men in the service of their union, what are these men called?"

"Lawbreakers," I say.

"Rioters," Fedya calls.

Sasha bangs down a flour sifter. "Here, government can aid business but to aid labor—no! That is socialist. Capitalists can combine, and it is all ordained by natural law. Let labor combine and it is a conspiracy. And what are strikers? Foreigners, anarchists, nihilists, communists. And who are the unemployed? Loafers, bummers, no-goods. If you are a discontented worker, then you are a dupe of the agitators. If you are a striker, you are a wild-eyed Russian."

"Like you, Sashenka."

"Like me!"

He straightens his eyeglasses. His hair is dusted white with flour, and his forearms.

"We need to get more strawberries at that farm, Sashenka. They are quite good."

Maybe we should stay here after all. Maybe there is hope, given this strike now. I go out into the dining room to serve a customer who has just entered, but cannot help admiring the meadow scene Fedya has painted over our soda fountain and shelves—brown cows, a stream and meadow, distant blue hills, and in the near distance, a stand of birch. Fedya loves birches above all trees. He has several small, framed landscapes for sale, hanging near the tables, but no one asks about these. Our customers are only interested in the baked goods, the ice cream, and the sandwich and soup bill of fare. At times I pity Fedya. What he can do so well, no one wants, yet he continues painting—a true artist! Will he paint in Russia? I worry that the comrades there may not allow it. I worry that he will be considered an aesthete and scorned because of his narrow frame and girlish eyes, his love of fine cloth and color and poetry (like me!).

Quite apart from the Homestead strike, that is another reason for staying here, though Sasha will be enraged if I voice this opinion.

Our customer is a disheveled young man in a too-large jacket. He has the copper-colored hair of an Irishman or Scotsman and the fair skin. He limps. He looks about himself skittishly. His hands are not clean, nor are his clothes. It occurs to me that he is a thief. I go behind the counter and stand just where we have placed a twelve-inch meat cleaver on a shelf under the counter. Against a gun, though, this cleaver will no doubt prove useless. Across the room, Fedya paints, oblivious to this supposed customer.

The backroom is quiet. Sasha may have gone upstairs to rest. "Friend," I say in my new English, "you look hungry. Let me give you some of our good Stroganoff. It is a stew."

The words confound him, or else it is my accent. He lowers his head. "I can't pay," he finally says.

My heart bangs out its alarm. "There is work here to do, in trade for a full meal. With pie and coffee," I add.

Soon he is seated, eating his fill while looking at advertisements in an edition of the *Boston Herald*, one of the newspapers we keep here for our customers. So I was right. He is out of work and might have been about to rob us. I refill his coffee cup and serve him a piece of strawberry-rhubarb pie crowned with vanilla ice cream. He gives me a nickel, which I refuse. "When you are finished, the backroom needs sweeping and a good mopping." I keep my voice neutral and pretend not to see that his eyes are filling. "These berries you will like. They are from a farm near the lake." The word Quinsigamond is always hard for me to pronounce, but I try—and sound quite the foreigner. "Sometimes they want workers at that farm. I give you directions."

He eats the pie. I bring a second piece, and soon he is mopping the backroom floor. I serve a few other customers, worrying all the while that the fellow just may change his mind and come out into the lunchroom and rob these unsuspecting Americans as well as our cash register. But no. When I go in back to check on his work, he is not there. He has slipped away, using the back door. Nothing is missing. The floor is clean.

After the three of us have closed for the night and have finished the baking for the next morning, I go back into the lunchroom to tidy up the chairs and tables. In the *Boston Herald*, a notice has been torn from the advertisements. The boy's doing, I'm certain.

I sit for a minute to rest my legs. This edition of the paper carries a story about the ongoing Republican convention in Minneapolis, and I work at deciphering it in order to learn more English. It is very hot there, over ninety degrees, it says. I do not understand the process of balloting at conventions. I thought that people in America voted for their rulers in elections and not at conventions. But the paper says there was a move to nominate William McKinley, the governor of Ohio, on the second ballot if Benjamin Harrison did not make it on the first. Whenever McKinley appeared on stage—and he had to quite often, as chairman of the convention, there was rousing, foot-stamping applause. Now there is talk of a "boom." A McKinley "boom."

I also do not understand about these booms and must ask Sasha. And what are these ballots and deals made at conventions? Is this what Americans mean by "democracy"? Booms and deals?

In another article there is more about the troubles at Homestead. My ignorance dismays me. Again the word "boom" is used, this time concerning the steel industry. There is a boom now because of protective tariffs. Tariffs protect the industry here. Then why cannot workers get the modest raises they ask for? Not only that, but at Homestead, union workers are going to be penalized by having their wages cut even more. Mr. Frick is saying that he is not even going to talk with the union, only with individual workers who want to work.

I think he is like the czar, this Frick.

In a prolabor paper an editorial asks, *What next, Mr. Frick? Pinkertons? The Pennsylvania militia?*

Is anyone at the Republican convention talking about Homestead? I go back to the first article and read about resin dropping from green lumber in the heat and gumming the hair and spoiling the suits of the delegates. I read of a lithesome girl snaking through the convention hall, half-wrapped around in "Old Glory"—I must ask Sasha what this Old Glory is. But no, I find nothing about Homestead.

Out of habit I glance up at Fedya's birches and imagine Fedya and myself on the riverbank, with a picnic basket.

Perhaps, I think, before we leave for Russia we will do this. Just once.

I stack the newspapers and draw down the shade on the front door. Today we have made seventy-one dollars.

EAMON

Up ahead in our train car, college boys are buffeting army boys with questions the army boys won't answer. The train slows, and one of the college boys walks to a guard and asks to be let off. The guard is also from the army and he shoves the boy back down into a seat and says, "Nobody leaves!"

The sour-smelling fellow sitting alongside me draws from his flask and says, "Want some?" while the college boys in our car start yelling Homestead, ain't it? Ain't it Homestead where we're headed?

Homestead? Where all the strike trouble is going on? That is my thought when I hear the word *Homestead.* Can it mean any other kind of homestead? A homestead is a farm with land, right? If it's where the strike is, that's a steel mill outside Pittsburgh. But why would anyone call a steel mill Homestead?

It don't make sense but one thing does. I am thinking how a man named Harrington bought me for one dollar, he not caring that I cracked my knees in the Lady mine out west, falling like that, coming out of a tunnel that dropped, and then they did not heal right. He did not even care that I got sent away for thievery after I could not find any honest work. He just shoving a dollar at me and buying me a steak dinner, so I am thinking, sure, it has to be Homestead where we are going, that steel mill, because otherwise he would of cared about my knees and about the prison term. The newspaper said *Guards needed to secure property*, and

I not wanting to thieve again, and so when he shoved that dollar in my direction, I nearly shamed myself with tears. And when a man gives you a dollar and buys you a steak dinner, you are not inclined to ask too many questions. But now I see it. Sure, Homestead is where we are heading, with this parcel of army boys. How in the world, though, did he get these college boys to come along?

After some hours of the college boys hurling their questions and army boys spitting out answers that are not answers, the train stops. More guards—all regular army boys—enter the car and say we are getting off now. Outside, in the dark, we have to walk between two rows of them and their rifles, toward two barges that lay low in some fog-hung river like the backs of critters from hell. These barges have some kind of top over them, black, and so they do look like crocodile critters in the poor light. We climb down a few steps into a space fitted out with bunks, and I go to the ones in back. I know by the smell that the foul-scented fellow is following close behind. Guards are telling us to sleep, we'll need it, and so we lay down on the wood planks with no blankets, and that is the calm before the storm. In no time at all, it seems, a couple of army boys are ripping open wooden crates and lifting out blue jackets and white shirts and telling us to put them on. We obey this order. Is this what guards wear? The foul-smelling one has told me his name—Gilliat—not that I cared to learn it. He says they are fitting us up for a parade, then laughs like an eejit. He is all but drunk and nothing matters to him except that his flask is near empty now.

Soon there is a dinging against the top of our barge, like stones thrown. Rifle shot! an army boy yells, and we know for sure we have come to where we were going—Homestead. The college boys turn into whimpering babes as the captain goes around handing out rifles but not to them. He's not going to give them anything but a good boot if they don't stop snuffling, which makes them snuffle all the more. Then the captain is asking for some boys to cross over to the other barge and fortify that one. Gilliat grabs my arm and holds me back. When the forward hatch opens, we can hear yelling not too far away. Sounds like they're saying *Kill the black sheep!* Don't let 'em land! Kill 'em!

"Black sheep," Gilliat says. "They think we're scabs."

"We aren't," I say. "We're guards."

He just laughs again and tries for more of whatever used to be in his flask.

The captain pretends to courage, and maybe it is as he climbs up the steps to the open hatch and hollers that we are taking over the works no matter what. The dinging against our barge worsens. An army boy yells the news. "Strikers are running toward the gangplank! The captain is kicking one of 'em. The captain's hit! He's down!"

Inside the barge, there is again the crackle of splintering wood and then more rifles, this time good Winchester ones, are passing from hand to hand. Soon we are climbing up out of the barge with our Winchesters. I am surprised to find that it is dark and I do not know whether it is night or morning. Lights from the works make starry spokes in the fog. As we clump together on the shore, someone shouts an order, and the army boys fire as one, directly into the crowd of men farther up the slope leading to the works.

"Gilliat," I say, "what the hell?"

"So how d'you like being a Pink?" he says.

From what I can see, the men on the slope are shoving each other backward, up the hill, and then they're hiding behind piles of scrap iron and are firing at us. A number of bodies lay on the incline. Behind them, the works looks like a fort. I have yet to raise my rifle because it is not in me to do so. *Pink? Pink what?*

One of the college boys jumps off our barge and into the river. At once he is fired upon by shooters out in skiffs.

One army boy calls out at us not to try that, but two more college boys do so. Each time one is hit, there is hurrahing from the men on the slope. And so I finally understand that this is a war. We have come to guard property, Harrington said, but it is a war instead.

From behind the scrap iron, someone comes running down the slope with a basket of what must be dynamite sticks, for we can see burning fuses. We scatter to either side, and then there is a wrathful explosion. Boys struck through with pieces of metal from our barge bleed and cry. The captain has retreated into the barge, and we are on our own. Now the river is burning, and cannonballs from across the river are casting up waterspouts that disturb the flames. An army boy yells that the strikers got a railcar full of burning oil aimed right at us.

It is something to know that you are trapped. You don't believe it at first because that is how the body is, so full of itself and its powers for such a long time it is blind to any other thought, but then the blindness lifts like the fog and there you are. A done-up case. Gilliat curses his lack of whiskey.

We hear hurrahing as we retreat to the half-blown-apart barge and crawl under bunks and await Kingdom Come. But then one of the army regulars yells how the car jumped into the air, at the end of the track, and dropped down a few yards short of us. We can smell the burning. The same army boy tells us to calm down, a tug is coming for us, he can see it. Then *he* is cursing. There's a burning raft on the river twirling toward us, he says, setting more of the river on fire. The tug is turning back. "Don't lose heart, boys," someone yells. "It's going to try again."

It does not try again, that we know of, and all around, wounded boys are moaning. A fellow lies dying not far away, blood leaping out of him in spikes. Gilliat took off his blue jacket and tried to stop it, but in no time at all the jacket was useless.

An army boy grabs a white shirt from a crate and makes a surrender flag, using his rifle as a pole. This he sticks out the open hatch. The shirt is shot to shreds in minutes. But after a time, it is quiet, so quiet we are all wondering what infernal device they have got for us now. Instead, a dapper fellow in a brown suit appears in the open hatchway and looks down in at the wretched lot of us before saying in an Irishman's tongue, "There is enough of the killing. On what terms do ye wish to give up?"

Soon we are surrendering our rifles and pistols, those that have them, and ammunition. We put on the big hats and button our coats, those that can, and climb out into the day. Hundreds of strikers stand in two clumps on the slope leading to the works. They are quiet as death, just watching us. As we are led between the clumps, strikers begin poking off our hats with poles. One of them grabs my jacket and pulls it off. Another striker is throwing hats and jackets into the burning river. Behind us, the barges burn. Ahead, a striker is slapping at those in our line with the knuckled side of his hand. Others are throwing stones at us. I see a club studded with nails come down upon a head. Army boys are falling to their knees. College boys, too. I do not see the pouch of rocks before it hits me full in the face. Gilliat holds me up and we get out of range. "That was a woman," he says, and damns her to hell along with all the rest of them. There is an uproar of sound now, coming from us and them. Women prod at us with furled parasols. We try to move forward to wherever, but it is hard, with so many of us falling. Gilliat must be cursing but I only see his mouth moving, and I don't see what comes next. It is like walking straight into a branch, not seeing it at all, just feeling the stab in the eye. I close both eyes at the blaze of pain. Wet is seeping out around my fingers, and I fear it is my eye or what was my eye. Pain worsens and it nearly puts me under. Gilliat has me in some fierce hold. Sometime later we are inside a building, in a room with seats like in some theater. Gilliat is saying, "Want to come, boy?" And I think, *Where?* Where does he want to go and how can we do it? So I shake my head because no one could do it, with all them out there, but then he takes a case knife from his boot and parts the flesh of one wrist and then the other, and the blood beads at first, then seeps outward like a spring from mud. He lowers both arms and lets the blood slide out upon the floor. Then I am crying like any one of those college boys who have somehow lived through all this.

I wake to quiet and stillness. It comes to me that I am in a bed, in a white room, so it is reasonable to think that I have been dreaming. Inside me relief fills every bone, every muscle. I touch my face. I touch my left eye but feel bandages. I touch my other eye. No bandages. I remember the women with furled parasols jabbing at us. I remember the man Gilliat, his case knife scratching a line across each wrist. I remember the barges, the burning river, the surrender flag shot to nothing. I remember the man Harrington and the steak dinner. Soon I am wailing bad as anything.

Son, someone is saying. *Son.* I think it is Gilliat and try to stop. Soon I can. With my good eye I see that it is not Gilliat. It is someone I do not know. This man has dark hair and a white-pale face. He has a hand on my forehead. Then he is rubbing the right side of my forehead, and I feel my heart slow. He says "They feeding you all right in here, son?" I nod even though I do not remember any food whatsoever. He says "I am going to tell them to see to it that you get something special." He keeps up that rubbing, and I do not want it to stop. I raise and lower my head as much as I can and make sounds that I hope are *Thank you, sir.*

He stays a long time rubbing my head like that, knowing just how to do it.

Later I find out his name. William McKinley, who is the governor of the state of Ohio, where I now am.

Governor? This I can hardly believe.

Were it not for my bandaged eye, I surely would not believe any of it.

EMMA

About four thirty, a man enters the lunchroom carrying an afternoon edition of the *Herald* and orders ice cream. I bring the dish of butter pecan to his place at the counter and then notice the headlines. *A day of Rioting, Bloody Work at Homestead . . . Twenty Killed in a Battle between Strikers and Pinkerton Men . . .*

I drop the damp towel I was holding and tell him I need to close the lunchroom. "There is emergency," I say. "Do not pay for ice cream, but may I have your paper?"

"I beg your pardon?"

"I must close!"

He rushes out, and I take the paper upstairs. "Sasha! Fedya! Wake up. You must read this."

Shortly after midnight, we are on a train to New York.

"You folks are plain loony," our landlord Mr. Dereck told us, "leaving a gold mine like this. What's the matter with you? You folks could be rich by summer's end. Never heard of such a thing!" I hardly hear these words. I sense that Sasha does not hear them at all.

Fedya has his paints but has left behind several canvases. We have left behind all the cooking utensils and the soda fountain assembly. We take only that day's receipts and a few pieces of clothing each. The next morning, in New York, we go to the flat on the Lower East Side of a couple we'd met in the anarchist group Autonomie. The woman, Marthe, opens the door. It is still very early, and we apologize. She appears exhausted and unhealthy, with liverish skin. Her hair is in long braids not yet pinned up. She looks at us and then at our valises.

"Marthe! Listen, please," I begin.

Our manifesto calls for the workers of Homestead to unite in the creation of a new social order based on justice and cooperation. We find a translator and a printer. We connect with old comrades. We write letters and give talks in halls, cafés, and in the streets. Our lunchroom in Worcester seems very far away and of another time. I no longer plan menus or see my customers' faces, nights before I fall asleep. There is no regret in my heart, just a rampage of questions. Who to see next, who to ask for money, who to ask for help? At night I ache everywhere, but it is good. It means I am wringing myself out again for a cause greater than any one person, a cause international in scope. Russia, America—what does it matter where it takes root, only that it does.

In a café near Union Square, Sasha takes our hands and says, in Russian, "Comrades, when I say it is time to act, I mean it is time to die. I have been preparing myself for this moment for years. Now it is here. I have decided that since you, Emma, are the natural speaker, you must live to explain the *attentat*. The capitalist press will distort it. You will have to clarify and explain that what I did was not directed at Frick the man, but Frick the symbol of the corrupt system. Nor was it the result of some selfish need for self-aggrandizement but rather the need to avenge the spilling of innocent workers' blood. You must make it clear that I have no personal grievance against him. Fedya, your task will be to help Emma and take care of her, if necessary."

"But Sashenka," I say, "the workers may rise up. There is no need to die! Please, Sashenka, do not say you must die."

"Emma, you are being naive. Frick will have guards there who might be reluctant to rise up. And this is only the beginning. There may be open warfare, and the capitalist press will wage its own war. You must counterattack with words. Yours will be the more difficult task. Mine will be over in a few minutes."

"Sasha, I do not understand. Why must you die, as part of the *attentat*?"

"Because I will not permit my enemies to kill me just as Lingg did not!"

Fear and horror wrench my stomach.

"My friends, my dearest," Sasha is saying, "why so dark? We should be joyful. Is this not what we have been working toward?"

Yes, Sasha. Yes. But my heart rejects it. My bourgeois heart.

No, my whole body.

A summer thunderstorm is bringing people into the café. They are wet and laughing. It shames me that I envy them.

"We must get more money," Sasha says. "I need supplies. Also, a suit of clothes and a railway ticket. We must canvass for funds."

I hold back words but clearly see, now, that our former landlord was right. We were fools to give up our lunchroom.

Sasha can obviously read my thoughts, or at least my expression. "Emma," he says, "a revolutionist does not look back."

"At least let us go to Pittsburgh with you, Sasha. As a woman, I can help gain access to Frick. Besides, I *must* be with you for the short time we now have."

"I alone will go, Emma."

Fedya has been so quiet through all this. He is looking out the window at the rain, the street, the hurrying people.

Sasha raises his glass. "Comrades. Let us drink, now, to the people. *V narod!*"

His expression does not ease. It is the expression of a man on the face of a boy.

"*V narod!*"

SASHA

That night I begin my study of Most's *Science of Revolutionary Warfare*. I will need to purchase, I learn, some high explosive—guhr dynamite if possible. This is a granular composite of kieselguhr and nitroglycerin. If I cannot obtain that, I will need some straight dynamite composed of nitroglycerin and wood meal or charcoal with a little calcium carbonate added. I need to handle it carefully though the nitroglycerin should be relatively safe, in its bed of inactive substance. Then I will need a blasting cap or detonator. These are dangerous because they are made of initiating explosives and are very volatile. Mercury fulminate is one—Louis Lingg comes to mind, the man's great courage after the Haymarket massacre. Swallowing mercury fulminate rather than hang—an act you may have to emulate, Sasha! Reading further, I learn that lead azide enclosed in a capsule of copper or aluminum may also suffice. I will have to scrutinize it in order to see if the capsule has come unsealed at any point. That means exposure to moisture and a ruined detonator. Also, dynamite itself is highly sensitive to moisture as well as freezing temperatures. So. I must find a reliable source.

I lean back and rub my eyes. Something is warning me that it is too much for one alone. In novels, perhaps. But this is life.

I go back to Most's book, dense with instruction and warnings. The man knows so much! Why can't *he* act?

Because, Sashenka, under all his braggadocio, Hannes is a small man paralyzed by a thousand bourgeois sentiments and emotions.

So, then, I must:

1. Buy the best dynamite possible.

2. Get the right size blasting cap. They come in sizes one through eight. If I get one that is too small, it will not detonate the secondary explosive.

3. Consider the type of fuse. I can use a safety or delayed fuse, which is hollow cord filled with a composite material that produces a slow and steady burning rate. Or, I can use an instantaneous fuse, a hollow cord filled with a substance that defeats me in my attempt to pronounce its name correctly. Simply, it is called PETN. This will produce an exceptionally fast fire, 6,000 miles per second. I will, in all probability, blow myself up with it.

I consider this possibility.

1. There will be no time for pain, for regret, for doubt.

2. Emma will be my voice—if she does not succumb to faintheartedness, which I fear she may. Fedya is not such a good influence, with his paints and his doe eyes.

It appears that I am a general with an army of two, only these two! Who can accomplish anything with such an army? So many comrades here in New York, but I cannot trust them. Flawed by human weaknesses as they are, I fear that any one of them will gladly betray me to the highest bidder.

All right, then. So. How do explosives work?

1. They work on the principle of changes in pressure.

2. Heat converts volatile substances into gases, which have a larger volume in relation to the surrounding pressure than their original volume. Hence, the explosion.

3. An explosion involves simple causality. Action. Reaction.

When I am confident, the following week, that I have learned everything possible about bomb making, I take the first morning ferry to Staten Island and there buy the necessary supplies from a man as nearsighted as I am. He speaks little, which pleases me. Having only forty dollars, the remainder of our money from Worcester, I cannot afford the guhr dynamite. Also of concern is that the fulminate capsules the man offers appear small, old, and tarnished, so I question him. When he begins to close the lid on the padded metal strongbox, I say, "All right. Never mind. I will take four."

Although I did not tell him my intentions, why could he not sense something extraordinary and so give me the guhr dynamite anyway?

On the ferry, an August sun ignites The Narrows into a flaming expanse. I carry the fulminate capsules in separate pockets. The explosives are in a valise. If anyone should jostle me, it will be the end for all of us. But no—soon I am walking through the streets of the Lower East Side. At Marthe's tenement, I go directly down into the damp and dark of the basement and begin to assemble two bombs.

A week later, it is done. I again take the ferry and carry one bomb in my valise to Staten Island. In a hidden sandy area, I ignite the safety fuse and run to a black willow fifty feet away and wait.

Overhead, a gull shrieks.

The black willow tosses its narrow leaves, its branches creaking like ship rigging.

Light falls through the branches of the tree, falls in shifting patterns upon the sand near my feet. In the clearing, a chip of pale flame crawls along the fuse, inching closer to the small black case. When it reaches the case, I close my eyes.

Then open them.

The case is still there, along with its blackened fuse on the yellow sand. Around it, everything else burns with light.

That evening I arrange to meet Peukert at Sach's. In the rattle of dishes and talk, he leans close.

"Josef," I say, "I must have the loan of your gun."

He leans back somewhat. "What for?"

"Afterward, you will hear of the deed and know."

"You do not trust me?"

"I have vowed to tell no one."

"Not even Emma?"

"No."

"Because she would object?"

"Because I do not want her in danger."

"Berkman, it is my gun. I have a right to know how you plan to use it. And to say whether I agree or not."

"I cannot tell you."

"Do you think I am a spy, then?"

"No!"

"Then tell me."

"Emma," I say later, "we need a gun."

"A *gun*, Sashenka? We have no more money!"

I pretend to rub eyestrain from my eyes. "Peukert won't let me use his. Are such men really comrades?"

"What happened with the bomb?"

Even my legs quake with emotion. "I threw it into The Narrows. The other one lies on the bottom of the East River. The man cheated us. Or else I made them wrong. It is also possible that Most's directions are incorrect."

She sees through my pretense of eyestrain. We hold one another, and in our small bed she tries to comfort me but that is impossible.

"We will get a gun, Sashenka. I can perhaps do some sewing."

"That will take too long! We need it now."

"Then, Sashenka, we will get it."

Emma is worth fifty Peukerts. A thousand!

EMMA

The night is vaporous and still too warm. I step around piles of liquefying garbage on the sidewalk. What I am wearing, what I have painstakingly put together—white linen and embroidery, white gloves, and the painful white shoes—is not appropriate. My handbag is too childish! Other birds of prey are better suited to the night, in their richer, darker plumage, their bearing assured as they drift toward me in pairs, their eyes taking me in. Sometimes they laugh, their heads inclined toward one another. Men approach them, and then one or sometimes both women enter a carriage or automobile, a café, a lodging. But whenever a man walks toward me, I slip into a storefront and huddle in shadows until he passes. I shouldn't! It has been hours, and I've achieved nothing.

My corset is causing a backache. My feet are cramped in these tight shoes, the same ones I wore to the opera with Most, so long ago. Each time I look down and see my white handbag I sense tears rising. Drunks are now wandering about in groups. I wish I could return to Marthe's flat.

A man nears and I vow to speak to him, but he passes on my right without my uttering a single word. In the next moment, he is walking alongside me, and my step falters, my legs have weakened so. "Rather late," he says. "But care for a drink?"

The drink helps. He has chosen an unfamiliar saloon and a table in a far corner, which also allays my anxiety. I sit with my back to the room and gradually relax. He is an older man with a somewhat yellow moustache and gray, almost white hair, and he seems as tired as I am, which tells me that I must be an afterthought. His suit is well cut, and there is a bit of color to his loose skin, color the whiskey heightens. Although I am not attracted physically to him, he seems a decent sort.

"New to the game, Marthe?"

"How can you tell? Is it my dress?"

"No, actually. Your shoes. They're all wrong for your outfit and look cheap. Your dress is nice, though."

"It's too white."

"Too white!" He laughs in a cultured manner, quietly.

"It makes me look too young."

"Well, you *are* young, and quite pretty." He orders another whiskey, and for me more sherry. *New to the game.* I hardly know how to speak to this man. What does one say, under such circumstances? I imagine you must try to make them laugh, feel at ease, feel drawn to you. Well this, I realize belatedly, I do not know how to do. In all my hours of walking, I did not plan it out. My thoughts were too much with Sasha. Still, it gratifies me that I was able to make this man laugh.

"You didn't answer my question, Miss Marthe. Are you in fact new to the game?"

"Is it so obvious?"

"My dear, find other work or starve—that's how obvious it is. What, may I ask, led you to it tonight?"

"I . . . had to."

"Are you from a brothel?"

"No, it is for . . . my family." As in Dostoyevsky's great novel—this I do not add.

"I see."

He drinks and broods a while. I try to think of something further to say about "my family." But he speaks before I can embellish my lie.

"Do you have a child?"

I am wondering if the other women I saw about the street tonight have to answer such questions. "No," I say.

"Yet you are doing this for someone you love."

"Yes."

"A husband, perhaps?"

Now my face heats. "I am not married."

"Ah. And is this all you can tell me, Miss Marthe?"

I see I am failing with this man. There will be nothing for Sasha tonight. Tears hover and spill. "Yes," I whisper.

He shakes open a scented handkerchief and wipes my face, first under one eye, then the other. His touch is very careful. Now I am drawn to the man even if he is not, to me. But then he leans back to regard me. "Miss Marthe, I am tempted to ask you to be my mistress, but I fear that your heart may not be in it. Do you know what being a mistress means?"

Mistress. Of course I do, but I shake my head because I am incapable, right now, of any spoken word.

"It means, my dear, that you will have a fine apartment as well as money to help your loved ones. It also means that you will not have to come out on Fourteenth Street at night again in a beautiful white dress and awful shoes. You will belong to me alone. It will be very much like a marriage."

"So," I finally say, "you are not a minister, then."

"Is that what you thought?" Again, he laughs but louder, more boisterously. "A *minister?*"

Now the handkerchief goes to his eyes. "Hardly a minister, I assure you!" After a while he catches his breath and pats his chest. "That alone was worth it."

"Being your mistress would mean a life of servitude," I say.

"And what you are doing tonight is not?"

I have no quick rejoinder.

"Where does a pretty young woman like you come by that sort of talk, anyway? *Life of servitude.* Look. You have something to offer, and I have something to offer. In fact, we have what each other needs. So we come to an agreement just as people do in business, just as companies do. We merge our interests in order that both might benefit. Do you see it?"

We merge our interests . . .

I am tempted to tell this man my true purpose. Will he then help the cause?

"Marthe? Do you see it?"

Will Sasha approve of him? There is no way of knowing—he is already on his way to Pittsburgh, where I must send money—soon.

"Marthe? You might be living a life of ease if you accept. I will see to your every need now and . . . make provision for you after my death."

"Ease and prosperity . . . for me alone."

"And your family, at least to some extent."

"But not everyone."

"Everyone? I don't understand. I can't provide for everyone, my dear. No one can."

"You are mistaken."

"Yes? Well, it doesn't strike me as something within the realm of possibility."

I push back my chair and stand, pain immediately assaulting my feet.

"So your answer is no, Marthe?"

"I cannot be your mistress. I must go now."

"Wait, please. Take this."

He presses a folded bill into my hands. "You've earned it. We've talked a while, and you've given me a fine laugh. If you'd rather not see it as payment, think of it as a gift for a new start. I hope I won't see you here on Fourteenth Street again, Marthe. Unless of course you . . . change your mind."

He releases my hand, and I hobble from the saloon, each step causing a streak of pain. At Marthe's finally, in the dark of her sitting room, I remove my dress and the hand-embroidered underwear and stockings. I hold each hot swollen foot in turn. Then I remember my handbag.

I raise the bill to the light from the window. *Ten dollars.*

I will see to your every need . . .

The man's vision, such as it is—so mired in the personal— disgusts me, and yet in the flash of a moment, I imagine myself in such a setting. The apartment, on a charming, quiet street off Fifth Avenue, will be beautifully furnished and decorated with paintings. There will be flowers and books and on certain nights, friends to discuss these books. (What friends? What discussions?)

You folks are plain loony, throwing away a gold mine.

And look, I've just thrown away another one, Mr. Dereck.

A thought bringing no pleasure, no exuberance this time, just anxiousness.

Sashenka, I need you tonight.

Lying on Marthe's cot, in Marthe's sitting room, I touch myself with fury and then stifle the groan, as in the old days with Yakov.

SASHA

The Cumberland Valley at first reminds me of Fedya and his paints. Then it reminds me of Russia—the shorn hay-fields, their sinuous curves of raked hay leading to tree line and blue mountains in the distance. I lower Cherny-shevsky's, *What is to Be Done?* and look out at this scene.

But that is a mistake because in the next minute a tumult of foolish emotion has me in a hard grip. I am again in my family's country house outside of Saint Petersburg, the land there a sea, and peasants afloat on it, scything, and my mother dying in her bedroom. She asks me for ice water. She asks me to turn her toward the wall. This I do, but I do not kiss her as I in fact desperately want to. Instead, I withhold any sign of my love for her because my heart still aches from her blow months earlier. Even now I can still sense the heavy silver ladle striking the tops of my knuckles when I took the part of a servant girl slapped by my mother for some small infraction I cannot even remember, now. *You have no right to strike her! This low servant girl is as good as you!* Then came the blow spatter-ing gravy all over the white tablecloth, a blow I thought must have broken my hand, but no—just my heart. With my left hand, I hurled a heavy saltcellar not at her, but at the mirror directly behind her, shattering it. Now she asks me for ice water, and I go to get more and carry it upstairs myself—all that other still between us, still unspoken and unsettled, while out in the fields, our servants chop at the flowing hayfield and I wish I could be with them, out in the open air and wind and sweet scent of cut hay. When I return with the water, she is gone, her body still turned to the wall.

I remove my eyeglasses and pinch shut my eyes awhile, but the scent of smoked ham and cheese again reaches me, and then I am staring, enraged, at the woman across the aisle who is at her lunch basket again. Will she *never* stop eating? My stomach complains loudly, and this further enrages me. The cup of coffee in Washington should have sufficed! A revolutionist emancipates himself from the human. A revolutionist must be *that* first, and only secondly, a man. In Chernyshevsky's novel, the main character puts himself through deprivation and physical suffering to fashion himself, body and mind, into a revolutionist. But as I ponder this again, I arrive at a different conclusion. A revolutionist need not go through the agony of saints because becoming a revolutionist is not an act of the body but of the will. We need only detach ourselves from the clay. Once that happens, a calm descends and *there* is the physical strength. There is the perfect will.

So those tears over something so far in the past shame me, as does my desirous stomach. And, too, my hypersensitivity to everything, each detail so absurdly vivid—the sunrise this morning, illuminating the dome of the capitol, for instance. It captivated me—enslaved me, in fact. *Berkman, what is the matter with you? How can you allow such weakness?*

We leave fields behind, and I doze, then jerk awake and immediately feel for my wallet. In it is a dollar bill, a clipping showing a lithograph portrayal of Henry Clay Frick, a calling card with the name *Simon Backman* printed on it, and finally a slip of paper listing two addresses of comrades in Pittsburgh.

The wallet is not in my pocket.

I fear my heart will set off the cap of fulminate.

And then my right foot bumps something on the gritty floor.

The wallet, its contents all there.

❖

Why did I hesitate?

I recognized him on Fifth Street and then ran up four flights of stairs in his building while he took the elevator. Both he and I emerged in the hall at the same time, in the empty hall!

"Can you help me, sir?" I said. "I am looking for the office of Mr. Frick."

Oh stupid! The thing might have been done. Sasha, what is the matter with you?

He is a larger man than I imagined. Dark head, cold eyes, black beard and suit. He simply pointed, not even deigning to answer in words. How dare I ask him anything? How dare I not recognize the great Frick?

But of course I did recognize you.

And ran back down to the street, where I now stand like a dummkopf, outside his building. The building resembles a great-tiered stove, with isinglass panel and squat pillar legs. Before it, a lunchtime crowd passes in the summer's day. Businessmen, clerks, stenographers, and typewriters— the proletariat, most of them. I must do this thing. A revolutionist is an instrument of change.

I reset my derby, clamp my eyeglasses on more firmly, and this time take the elevator up to his office. Employees are returning from lunch now. It will be more difficult but not impossible.

In the reception area of the Carnegie Steel Company, I give my card to a Negro clerk. *Simon Backman, Labor Broker,* who can provide Mr. Frick with replacement workers for the Homestead mills and all the other mills now striking in sympathy with the Homestead strikers. I sit on a wooden chair while the clerk directs another man into Frick's office. The clerk returns and says Mr. Frick will see me in a few minutes.

I place the capsule of fulminate under my tongue. I touch the right hand pocket of my pants. Something tells me not to wait. Something tells me to act. I stand and then am walking toward Frick's door. The Negro clerk moves toward me, saying something. I push him aside.

Frick is seated at a long table, one leg insolently over a chair arm. The other man is also at that table. Behind them is a large window. There is too much light, and the men at the table look like silhouettes. "Frick!" I say. He looks up, and I aim for his head, that large head, and then fire the gun.

He falls to the carpet as the other man comes after me. I throw him to the side and approach Frick. The wound is in his neck, I think. I fire again. His shirt collar is red. There is blood in his beard. Frick gets up and moves toward my outstretched arm. Just as I fire the gun a third time, the smaller man knocks my arm upward, and the bullet hits the ceiling. A fourth shot misfires. I pull out the sharpened file from my left coat pocket and at first stab air, then Frick's side, his right knee, his hip, his buttocks. We are under his desk now. My glasses are gone, and he is a blur to me, but still I stab, and still he moans.

And then one terrible blow after another strikes my head. Everything becomes blinding flashes of light and then darkness. Sometime later, men have my head in their grip and my mouth open. Fingers scour behind my teeth and pull at my tongue. They find the capsule I have forgotten to bite down on. I hear a trigger cocked, but someone— *Frick?*—is saying "No! Let the law do it!"

"My glasses," I say. "I can't see!"

"Yer lucky you still got yer head, man. Get yerself up now and stop the sniveling."

EMMA

I refuse to believe it! Carpenters bringing down Sasha? *Workmen? Using their hammers?*

Surely this must be some fabrication of the capitalist press.

And can it be true that Frick is still alive? The newspapers say he refused ether so that he could help the doctors find the bullets in his neck, and after they were removed, he went on to finish the day's business at the Carnegie Steel Company.

Impossible. The press must want to glorify him.

From my window seat in a café, I look out upon a world unchanged.

The world. And in the newspaper of that same name, I read Frick's words to the press. *This incident will not change the attitude of the Carnegie Steel Company toward the Amalgamated Association. I do not think I shall die but whether I do or not the Company will pursue the same policy and it will win.*

Peukert brings his coffee to my table. He has pulled his cap low and sits hunched forward yet attempts a light tone as he congratulates me. "You know, Emma, if I had known why Berkman needed the gun, I most certainly would have given it to him."

"Of course you would have, Josef."

Ignoring my tone, he says, "I am hoping that you will write a defense of Berkman for our paper. We will publish it at once."

Anger scalds my face, but I cannot indulge it.

Autonomie's *The Anarchist* does in fact publish my article the following day, but the day after that, Most's *Die Freiheit* comes out sneering. *Berkman used a cheap pistol. His act was carried out in ludicrous, bumbling fashion. Even the Pittsburgh comrades hadn't trusted him.*

Of course. Hannes still hates Sasha for having taken me from him. That is what is *ludicrous*. So I must repeatedly attack him in *The Anarchist*.

In Pennsylvania, the militia of the commonwealth has entered Homestead to protect the mills.

Here, Marthe turns us out of her flat. She fears the police, of course. They have been tearing through flats and destroying printing presses not only in New York but everywhere in the country, and everywhere they are arresting comrades as accomplices. Hannes Most publishes an essay—how, I don't know, haven't they broken his press, too?—repudiating what for years he'd held sacred: the *attentat* or *tat!* Propaganda by deed.

This I cannot bear. When Fedya and I learn that he is to speak at a hall on Bridge Street, I take a horsewhip from a carriage, and at the first castigation of Sasha, I step up on the platform and snap the whip against his misshapen face. "Coward! Jealous coward! Pompous hypocrite!" I snap it against his back, his arms, his legs while he cowers and people shout, *She's mad! Stop her!* I break the whip and throw the pieces at him before Fedya pulls me off the platform and out the back door.

In the alley, we run.

At another such hall, but in Baltimore, where, this time, I have been invited to give a talk about Homestead, a young man hands me a telegram, which I silently read. *22 years. Western Penitentiary of Pennsylvania.*

When my eyes clear and I trust that I can speak, I raise the piece of paper for the audience to see and read it aloud. There follows a vast silence I begin filling with words.

LEON

Saloons along Wire Street roar like blast furnaces. Sweating detectives walk about in pairs and look worried. It is ten o'clock at night and still too hot. Maybe eighty degrees. Today it was ninety-nine, with a steady hot wind from the southwest. In the newspaper it said to watch out or there might be a fire here in Cleveland as bad as the one that time in Chicago. So we cannot have open fires and must be careful with lanterns. The real danger, Waldeck says, is not a lantern but *words*. Officials wanted to ban all meetings, Waldeck said, but decided not to because that might cause more trouble than good. Now Waldeck wants to hear Dyer Dhum talk about Berkman. I, too, would like to know what happened there and so have agreed to go with him.

The hall behind Kapek's stinks of tobacco and too many men. We cannot see Dhum very well because we must stand at the back, behind other standing men. We can hear him, though. He is fairly hollering. "I do not want to incite anybody here to violence. I do not think anybody needs inciting. . . ."

What does he mean by that? I think he means that we are already incited.

". . . If you and I want anything done, do not let us urge others to do it, but let us, like men, do it ourselves. We must teach these rich people that we care nothing for their law and order. We appeal to that spirit to release us from slavery which has caused men to wade through rivers of blood. . . ."

I look at Waldeck. Is he thinking the same thing?—that anytime you talk about rivers of blood, you are urging them on. Waldeck's bony face shows nothing. He is staring in the direction of the speaker as he sometimes stared at our stepmother, seeing but not seeing.

". . . We glory in the fact that the strikers at Homestead shot down the hired Pinkerton thugs, but we glory more in the fact that among us there was a man—only nineteen years old!—with courage enough to go to Pittsburgh to do his work and then honestly say I came here to kill Frick. Think of it! It is such a man that will free our race from its present slavery."

There is sudden laughter from the adjoining saloon. Someone closes the door, and the hall grows hotter, the smoke from so many cigarettes denser. Waldeck grabs my arm and bulls us through the standing men and into the saloon, where we quickly swallow one beer each, and then are out on Wire Street again. At one end it stops at the Cleveland and Pittsburgh Railway tracks and might be blocked easily enough by police. The other end opens onto Broadway, and we walk in that direction.

"What's the matter, Waldeck? Why didn't you want to hear him out?" I speak in Polish because we are passing men who might be plainclothesmen.

"That room's a death trap. A fire could start, police might come and shut the doors, anything—and then what? I recognized a couple plainclothesmen there. They could signal, anything! That's no way to die."

"The speaker didn't seem afraid of anything."

"They have a secret door for them."

"A secret door!"

"For the *panowie,* they have them."

The higher-ups, he means. "You didn't care for him."

"I get tired of the talk. Something happens and then everybody talks and talks and sounds important, but nothing changes. Like with the priests. They talk and talk and what? People do what they want anyway."

"You're in a good mood tonight."

"Or those papers, *The Alarm* and all the rest. Talk! It seems like it's the only thing they can do."

"Except for Berkman."

"*Ja,* but I'll tell you something, brother. Nothing will change. He's one man, and there are a million capitalists."

"But it's a start, no?"

"What start? As for Berkman, even those carpenters there don't help him. It's useless. People in this country don't want any revolution. They just want some excitement and their beer. As for those speakers, they do it to puff themselves up and make some money on it, that's what I think."

On Broadway we jump on a car heading toward downtown. Why?—I don't know. I am just following him. "Waldeck, what's the matter? You don't usually sound so bad."

"I think we're going to strike."

"Then we will! You don't think we should?"

"Look at Homestead."

"We can't let that scare us."

"Sometimes I think I taught you too much and then again not enough."

"But if we all hold together—"

"This time is different, Leon. This time they're good and scared and it gives them power."

"How, if they're scared."

"See—you know nothing."

"So tell me!"

"Because now they will do anything. They will break us like a branch because they have to. They have no choice. An attacked animal has no choice but to fight to the end."

"Well, but if they're *dying*—"

"You're being stupid! You have to think, Leon. *Think!*"

I'm afraid to say anything more. We get off near the central viaduct and walk east on Central Avenue until Waldeck turns into a walkway leading to a frame house with a blue door and two narrow sidelights outlining it with dusty yellow light.

"I'm going to introduce you to a socialist," he says. "You can ask her all your questions."

A woman in a red kimono patterned with gold bamboo trees opens the door and smiles. Many of her teeth are missing except for the front ones, which have a gap. Her face is powdered white; her eyebrows seem to be missing and her eyelashes, too. I turn to leave, but Waldeck grips my arm.

"Charlena?" Waldeck says.

"Come in! I go see." Hanging onto her kimono with one hand and the bannister with the other, she climbs the stairway one step at a time.

"Waldeck—"

"You'll like her! A real socialist!"

Soon a young woman is coming down the stairs, her royal blue kimono sliding open to reveal pink knees and slender, blue-veined legs. Her gold slippers turn up at the ends. A red bundle of hair sits lopsided on top of her head. Waldeck loosens his grip, and I pull away and run out to Central Avenue. I hear them laughing before the door shuts.

I take a car back to my father's saloon on Todd Street, words and phrases jangling in my head. *Plainclothesmen. Incite. Pittsburgh. Rivers of blood. Socialist. Glory. Berkman.* The saloon thrums and vibrates with talk and heat. Men stand three and four deep at the bar. At a table in the back, there's an old issue of a newspaper that tells about the assassination attempt. One thing I can't get over— Berkman just nineteen years old. My own age exactly.

Then the strike is on at the wire factory, and we have too much time, Waldeck and I.

"Waldeck, what do you say we read the Bible from first page to last?"

We're in our father's saloon when I say this. He sets down his bottle. "Are you crazy?"

"So we can know it for sure."

"What do you want to know? The priests tell you at church."

"But it's all broken up. I want to know it for myself." I cannot admit to Waldeck that it is not a matter of knowing, so much, as feeling—something. Waldeck's words about Berkman have discouraged me, and the strike is getting bad. There's talk we won't be hired back, once the strike is broken. So I think Waldeck was right. I want to be hopeful again, but what I feel all the time is just worry. Also, I'm tired too much. Who knows? Maybe I can become a priest, if I learn what priests have to know.

I order a Polish Bible from a bookseller advertising in the newspaper, and when it arrives, Waldeck and I take it to the woods southwest of the mills, far enough away as to seem miles. There, sitting near a creek and leaning against trees, we begin.

In the beginning God created the heavens and the earth; the earth was waste and void; darkness covered the abyss, and the spirit of God was stirring above the waters.

God said, "Let there be light," and there was light. . . .

Waldeck and I make it most of the way through 4 Kings, the part where the Moabites are defeated by the kings of Israel, and the king of Moab offers his own son as a burnt offering upon the wall, when the strike at the wire factory is broken. The bosses begin hiring again but say they will not hire strikers. All the strikers are on a blacklist. Waldeck thinks we should try our luck anyway. The foreman of my division has always been friendly to me so I decide to go with Waldeck and see. On a cold day we stand in line outside the gates well before dawn, and finally at six in the morning, someone opens the gate and allows one person in at a time. I pick the name Nieman because it sounds strong. Waldeck is going to try *Kaiser*, he says, and laughs. Our breath makes plumes in the still air. The line of us goes back for three blocks at least, but Waldeck and I got here earlier than most and have hope. We stamp our feet and try to shake cold from our hands. Finally when it is my turn to go inside the gate and to the office, I pull my cap down over my forehead as far as it will go and say my new name in a low voice. Fred Nieman. The foreman looks up from his book where he is writing down names and recognizes me but says, "We won't have troublemakers in here, Nieman. One peep out of you and you're out." I nod, and they let me pass into the factory. My heart takes a long time to settle. Everybody knows who I am but nobody says anything. I go to my place in the wire line and start dipping wires, just like that. Waldeck, they keep out, and I think he will probably go and get drunk.

Soon I am seeing little but wires and hearing that screaming sound of rods being rendered into strings. All through the shortening days and long nights, I hear it, and each day I feel worse. In advertisements for Dr. Greene's blood and nerve remedy, Nervura, people are invited to consult with Dr. Greene, who lives on Fourteenth Street in New York, either in person or by letter. So I write to him, asking how I might be able to breathe better and in general improve my health. Three weeks later my sister Victoria gives me a letter from New York. I told her to watch for it. Dr. Greene writes that I should continue taking the Nervura but to increase the dosage. I should also avoid all shocks to the system, get abundant rest and fresh air, and eat barley as often as possible. Waldeck laughs and says beer might do the trick there. Dr. Greene ends his letter with the words, *Now it is for you to decide whether you will remain in your condition of weakness and ill health, or be cured as you surely can be, by this grand restorer of strength and vigor.*

It gives me hope. Waldeck gets more Nervura for me, and I double the dosage but after several weeks there is no change in my health. I try Hood's Elixir and then Ayer's and all the while wait for some change for the better, as I watch the wires dipping and rising in their passage through the factory. One day in Lent, though, I can't, anymore. Men carry me out into the air and lay me down on cindered ground. The foreman stoops alongside me and says to go home and get better, then come back. He helps me sit up.

Two days later, the same thing happens—a clenching of chest and wheezing and no way for air to get out or in. "Go home and get well," the foreman tells me. "When you come back, I try to have job for you again. You're a good worker, it's too damn bad."

By then our father has found a farm to buy, and he wants Waldeck and me to come in on it with him. What can we do but say all right. As for our stepmother, she will just have to get used to Waldeck being there.

SASHA

I sit hunched over a loom, trying to make textile mats. Our workroom is cramped and hazy with dust that burns the lungs and scorches my eyes. I cannot see well and have to lean in close to the loom, which makes it worse. The mug at the loom alongside me coughs himself purple every so often and hacks up red phlegm. I don't want to think that this will be me in a few years, so I think about *you,* Emma, but that is almost worse. I sense your disappointment in me, yours and Fedya's. What I think is that you are confusing motive and act with result. How could you use those words *failure* and *lessened moral effect!* As for suicide, I sense that you're both disappointed that I'm still alive. Disappointed that I'm not a true martyr for the cause. And yet, my dear Emma, you didn't *want* me to die! Do you remember? In that café the day it was raining so hard?

Of course I wanted to kill myself afterward! Thrown, that first night, into the darkness of my cell, the stink of it and assailed by the thought, *twenty-two years*—of course I said to myself, *no.* Then I spied in the murk something reflecting a bit of light from somewhere. A spoon! I knew then what I'd do with it—use the narrow end.

But an officer found me lying down in my cot when I wasn't supposed to be there and as I hurried to get up, the spoon fell to the floor.

Soocide 'tempt!

For that they gave me three days and nights in the hole, and when they resurrected me, ordinary light blinded. And in some stunning reversal, I wanted—want!—the exact opposite of death, perhaps to be able to show you, *teach* you the error of your viewpoint. Now, as I work this loom, pulling the warp of threads toward me, I see not the pattern they begin to make but words, *my words*, arranged this way and that. I have time enough to get them right, to prepare for the time, nearly a month away, when I'll be allowed to write down the few chosen ones on paper and send them to my dearest Emma, the "Sonya" of my letters.

  . . . I sense bitterness and disappointment in your letter. Why do you speak of failure? You, at least, you and Fedya, should not have your judgment obscured by the mere accident of physical results. Your lines pained and grieved me beyond words. Not because you should write thus; but that you, even you, should think thus. Need I enlarge? True morality deals with motives, not consequences. I cannot believe that we differ on this point. . . .

THE MAJOR

I cannot concentrate on the music. Mrs. McKinley's recital is being played with mighty gusto and verve, the celebrated violinists working hard, but it slides into the far away, and I keep seeing that ship, the *Maine,* lovely and white, at the mouth of Havana Harbor. A white ship on a calm night sea, the lights of Havana in the near distance, and then a terrible explosion shatters the quiet, and the Maine becomes a flaming waterspout that drops in burning pieces back into the sea. Two hundred and fifty men dying. *Two hundred and fifty.* Sabotage? Or accident. If sabotage—who? Spain? Or war mongers here? Why would Spain wish to start a war with us? Because of our meddling in their Cuban affairs? Because they believe they can *conquer* us? There's no question in my mind that they have the superior force. They certainly have the greatest navy in the world, and what do we have? I don't even know!

Oh my Lord. *War.* I have been in one war and do not want to see another. Only those who have not been at Antietam or Gettysburg or Cold Harbor or the Wilderness or any number of other blood-soaked battlegrounds could be so rabid, now, for war.

And if the *Maine* in fact exploded by accident, its powder stores spontaneously combusting . . . but no, they say that couldn't have been the case, it's all there in the naval board of inquiry's report. Up until receiving that report, I had hope, but now *peace* is a despised word. Imagine! On the Hill, I'm told, they make the word sound like a snake's hissing. No matter that Spain *disputes* the report, so then they cannot *want* war, can they? And if they don't want war, then it follows that they *didn't* sabotage the *Maine.*

Am I thinking clearly? I fear not. I haven't been sleeping, and Dr. Rixey prescribing his bromides, which only make me groggy. How can I reason with them? How can I keep urging diplomacy when the air itself seems chemically treated and wants only a match. I've failed, that much is clear.

They'll bombard and burn our harbor towns . . . blockade the entire eastern seaboard and the gulf coast.

"Excuse me . . . so sorry . . . excuse me . . ."

Music purling joyfully, and my eyes shamefully wet as I hurtle myself out into the cooler air of the hall and find a room, empty, thank God, and fall onto a rose satin lounge, in the dimness. They will *defeat* us, and then what? Surrender? Surrender to *Spain?*

Become a conquered nation?—after all we've been through, and all the bloodshed?

Oh my Lord, let this not be.

Someone is gripping my shoulder. I open my eyes. It's Kohlstaat, my old friend and advisor. "I felt a little . . . faint. It was awfully warm in there."

"Sir, I'm afraid we aren't going to be able to stop 'em on the Hill. They're all crazed. They may just go to war without you."

"Do you know how many battleships we have? Three? Four?"

"I don't know. A few. I'll find out. Shall I call Dr. Rixey for you?"

"No, no. I have to go back in there or it'll upset Mrs. McKinley. I don't want to ruin her evening. Just give me a moment."

Lord, let it not be. Turn them back from this chasm.

All right, Mac. Up, now. Back to the fight.

I heave myself up and trundle past tall vases of for-
sythia I hadn't noticed before and reenter the music
salon, where they're just finishing up. There's bowing and
applause that sounds genuine. As I take my seat alongside
my wife, she glances worriedly at me. I smile and applaud
with vigor. A wonderful recital, indeed!

EMMA

It sells papers. Dailies screaming *Treachery! Vengeance!*
It's selling other commodities as well. Children and adults
buying and sucking on candies imprinted with the word
vengeance in sticky red. Is vengeance that sweet? People
buying chemically treated flimsies of the *Maine* by the
dozen and setting match to the matador's torch that in
turn ignites the paper into a curl of flame. Editors whip-
ping everybody up into madness. *The president a coward!
Scared of Wall Street. Indecisive, weak, vacillating! Lost control of his party, and rightly so! Should step down; get out
of the road. Let that firebrand Roosevelt through. Put him in
charge of the navy—get rid of the old goat Long and those
other goats, too. Roosevelt!—now there's a man. Send me,
he says. I'll fight.*

Vox populi. The voice of the people.

I hate this war frenzy. The sneering, swaggering sense
of superiority and self-righteousness that goes with it.
Blood lust disguised as piety, patriotism, love of country—
a sentimental lie! But people are blind now to anything but
war. I see it in their faces, a lust—for territory, brutality,
the sanctioned joy of beating another to death. Above all,
I hate how this war lust strips people of their ability to
reason and implants a mob mentality, the devilish ability to rationalize, twist anything, everything, to its own
demented purpose.

From lecture platforms, I conduct my own war. My talk
on patriotism is drawing crowds from well beyond the

usual anarchist and socialist circles. "Please define the word *patriotism* for yourself," I ask my audiences. "Is it love of birthplace? Love of that place where a child first innocently dreamed, looked at the stars, and aspired to greatness, that place where a child heard noble stories at mother's knee? Well, if so, only a few today must experience that sort of patriotism since one's birthplace is more often a grim place; one's fields and pastures, the factory and mill grounds, and the stories one heard did not recall great feats of courage but rather times of sorrow and tears. So what, then, *is* patriotism?

"Dr. Samuel Johnson believed it was the last resort of scoundrels. Leo Tolstoy called it the principle that justifies the training of murderers. Gustave Hervé believed it to be a superstition more inhumane than religion."

At this point in my lectures there's usually a great clattering as people climb through their rows and bang out of the hall. I always pause until the ruckus dies down, and the audience turns to me again. "Too bad!" I say. "It's people like that who need the truth!"

Many stay out of curiosity, wanting their money's worth. Mine is a show bordering on the scandalous for them and well worth the ten- or fifteen-cent price of admission, provided that the police don't bust heads before Red Emma can get to the good stuff.

"Conceit, arrogance, and egotism," I cry out, "are the essentials of patriotism! Patriotism assumes grandiosity on the one hand and worthlessness on the other. Killing is duty. Asserting one's superiority over another a duty, a good, and proof of love of country. Now imagine this: children in the supposedly ruthless—and worthless!—lands being taught the very same thing, being poisoned by the very same bloodcurdling stories about Americans. Children being poisoned by hate from the very beginning of their lives. Just as ours are, right now.

"Friends! This clamoring for a greater navy, more arms, more munitions . . . don't you see that millions of dollars will be taken from the people? From the produce of the people? Not from the wealthy, but from the working man. The wealthy are only too happy to squander their fortunes in foreign lands, invest in foreign lands, make deals with heads of foreign lands. It is the poor who pay for the military and pay in another and most terrible way . . . with their children.

"Friends! Patriotism is nothing but a menace! A menace to liberty! Open your eyes, please. Use your powers of reasoning. Patriotism, clothed in such glorious associations, is but an *obstacle* to freedom. It turns men into mindless machines as surely as the military will turn your children into killing machines. It does not enliven. It exhausts, it expends. It depletes. It is a waste, a disease!"

Ed Brady, whom I had once deeply loved, writes: *Emma, I'm saddened to read the reports of you in the dailies. Pause and reflect, please. If this country were against the war, would you be for it? They're suffering badly, you know, the Cubans.*

Inexplicably, we become lovers again when I return to New York. Lovers until the evening he comes to my room in his dressing gown while I'm organizing notes and papers. He sits watching me, his legs crossed, one slippered foot jiggling. "An interesting thought just occurred to me, Emma. It's how you could be in Cuba right now. In Havana, working with Clara Barton. She's doing the work of five, they say. Actually saving dozens of lives every day. I was just thinking how she's on the side of life, real life, whereas what you're doing . . . your speeches and all—"

"And I'm *not* saving lives? At least trying to?"

"Listen a moment, please. I don't think you know how . . . divisive you can be. How you set people against one another. You believe you're doing good . . . I understand that. Yet in fact, I think, you encourage . . . hatred."

"That's just not true."

"It very well may be. Tonight I've been reading how you entertain them with cheap irony and name-calling just as during the strikes. It shocks and entertains them in some dark, destructive way, I think. Carnegie wants his workers to like him, too, but at least he gives them free books. I don't understand how you seem unable to—"

"You were drawn to me, Ed, because of my speeches on Sasha's behalf. You, a thoughtful, cultured man. And once imprisoned for *your* writings. What's happened to *you*? Why this caution, this timidity now? Well, not just now. In fact, you were like this during the strikes, too, not wanting me to lecture or address any rally. I don't understand you, really I don't. What was good before, when we first met, isn't now? Why not? What has changed? I certainly haven't. So it must be you, Ed. Look at you now, in your fine silk dressing gown."

"During the strikes, I didn't want you imprisoned, Emma."

"Well, I was. And survived it."

"You'll be imprisoned again, possibly for a far longer time. You'll get sick again."

"I don't care."

"If you don't care, that must mean you don't love me. At least not very much. What am I, just a convenience for you? This house, my food . . . is that why you've deigned to put up with me? Is that why you've been *pretending* to love me, these past years? It's rather dishonorable, my dear. You should be able to discern that, with the acuity of *your* mind. Come to think of it, prostitutes have more honor."

"Please leave my room."

"And another thing. Have you ever considered that your devotion to your so-called cause may in fact be, simply, thwarted motherhood?"

"Ed, leave."

When he does, I close but cannot lock the door. There is no lock. Instead, I stand there a while, my back against it. For three days, then, we don't speak to one another. I change my schedule so that I'm not there, evenings, when he returns from his publishing job. But on the fourth evening, I'm home. He sits in his chair near the fireplace, reading as usual, in a sitting room filled with books and his treasured Chinese vases and other *objets d'art*. I take the opposite chair and wonder what he's reading. Probably one of the Greek classics. I remember how, several years ago, he took so much time, schooling me in those classics.

"Ed? I've come to a decision."

He looks up from the book. Obstinately, he won't speak now, of course. "Yes," I continue, as if we were having a pleasant chat. "I'm going to enroll in medical school. In Europe. Friends of a friend have offered to stake me. I haven't said anything before because I hadn't made up my mind. But your words about Clara Barton . . . I guess they struck deep. Only, I plan to become a medical doctor. Like your beloved Chekhov. And mine, I should add."

He takes this in, slowly. I'm about to leave the sitting room, thinking he still is refusing to speak, when he asks, "For how long?"

"In Europe, you mean? I'll be in Switzerland for three or four years, at least."

"You won't come back, will you."

"I don't know why not."

"Well, Europe's your home, after all. Why should you come back? There's nothing to hold you here. Oh, but I'm forgetting Berkman."

He isn't over his pique yet. I should have waited with this news, waited until all was set. "I thought, Ed, that we might discuss all this rationally."

"Do you know something? I'm tired of deluding myself. I'm tired of this . . . arrangement. And obviously so are you. So it's for the best. I wish you well! Write me some-time. When do you leave? Tomorrow?"

"I've only just decided. I don't know when, for sure. I still have to make arrangements."

"Well by all means make them and let me know. I'll fix up a nice send-off for you and your friends."

I hear the demeaning emphasis on the word *friends* and stand. "Tomorrow, maybe, we can talk some more about this."

"Tonight's no time to *talk*, I agree."

In my room, I begin clearing up notes for an article I'd written, but one of the notes catches my attention. Soon I'm reading and then writing. Time passes. I don't know how much—it might have been hours; I always go into some kind of trance while working—but then my hand involuntarily jumps up from the page at the sudden sound of violent shattering. It comes again and again from the direction of the sitting room. Opening the door an inch or two, I see him heaving his antique vases and plates at the andirons. I close the door and sit on the bed, shaking. Then it is quiet except for his moaning. I stay there, on the bed.

Leaving the house at dawn the next morning, I see shards of porcelain scattered all around the fireplace and on the rug. He has also torn a sketch of me that Fedya had done. Strips of it lie scattered around. The frame is broken, the glass crushed. I leave quietly, and when I return extremely late that night, determined to get the remainder of my things, I again hear moaning, like some animal's. He is lying in his bed, his wrists bleeding into the bed linen. I run to my room for my midwife's bag.

LEON

Dr. Thelonius Lund is a small man with a large smooth head free of any hair and polished to the same gleam as the cabinets and desk and tables in his office. There are many initials after his name, none of which I understand except for the M and the D. Blue veins cling to his head like tributaries scattering downward. He is very calm as he tells me that he does not believe in knives or drugs because, really, there is only one disease. Abnormal or impure blood. And so there is only one cure: *hydropathy.*

"Hydropathy," I repeat. Here is another word to learn.

"Yes. It is nature's cure."

He makes a round cage of his fingers as he explains. "To fight bad blood you have to throw surplus water out of the organism. Dryness then prevents further decay. In the usual doctoring, deposits of waste are just shifted around by the body. But then what happens is that you have pockets of decomposed substances here rather than there, that's all. And different symptoms to go with the new location. The liver, say. Or kidneys."

I would like to ask a question of Dr. Lund because something confuses me. How, if the disease is present in the blood, will dryness elsewhere help? Isn't the blood a liquid? But I don't interrupt the doctor. He is saying how "renovating agents" will take over once the body has dried out enough. These agents will restore the organism to full health. "So refrain from liquids," he says, giving me a packet of powders. "What gives life also gives death. The very air—think of wind, a windstorm! All four elements! We will be on the road to salvation when we begin to understand this."

In the next days I burn with fever. My hair begins breaking off and falling out. My voice slurs. Our stepmother says I am drunk, a drunkard, but I am not drinking anything and hardly eating, except for the powders. Waldeck wants to know what is wrong with me, I should see a doctor, he says. I have, I tell him, and he is curing me. Waldeck says that the cure, then, is worse than the disease and it's going to kill me. No, no! I argue. I am doing what he says. After the third day I cannot stand. I cannot walk. I am seeing things, as drunkards do. I see Dr. Lund's skull rising out of his head. It is a knot of oiled maplewood. It floats about the room and I scream the doctor's name. After that I don't know what happens. When my eyes open, there is Waldeck with a bowl of soup. He feeds me spoonful after spoonful. "No more quacks, brother," he scolds. "What the hell's the matter with you? We had Dr. Lipke here, and he said you might have died, in a day or two. By the way, I took care of the quack."

"Waldeck—"

"Don't try to talk."

Nobody can cure me. I want to say these words but can't. Besides, Waldeck will just argue. I drink our mother's soup while they are at church. Their Sunday soup. I can't stop drinking it and now she will beat me, probably.

Waldeck, I must find *work*. So I must be well. It's no good here. I can't say these words, either. But the soup, the soup is heaven itself.

In early May, the sky is the color of the sea on maps. I rest on a knoll in the pasture, under an apple tree. The clouds, which first looked like fluffed up *pierzsynas*, have become lead gray. Now they look like the country's few battleships. We will lose against Spain, I think. They have the greatest navy in the world and what do we have but a few old tubs painted gray.

Our stepmother and my sister Victoria pass nearby, their buckets full of mushrooms. Victoria waves and calls out, "Mother killed a rattlesnake with a hatchet! We found lots of mushrooms!"

Our stepmother says nothing. She swings the hatchet in one hand, a bucket in the other. I know what she thinks. *Let the old stump rot. Maybe he'll grow some mushrooms, anyway.*

That night I tell Waldeck that maybe I should enlist. Waldeck is in a bad mood because of an ailing cow and rain that has stalled the planting of a field. He says, "You won't last a day. Besides, they don't want sick men."

"Do you think it's a good thing, Waldeck, to free those places from the Spaniards?" The dailies, I tell him, think so and Congress, too, even though at first the president dragged his feet.

"Brother, you don't think deep enough. This is a war of imperialism, of cabals—"

"Waldeck, explain, please, cabal."

"It's . . . it's when some small group gets together in secret and hatches some secret plan. Who knows who blew up the *Maine*? Maybe we did—to get the war going."

"So what is the secret plan?"

"To get more territory! To have more markets, Leon! Don't you know by now that the rich always find a way to get richer? War is just one of those ways."

"But against *Spain*, Waldeck? Isn't that crazy?"

"Maybe yes, maybe no. I hope we don't get whipped because maybe then we'll have to learn Spanish. On the other hand, I hope we do."

"If anyone heard you, they'd say *treason*, Waldeck."

"Prison would be no different than this place. It might not stink as bad." He stares at the cow and says, "I don't think she'll make it."

The cow stands hock-deep in manure, her head down, her ropy tail all stained. Her flank is hot to the touch.

"We should call the veterinarian."

"There's no money for that."

I know this. I also know that we should not have this farm, not have these animals. If treason is a crime, what is this? I leave Waldeck and go into my small workroom and work on the metronome I am trying to fix. Waldeck won it in a card game and gave it to me. I clean it again and oil it a little more with machine oil. Above me, the roof strains in the wind and boards vibrate. Then rain hits the side of the barn like stones—more rain! Waldeck will be fit to be tied. I remount the parts in a slightly different way and release the pendulum. It begins to move. *Tock-tock.* I raise the weight on the stem, and release it again. *Tock-tock-tock-tock!*

Yes. All right. Sell it. Maybe it will bring enough tomorrow to pay the veterinarian something. I go out to tell Waldeck, but he's not in the barn. The trench has been cleaned of manure. The cows crunch their hay, but one place is empty.

Outside in the wind, Waldeck is standing with the cow.

"What are you doing?" I yell in the wind. "She shouldn't be out here!"

"She's dying. I don't want to have to haul her out of the barn tomorrow."

"Waldeck, take her back inside."

"Leon, you're too damn softhearted, and you want to go to war? What a joke."

"Take her back in. I'll help you tomorrow. I can sell the metronome. It's working. We'll get the doctor."

"And who's gonna give you more than fifty cents? You're crazy. Go inside before you get sick. Sicker."

I throw myself at my brother, and he pushes me down. I get up and heave myself at him again.

"*Leon!* I don't want to hurt you, dammit."

He's trying to hold my arms, but I keep shoving against him, pushing him backward, toward the barn. "Let her die in the goddam barn, Waldeck! What the hell's the matter with you?"

We fight. We curse each other. Part of me sees how idiotic it is. The other part can't stop it. Soon we are both covered in stinking mud, and then I am coughing, fit to die myself. After I stop, Waldeck grabs the cow's forelock and I push from behind, and we get her back inside. Later that night she does die, but at least she's inside and covered up.

Waldeck was right. I get only fifty cents for the metronome. After buying an issue of the *Plain Dealer* and a cup of coffee in town, I read, on the train, about how Admiral Dewey entered Manila Bay in the Philippines and destroyed the Spanish fleet. He had only four light cruisers and one old gunboat. So how does he do this?—destroy a whole fleet that is protected by a gun battery on land and batteries at other fortifications at the mouth of the harbor. Yet he does, and with no loss of life or boat, and now he is a hero. An old man does all that. Reading, I miss my stop and have to walk back a quarter of a mile. Woods beyond fields and pastures are rocking in a strong wind. The day is all fast cloud and wind roaring like the train itself. At the farm, I find Waldeck in the barn, throw the change at him, and go back to the house.

When a cow, a tree, or anything, commences to die— what?

It dies.

THE MAJOR

Tabletop, chair arms, pen, papers, everything sticks to one's fingers. The faces of the nine men arranged around this table gleam like Mrs. McKinley's bone china, and I imagine my own does, too, in this damp heat. If one of us happens to gesture with a raised hand or arm, the humid, smoky air stirs, and I get a faint whiff of the floral centerpiece Mrs. McKinley ordered from the greenhouse, an arrangement of white and pink lilies, their scent funereal, though not one of us dares to complain.

"So," I begin. "The Philippines—once again, gentlemen."

Our mahogany chair backs creak. Damp papers are taken up. For the past several days we have been formally and informally deliberating about the contents of the note that must soon be sent to Spain, in reply to her request for an armistice. On two points we have quickly agreed: Spain must give up Cuba and evacuate from the Caribbean. And in lieu of compensation for costs of the war, the United States will have Puerto Rico and the other Spanish-held islands in the West Indies as well as the island of Guam in the Pacific Ladronnes. But as for the Philippines—the third point—we've been deadlocked. Not even during our refreshing excursion down the Potomac, which should have helped clear our heads and break the logjam, were we able to come to any agreement. So, again, here we are, on a steamy Washington night, in a closed room that, I'm sorry to say—forgive me, my dear—smells something like an undertaker's parlor.

I finger the memo in my right pocket, which I jotted down three days ago when the French ambassador to Spain, M. Cambon, first presented Spain's request for an armistice. My original impulse was so clear, I immediately scribbled it down, but now I'm not as certain about it all. If we have Cuba, Puerto Rico, and other Spanish islands in the Caribbean as well as that obscure one in the Pacific somewhere, what in the world are we going to do with the Philippines as well? Two years ago I hadn't even known where these islands are. Imagine. All this is still so stunningly unbelievable and dreamlike. *Winning the war against Spain—in just a few months and with limited casualties.* There seems to be something of destiny in this.

I regard my secretary of state, whose rust-red moustache always cheers me up. "Judge Day, if you'll kindly tell us where we've gotten on this matter thus far, we might be able to move forward."

The judge gives his usual fine recapitulation, and I reiterate that we've already reached formal agreement about two of the points, so let us focus solely on the Philippines.

"Mr. Alger?" I say, "I defer to you."

Secretary of War Russell Alger turns slightly to face me but can only open his mouth slightly, behind a goatish moustache and beard. He is a thin, narrow-framed man whose pale hands tremble.

I've been a schoolteacher, so I recognize the signs. This pupil has nothing in his brain at the moment but confusion. The secretary of war hasn't yet recovered from the humiliations he suffered this past year at the hands of the press—and not just the opposition press, either—over the bad-beef scandal that caused worse casualties than the war itself. And he's had to face a number of other accusations of negligence and incompetency, mismanagement and corruption. But above all, the American people can't forgive him for allowing American soldiers to suffer malaria and other awful illnesses in filthy, diseased camps and transports. They want him out, and I should comply, and quickly, and yet the man is so destroyed already. His heart is broken, quite literally, a condition that will soon do him in, I fear. Up to now, the poor man's life might have been a story written by Horatio Alger, no relative, by the way.

Now Mr. Alger's breath comes in laborious little bursts. "I cannot say . . . just yet."

"Judge Day," I go on, glad to release Alger.

"If it's all right with you, sir, I'll wait a bit until the others have their say."

"Take your time, Judge." I turn to my attorney general, who occupies a somewhat constricted space at the table, wedged between the mound of lilies in front of him, and the large floor globe behind.

Mr. Griggs is an easterner, polished and forceful and a tad hard to warm up to. He's also in excellent physical condition, which is rather a rebuke to me, I must say. Leaning toward the lilies, his face somewhat scornful, that regal face, he offers his usual volley. "I've said it before and haven't changed my mind in the least. I say we take them and take them all. To do anything less will present us with enormous problems."

"Take all the islands in the Philippines, you mean, and not just Manila and Manila Bay."

"Everything! We can't trust that rebel Aguinaldo. And those people there aren't capable of standing up to a military despot. They're also incapable of self-rule, at least for now. Also, don't forget, the Germans have an eye on those islands too. And Japan does as well. The British in Hong Kong want us there. Even Spain does! We, at any rate, will protect the people there. Who else will?"

"So you're absolutely opposed to holding just Luzon."

"Wouldn't work! Too vulnerable. Think of all the surrounding islands, all the insurgents there. Won't work at all."

"What about some form of joint protectorate?"

"Clumsy. There'll be problems with trade policies, for one thing. This leads me to another point. I believe we should be concentrating on the tremendous possibilities for commerce in Asia, but we have to be bold, not half-hearted, or we'll lose the whole thing."

Mr. Griggs's heated face has gone quite rosy. I let his words hang for a while before calling on my secretary of the navy, John D. Long. The man of the hour—along with Admiral Dewey. With his broad round face and flaring, sand-colored moustache, he resembles a scrappy Irish boxer, but tonight he looks done in, his hands held limply over the table, his shoulders sagging forward.

"Manila. And Manila Bay," Mr. Long says. "Possibly Subic Bay to the north. I'm inclined to stop there, with those."

Mr. Griggs shakes his head but says nothing. Like all of us here, he's respectful of Mr. Long, who has served the country so well despite being on the verge of nervous exhaustion.

"Well, it's a good point," says Jim Wilson. Tama Jim, as he's known, the big Scotsman from Tama County, Iowa, and my secretary of agriculture. The rest of us are drooping around this table but not Tama Jim. He sits there like a proper minister, his back ruler straight. His baritone is soothing. Here's a man, it tells us, who still plants his own fields and shears his own sheep. Here's a man who knows the seasons as well as he knows the Bible—and his fellow man. We always pay close attention to Tama Jim. "A good point," he repeats. "But I've had some words rolling 'round my noggin' these past days, and it's about time to share 'em with you: *Go ye forth and preach the Gospel to all nations.* Now, I couldn't figure why in the world those words have stuck like that, but now I know. Here it is. Don't we have an obligation, gentlemen, as upstanding Christians, to our fellow man out there? And isn't this a

God-given opportunity as well as a sign, a true sign, of just what we have to do now? Why, to bring down Spain in just three months! *Spain*—a Christian nation but ruined by power, greed, and an insatiable lust for cruelty. I believe it was all meant to happen in just this way, gentlemen. So now we should follow through in our moral duty to those poor folks there. Not only do we have to inculcate a democracy out there and take care of those people, but we need to bring them the enlightenment of uncorrupted religion. We need to liberate them physically and spiritually. To let those islands just drift to whatever fate, now, would truly be reprehensible. I shudder to think how we'd see ourselves in years to come if we allowed *that*."

"You Scotchmen," I say smiling, "are in favor of keeping everything—including the Sabbath, aren't you?"

"In this case, yes sir, I am!"

Mr. Griggs rubs his closed eyes with forefinger and thumb. Lyman Gage, my secretary of the treasury, lowers hand from chin. "Go ahead, Sophocles," I say. I like to call him that, not so much on account of any great wisdom, though he is sharp as a tack, but mainly because of the oblong shape of his head, the cloud of white hair, and his usual daydreamy expression.

"I was just thinking . . . idealism is a wonderful thing. But I believe we have enough—nay, more than enough—to look after in our own country. I agree with Mr. Long. Let's stay with Manila and Manila Bay. Anything more may be courting some big trouble. It's like—"

"Excuse me," Mr. Griggs interrupts. "We're getting ourselves lost in the clouds of speculation, gentlemen. Let's bring this back into the practical world. We *cannot* hold part if we don't take the whole. And if we don't take the whole, there'll be a very real and very great threat to world peace. As I see it, we have no choice. This is not speculation, by the way, gentlemen. It's plain logic. If we don't hold the whole, we cannot hold a part. It's impossible, given the realities."

I glance around the table, trying to determine the effect of these words. Judge Day is writing furiously, his expression, though, calm as ever.

"Hubris," Lyman Gage says mildly. "That's the word I was looking for." He draws forth a cigar. So do I, and so does Charles Smith, the new postmaster general, who, like Secretary Alger, hasn't yet ventured an opinion. "Pride," Mr. Gage goes on, while we light our Cuban cigars. "Going too far. As in the Greek tragedies."

Mr. Griggs noisily, rudely, expels a mouthful of air.

For the next half hour I listen while my cabinet holds to its battle lines. In a lull, I say, "Judge. Still haven't heard from you."

He raises his head from his writing. "Not sure you want to."

"Go ahead. We'll listen anyway. We're getting good at that, at least." There's a bit of laughter, a great deal of cigar smoke expelled upward, and then Judge Day is saying, "I've been assailed right and left by Senator Lodge and others and that didn't do it, but I have to admit, hearing Mr. Griggs's argument tonight has shaken some of the starch out of me, though not all. I think we need a naval station out there, but as for the rest . . . I'm pretty bothered. What we have is an archipelago of *thousands* of islands and millions of people. Think of it! For a hundred and twenty-two years we've been priding ourselves on our way of government, which governs with the consent of the governed. How in the world are we going to do that, now, with all those people over there? Over that whole area? The consent of the governed! Don't you think that's a pretty tall order? Millions of unlettered folks scattered over thousands of islands?"

The judge stands and goes around the table to the globe behind Griggs. "What kind of sense does it make to try to annex a land that's half a world away?" he says, spinning the globe. "And as different in every respect. Now that's apart from my objection on *principle*."

"I don't believe we have the luxury of choice," Mr. Griggs interjects. "Not now."

"No," Tama Jim adds. "We may not."

Around and around we go again, as in some children's game. Finally, in another lull, I say, "Gentlemen, we don't have to rush into this. We have time. We can be very careful as to what we say, now, to Spain. I suggest we leave this aspect of the issue open. But we are agreed, are we not, that we must have Manila and Manila Bay, at least?"

Yes, their silence says. As a naval station. And for potential trade in the Far East.

"So that much, along with our first two points, we can now tell the Spaniards. What if we state that the disposition of the Philippines is to be left to further deliberations by a peace committee?"

They take this in, wary.

"At any rate, let's begin there tomorrow morning."

Judge Day's papers curl in the humidity. His fingers look heat-swollen. Griggs rubs his eyes again. I know he's perturbed, and I'll be getting that wind shortly. Tama Jim stares complacently before him, but Mr. Alger appears stiff with anguish. Sophocles Gage and the postmaster general send new eddies of smoke into the blue-gray canopy. John Long rubs his hands worriedly, while Cornelius Bliss, my secretary of the interior, who has been quiet all night, now chooses to speak—to Mr. Long.

Ah well.

Finally alone in the cabinet room, I stand alongside the marble-topped table dating from Lincoln's time and look out into this tropical night. A little walk surely would be nice. I can't recall the last time I've had a good little walk. Sometime before the fight with Spain, I think. Imagine—*Spain.* I still can't get over it. And all this new territory now, and the country mad with joy. And perhaps strangest of all, I, having been so roundly reviled this past year, am now a hero of the highest order, along with Long and Dewey.

I walk over to the globe and study the vast distance separating us from the Philippines. And yes, the archipelago does stretch out for hundreds of miles. As I spin the globe, its surface buffs my fingertips, the slightest force I exert slowing it or bumping it to a halt.

Then I remember the memo I've written to myself and read it again: *Take Cuba. Take Puerto Rico and the other Spanish islands. Take that island in the Pacific. Take the Philippines.*

Griggs is right. Take them all. Despite the heat, I shiver with gratitude and awe and a deep, deep happiness.

And yet. *And yet.* Some American soldiers, I've been told, have been calling the Cuban fighters niggers and mongrels. How, then, will they treat the Filipino people? How will *we* treat them? It's puzzling—people wanting to free Cuba, free the Philippines, and hating me for my indecision about going to war, but now we're calling people there mongrels and niggers? I should have brought up this point tonight. Why didn't I?

It's late. I need to go up and see to Mrs. McKinley.

EMMA

In the sky to the west, sunset clouds are arranged in bars tinted carmine and purple. Under them, a panel of bronze light touches the diminishing coastline of America as this ship, the *Great Eastern,* the famed floating palace of the Cunard Line, ploughs gently through humps of gray Atlantic water. The ocean wind, after the heat of New York, is as good as chilled wine. Feet braced, my hands gripping the deck railing, I watch America receding as once, some thirteen years ago, I watched it appear— Helena and I so excited, standing at the railing in the fog and seeing the Statue of Liberty suddenly there before us. Now the steamship's wake seems a wide lace ribbon streaming behind us and only tenuously connecting us to America. The ship's three smokestacks scribble lines on the evening sky.

Medicine my lawful spouse but writing my mistress— Chekhov.

So it's possible, yes? What I'm attempting? Surely I can do both. Medicine my lawful spouse, but speaking, working for the cause, my lover?

Can you really, Emma? Do both well?

The wind is no longer pleasant, and I feel a need to sit somewhere, out of it—the effects of doubt, I suppose, which can drain exhilaration in an instant. From a lounge off the second-class deck comes the sound of a gramophone playing Paul Dresser's latest hit, "Gold Will Buy

'Most Anything but a True Girl's Heart." It should lift my sudden dark mood but doesn't.

At a bookseller's on Charing Cross Road in London, I slip a heavy volume from its place on a shelf and take it to a nearby table. The book is far too heavy to hold with one hand and page through it with the other. The print is small; the chapters long. *The Arteries. The Brain. The Alimentary Canal. The Connective Tissues. The Ear. The Eye. The Liver. The Heart* . . . This volume is well over a thousand pages in length—and it's merely an introduction. I leave it on the table and remove other volumes from their places on the shelf. *Histology. Embryology. Pharmacology.* Should I purchase the books here or wait until I reach the school in Zurich? Wait, I think. The school may require others. Each of the volumes I've removed contains hundreds of pages, and there must be other volumes, in addition, to be studied as well. Of course there are. Don't be stupid, Emma. In this one bookseller's alone there are three or four *cases* of books devoted to medical texts. An ache has begun behind my left eye—perhaps I should consult the chapter on the eye, or is the ache actually in the brain? Or in the nerves leading to the eye? And what has caused this ache, Emma?

Fear?

How can something nonmaterial cause physical pain? Now there is a mystery.

I'm thinking again of Sasha in Pittsburgh. How my words, after the failed *Tat*, hurt him so. I should not have written of failure even though in one sense it was. A failure we all shared, the three of us. After several weeks, the pain of it eased somewhat, for me, but each time I think of it—still!—there's a scalding sensation, not as intense now, but there all the same.

So what do you fear, Emma? That you, too, will fail—at this double endeavor?

I fear that I am thirty years old, and this study will take many years.

Many years.

I fear that I will do nothing well.

Oh, the bleakness of this London day—a cold rain and people hurrying by outside, hunched and wrapped up, their umbrellas lacquered with rain and dripping.

I reshelve the volumes and leave without buying anything. Walking down Charing Cross Road under my own umbrella, I don't know where I'm going, perhaps back to my room. I need to think this through again. And yet what is there to think about? I have the funds, all is planned: see comrades here, give three lectures, then depart by train and boat for the continent.

Perhaps it's only being so far away from Sasha that's so unsettling. The thought brings with it, again, something of the old pain.

At one end of Trafalgar Square a man is addressing— or trying to—passersby who are ignoring him, except for one or two. He's very thin and wearing brilliant yellow gloves and holding over his head the bare ribs of a broken umbrella.

"You think this is ridiculous?" he shouts, accenting the third syllable of the word *ridiculous*. "You think *I* am the fool?"

His few listeners don't respond. I move closer.

"I will tell you something, my good people. I am no more ridiculous than this society in which you are living! And I will tell you something else. They once put me in an insane asylum, and do you know why?"

"Because yer barmy!" a newsboy calls out.

"No, my lad. Because, they said, only a lunatic could disbelieve in government! Now what do you think of that?"

People walk on. I remain.

"And then what happened? I will tell you, my friend," he says, addressing me now. "A professor—a professor!—had me released. He said, 'That man Hippolyte Havel is saner than all of us. Saner than *all* of us!'" Rain falls through the ribs of the umbrella onto the man's hat. It darkens the yellow glove on the hand holding it. I step forward, then, and introduce myself.

⁘

In our room in Paris, I see that I have a letter from America. My hand trembles somewhat as I open it.

. . . I thought it was understood when you left for Europe that you were to go to Switzerland to study medicine. It was solely for that purpose that Herman and I offered to give you an allowance. I now learn that you are at your old propaganda and with a new lover. Surely you do not expect us to support you with either. I am interested only in E.G. the woman—her ideas have no meaning whatever to me. Please choose . . .

Not reading any further, I hand this letter to Hippolyte. When he finishes reading, he regards me with fear in his eyes. "Emma," he says, "I gave up my job in London to come to Paris with you, then Zurich. You said we'd both study. Live frugally, study medicine, and be useful to the movement, but now—"

"Your *job*, Hippolyte? Every menial task in a boarding house?—floor washing and polishing boots and carrying coal scuttles. Surely you can find such a job like that here."

"It was work. Here, with my background, it won't be so easy. I had to flee Europe, you know. Really, I shouldn't be here at all."

"Now you tell me this! Yet you were willing to come with me, yes? You made that choice."

"To study medicine, Emma. It was a great opportunity and—"

"Ah! You came for that but not for me."

"For you, too! Of course! Both!"

"Something relevant, if also unsettling, has just come to mind. Do you remember, at that party in London, when we met the revolutionist Tchaikovsky? Do you remember the remarkable illustration he used?"

"I don't know. Maybe. You probably were talking to him on your own."

"I think you were with me when he told us how, in his youth, he'd achieved notability as a chemist but chose to give up science. 'Why?' I asked. He went on to talk about cats! Surely, you remember."

"Yes, yes. Something about their hunting."

"Really, Hippolyte, what he said was profound. I'm surprised you don't remember it clearly. He said how we should learn a lesson from the domestic cat. Observe how she doesn't try to clean herself while waiting for a vole to show itself. Nor does she pause to feed her own kittens or lick a wound. And if you call her or even shout, she won't flick an ear. No. She is pure concentration. She becomes will and purpose and power. She melds herself to the act. Or else—goes hungry and her kittens die."

"I do remember him saying that."

"So then, remember? He went on to conclude that only we humans foolishly believe we can do everything at the same time if we will it. Only *we* are that proud. We don't understand the wisdom of extreme humility. He made a strong argument. But I said, 'What we imagine, we should be able to accomplish, no? We simply need to push ourselves. Not settle for the paltry achievement. We are not cats! And we must, we *must*, disregard failure—after, of course, we learn from it.' He said that I'm young. That mine is the view of youth. Inwardly, I disagreed, but now this letter . . . it clarifies everything for me and in fact substantiates his point!"

"But how will we live now, Emma? Maybe we should go back to London. I could try to get my old job back, and you may find something, too. And we can work for the movement there."

London. London, I'm ashamed to admit, frightens me. I'd been relieved to leave the East End, where prostitutes worked in alleys while their babies and children lay in prams outside pubs, sucking on sweets imbued with whiskey, their faces wet and hectic red in the fog. In those alleys, dogs savaged bodies, and women fought each other, and the Thames was turgid with human waste and carcasses adrift in the oily water. But even that wasn't the worst of it. The worst was their eyes, the eyes of the poor staring warily at me, and often with outright malice, and hecklers calling out, *What do you know of our lot when all you do is travel around and enjoy yourself at our expense? You aren't a blue shirt, you probably never worked in a factory or if so, not for long . . .* Sasha could have withstood all that, could have looked beyond it to the *what can be* instead, but I, I'm sorry to say, lost heart.

"At least, Hippolyte, their money paid for Sasha's escape tunnel! That house we had to buy there to hide the exit part of the tunnel. So. That much to the good. I think . . . what I think we'll do now is— But first, I'll write a response and then we can make plans."

He reads their letter while I go to the table and write: *E. G. the woman and her ideas are inseparable. She does not exist for the amusement of upstarts, nor will she permit anybody to dictate to her. Keep your money.* "There. That's done. Now I want to stay here for the anarchist congress. And too, there's the exposition. Maybe we can be tour guides for English—or German or Russian—visitors. After that, maybe we might even go to Russia ourselves. What do you think? We could do that, no?"

As he reads my response, he taps the tabletop with two fingers. His hands have finally healed—all those inflamed cracks and blisters from the boardinghouse work in London—and he no longer has to continually wear his yellow gloves. I go to the window and look down into the angled street leading to the Rue de Charenton, which in turns leads to the Gare de Vincennes and the Place de la Bastille. It had been foolish of me to put myself in the role of a dependent—again. And not long after the years of dependency with Ed. Sasha was understandably heartbroken and angry when I accused him in that letter of failure. If his act was a failure, what in the world have mine been, so far? *Acht,* Emma, how stupid to have sent that letter to Sasha before thinking deeply, clearly. How stupid to have forgotten my earlier terror and heartsickness at the thought of his death. How muddied my thoughts—and life—have been compared to the purity of his.

I stand there a long while, thinking of Sasha and his great sacrifice.

"My so-called benefactors have done us a favor, Hippolyte," I say finally, still looking down at the street.

So why, then, tears?

Waving that morning's issue of *Le Monde*, Hippolyte wakes me from a deep sleep. Sasha's tunnel discovered! At one end, children getting into the house, seeing it, and tattling; at the prison end, prisoners unsuspectingly dumping a huge pile of bricks over the disguised entrance. He has been placed in solitary confinement for weeks. I look up from newsprint.

"I must go back. Come with me or not—whatever you wish."

IDA AND THE MAJOR

There's much wind tonight. I dislike wind. It harries this shabby mansion, pouring its cold through the sieve of cracks. The ancient coal furnace in the cellar can hardly offer any counterforce. In Arizona, where the Grand Canyon is, it must be warm. Imagine a rift like that in the earth! And so red, like a wound. I remove the slide from the stereoscope and insert one of Niagara Falls, but I fancy I hear voices and look up. Children laughing somewhere? In the next room? Or downstairs? I don't believe anything was scheduled for tonight. No, of course not. My Dearest and I always go into near-seclusion for the month of December. My Dearest tells me that this is a holy time when we can meditate on God's many gifts to us, but for me, Christmas Day, the anniversary of our Katie's birth, is . . . hard. I go downhill starting at Thanksgiving, and there's just no helping it. I cannot bear to see others' joy in the season. So we do not open these doors to guests until the first public reception of the new year. Therefore, there should be no guests here tonight, no gatherings, no festivities whatsoever. I wish Jennie were here, but she had to return to New Jersey after her husband's death at Thanksgiving time. Garret Hobart, Mr. McKinley's vice president and friend, dead, at forty-five.

I am fifty-two.

"Clara," I ask my maid, "do you hear anything? Is there some gathering in the mansion tonight?"

"No, ma'am. Least, I don't believe there is."

I strain to listen and—yes. "There. Again. And you don't hear it?"

"Is it the wind in the chimley, ma'am? Sometimes there's a hum, I noticed. Like faraway music."

"It's not that. It's voices. There are children talking somewhere. A party."

My maid sets aside her knitting and opens the hall door, letting in a good deal of cold air. Then she closes it again.

"Nothing? Go down the hall a ways and listen."

Clara does so, then returns with my nurse, Miss Larrison, who places both hands on the oak table and lowers her head and concentrates as if she were at a séance. "The silence," she declares, finally raising her head, "always sounds that way to me. Like a humming, sometimes like faraway bees buzzing. But as for voices, I hear nothing, ma'am."

"But I heard them distinctly. Someone is here."

Miss Larrison nods to Clara, who goes to the telephone.

"Ma'am," Miss Larrison says, "it's late. Your imagination is getting the better of you, I think. You need to be in bed now."

"But I'm not tired! How can I sleep if I'm not tired? I'll turn and turn."

Miss Larrison finds a mohair shawl to drape over my shoulders, and just as she begins to massage my temples, there is My Dearest, rushing forward and then dropping to his knees before me.

"My darling's still awake? She'll have to sleep all of tomorrow, then, and she won't like that when she could go into the conservatory and visit with Mr. Stevens. See how he's coming along with the daisies and what-all."

"Not . . . daisies . . . amaryllis. Roses."

"Indeed. Roses. And what'll he do without you to help him?"

"He'll be glad."

"On the contrary! I'll get an urgent call."

"Nobody wants me with them. Only Jennie, and she—"
I sense my face crumpling into an ugly mask.

"Miss Larrison, will you kindly help Mrs. McKinley with
her medications?"

"Stay!" I beg him. "Don't leave. What have you been
doing? There is no party anywhere here tonight, is there?"

"Party? Of course not. I've been getting the news from
the Philippines. It looks like the rebels there will soon
surrender. I'm going to work this news into the annual
address."

"Then it's all turning out."

"Not in time for New Year's, unfortunately, but yes. And
I'm not superstitious, as you well know. It'll come when
it will. You, though, shouldn't be thinking of such things
right now. It's time for rest."

"I haven't been thinking at all. But I could hear voices
somewhere, and laughing. It seemed to be Katie's voice
mixed in with others. You remember how fast she talked
sometimes."

My Dearest has to push himself up in order to stand,
I'm pained to see. He lowers his head to listen, then says,
"Can you hear anything now?"

"No. Now that you're here."

When she has fallen asleep, I walk back down the hall,
but pause halfway to listen. All the doors to the bedrooms
and parlors are closed. I hear nothing, but then think I do.

It must be the wind.

In the cabinet room I sit down in my usual chair at one
end of the long table, an area I call my desk. Cortelyou
is still there, with his typewriting machine, and ready to
go on with the dictation. I take out a cigar and light it.
"George," I say after a while, "Don't think I shall run again.

Might be better to make the decision now and have done with it . . . so it won't get in the way of other things."

My "boys"—George and Eamon. George all put together and proper; Eamon all rough and still boyish. I wish they were both my sons. There. I've admitted it to myself. The longing and the pain of that longing. So of course I understand my dear wife. And of course she has a right to her sorrow, but I only wish . . . that it hadn't made such an encampment within her.

"So many people will be disappointed, sir," George says. "And of course, Mr. Bryan, should he win this time, might renew the silver issue. There could be another panic, another depression. He might even withdraw troops from the Philippines, which may be awful bad for the people there."

"I don't believe Bryan can win."

"Not if *you* run, sir."

"So you think I should—in order to stop Mr. Bryan. You think it's my duty, then?"

"It will be a loss if you don't, sir."

"I don't know. What I'd like most is to be home. I've been thinking that one term should be enough for any man." I smoke a while and consider, and then run at it again, with words. "It's strange. A man might think he's making a single decision, but it's never that. A hundred choices can spring from just one, I'm beginning to see. Every so often I get some glimpse of . . . I don't know, exactly . . . almost a confusion of things and no sorting it out. The march of events ruling and overruling human actions, though 'march' may be a misnomer. More like some rout. Yet I also believe that we're firmly in His hands, and that we each have a certain destiny. It's possible that mine is to serve a second term and what all that leads to. I wish I could be certain. There's nothing, you know, like single-mindedness. If General Grant had been divided to the extent I feel that I am at times, imagine where we'd be now. It's all . . . puzzling."

"It's late, sir. It all might appear differently to you in the morning."

"True. But sometimes it's just good to spout on a bit, and you're a good listener."

"Thank you, sir."

I wish I could appoint George as my official secretary, in place of Mr. Porter, but I just don't have the heart to fire the old man. The ineffectual and pompous fellow, I should add. But at least I don't have to see that much of him, thanks to George.

We work for another hour on my address until the young man insists I retire for the night and that we'll go over a fair copy early the next morning. I agree and send him off, but as for me I'm not so tired. I like this time of night when everything ceases and there's not one jot more to be done, for the moment. In my vest pocket is a note, and I take it out and read it for perhaps the fiftieth time. *Tell him for me that he has not only done well, but that he has done the best.*

Mrs. Hobart. A widow now. A beautiful woman. Kind— and so kind to Mrs. McKinley. Also, intelligent.

Jennie.

1900–1901

THE MAJOR

The people! They're coming from all over the state and even the country, imagine that! Every railroad is offering excursion fares to Canton, Ohio, making it cheaper, advertisements announce, than staying home. So my dear Ida and I are free to stay put at our beloved home, receiving hundreds of people each day while my opponent Mr. Bryan—once again!—has to career about the country in search of 'em.

Our poor yard, though. Ida's blaze of geraniums is no more, and the lawn has been reduced to its primal element of plain old dirt. The porch roof is propped with two-by-fours of raw lumber because the porch is sagging from too much weight, and people have been hanging onto the pillars and stressing the roof. Well, it can't be helped for now. Come fall we'll put it all to rights. So far I've spoken before groups of meatpackers and coal workers, railroad machinists and stonecutters and farmers, silver miners and silverites, gold bugs and protectionists and free-traders, seamstresses and cigar makers, leather tanners and shipbuilders. Today, it's a huge gathering of The Women of Northern Ohio on this very warm and humid day, which leads me to hope that any thunderstorm will hold its fire in deference. These ladies appear to be wearing their best summer frocks, and they are standing under a silken canopy of open parasols veiling them in diffuse, multicolored pastel light. Truly, it is an inspiring sight!—one that in fact inspires me to say, "There is *no* limitation to the influence that may be exerted by woman in the United States, and *no* adequate tribute can be spoken of her services to mankind throughout its eventful history."

True! Absolutely true! Looking out over this expanse of color, I feel this truth as a great warmth within. I am up on my dining room chair, on the porch, as usual, and it seems I am looking out over a lovely pacific sea, one from which we can all take sustenance. *"Everywhere"*— I smack my palm for emphasis—"woman is appreciated and recognized. She is a power in every emergency and always for good. In calamity and distress she is helpful and heroic. She is indeed a splendid example to the other half of our species. Her efforts for the public good are noble. But excuse me, ladies, please! I should be saying *you* and *your.* So. *Your* influence in the home, the church, the school, and the community is powerful and nothing short of sublime. But where is your power the greatest? In the quiet and peaceful walks of life. John Stuart Mill's famous words about his own wife oft come to mind in this regard. He said, 'She was not only the author of many of the best things I did, but she inspired every good thing I did.' And this is true as well of my own dearest Ida."

The sea of color shimmers somewhat, but these ladies do not beat their gloved hands one against their other. Their throats make no raucous sound. They stand like deities, elegant and lofty, as I tell them that one of the *best* things about our civilization in America is the constant advancement of women to a higher plane of labor and responsibility. I assure these deities that opportunities are now greater than ever and that nearly *every* avenue of human endeavor is open to them, especially here, in this country. "And in this country, too, respect for womankind has become a national characteristic, a high and manly trait. There is none nobler or holier. The man who loves wife and mother and home will respect and reverence *all* womankind."

At these words, one of the ladies appears to faint. I notice first her parasol catching on the shoulders of the women standing nearest her. I descend from my chair and the sea parts for me as I quickly go to her aid and carry her into the cooler part of the house, where she revives. I ask our housekeeper to give the poor woman a cold drink of lemonade.

Outside again, up on my well-used chair, I am struck with a powerful thought, engendered perhaps by seeing that delicate lady in my own simple home. "From the plain American home," I say, "where virtue and truth abide, go forth men and women who make the great states and cities which adorn the republic, which maintain law and order. It is *this* citizenship which aims at the public welfare, the common good of *all*. And what is its origin?" I pause and look out at my audience, seeing an occasional smile but mainly a calm goodness in the countenances of both young and old. "It is . . . *woman*."

I bow to the ladies and hold the bow as gloved hands finally come together. My heart beats mightily at this acclaim. But then Ida's nurse is near, saying that the lady in the kitchen is fine but my wife needs me at once. I step down from the chair and rush inside. I fear that, from her upstairs window, she has seen how the young woman fainted and how I rushed through the crowd to help her and then carry her inside. Foolish! I should have known this might happen!

I am right. The nurse confirms it. Ida had wanted to hear the speech. Up in our room, my dearest is shaking fearfully.

We get her into her bed and I proceed to massage her temples, all the while saying, My dear, my dear Ida. Ida Ida Ida, my dear . . . my dearest . . . saying those words for an hour, then longer, then off and on throughout the night.

LEON

I get three rabbits before I have to lean against a tree for a while and rest. Geese are skidding their way northward on heavy waves of moist wind. Snowmelt has been sending up tilting figures of fog. This morning the creek and its banks were frosted in the stillness as if all the cold in the sky had fallen there overnight. But now a wind has come up, and the earth smells of mud.

I leave the rabbits on the back porch. I don't like their still-warm limpness, the clouded eyes. And though I am a fair marksman, I don't care for the shooting, either. But now I can ask for a little money. All in all it is a kind of job.

My stepmother appears at the screen door, sees the rabbits, and then says, "Somebody is here for you."

I try to think if I owe anyone money as I scrape mud from my boots with a stick.

"Who?"

She gives me a look and some kind of smile—why?

"Go see for yourself! In the front room! But don't go in there with those boots of yours."

I take off the boots and wash blood from my hands at the kitchen sink. I put on my old slippers and go into the front parlor, my heart too much at work. A woman? Maybe she wants Waldeck instead? My jacket is damp. My old trousers are frayed at the cuffs. It is no way to receive company. On the other hand, what does it matter?

The stove in that room has not been lighted, as usual. The carpet, though, is clean. I know that the spittoon is clean and so is the white doily on which our oil lamp rests. Our stepmother takes good care of this room. When I look up, I see, sitting in the center of our black horsehair sofa, under a framed picture of Our Lord, someone who looks like Lucy.

Lucy?

Whoever this person is wears a deep green suit under a brown cape. Her eyes are large behind silver eyeglasses. The dark hair is pulled back, and yes, there is the heart design at her forehead.

I try to breathe slow. In, out. In, out.

"Leon," she says, "Let's walk. It can't be any colder outside than it is in here."

Lucy.

We walk along wet black fields after I changed into my one good suit and coat. The stream flooded this past January, throwing chunks of ice and stones into the road. Now these chunks, pulled to the side by teams, have all but melted. I am conscious of Lucy's long strides, the fearless way she steps through mud and around stones, the way she holds her face to the wind. While stopping in Cleveland for a while, she tells me, she searched for me by checking parish records.

"But why did you think to search in Cleveland?"

"Oh, I was naturally curious after not getting a response to any of the letters I wrote you, Leon, and—"

"You sent me letters?"

"Yes, over a dozen, right after I went to Pittsburgh. You couldn't have moved by then, and I thought maybe something happened to you, so I wrote to the librarian in Natrona, you remember her, right? And she told me she'd heard something about your family moving to Cleveland."

"You wrote a dozen letters?"

"Yes! I did. At least a dozen. I didn't know what to think when you didn't write back."

I stop walking and look down at the scattered stones in the road. *Let me breathe! Later be sick!* "I was still at the bottle factory, working fourteen-hour shifts. If you wrote and they came to the house—"

"You think she took the letters?"

My eyes water, but I don't want to draw out my handkerchief.

"Of course she must have, Leon! That's the only explanation. I'm certain I used the correct address. Leon, why are you still living with them? When I told her my name, you should have seen her expression. It was . . . she looked so hateful! Then she said she didn't know where you were, that you might not be back for hours and hours, and that you like to go off in the woods by yourself and just brood in order to get out of doing any work. I sensed she was lying, so I said I'd wait a while, if that was all right with her. She showed me into that cold room and just left. I waited for over an hour out of sheer stubbornness. I was finally going to leave when I heard you coming in."

"I was hunting rabbits for her."

"Not brooding."

"No."

"You have to get away from here."

While we walk toward Warrensville, I explain as briefly as possible that I cannot leave until I feel better and can work again.

"Are you seeing a doctor?"

"They don't help. Sometimes one will give me some kind of powder."

"There must be knowledgeable doctors in Cleveland, Leon. You shouldn't go to quacks. If it is a question of money—"

"Thank you but no, I cannot take your money, Lucy."

"I have more than I need now. Please! It means nothing to me."

I try to draw in air and then try to exhale. It is hard. "Without . . . work . . . I cannot repay . . ."

"Later you will be able to repay me. Don't worry about that now. Just get better."

We are nearly to Warrensville, and she tells me she must take the train to Cleveland soon and then go back to Philadelphia. They are expecting her.

I wish to know who but am afraid to ask. Her family? *I have more than I need now.* Has she married a wealthy man? These questions will take many words. I am afraid that I will not be able to say them all so I say nothing.

In Warrensville she insists we stop for coffee at Bower's Bakery and Café—she nearly froze in that parlor, she says. At a small table we sit almost knee to knee, and she tells me about her work in Philadelphia. She is a chemist who makes soap. I am ashamed, but I must ask what a *chemist* is and how do chemists make soap. The explanation takes a long time and while she talks, laughing every so often in her quiet way, I can see how happy she is, how knowledgeable, and how traveled—she visits factories! Like a boss.

"What do you think of the name 'Floating Cocoa'? That's my newest soap, and they're making it in Cleveland. That's another reason why I had to come out here. I proposed the name 'Kalmar,' after a pretty town in Sweden, but the higher-ups thought that was too dull. People apparently want to be entertained by the odd and whimsical, even the pompous. One of my soaps was actually named 'Cyclone' and another 'Centaur.' I really don't care what they call them, though, as long as the soaps lather well and their fragrance isn't overwhelming."

At the farm our stepmother makes our soap from lye and wood ash. It lathers a little but mainly turns the water gray. "You have been to Sweden?"

She looks down at her coffee cup then, maybe thinking that her words sound like bragging. I want to tell her

I know she doesn't mean to brag, just say how things are for her, now, but I have to work too hard breathing.

"I was in Sweden just for a short while."

Now I look down because it is hard to meet her eyes straight on, they are so lively and intense. If Sweden, I think, then other places in the world, too. Not just here in America.

"Leon, let me give you some money. Please don't be proud. It's not worth it."

She opens her handbag and puts fifty dollars on the table. *Fifty.*

I would have taken it to save that cow, but now I do not want it. "Leave the farm," she says. "Go to Chicago, maybe. Or Pittsburgh. I will wire you more money in Chicago if you let me know where you are. Indianapolis, Cleveland, anywhere! Get well, and then you can work in one of the soap factories. I'll see what I can do. It's no time for vain pride now."

"On the farm . . . Waldeck has no patience with . . . machinery. When he tries to fix anything . . . he makes it worse."

I am thinking how she did not say *Philadelphia.* All of this, and the day, the whole day now, is a torment inside. It is going to happen, I think, and then it does, and I am doubling over in the café, making terrible sounds. Some person comes over from the counter and helps me outside.

Lucy stands alongside me while I hack and wheeze and choke. When finally I stop, I see that all color has left her face.

"I'm sorry," she says. "I have to leave now. Remember what I said." She gives me a small card with her name engraved upon it. And then, like that, she is gone. The man who helped me outside goes back in and returns with the five ten-dollar bills. He gives me a look.

When I get back to the house, Waldeck, my father, and my stepmother are having a supper of stewed rabbit.

When my stepmother raises her eyes, I say, "You took her letters to me. Why did you do that?"

"You're crazy! I don't know what you say. Take? You're the one that takes all the time but don't give back nothin'!"

I can see it. My hand striking her round thick face, her head snapping backward, breaking like a rabbit's, but instead I pass behind her chair and climb the stairs to my room. All the way up, I can hear her *wiedzma* voice. "That's the trouble with him. Not enough to do! On his *dupa* all day. Thinking too much. What letters? I don't take nobody's letters, and he calls me a thief. He's crazy. All the time has it in for me—"

"Enough!" my father shouts.

"When somebody calls me a thief I don't let them get away with it, and I won't in my own house either, crazy or no. He broods like some old hen and thinks evil all the time and gives me the evil eye. You saw it just now! That's how he is."

"Quiet!"

I sit on my bed and chew at a thumbnail and keep seeing Lucy, as she has become. A chemist! *Chicago, Pittsburgh, Indianapolis, Cleveland . . .*

It is like seeing a train schedule board. And then I'm thinking, maybe yes.

Chicago.

The thumbnail tears into the quick, and there is blood, which I let drip on her floor.

GUSTAVE MEYER

In my best knickerbockers and cap I wheel down Washington Street to the Western Union office in Hoboken. There, I take a piece of paper from my vest and hand it to Mr. Holt. He is wearing his usual green visor. His forehead is pink, and so is the top of his head where a few hairs can't do the job of covering it. As he reads my message, his forehead bunches in wrinkles, above the visor. Then he looks up and says, "Can't send this."

"Sure you can. I'm Gustave Meyer. I predicted his landslide victory, didn't I?"

"I know who you are, lad. I still can't send it. You're just calling for trouble with this, you ask me."

I give Mr. Holt my usual blank look when people are so rude and, well, stupid. After a while he makes some quick, angry gesture with the piece of paper still in hand and then turns to his apparatus and begins transmitting my message to the president of the United States, who is now in San Francisco, at the bedside of his ill wife.

Your wife will live another year—until about next February or March—but be careful of yourself. You will be shot or stabbed during the month of June, or else in September.

After paying Mr. Holt, who is still as rude as anything, I wheel to the park nearby and join a parade of other wheelsmen and ladies filling the paths. It's a very nice morning, and I have enough money left for a cup of vanilla ice cream.

How do I know what will happen? I'm not sure how. I study my charts of the stars, but it's more a feeling than anything else. A certainty a person just can't ignore.

Inside me now is a good feeling that I am doing my duty.

Now he can do something about it so it might not happen.

The good feeling goes when I think how certain I am that it will.

A JOURNALIST

Buffalo, New York. The Pan-American Exposition. They are coming from every state of the Union and the territories of Alaska and Hawaii and our newly acquired Puerto Rico, Guam, and the Philippines, as well as from Cuba, Central America, South America, Europe, Africa, and Asia, everyone wanting to see the Esquimaux and bare-chested Island beauties, Fatima, the Bewitching Black-eyed Couchee-Couchee Dancer of the Orient, and Chiquita, the Smallest Woman in the World, as well as the Winnebago dancers and Hula dancers, the camels, dervishes, and rickshaws, the acrobats and Arabs, Egyptians and Mexicans, the child savages and Amazons and ostriches, snake charmers and trained tigers, Italian gondoliers and Venetian canals, and the *three million dollars' worth* of weird and wonderful Illusions on the Midway. But let's not leave out the savage beasts and aboriginal combats, the Indian chiefs and ponies and villages, the fountains, lakes, pools, and pavilions, the classical statuary—nudes and steeds and standard bearers rivaling those of Ancient Greece and Rome—the colonnades, gardens, restaurants, and Kubla-Khan buildings, each painted a different hue and torturing the sky with a fantasia of curves and angles. And if all that isn't exciting enough, they will also find battle reenactments, basketball and football games, track, canoe, and bicycle meets, lacrosse and Scottish games, Volksfests and firemen's tournaments and cattle shows. But above all, visitors are no doubt coming from the four corners of the globe to see for themselves the three hundred thousand miniature man-made suns illuminating pools and basins, canals, walkways, archways, columns, domes, towers, finials, and turrets, each Spanish-Renaissance façade, each neoclassical dome, each Palladian arch bejeweled as an Elizabethan gown with rows of 7-watt bulbs as the power comes up slowly at twilight while a military band plays the National Anthem, and the periphery of every building smolders dusky red deepening to the demonic before burning a paradisiac gold. Electricity mounting her throne, electricity creating not daylight but refined daylight, a glow transforming the grounds of the exposition into a radiant realm of romance.

LEON

The City of Buffalo rears upward and plunges down again. This lowest deck is wet, and it tilts forward and back and from side to side. On the upper decks, people are hanging on and laughing. On this deck, too, they are laughing though I am not. Waves splash us. I should go inside the cabin but dare not move. In the air around the steamer's side-wheel, there are rainbows. Now we can see Buffalo's grain elevators. A man nearby is saying that when it's cold, you can see big white clouds of steam from Niagara Falls. Today there are no clouds of steam, only a brown haze over the city.

Soon we pass into the green water of the harbor. Now the side wheel is churning up shingles, barrel staves, and the carcass of something, its entrails all frayed. I must turn away. When we dock, everyone around me moves at once, but I stand there weakened by what happens in my chest, the drowning in air that cannot get out. So I wait, trying to breathe. A deck hand comes up to me and says I must get off.

"Lake sure was rough today. You'll be all right in a while. There's some benches on the wharf."

I am wheezing as he walks me down the gangplank.

"You here for the fair?"

I am able to say yes.

"Lots to see!" He latches a chain across the gangplank and walks back up to the steamer.

I sit on the bench until I can breathe well enough again, then I make inquiries in the steamship company's shed and proceed to a trolley car.

At the last stop, I get out. The air is good, and I no longer feel like I am drowning. On both sides of the road wheat fields sway and sigh. Over the tree line are white clouds like on a church ceiling. To the west, the city is covered with brown smoke. The sun is a red ball.

I begin walking. After some time, I see three men standing near a thresher in a wheat field. I part the wheat and walk over to them.

I know this type of thresher—a Buffalo-Pitts. In Polish, I ask if I can help.

"What you got, a goddam new thresher in your pocket?"

A while later, it shimmies into life—the fuel line was just clogged. Then I am sitting in the farmer's kitchen, and his wife is bringing out cold chicken, bread, butter, and a bottle of beer. While the men stay with their work, I eat a little bread and butter. The woman goes out into the yard to stir blackberries simmering over a fire. The scent of those berries finds me, and I am in Michigan again, at our farm, and it is Mother making blackberry jam, and I think, I cannot be doing this thing, can I?

She comes in and wants to know why I don't eat more. I tell her I have been ill and cannot eat much.

Of course she is nosy. All farmers are. "Where are your people?" she asks.

"Cleveland. I am here for the fair. Have you seen it?"

"No. There is too much work here. Your shirt is dirty. Do you want me to wash?"

I give her a dime for the work and clean my dish at the sink. Then I go upstairs to the room where I am to share her son's bed. He is a boy of six or seven. I listen to him breathing so nice and can sleep a little myself.

In the morning, I sit on the porch and once again read the notice I have torn from an issue of *Free Society*. It is possible, I tell myself, that I misinterpret, for the notice is in English. They have it under a headline that says *Attention* and around it is a black box like you see with death notices.

The attention of the comrades is called to another spy. He is well dressed, of medium height, rather narrow-shouldered, blond and about twenty-five years of age. Up to the present he has made his appearance in Chicago and Cleveland. In the former place he remained but a short time, while in Cleveland he disappeared when the comrades had confirmed themselves of his identity & were on the point of exposing him. His demeanor is of the usual sort, pretending to be greatly interested in the cause, asking for names or soliciting aid for acts of contemplated violence. If this same individual makes his appearance elsewhere, the comrades are warned in advance and can act accordingly.

Are my shoulders narrow? Yes, somewhat.

My hair is not truly blond. Light brown, with some yellow maybe.

Did I ask for names? I don't think so. I did not solicit (does this mean *ask?*) aid. What is *aid?* In Cleveland I asked a man named Schilling for work.

I am of medium height, yes. I dress well, in my one suit, which I try to keep clean and brushed.

Yes, I was at meetings in Cleveland. And yes, I was in Chicago.

I am not twenty-five years of age. I am twenty-eight.

How will they act accordingly? Shoot me?

Or do they mean someone else?

The boy, Tony, comes up. He wants to play. "Play what?" I ask. He has a stick, and he lifts and lowers his shoulders in indecision. Then he sits on the porch and looks out over the field where the thresher is passing.

I take a dime from my pocket and tell him I will hide it so he can search for treasure.

My chest hurts from that notice and I don't feel like playing with the boy, but I place the dime near a rosebush while he covers his eyes. Then he jumps up and begins searching.

When he finds the dime, I let him keep it. "Again!" he says. I hide another one, this time in the birdbath. It shines there, and I think how he'll find it right off, but he doesn't. It takes a long time. After that, I go in to rest, but it's the words I keep seeing, that notice, with its black line closing it in.

THE MAJOR

As our train approaches Buffalo, I take her hand. It's warm, which is reassuring. I am still most concerned about her health and whether or not she'll be strong enough for the coming events. I fear I should have listened to Cortelyou, but the man has been such a fussing hen lately that I knew what he would say, just out of habit. *Stay to home, sir.* He showed me a telegram from one of those so-called psychics, a poor soul who needs to publicly demonstrate—or maybe prove!—self-importance. This fellow is all the more pitiable because he's just a boy. Lad in Hoboken, New Jersey. He predicted my landslide victory in the last election, but that might not have been hard to do, I remonstrated with my secretary. Anybody might have. And Cortelyou said, smiling a little, "Anybody but you, sir!"

And Eamon, too, catching the jitters from Cortelyou. Mumbling in the stable about my needing to stay in Canton. I suspect that Cortelyou, who has been trying to teach Eamon to typewrite, may have shown him the telegram. Your wife will recover from her illness, it said, but, *You will be shot or stabbed during the month of June, or else in September.*

I am not a superstitious man and I do not believe in such devilment as predicting the future. Yet it seems diabolical in some greater sense, as if those words, by their just being out there, unloose some malevolent power. Sometimes I think that—as, I confess, I do at this moment.

So it is important to fight against it, as I did in the Shenandoah during the war, when fear tried for the upper hand and our forces were in fast retreat, stampeding to the rear. But now, July has come and gone. Mrs. McKinley has all but recovered from that blood sepsis, and I need to take my speech to the people—even if it is September—and where better to give it than at the Pan-American Exposition, where thousands daily converge.

"You know, my dear, it will be magnificent. Every building painted a different color, unlike all the white buildings at the Chicago Exposition four years ago. I'm told that at the Pan-American Exposition the brightest, savage colors will be at one end of the fair, and those colors gradually lighten, becoming the palest, most heavenly and civilized imaginable at the opposite end of the grounds. Whoever thought up that scheme to show our progress is awfully clever, don't you think?"

Ida gives her faint smile. Again I scan her face, trying to read it for warning signs. "And there are many statues and classical groupings, I'm told, but I know you're going to like the gardens best of all. The roses and lilies and water gardens."

I hear pleading in my voice, and it occurs to me that I might be trying to convince myself of the wisdom of this trip.

Dr. Rixey, our physician, is seated on her other side, with his bag of medicines. All will be well. I must believe this. I have always believed it. It is something a man just knows, at his best of times. I don't mean when things are going well, but rather when we are fully and most profoundly human, giving ourselves over to His care.

Even when the first explosion shakes our train carriage, remnants of this thought persist. Objects slide from shelves, shards of glass from shattered windows drop over our seats. Ladies are screaming, and men shouting that anarchists have bombed the train. Dr. Rixey urges Ida to inhale from some infusion, while I hold her, my handkerchief ready. We've reached a station, and on the platform, people are running about while pieces of window glass from a nearby building fall, glinting.

Cortelyou and Eamon rush into our carriage. Cortelyou's face looks like paste glue; poor Eamon's is fiery, and his one good eye wild. Cortelyou has him by the arm. "It's not anarchists, sir!" Cortelyou says. "The fellow they caught only had a few bits of coal in his sack. It's a Marine *corporal* firing his twenty-pounder too close."

Another explosion jars us. "Tell him to stop! Get word to him quickly. Dr. Rixey, stay with Mrs. McKinley. I'm going out there."

"No, sir!" Cortelyou shouts.

"I must! People need to see that I'm all right."

I grab my hat, and we push through the jumble of fallen baggage in the baggage car. At the door to the observation deck at the end of the train, Cortelyou and a Pinkerton try to hold me back, but I have a few pounds on both fellows and easily break free. "Just hold onto Eamon. Don't let him run out there or they might think *he's* one!"

Then I'm outside in the clamor, window glass still tumbling and people shouting, *Get the anarchists! Get 'em!* Some men down on the tracks are beating a fellow senseless. I raise both arms and shout at them to stop.

"Folks!" I holler. "Folks, calm down. That was just cannon fire. Nothing but *cannon* fire!"

After a while mayhem becomes big gusting cheers, and our train goes on.

LEON

It sounds like a storm, only there are no clouds. People are running toward the lavender station. Women are holding their hobble skirts and big hats. Men have their boaters in hand. Children run, too. So do I. On the platform, there's a line of victorias hitched to matched teams. There are mounted riders forming a column that stretches out along the tracks. Policemen are shouting orders. In the heat, I go lightheaded and fall against a gate. A man clamps down on my shoulder, something strikes my back, and I fall to the gravel, a horse's hoof only inches away. It is oiled and shiny and ribbed like a shell. I roll away from it and cover my head. There are whistles and cheering, and the earth sinks under the weight of a slowing train. In the next minute, the teams and carriages and mounted horsemen are all clattering away.

My shirt is not torn. No button of my coat is missing. There are some scrapes on my hands. I brush myself clean, after standing, and then begin walking. I see I am on Elmwood Avenue. It leads to another entrance to the fair and I go in once more and just sit by the lake. White parasols in rowboats look like small raised sails. Along the shoreline ducks tug at grasses or float in lines, bobbing on ripples.

It was him, but here I am, still, in the day.

The sun is warm against my hands and face. The air smells like lake water. Part of the lake is silver, the rest a deep blue.

Then I feel where someone hit me with a club. It is throbbing.

I walk to the midway and into Bostock's Wild Animal Show, where tigers must jump through hoops of fire. They snarl and get whipped for it. Finally they jump. Saliva hangs from their jaws. Their long tails flick back and forth. The tent fills with the smell of singed fur. One tiger keeps twisting back to lick at a place that maybe is burned. The trainer shouts at him and cracks the whip. The beast jumps through the hoop.

My palm finds the handle of the Iver Johnson in my pocket. But the act ends, the trainer leaves the ring, and soon there are chimpanzees doing acrobatics.

THE MAJOR

Before me, the far reaches of the crowd on the great esplanade appear to be no more than dots of color. My dear Ida and I are seated on a stand shaded from the sun and festooned with American flags and purple drapery. Below us, eighty red-plumed horses and their riders stand perfectly spaced. Beyond the horses is a cordon of national guard and marines. Beyond the guards are thousands upon thousands of people, some thirty thousand, I've been told, their small flags and handkerchiefs lively.

"Ladies and Gentlemen," John Milburn, the director of the exposition, cries out, "I now give you . . . our esteemed *president!*"

I stand and raise both arms up into the cyclonic sound. It gusts and roars, washing away all worry and the oft-debilitating effects of the vilest yellow journalism, the cowardly political attacks, the distortions and lies in the Hearst papers and elsewhere. Here is truth in its simplest, most elegant form—*the voice of the people*. I am not a philosophical man in the least, nor has my religion of Methodism ever transported me to the borders of mystical experience. But such acclaim from the people almost always does.

Then I am speaking, words coming easily, flowing forth on well-oiled tracks. I welcome the illustrious representatives of other nations and praise expositions as the great timekeepers of progress. I note the positive effects of competition and praise the relatively new practice of settling international disputes and differences in courts of law rather than on battlefields. Then it is time to say what I have come here to say. "My fellow citizens, trade statistics indicate that this country is in a state of unexampled prosperity. The figures are almost appalling. They show that we are utilizing our fields and forests and mines, and that we are furnishing profitable employment to the millions of workingmen throughout the United States, bringing comfort and happiness to their homes and making it possible to lay by savings for old age and disability.

"That *all* people are participating in this great prosperity is seen in every American community, and shown by the enormous and unprecedented deposits." I go on to the heart of my speech, that in this golden age—the crowd applauds the unintended allusion to the gold standard—there is a crucial need, now, for *free* trade. We need more markets. If we don't have these markets, we risk a return to the hard times of '93. We also need, I tell them, more steamship lines and a canal uniting the Atlantic and Pacific Oceans through the Isthmus of Panama. We need a cable linking the United States with Asia. "Nothing in this world brings people as close together as *commerce.* Forces that have so recently been directed toward warfare and strife must now be redirected to cooperative effort in this new century of light."

Boaters spin upward at those words and handkerchiefs wave. I have to brace myself against a swell of emotion. It verifies the truth that our God is a beneficent God, and that all things move us toward fulfillment.

But later, in the banquet hall at the fair's only true marble building, my eye keeps straying to a closed door made of handsome walnut. I'm wondering where the door leads and so I ask one of the waiters. He goes to inquire and then soon returns, a quite nimble man.

"The door leads, sir, to a small garden. There's a pool there, a reflecting pool. The door's locked right now. It can be opened if you wish to see the garden, sir."

"Not at the moment, thank you. You look very familiar to me. Were you at the convention in St. Louis? Did you serve us there, too?"

"Indeed I did, sir. Frederick Constable's my name, sir, at your service again."

"And very good service it is, Mr. Constable." A coin passes from my hand to his—he at first refusing but I insisting. Then I turn again to the Bolivian coffee and warm apple pie made with New York State's finest apples. But still the eye wants to go there, to that door, and does. Why? It's just a door. Six-paneled. Step through it into a garden and see yourself in its reflecting pool. Why should that worry a person?

LEON

The lights come on at dusk, outlining domes and roofs and arches. So many lights! At first they burn red and then gold, while a band plays the National Anthem and people all stand still, watching. What he said was *a golden age.* Up on the stand, surrounded by purple drapes, he looked like the Emperor Napoleon. The many horses were there again, in front of the stand. The riders in red, with plumes in their hats. He went away in a carriage, the horses surrounding him. Just like Napoleon.

I told Waldeck to vote for William Jennings Bryan, but Waldeck only laughed at me and asked what would it change. I thought it might change some things and told Waldeck there would be income taxes for the wealthy, work projects for the poor, fewer labor injunctions against workers, and more money all around.

"More money!" Waldeck shouted. "And higher prices for everything, too, so what will it matter, more money? You're too gullible, brother. You need to think of politicians as out of work and looking. When they need a job, they will say whatever they think will get them one. Look who that Bryan's running with—a millionaire!"

It did no good, saying that Eugene Debs wanted Bryan and so did Bellamy's nationalists, and the socialists, even the prohibitionists. "Is that why you don't want Bryan," I said, "because the prohibitionists do?"

"*Ja,*" Waldeck said. "You hit the nail, there."

Bryan tried again four years later, but once you fail it's hard. And now look. Now we have the emperor again.

In the Electricity Building I read how water passes through a generator at so many cubic feet per second. This produces electric energy, which is power, and that power makes light. Electricity is nothing more, I read, than bits of some invisible material called electrons and protons. These are the building components of all things, and each of these bits is two thousand or so times smaller than the smallest bit making up an atom of water.

What is an *atom?*

Does water hold these atoms?

I don't know. The card says that these smallest bits move through wires, any kind of wire though copper is best. I did not know this while I was working at the wire mill! The bits move. They flow. So that may be why they are called a current. The number of bits flowing past a certain point in one second determines what is called an amp. In one amp alone, there are many bits, but I cannot decipher this number. There are too many zeros, a whole train of them.

These many bits create electricity, but I cannot understand how.

My children, the time will come when you will be learned and know much.

No. It had not happened.

If you have enough bits, can you make a sun? Make a sun and light fields at night so crops might grow? Melt the snows of winter? Dry rain clouds when there is too much rain?

Think, Leon! The lightest things in the world are somehow the most powerful. How can it be? How can a thing that weighs next to nothing be so powerful? Yes, but also think: a man's mind might be said to be the lightest thing about him and is it not more powerful than the body?

For some, perhaps.

What about the soul? It is said to be immortal. It is said to live forever. Therefore, is it not more powerful than the mind, which dies with the body? And if the soul is so powerful, does it mean that it is made of more amps than the mind?—if they exist everywhere, in the earth and sky and within oneself? So when one prays, does the soul conduct some current to heaven, if there is such a place? And when one thinks a certain thought, is one flooded with currents of light? Where *is* the origin of ideas? What machinery, what waterfall generates them? And who or what moves everything in the first place?

God?

Maybe. I don't know.

People are leaving the Electricity Building. Out on the esplanade I walk with everyone else in the direction of the lake and find a place near the shore but far distant from a viewing stand they have built for the emperor out on a dock. I watch as the pyrotechnic king blows up the battleship Maine in the sky above the lake. He stages the battle of Manila, and it comes back to me how I tried to enlist but they would not take me because of my lungs. Now there is the Southern Cross on the sky and soon after, Niagara Falls. It is foaming and pouring down over the lake.

How is such a thing done?

The applause coming from around the lake sounds like rain, but it is light that pours over us. Shells climb and explode and I see shapes that look like the United States, Cuba, Puerto Rico, and a group of colors that might be the Philippines. These shapes and colors expand and then fall from the sky. The next shell explodes, and there is McKinley's face, all light against the dark of sky. And then, just like the handwriting that appears on the wall of Nebuchadnezzar's palace, words form. *Welcome McKinley Chief of our Nation and Our Empire.*

Face and words expand into embers that fall into the lake.

EAMON

In Mrs. Milburn's garden I pick three carnations. They are white as porcelain and frilled like a young lady's gown. Smelling them, I think of a spice cabinet. I think how life is like that, too, if you can let it be. If you can keep out the dreams and all the rest that's over and done with and only haunt a fellow. Keep all that away, and it's good. I carry the flowers into the house and up the back stairs, all varnished oak, no sagging or creaking, the railing mounted hard and true. Upstairs, I fill a stone crock with cool water, hearing it gush, and then I drop the carnations in and set it on the Major's dressing table. I go back downstairs and get the Major's clean Piccadilly collars from the laundress, and his clean cuffs. Upstairs again, I find new cuff mittens in the Major's trunk. I put out some coins—he always likes to carry a few coins with him. I put out a new pad of paper, five collar studs, three clean handkerchiefs, and altogether the top of the dressing table looks like a fine store display. Then I turn back the covers on both beds and admire everything. This is a fine house, grander than the one in Washington, which is a tatter, with its leaky pipes and windows, its sagging floors and thready drapes and huffing furnace. Not so, here. Here, everything is mint and plumb and first-rate. I look about for something else to put hand to but there is nothing else.

After bidding a good evening to the two men who are guarding Milburn's front door, I walk along Delaware Avenue under old trees that look like big vases. The evening is fine. The breeze carries the scent of flowers. But then there's some explosion and then another, and I am limping away from those explosions even as I know I should be going toward them.

The Major.

But I can't. I can't turn and make myself go the other way. Instead I get lost because all the houses look the same now, and all the trees. When I cannot go any farther, I drop to the grass under one of those trees. Gilliat is saying *Want to come, boy?* and blood is sliding from his wrists, and my eye is gone and it hurts bad, so I holler out and keep hollering and then men are dragging me somewhere. *Eamon, Eamon, it's fireworks, boy, nothing but fireworks, you know fireworks, don't you?* And I say they got the Major, and whoever is dragging me is saying *No, it was fireworks over at the fair, you're just crazy again, is what.*

In Mr. Milburn's carriage house, one of the Pinkertons keeps guard over me as I come back into myself. I can smell hay and horses. This calms me some, but Milburn's team is not back yet.

"Were you lying to me?" I say.

"Why would I do that, boy? He'll be here any minute now. They got a big day tomorrow. He'll be here any minute, wait and see."

Then I am curry combing the piebald pony and listening for the clatter of horses and carriage.

A JOURNALIST

St. Louis. The Sons of Liberty Hall. She is a remarkably small woman for someone of her stature within anarchist circles. Four-foot nine, at the most, perhaps, with a head of curly brown hair that makes her look quite a bit younger than her reputed thirty-two years of age. For an avowed anarchist, she is quite fashionably attired in a blue cheviot skirt and blue-striped waist. Throughout her speech, "Influences on the Child," her eyes remained keenly, if not fiercely, focused, her famous jaw, for the most part, outthrust.

"Miss Goldman," I ask during the question period, "can you tell us how you happened to come to America? Your English is quite good. Did you come as a child?"

"I came with my sister when I was sixteen. We journeyed together, the two of us, from Saint Petersburg, in December of 1885, to Rochester, New York, where we had family. Friends, allow me to expand upon this answer, for it has great bearing on our talk this evening. Why do we leave one place in favor of another? Because, I think, we are looking for *life.* Life? Do we not have life? Yes. It may be choking us or starving us, but we have life. What I mean is nourishment, freedom, possibility! As I told you earlier, I could never manage to please my father. He did not think I resembled him or my mother, so he often said that I must be from the pig woman at the market. I saw this woman many times when I went to the market with Mother. She sold slabs of pork hanging on hooks. She sold live pigs and piglets. And she had jars of pigs' feet and hocks on a table. Her arms appeared crusted in blood. Whenever I displeased my father, he ordered me to sit still in a corner, and there I'd imagine the pig woman sitting alongside me, calling me her little dumpling. Whenever my father commanded me to carry a glass of water back and forth—and if I spilled a drop he would beat me—I imagined the pig woman walking alongside me. I had to walk very slowly, and I would stare at the water just below the glass's rounded edge, water wanting to breach the lip. I understood that I could not weep for that would make the water spill. It was the pig woman who kept me from crying. And, friends, in my imagination it was the pig woman who kept telling me to go to America. There, my father could not beat me for reading books. There my father could not call me his disgrace or strike me suddenly, from behind, the heavy comb I wore in my hair digging into my scalp.

"Czar Alexander's early beneficence had been giving way to despotism, after 1848. Everywhere peasants were being flogged with knotted ropes, everywhere Jews were being repressed, and everywhere there was illiteracy, drunkenness, and despondency. Yet revolution was in the air, and the czar and his minions, looking at the setting sun, perhaps saw blood there or a great wheel turning. Were they to be crushed under it? Crushed by the *common people?* By *peasants?*

"You all know what the czar did then. He tried to break the wheel, crush it before it could crush him. And so he ordered more floggings and hangings, more tortures and imprisonments. But the wheel was finally too strong for the czar. On March 1, 1881, he was assassinated by the *Narodnaya Volya.* These words mean *Will of the People,* but do they not sound like a woman's name?

"And here are some others. Listen! Vera Zasulich. Catherine Breshkovskaya. Gesia Helfman. Sophia Perovskaya, Vera Figner. All woman. All revolutionists. And each the equal of any man. Sophia Perovskaya hanged with her lover Shelyabov although she could have run away and saved herself, as many urged her to do. What twelve-year-old girl would not weep for her, as I did. Repression begets repression. The weak only prey upon the weaker. And so my father beat me and berated me until I cried that I would throw myself into the Neva River unless he allowed me to go to America, to our married sister there. He finally allowed, and we began our journey, my sister Helena and I. As for my English, thank you for the compliment. Now. Any further questions this evening?"

"Yes, if I may. One more. You appear to greatly admire the women revolutionists you spoke of just now. Do you believe that violent force against a despotic ruler is always justified? What I mean to say, Miss Goldman, is, do you yourself advocate violence as a means of political change?"

"Are you an undercover agent, my friend?"

"No, merely another journalist."

"Well, that's a good cover, too! I've been asked this question many times, sir, and my answer never varies. I do not advocate violence, but my sympathy is always with the one who carries out the violence."

"Is that not a contradiction?"

"I believe it is not. If you do your reading, you will find that nearly always these individuals are sensitive souls who cannot abide cruelties and above all injustice."

"So their sensitivities excuse an act of murder?"

"They earn my sympathy."

"Could you yourself have possibly murdered your own father, Miss Goldman, given his cruelties and injustice toward you?"

"It is entirely possible, and thus another good reason for fleeing to America—though he and Mother came, too, not long after. Any further questions?"

THE MAJOR

I hear nothing from the next bed and raise myself to look. Her eyes are closed, her face restful. Her breathing is even. I lie back thankful that my crying out hadn't wakened her. It was a dream, only a dream. I believe I ate too many oysters at the banquet yesterday. Too much of everything, in fact, and my stomach still in rebellion. Well, never mind. *Back to the fight, boys!*

Bathing, I think how I've put on far more than a few pounds since those days in the Shenandoah, my horse blazingly fast and I just a stick atop it. *Back to the fight, boys!*—and that fleeing regiment turning. It astonishes me to this day, how they listened, even in their panic. Quietly I shave and dress. Eamon has everything laid out perfectly, as always, which makes the task easy. I load up pants pockets again with three knives, a key on a heart ring, two loose keys, a gold nugget, and six keys on a steel ring. The need to carry all these keys is something of a mystery to me. Several are to the Canton house, and it's a comfort, carrying those. I put on my newly starched shirt and white vest and fasten my gold watch and chain. I put on the morning coat and in various pockets distribute gold pencil and note pad, glasses and chain, one dollar and twenty cents in coins, three clean handkerchiefs, and five collar studs. Finally I take one of the carnations from the jug and affix it to my right lapel. Then, top hat, and checking on Ida once more, and I am ready for this day.

The guards at the front door greet me, and I them. Yards and shrubs along Delaware Avenue are resplendent in the morning light—there must have been some dew in the night; I didn't hear rain. Two guards are following me at a slight distance, but that's all right. They're quiet about it, and I can savor the early morning peace. Six o'clock, by my watch. What I like is to see the moisture in the air, mornings, and sunlight making spokes and shafts as it falls through the trees. Those pyrotechnics last night were a fine sight, if somewhat unsettling there at the end, my face—so large—up on that dark canvas, but this, the morning air and the smell of wet grass and earth, and the light itself is, to my mind, equally fine. If not more so.

The big houses along this street are set deep in their yards, and around each, wet hedges and lawns are silvered with dew. The air holds night's coolness though I've been warned it's to be quite warm again. I'm tempted to leave today, a day early. After so much bustling about and adhering to everyone's schedule, I long for the peace of Canton and our quiet house. Ida's fall flowers will be blooming out back. She can tell you the names, but to me it looks like some artist's palette of mixed-up colors. A fine sight! I have so much to be thankful for—my speech given yesterday—but mainly, I'm thankful I didn't lose her this past spring to that blood sepsis. And though I couldn't get a lick of work done on that western tour or give my speech, that's all right. The people there were so kind, everyone so helpful, restrained and considerate. The *people!* That's what I meant about what's important, what's true. All the rest, the political attacks and such, are more or less petty annoyances nipping away at a person's heels.

Nearer my God to Thee, Nearer to Thee
E'en though it be a cross that raiseth me . . .
A fine hymn, that one.

I walk briskly along barberry hedges and silver lawns for a scant few minutes, cross Delaware Avenue, and turn back the way I've come. All the while, I finger the ring of keys in my pocket. *Canton.* In this fine weather we could be sitting out on the porch. The thought tugs. *Leave. Leave this morning after breakfast. The main work here has been done.* I could say that the First Lady isn't well. But that would be something of a lie, and I've never countenanced lying. Still, it's a half-truth, anyway. The heat has been hard on her, and the schedule. Today, Niagara Falls, followed by yet another reception. Well, she needn't attend the reception, at least.

Into my thoughts comes a picture of the thousands of people who'll likely be there—from every state, Milburn has said, and many countries as well.

The voice of conscience, I suppose. Well, I cannot disappoint so many. And Milburn has gone through so much trouble for this visit. Even refurbishing his home. There it is now. Covered to the roof with ivy and handsomely fitted out with patriotic bunting and flags. The man has spared no expense. It's a fair sight.

I take a last breath of the good morning air and go back in.

LEON

In my room above a saloon on Broadway, squeaky bed-springs tilt at each move. The bedstead is metal painted brown. Under chips in the paint you can see other colors—green, white, and even yellow. Everybody with ideas. Above the bed is a tintype of Niagara Falls in pink and blue and white. Behind the tintype is a spear of Palm Sunday palm faded to the color of a cornstalk in fall. There is a calendar from the Germania Brewery, but it shows the month of April, not September. The stained ceiling in this room looks like a storm brewing. There is my suit jacket on the back of a white kitchen chair. And on the chair, my pants. My shirt hangs from an iron hook near a darkened mirror. My gray hat hangs from another hook. My shoes are side by side underneath the mirror, clean stockings placed inside them. In my valise on the floor, one clean shirt and one pair of clean underwear and two photographs of me, one for Victoria and one for Waldeck. Also the Iver Johnson five-shot automatic pistol. In a way it is hard to believe I have purchased this gun just yesterday. I have been awake this morning for a long time already, thinking about this. A clanging fire alarm woke me before dawn. Horses and pumpers racing by in the street below. Then wagons delivering goods to the Broadway Market just down the street, then the clink and rattle of bottles in cases carried into the saloon below and thumped down. Then church bells. Then factory whistles. Then somebody cursing in the street. Then more horses. Then someone in

the next room pounding around, coughing and then dropping something heavy. Then another fire alarm, another
team of horses, another pumper. Each new sound sends
blood booming harder through each temple. Each breath
brings with it the stink of beer and cigar smoke and horse
urine. I can hear my heart. It is like someone running,
hesitating, running again. My shoulder is stiff where they
clubbed me yesterday. The powders fog my thoughts.
Maybe I shouldn't take them today?

   Maybe yes, maybe no
   Maybe fast, maybe slow . . .
   There is too much noise here. I get up and swallow the
last of the powders.

   The airship Lunette takes me to the moon and back.
Then I go see the Johnstown Flood, Chiquita, the Smallest
Woman in the World, and the Hawaiian dancers. I walk and
look and walk some more, and everywhere there is meaning, ideas, events, disasters the mind wants to understand.
Why this? Why that? The classical statuary on either side
of the esplanade, the all-but-naked figures in pools, others
in flower gardens, the rose court, the lily court—who are
these figures? That they are important is clear, yet their
significance is a mystery to me.
   But I stop before the United States Building and see
something that *is* clear. A chariot with an emperor figure
standing and holding reins that lead not to horses but
six human figures. They are bent over and bony as they
attempt to pull the emperor's chariot. Being dragged
behind the chariot is a nude woman in chains. The slaves
pulling the chariot must be the people. The woman being
dragged behind is—what? The state? The nation? Or, is
the woman the people and the slaves just that, slaves.
Real women clothed from ankle to neck glance at these
statues and then quickly look elsewhere, but I cannot.

The Despotic Age, it is called. A despot is a tyrant.

I tap a finger into the empty tin of stomach powders and touch my tongue. The sun presses down. The sky is so blue it wants to be purple. From somewhere there are rumbles as of thunder moving in, but the sky holds not one cloud, just the press of sun and that blue, wavering and wheeling in a circle. Under it, the buildings along the esplanade look like fancy cakes about to melt.

As I leave The Despotic Age and walk toward The Temple of Music, the sound of thunder grows louder. An organ, I realize. Someone must be playing an organ, maybe practicing. It is like a carpenter building something that goes up and up and then falls down. So he tries again. Up. Up. Up. Then, down. He does this again and again while real carpenters are hammering in nails, three bangs at a time, often, the way carpenters do, the last one the hardest, ta ta *ta*, the nail going in and in, then stopping when it cannot go any farther.

They are building something for him, maybe. A stand, like at the lake.

Sometimes two carpenters are pounding nails. They start out together, but then the bangs go one after another, making a pattern a person can almost see.

It is too early so I walk toward the lake at the southern end of the fairgrounds. Lake water is something I know. How it smells. How light rides on the surface. So I go there and sit in shade, on a bank where there are no others. Like yesterday—*just yesterday?*—one part of the lake is silver, the other, deep blue. Rowboats slide from one part to the other, then back. Sometimes there is an open parasol in a boat. Ripples wash in to shore and cause a line of ducklings to bob.

Leon, Leon, what do you think? Yes or no?

IDA

We sit in an exceedingly small railway car, its seats arranged so that each faces one side of the car. The upper half of the car is entirely open, and we can see the river, just a few feet below us. It pulses and froths and I do not much like it. On either side of the river are high walls of rock. This bit of railway track has been carved out of one wall. The river carries tree trunks and limbs, boards, logs, and every now and then a cask or barrel. Everything is moving fast. Suppose one fell into the water. Or, suppose one went over the falls in a barrel, as some do, it's said. What would happen to the barrel? The whirlpool looks like a cauldron of some kind, filled with boiling water. It bulges at its center. On its circumference, green and white water swirls at a slower pace. My Dearest takes my hand while our niece, who has brought a guidebook, explains that some twenty-five thousand years ago, the great Canadian Glacier changed the face of the earth so that at the end of the Ice Age, all waterways had to find new courses. That is when this river, the Niagara River, was formed. And that is what formed the Great Gorge, where we now are. "Look there, Aunt Ida!" our niece says. She points to a wooden keg that has popped up in the center of the cauldron. Now it dips under and appears in a different place. Then it is gone again before appearing elsewhere. Boards, too, are appearing and disappearing. Someone says, "They can go on like that for days, sometimes even weeks, before they break free and make it into Lake Ontario." People in our car are laughing at the erratic display. As I watch, the cauldron begins to shimmer with bands of light. The outermost are lavender. I grip my Dearest's hand harder. Soon spasms overtake my jaw, and my teeth are banging against each other.

"Ida," he whispers. *"Ida."* He rubs my temple, but it does not help. He opens a clean handkerchief and covers my head. In the sudden whiteness, I see him in the cauldron, going around and around, appearing and disappearing, and there is no one to help.

Sometime later I awaken.

Where? California?

I am able to ask this question, and my Dearest, who is sitting beside this bed, replies, "No, at a hotel in the village of Niagara Falls." I must rest, he tells me. He will see me soon, after the reception at the fair. Cortelyou and Eamon will take me back to Mr. Milburn's house after I have rested.

The drapes are drawn. The light in the room is kind.

LEON

Ahead of me a woman is saying how she met the president once in St. Louis and shook his hand. He was the epitome of graciousness, she says. I nod but don't wish to talk with her. I know the word *epitome*. She means that the president embodies this great thing *graciousness*. I did not know that you can link the word with a person. Thinking of this word makes me remember Lucy and the library at Natrona when I was the epitome of hope. What is hope? I think it is faith. Lose one and you lose the other. And when that happens, you are what?—the epitome of nothing.

A tall Negro man stands behind me in line, breathing out in huffs every now and then and saying to the man behind him how it's hard work just standing there in the sun. Waiting was never easy for him, he says, but this time it'll be worth it. When he says that, my stomach twists like when you touch a worm and it curls up on itself. Ahead of the woman there is a young boy. It would be better without him there. Again my stomach twists and curls upon itself. It is possible I will keep walking, no? The hundreds of people behind me will keep walking past him, too.

Somebody is still playing an organ inside. It sounds like in church. The carpenters must be finished because there is no more banging. I can leave this line and walk away.

And then do what?

Go back to them?

They won't have you, Leon. They say so in the newspaper.

The man behind me breathes out again. He says loudly that he works in a restaurant but took the day off today. "Where do *you* work?" he says.

I think he is talking to me, but I say nothing, like I don't hear him or don't speak English.

It is so hot now. The sun is a flame singeing me. In the Bible, God touched Isaiah's lips with a hot coal to purify him so that he might speak what is true.

But what if this heat pressing down is a taste of hell?

The big doors open. The organ music is louder now.

Well, Leon, soon you will know everything or nothing.

The woman ahead of me is moving forward. I am, too. The Negro behind me says, "'Bout time!" I am walking fast as I go through the high doorway into a place like a church. It is dim and much cooler inside, and at first I can't see anything. The line stops. My left hand holds my cap. My right hand, bandaged with my handkerchief, hangs at my side. Now I see why we stop. Two guards are pulling someone from the line, up ahead. He has dark hair. They search him roughly but then raise the red velvet rope and let him get back in line. We are moving again. One of the guards gives me a hard look. What does he see?

A light-haired fellow. Fair skin. The right hand hurt somehow. Well, you know workers. They're always getting hurt, no?

The guard is now looking at the Negro behind me. Will they stop the line and search him?

No. We keep moving. I can see him up ahead—Napoleon on a chair that is placed on a little stand. So that is what the carpenters were making.

It seems now that I am inside some kind of thresher. There is every kind of sound. And particles of light falling all around.

The Negro behind me is saying, "You don' wanta go, then step aside and let the res' pass! We been waitin' long enough."

I raise my bandaged hand so that it is level. I move forward.

THE MAJOR

Sitting in the straight-back chair at the edge of the dais, I lean forward, smiling and shaking hands while drawing people toward me with my left hand. This is my way, pulling and discarding, pulling and discarding, the line a long string of Ida's yarn. It keeps things moving nicely. But here comes a disabled fellow, bandage about his right hand. I break rhythm to reach for the fellow's left hand, but the fellow hesitates, maybe not wanting to shake hands with his left. Such awkward moments are common during receptions. Nor am I surprised by the expression overtaking the fellow's face, the incredulity there, but why fireworks now? That sound of. And whip-sting of pain.

"Am I shot? Did I just get shot?"

"Afraid you did, sir."

"Go—

". . . easy on him, boys, and—

". . . take care how you tell her."

Then I am following something heading down a hole where it is cool and dark and quiet.

EAMON

Hands were supposed to be out in the open! The detectives saying that. I heard them. Surely I did. Hands in the *open*, not in pockets, but a bandaged hand is not a hand out in the open, and they let the fellow through.

This fact wants to strangle me as I run toward the fair, a whole slew of people out on Delaware Avenue, all heading in the same direction. Running, I keep saying *alive alive alive alive alive*. It ain't a prayer. Just another dream you make to push against the one you don't want.

They have him in some small building. Cortelyou spies me and yells, "O'Keefe, out of the way! You're blocking the door!"

He shoves me aside to grab at fellows behind me, trying to haul them in. How does he know who they are? Doctors, they're saying, and Cortelyou is taking them at their word.

"Find out if they're *real* doctors!"

A strange sound, me hollering. This stops Cortelyou. He is a house coming apart. Hair fallen out of its clean lines. Pocket watch banging his leg. Shirt escaping pants. Eyeglasses dangling on their ribbon. He grabs two of the men just entering and whirls them around. They scowl but then show pieces of paper. He grabs two more before pushing the lot into another room. Soon he is back, a shambles.

"We need to hook up some kind of light. It's blasted dark in there. They can't see."

Cortelyou and I rampage through rooms the size of stalls until in a cabinet I find a woven cord and electric bulb. Cortelyou takes it and runs to the closed-up room.

I go too. At the door guards block me, their eyes alight, and I am on that river again, shot pinging off iron plate and boys moaning, but Cortelyou is there, baring teeth at the guards and saying, "Let him through! He's apt to go crazy on us otherwise," and then I am in the room with the Major who is laying on a table, and there is Dr. Rixey holding up a hand mirror to aim the last of the sunlight into the wound while all around stands a picket of black-clothed figures.

Dr. Rixey sees me. "Eamon! Get up on that chair and hold the light over the Major. Hold it high but not too high."

I climb onto the chair and let the snaky cord with its light down, stopping just above the wound. I see what they are seeing.

"Steady, Eamon. You wanted to be here, now do your job!"

One of the men at the end of the table shouts, "Rising! Rising now!"

The door opens and another person comes in, this one's head and mouth covered with white gauze. He's tall and says not a word.

My hands clench around the cord and I nearly shout out a warning, but one of the men at the table says, "Park! You're in time, thank God!"

They make room for him right near the wound, but he goes down to the end of the table and just stands there at the Major's feet, still saying nothing, and I am thinking what if he ain't who they think, in that gauze, and I can all but see the shot flashing out and the way the wrong catches hold and keeps going, becoming ever greater.

But no, it doesn't happen that way. Instead, the doctors work at sewing up places in the stomach. They don't find the bullet. I have been watching for it, and they don't. Why? I want to ask but don't dare. That they are fixing him and that his pulse is still on the rise—this, I gather— eases my heart. Still, I wonder about the one in gauze. He just stands there watching it all. Some of the others asked him to take charge, but he said no because things were under way.

No matter. They are fixing the Major and he will live.

IDA

"It's become dark! Why isn't the Major here yet? Has he sent a note? He always does if he's to be late. No note? Did he call? Why don't you tell me, Clara? I don't like this. Already dark, and my Dearest not here? Light more lamps! Are you hiding something? You are, aren't you? Something happened. I believe I saw it. Something has happened to the Major!"

"Ma'am? Drink this, now."

"Why do you want me to sleep? Is he dead? *Tell me.*"

"The Major isn't dead, ma'am. But he was hurt. He's still at the fair. Doctors are with him."

"How was he hurt? Did he fall? Did he slip? Marble can be slippery. Is that what happened?"

"No, ma'am. He was wounded while at the reception."

"Wounded! That means he was shot? *Who* shot him?"

"They think an anarchist, ma'am. The investigators are trying to learn more."

"Anarchist?"

"Yes, ma'am. They are—"

"I believe I know! Criminals! Clara, I must go to him. Take me at once."

"Ma'am, they'll be bringing the Major here soon."

"They must bring him to me. Where is my diary?—the one the Major gave me."

"You haven't been writing in it, and I'm not sure—"

"Find it, please. And pen and inkwell."

My hand is shaking so, but I write, in the small space for today, *Went to visit Niagara Falls this morning. My Dearest was receiving in a public hall on our return, when he was shot by a*

The word doesn't come. My hand slides from the page.

LEON

"Who *are* you?"

"Nobody."

Something hard strikes my jaw. I gag on blood.

"We know that, you shit! Tell us your *name.*"

Another blow sends me backward.

"It is Nieman."

"Nieman? That your name? Who sent you to Buffalo? Who you working for, man?"

"Alone. My name is . . . Nieman."

"Yeah, you said. You one of them anarchists?"

"I am alone in it."

Streaky light cages me. Words are far away. "Keep it up, Nieman, an' you ain't gonna make it outa this room."

". . . alone."

"What'd he say?"

"Says he did it on his own."

"Like hell. Where'd that money come from?"

"I do . . . by myself." I want to die now, but they shake me.

"Listen here! *John Most.* You know John Most?"

"No."

"What about Emma Goldman, Nieman. You know Emma Goldman?"

"Emma—"

"You know her?"

"I am alone."

"You ever go to one of them talks of hers?"

"My shirt is—"

"Hell with your shirt. Hold him up, boys."

Again, blows. I hear them but feel little now.

"Bet you did it for her, didn't you? Say yes and we'll go easy on you, boy. Say yes and your troubles are over."

"For myself."

"You did it for them anarchists, that right?"

"For myself."

"We'll be takin' turns now, Nieman, until you talk—or die—whichever comes first."

"I act alone."

"Bresci. Had a clipping about him, didn't you. Didn't you, Nieman?"

"*Ja.*"

"Liked what he did, did you? King killer?"

"No."

"No? Then how come you kept that clipping?"

"I don't know."

"And what about this one, Nieman? Feels like a rag so you must have looked at it once or twice, right? '*The attention of the comrades is called to another spy. He is well dressed, of medium height, rather narrow-shouldered, blond, and about twenty-five years of age . . .*' That you, boy?"

"No."

"Them anarchist pals of yours think you were a spy?"

"I don't know . . . anarchists."

" '. . . *His demeanor is of the usual sort, pretending to be greatly interested in the cause, asking for names or soliciting aid for acts of contemplated violence . . .*' So you were looking for them to help you, were you?"

"No."

"No? '. . . *he has made his appearance in Chicago and Cleveland . . .*' When were you in Chicago, Nieman?"

"I was not."

"Bet you were. '. . . *If this same individual makes his appearance elsewhere, the comrades are warned in advance and can act accordingly . . .'* What were they going to do, Nieman? Shoot you? Should have."

They knock me from the chair again. I see sand, then grass. Where the grass begins, that is death. The grass will be wet, like in the morning, and cool.

"Where the hell you going, Nieman? Home?"

They are laughing now. It sounds like hail. I will die soon so it is all right.

"I am Leon Czolgosz. I act alone. She has nothing to do with it, Emma."

"*Emma!* So he does know her! Spell that name, Nieman. Boys, douse him, quick. He's going on us."

EMMA

Newsboys shout the headlines. *McKinley Shot at Buffalo. Woman Anarchist Wanted.*

I lower the veil on my hat and buy a paper. In a lunchroom I study the sketch of the would-be assassin.

Nieman. Large eyes. Full lips. The face darkened with bruising the artist has drawn in. Thick hair curling and disarranged. I know this man. He is the one who came up after the Cleveland speech and asked for something to read and I gave him several pamphlets. Which? Yes, I remember. *The Chicago Martyrs. Altgeld's Pardon.* So earnest. Wanting to learn. To know. A young man. Handsome. Diffident. Did he say his name? I don't remember.

I tell myself it was not this man sketched in the *Courier.* I tell myself I do not know this man. I want it to be true.

Useless to deceive myself. Of course it was him. And he followed me to Chicago, somehow learning that I was at Abe's house. It all comes back now. How he accompanied me to the station on a streetcar, and several comrades were waiting for me at the station and, seeing him, were amused because of course they knew: infatuated with our Emma! Another one!

. . . before, I was a socialist, but now I wish to join—

Mr. Nieman, there is nothing to join. Anarchism is a way of thinking . . .

I thought perhaps you could teach me about it.

I'm sorry, Mr. Nieman. My train leaves soon. Hippolyte will introduce you to the others. And Max—do you know

Max Baginsky?—he's quite the scholar and can advise you on what to read.

Hippolyte, take care of Mr. Nieman. Introduce him around . . .

He told me he'd been ill and was out of work. I'd hoped the comrades might find something for him to do, however small . . . *take care of Mr. Nieman:* our code for that.

Right then I wanted only my Chekhov and my train seat. Speaking tours exhaust me these days. They empty me of every word, nearly, and I crave solitude, as on that day.

Had I given him more time . . . perhaps even . . .

No, Emma! You did nothing wrong. The comrades did nothing wrong. This man says he acted alone.

But—

Out of work. Despairing. Possibly infatuated— And then that notice. I *knew* Abe meant him. I knew it!

Oh, Abe. How *stupid.*

A German alias. In German the word *niemand* means nothing.

I cannot return to the boarding house. They'll be looking for me there. I leave my paper on the table and go out into the heat where people are buying papers from newsboys, then standing in clumps and reading. I buy another and pretend to read as I walk in the direction of the station. We are all in danger now. Printing presses will be destroyed; houses wrecked, comrades jailed—as during the Homestead Strike and Sasha's failed *attentat.* And before that, the Haymarket. Time a circle only now it will be me who—

A hand grips my forearm. "Emma?"

My heart is wild as I turn to face this person who must be a plainclothesman. But then I recognize an old friend. "Karl!"

"My God, they're looking everywhere for you. What are you doing out on the street like this?"

"Lower your voice, please. Let's walk."

"They're saying you—"

"I know. There's a park. We can talk there."

"You shouldn't . . . I mean, you should leave, go somewhere, not—"

"Stop looking over your shoulder like that."

"I can't sit with you, and you shouldn't linger, either."

"All right, old *friend*. Just swear you'll not tell anyone you saw me here, in St. Louis."

"I swear I'll not tell anyone. Be careful."

He releases my arm and is gone. I cross over to the small park and sit a while to catch my breath and decide what to do next. A sparrow alights on an exposed root and tilts its head at me. I have nothing for it. When it flies away, I am still looking at the root but seeing the scaffold at the Cook County Jail and the four men with flour sacks over their heads and ropes around their necks, their hands tied behind their backs.

THE MAJOR

"Gentlemen! Hard enough being shot without having to be starved, too."

They smile at me, my doctors and male nurses, but shake their heads.

My right hand goes to my face, the bristles there. "Then a barber, at least?"

They smile again. Everything I say seems a witticism. Dr. Mann says, "Of course, sir. Soon."

I fade again—every few minutes asleep! But the dreams are generally good. Just now I was riding Sheridan's horse Rienzi in the Cumberland. How's that for a dream?

Then my dear Ida is here, holding my hand. "They tell me you're better," she says, "and asking for food. That's a good sign, isn't it?"

"It is indeed, but they're not inclined to feed me yet."

My wife is still so beautiful, even with her bountiful hair gone. It reminded me, once, of a field in autumn, the many glints of color. "You must not worry about this," I tell her now. "Strength is coming back. Soon we'll be home."

Her hand in mine is warm. I slide away on another good dream or perhaps memory, I warming my bare feet and hands on ground where cows have just lain, they warming the ground with their steamy bodies. I can see it all so clearly, how mist beads the pasture grasses, and the cows' flanks are runneled with that mist, their ropy tails dripping, and there's fog low in the branches of a stand of maples. The day is so still, the light so even, you can't tell what time it is by the sun. Dung dropped by the cows gives off wisps of steam. The cows move a step at a time, grazing, their jaws working as they walk through field grasses so green they'd confound an artist. God is in that green, surely.

This revelation brings a mighty happiness.

EAMON

They are saying no sepsis! Temperature down! Pulse not racing! Abdomen not swollen! The danger past! They shake hands with one another and with newcomers. Newspaper writers scribble, in the carriage house and stable, telling this news to the world. In the dining room, the big table holds viands to tempt any man. Ham and sausages and cold beef and turkey and cakes and pies, and the doctors eat and talk and shake hands, then one or two of them might break off and go upstairs to the Major's room to see how he looks. Well, I can tell them. Not so good. Then they're back down in the dining room, talking to others fancy as themselves and shaking hands and smiling until I want to yell again but dare not for they will put me out like some troublesome dog.

This house all aflutter, carriages coming and going and all the horses needing attention, but still there is time to slip upstairs, into his room when they are all down in the dining room, and he says, turning somewhat, "Eamon! What's the news, son?"

Hearing that word *son* each time, no matter how often in a day or how little, is like having the real sun in my chest and the warmth of it spreading out in every direction. I say, "The news, sir? It's good. In France and in England they like your speech, sir." Cortelyou said so and I overheard, and it is something, after all, to be saying that now to the Major, saying *France, England, speech*, as if somehow I am a part of it all, too, which I am, but I don't mean in the great way the Major is, but more like I am the blade of grass, green and getting greener, right at the foot of a big oak, and we're both drinking from the same underground spring and my small roots rest on one of his great ones.

He smiles at my words, but his face seems gray to me, and in his eyes I see something there, as with horses when they're poorly.

"Son, a little water, please."

One of the nurses nods so I give it to him, shivering inside lest I spill any. He is able to sip a little, and he says, "That tastes so good. I'm happy you came up to see me, son. They feeding you well enough downstairs?"

Like before, when he said that, only I in bed, that time after Homestead. It all comes back, and I spill the water over him a little. A different nurse comes over, takes the glass from me, and pats the Major's chest with a towel. The nurse gives me a look which means, *This is the last time for* that, *boy*, and I feel pretty done up. So I go back down to the horses and just keep brushing them. I think how he smiled and didn't get riled about the water. I think how he calls me son and how it sounds like I truly am even if I'm not. I think how his eyes don't look so good, and his skin, and I put my face to the horse's neck and just breathe in until the shameful tears finally stop.

EMMA

Signal lights at crossings leave bloody streaks on the night as the train rushes across Illinois. I cannot sleep, in my Pullman berth, because of the voices just beyond the velvet curtain.

"Hang 'er! Never mind no damn trial."

"Tar'n feather 'er!"

"Deport 'er!"

"Hell, no. That's too good."

Crossing bells clang, the train slowing from time to time, then rushing on again, faster, as if to make up for the loss of time. Finally it grows quiet in the corridor, but still I cannot sleep.

In the morning, I make my way, veiled, to the ladies' washroom, where a woman lurches against me as the train tilts into another turn. She begs my pardon and says, "Isn't it dreadful? My heart goes out to that poor woman! I can't get her out of my thoughts."

"What woman?"

"Why, Mrs. McKinley! She won't bear up, poor soul. This is probably the end for her, too. It's so tragic."

The woman rubs complexion cream on her face and neck. "She was made to mourn, I declare."

My eyes are pouched, my skin without any suggestion of color. My hair is mashed down on one side. I dip my hands in warm water. They appear red and large. Quickly I withdraw them, pat life into my face, careful not to lift the veil too much.

In the dining car no one appears to notice or care that a woman vaguely resembling the infamous anarchist has just entered. A Negro waiter in white uniform and wearing white gloves pours coffee from a silver-plated pot. A silver bud vase fastened to an oak panel between the windows holds a single red rosebud. I look out at farms sliding past, with their windbreaks of trees. In a pond reflecting coral morning light, a Great Blue Heron stands still as a stick. A flock of wild turkeys lifts heavily from a muddy field and flies low, away from the train, before lumbering down and settling again. In the dining car, men are dining more on their morning editions, while women scrape jelly on toast. The fine netting of my veil throws small black triangles over it all.

In Chicago, a detective stands facing my car, watching disembarking passengers. Net veil lowered, I go to the opposite end of the train and exit, pretending nonchalance. Inside the depot, two comrades are sitting on a bench near the doors. They follow me out to the street, then onto a streetcar. I change cars frequently, taking a circuitous route to the east side.

In Max's book-lined living room, I embrace Max's wife Millie first. She is all bones and fast-beating heart. I try to quash the pang of envy. Then I am holding Max and in the power of his arms sense his love for me, still.

My laugh, when he releases me, shocks them.

I apologize. I haven't felt myself, I explain, until just that moment. I've felt so unhinged, but now am better. "Tell me what you know about the shooting."

Nothing more, it turns out, than the dailies.

Millie serves a breakfast neither Max nor I can eat. Speaking in German, Max keeps his voice low but waves both arms about. "The police want our blood just as during the Haymarket affair. Do they care if we're guilty or not? No! Emma, they want to destroy you and in that way destroy the movement. Here is what I think. You must go to Canada. If they find you anywhere in this country, they will hang you. They see you as an accomplice. Proof does not matter. They can buy any proof they need. You know this!"

I do know that but say, "It is cowardly to run."

"You can work for the cause there, Emma. Toronto. Montreal— I have letters from comrades. I will show you!"

When he leaves the room, Millie turns to me and whispers, "Please, at least listen to his plan. You see how he is? He's making himself sick over this. He can't sleep, he will not eat . . . since Friday."

Returning to the kitchen, Max does look crazed, his hair, eyes, hands all in flight. "I don't know where they are! I don't know what I am doing anymore! I had them, but now they're gone. Millie! Find them for me, please!"

Pale Millie bumps the table, leaving the room.

"Emma, they are going to kill you."

"I will go to Canada, Max. And if he lives, I will come back in a few months. Only, we should help that boy now, no?"

"Who? What boy?"

"Nieman."

"Nieman! Do we even know who he is for sure? Tell me, please, who is he? They say he knows you, knows us. Emma, you are not thinking clearly. They have no real proof of your involvement, but if you try to help him . . . We cannot! That is all they need, now."

"Max, all right. All right."

"You must go to Canada. You *must* live."

"I will. And you, Max, must eat something now. Eat, and I will tell you *my* plan."

The house, not far from the lake, is Norman in design, with a tower at one end and tiers of curved windows.

Scarlet-leaved peony bushes line the walkway to the house's front entrance. A young maid opens the heavy door and ushers me into a small parlor off the hall. She is a pretty girl, her brass-red hair woven into thick plaits under her cap.

I sit on a brilliant green, silk-covered settee and for a few minutes look at the gilt-framed botanical prints on two walls. Below them, vibrant ferns drape down to the floor. There is a hooked rug with figured roses. Sun slants in from paned windows. Outside, there's a small flower garden. After several more minutes, Rosaline Marchand enters, smiling. Her skin is pink as the maid's even though her hair is gray. She might be an actress in powdered wig, an actress with fine dark eyebrows and eyes. I become conscious of my dishevelment and fatigue.

"So delighted to see you!" she says. "How many times have we said to come and stay with us and now here you are. Glad I was home. Usually at this time I'm in my office downtown, but we have a new girl in training."

Smiling Mrs. Marchand sits opposite me. *Office. New girl in training. Botanical prints and ferns.* I register these thoughts, but my heart is too burdened for any sense of superiority. After a perfunctory *I hope you had a good journey,* she ushers me upstairs to an opulent bedroom.

Lying on the high bed, my legs and ankles throbbing, I sense admiration for Mrs. Marchand beating out my usual need to censor and criticize. What appeared to be vapidity, I realize, is in fact a veneer masking courage. And, too, the woman is circumspect and cautious and smart, not uttering my name to be overheard by any servant girl. I roll to one side to ease my aching hip. The deep feather-bed envelops me like water.

Two maids—the beautiful young girl from this afternoon and another who might be her sister—serve a full roast beef dinner that embarrasses me, the circumstances of my visit hardly warranting any such celebration. Then I think that perhaps the dinner is not in my honor at all; perhaps Mr. and Mrs. Marchand often dine like this. I have little appetite and as they ask their questions, I find myself talking more and more. Their continuing questions lead me from topic to topic, and after a while I imagine myself, from their perspective, as *life* itself, plopped down amid all the Ecuadoran mahogany, the drapery—closed!—the silver, and crystal. So dinner table becomes a stage, and in no time my words find their satiric groove, transforming my fear, the previous night, into a hilarious anecdote about the good Christians on the train from St. Louis.

Laughing, we don't hear the doorbell. At the maid's whispered words, Mr. Marchand pushes back his chair and leaves the room. Mrs. Marchand smiles, exchanging a look with me.

"He'll take care of it," she says.

But then the dining room door slides open, and there are Max and Millie, their faces blanched in the chandelier's brilliance. Mr. Marchand slides shut the heavy pocket door behind them.

Max speaks in German. "I think we were followed! I don't know. We should not have come here, but I wanted to—"

"English, please, Max," I say. "It's all right."

His attention snags on the room's elaborate mahogany mantelpiece. In slow English Millie says, "He wanted to bring your disguise, Emma, the minute I finished it."

"Please do sit down," Mrs. Marchand says, "you're just in time for dessert and coffee!"

Mr. Marchand settles himself, and Millie sits, but Max does not. "We think you should leave now," he says. "At once."

He, too, is not using my name. "Max," I say, "sit for just a moment. We must discuss something."

Finally, he does but says, "What something? There is nothing to discuss!"

"I need to give an interview tomorrow morning."

"Interview!"

"Mr. Marchand has arranged it. We'll get five thousand dollars for an interview with a Hearst paper. I've agreed to do it. Five *thousand* dollars, Max!" I know he understands my emphasis—all this for Sasha's commutation fund.

But Max says, "Then they will have you."

Mrs. Marchand places a cake on the table, douses it with a liqueur, and ignites it. Flames roar an instant before sinking back. "We seldom have this," she says, "but tonight seemed special. It's filled with pecans."

Max stares at her. I can tell he has confused her meaning. *The night is filled with pecans?*

"I brought shears," Millie says in German. "He wants me to cut your hair."

"Let us speak English, friends," I say. "They want me to cut off my hair," I tell my hosts as I pull a strand taut.

"Oh no," Mrs. Marchand protests. "Not your lovely hair. We won't allow it!"

I turn to Millie. "After the interview you can cut it."

"There will be no after," Max says in German. He refuses the cake and the coffee Mrs. Marchand herself pours.

It's the harder way, I argue with Sasha in my thoughts much later that night. Living is always the harder way. To allow myself to get caught now?—what purpose would that serve? There'd be a frisson of interest in the papers, then nothing. This way I can continue working for *you*, Sasha dear, and the cause.

Indecision and shame infuse me. While in St. Louis I received word of Sasha's second suicide attempt, and this not long before the Buffalo shooting. They stopped him and then stuffed him into the "hole" again, where he'll be for months in solitary confinement—and where he is right this moment, while I lie in a high warm bed after a sumptuous bourgeois meal.

Emma, Emma, you have always liked luxury too much. You have always been tempted by it.

Only this one night, Sasha. The interview is tomorrow. Five thousand dollars! And I will be doing what you have always said I must—speaking, explaining the attentat. *Even you, my poor Sasha, must admit that continuing to live can be harder than dying.*

Then I am thinking, again, of that young man in Cleveland asking me what he should read. The sensation is like missing a step on a stair.

I get out of bed and rip out the inscribed flyleaves of the few books I've brought. I set match to several letters and notes and the flyleaves and then watch everything burn to ash on the grate.

That night I sleep little if at all and in the morning draw a bath, hoping it will revive me. The house is quiet. The Marchands may have gone to their offices, and the maids, if there, are making no sound whatsoever. The interview is scheduled for one this afternoon, and Mr. Marchand promised to return for me and bring me, in disguise, to the place, and then to the train station. It's a good plan, and if it works, I'll be in Toronto tomorrow morning.

But when I remember what happened to Sasha when he tried to escape, the sensation of lightheadedness and wrenching fear worsens. Then I am seeing Nieman's face again, those lovesick eyes.

Glass shatters downstairs somewhere. It is a loud crash—too violent to be some kitchen accident. Quickly, I get out of the tub and reach for my kimono and glasses but then stand there, my heartbeat erratic.

A minute later, I am walking down the stairs, my expression indignant. In what I hope will be taken as some Old

Country accent, I say, "Vatch yourselv you are not cut! Why you do not come through door? Or you are burglars?"

The dining room floor is littered with shards of glass and pieces of lead casing. Part of a stained glass panel hangs without much support. A man in a suit and bowler is climbing through the window, holding a revolver in his right hand. His left hand is bleeding.

"You break vindow like that and now drip blood all over? Vat is this? I call police!"

"I am the police, you idiot. Why the hell didn't you open the door?"

"I hear no ring."

"Well, go open it right now."

The maids may be hiding, or possibly they had orders not to be home today. Could the Marchands have betrayed me? Or had the police followed Max and Millie? But then, why not break in last night? I open the Marchand's front door to five more detectives.

"Vat you want?" I ask them. "More vindows to break?"

"You the maid?" one of them asks. They all resemble the first, in their bowlers, and all carry revolvers.

"I am, ya."

"Why didn't you open the damn door? You sleeping or what?"

"I . . . bathing. It is my day to bath."

"Well, la di da. Where's everybody else?"

"Nobody iss here now."

"Emma Goldman staying here?"

"Ve haf no gold here."

"Goldman! you dunce. A woman. Somebody not living here but just staying. She here?"

"I am here only."

"Search the rooms, boys."

All six run upstairs. I stand at the front door, shaking. Impossible to flee, in a kimono and barefoot. All six come running down again. "She's here, you dummy. We found her pen. Got her name on it, see?"

I turn to the one whose thumb is still dripping blood. "Gentlemen, before you smash up anything else—I am Emma Goldman."

"No, I didn't order him to do it. No, he is not part of our so-called group. We have no group. Anarchism is a *belief*, a philosophy. I had nothing to do with the shooting at the fair. I believe in freedom as a condition of life, a necessary condition. I believe that heads of government and government itself are unnecessary. In fact, government impedes the functioning of society. But no!—this *doesn't* mean throwing bombs or killing people. It does not sanction violence. And once again, *no*, he wasn't acting for me. How many times must I repeat this?"

Ad infinitum, it seems. Either my interrogators are stupid to the core or else they are trying to wear me down. Both, no doubt. Five sit at this metal table, three across from me and one at each end. Another man is standing behind my chair. I sense the small movements he makes. Perhaps there are two of them. The interrogators have been at it for several hours now, and I am most uncomfortable, having had to relieve myself for some time. On the table is a pitcher of water. The men refill their glasses every so often. More and more frequently my glance returns to this pitcher although I try not to look there, or at the glasses, or at the men drinking from their glasses. The pitcher is clear, so I can see the water. Twice, a woman has brought in a full pitcher and taken away the other, and of course the water appears, then, very cold and fresh. The woman never looks at me. There is no clock in this room, but it must be late afternoon by now. My throat burns; my words rasp. *Thirsty? Tell us the truth, Goldman, and you can have a good swig, have the whole thing, if you want. Or even a couple a pilsners.* An electric bulb on a long cord hangs over the table. It has begun to hurt my eyes. The interview with the Hearst reporter would have been over by now, and I en route to Toronto.

"But he did *know* you," the one directly across from me says. This man seems quite young; that he is here must mean he's good at his job. I look into his eyes, a pleasant blue but closely spaced, and I say, "Many know me."

"*That's* a fact," he shoots back, and all the men laugh. "He says he met you in Cleveland. Met you and probably more than that, right?"

Again they laugh in their snide way.

That day when he came to the lecture—it was an afternoon in May. New leaves and tassels gave the maples just beyond the hall windows delicate chartreuse filigree. Because of the warmth, the organizer had opened the windows; the doors were propped open with bricks, and the room filled with fine spring air. The sweetness of it all filled me, and I was eager to begin speaking.

"You better talk to us, Goldman, if you ever want to leave this room on your own two feet."

Friends, look at your hands. What do you see? Some dirt there? Scars? Don't be ashamed. What else? Nothing? Well, let's say it appears to be nothing . . .

". . . says you fired him up. Your words set him on fire. What do you suppose he meant by that, Goldman?"

"There are a number of ways to interpret it."

"Damn sure are!"

Of course they laugh again. And drink more water.

"So he listens to you talk, gets fired up, and goes and shoots the president. How would you interpret it?"

The power is in you to overturn this platform right now, but you don't. You choose not to use your power against me. Patrolman! You. Over there, nearest the door. Why are you here? To listen to Emma Goldman talk about the philosophy of anarchism? Not likely. No. You're here because you're forced to be here. You've surrendered your power to be elsewhere. Why?—because you need to get paid, so you follow orders . . .

"I did not advocate violence at that talk or at any other talk."

"Right. We heard you before. So, once again, sweetheart, let me read back your own words. 'It's a terrible thing for idealists to have to resort to violence. But when it does happen, my sympathy is always for the one carrying out the act.' So this fellow Czolgosz or Nieman or whoever the hell he is hears you say that, and he's already twisted up in his brain, and so he goes—"

"I said more than just that. Your detective probably didn't take down the rest, having gotten what he wanted."

"You planted the seed, right? You gave him *ideas.*"

"I did not tell him to go and shoot the president! And please correct me if I am in error, but I have been under the assumption that the constitution of the United States protects freedom of speech. It is my understanding that this is stated in Article I. It is also my understanding that you gentlemen profess to hold the constitution sacred, do you not?"

"Freedom is one thing. Inciting to violence another. We got laws against that."

"Here is also what I said. I'm sure you want to hear it again. 'Anarchists don't favor the socialist idea of turning men and women into mere machines of production under the eyes of a paternal government. Anarchists go to the opposite extreme and demand the fullest and most complete liberty for each and every person. This is so each person can work out his own salvation upon any line . . . as long as it does not interfere with the happiness of others.' I think we can assume that shooting someone would be infringing upon that person's happiness, no? So you see I was *not* inciting to violence. How many times must I repeat myself, or is it that you don't understand plain English?"

The detective behind me suddenly clamps both hands around my neck and squeezes hard while at the same time shaking me. The room darkens, all the faces recede. When I come to, I am slumped over the table, my face in water.

And I have wet my Scotch-plaid skirt. The men are laughing at the puddle under my chair. "No more water for you, girly, for look what you went and done."

LEON

The El, in Chicago, then an electric trolley, then a horse-car out to Jackson Park, I memorizing the signs on buildings so as to know how to get back. *Robert Burns Cigars.* *Electricity is Life.* Never did I think that I would be riding back with *her,* to the station. On the trolley back to the city, a woman across the aisle stared at us and was about to suffer some paroxysm because Emma did not bother to lower her voice. *Do you know that marriage sanctions the greatest evil?—the granting of power to one human being over another? It is a monarchy, Mr. Nieman. A monarchy in the home. Whereas I believe in freedom to love.* When we needed to transfer to the El, a hot wind had pulled my hair straight up from my scalp, disarranging it, and I felt very bad to think what I must look like to her. An *idiota,* a know-nothing, and ugly on top of it all. All too fast we were at the Grand Central Depot. They have a large clock face set into each side of its tower shaft so that anyone can know the time, no matter what direction they come from. It struck me that someone must have to climb up, inside that tower, to fix the clock when something goes wrong. It also occurred to me that I could do that—if someone would look past the illness and hire me.

"Mr. Nieman? Good morning, I am—"

In that house in Jackson Park, where she was staying, they had a silver bowl for calling cards. A silver bowl, imagine. What do anarchists want with silver bowls? And calling cards. In a garden there were tiger lilies. We had these, on the farm in Michigan. My mother liked them, so when I see them, all orange and spotted on their tall stems with those little black beads on the side, like a rosary, my eyes fill. She sees this, Emma, when she comes into the hall. I am ashamed.

"Mr. Nieman. Are you awake? My name is Dr. Joseph Fowler. I am the police surgeon. There are some people here who wish to speak to you. Can you sit up, please?"

In the hall, I felt bad because she was just leaving. She wore a white suit and a black hat with a red flower on the side. She limped a little, walking toward me. That surprised me—the way one leg dipped down a little lower than the other. I get there, coming all that way, and she is just leaving for somewhere else.

"These men are doctors, Mr. Nieman."

But she recognizes me! *Ah yes, you're the one who wanted to know more about the Chicago Martyrs. That was you in Cleveland, wasn't it?"*

Ja, I say. It was me.

"Nieman, you've been sleeping for hours. You need to be up, man. How's that face of yours?"

Face? What are they talking about? I sit up and then know. The pain wakes up and scatters over and through my face and head. My arms.

"Is it any better?"

I do not want to think about the pain or how I yelled and screamed and shamed myself. Or how they did not shoot me as I wanted. So I think how she took my arm— Emma Goldman! At the Robert Burns sign, we transferred again, and I tripped, stepping down, and the conductor said, "Watch yourself, boy," but she didn't care. She took my arm—

I scream. They are pressing something into my head, into the pain there.

"That's just a hatter's impress, Leon. I called you Nieman before, didn't I, but your name is Leon, isn't it.

The doctors want measurements of your head. Be still, it won't hurt so much. Just a minute, just a minute."

She talked about the institution of marriage, making it sound like a bank. She held onto my arm while she talked. I—

"That's it! They're finished. Now, you'll talk to these fellows, won't you? This is Dr. Floyd Crego, and to his right is Dr. James Putnam. They're from the university here, Leon, and they want to ask you a few questions."

Mr. Nieman, I'd like to introduce you to a few of my friends who have come to see me off . . . Havel! Take care of Mr. Nieman—

"Leon, tell us, please about that handkerchief you wrapped around the gun. Was the handkerchief yours?"

"*Ja.*"

"It's being said that it was a woman's handkerchief. Was it?"

"No."

"It wasn't Emma Goldman's handkerchief, Leon?"

"No."

"Last night you said that it was hers."

"No."

"You didn't say that?"

"No."

"I see. All right. Can you show us what you did with the handkerchief? Here. You may use this one."

I turn away from it. It is bloodied and torn and blackened.

"You don't want to use this one? Why not, Leon?"

I twist at a loosening coat button. *Good!—here's Max. Do you know Max Baginsky? He's quite the scholar.* My heart hurts when she says that.

"Leon, it won't do you any good not to cooperate. It'll go hard on you boy. Like last night. Do you want to show us with a clean handkerchief?"

"Our stepmother's apron, like butchers wear, was always spotted with blood. It looks like rust after a while. New blood does not."

"You had a stepmother, Leon? She good to you?"

"No."

"Ah."

"I thought I would shoot the president so I wrap the handkerchief around my hand and in that way hide the gun. As for who tells me to do that, no one, even though I hear people talk of such things."

"Where did you hear people talking of such things, Leon?"

"Everywhere."

"Can you explain?"

"At meetings."

"Where were these meetings?"

"In cities."

"Which cities, Leon?"

"Akron. Buffalo. Cleveland."

"Did you also read papers and books that discuss the shooting of rulers?"

"Look at my shirt. It is torn and bloody. I ask them to bring me the other one from my valise, but no. They don't bring. Did they take my valise? I will pay for a clean shirt. You know, the thing is done. Why does it matter what I read? Done is done. Now just shoot me, but I ask for a clean shirt first."

"We can't shoot you right now. There has to be a trial first."

They come back. The doctors—if they are doctors—and ask the same things. This time I tell them, "No, I did not shoot the president. I did not mean to do it and I did not do it. I don't know who did. No, I am not lying. Did I buy a gun at a shop in Lafayette Square? No, I buy no gun."

"What's the matter, Leon? Are you still in pain? We gave you something for that, remember?'

"Today there is little pain."

"Do you know who we are?"

I say the names, but I do not know which one is which. Each wears eyeglasses. Each looks learned.

"Do you remember what we talked about yesterday, Leon?"

"I did not do it."

"What didn't you do?"

"Shoot nobody."

"But you already confessed that you did."

"I am happy that I did."

"Take this and show us again what you did."

Handkerchief. Clean. White as the flank of a newborn calf. I can see the calf as I twirl cloth around index finger— so white the word *immaculate* comes to mind, and its black patches pure in their own way too. You watch the mother lick the calf clean, the thing lying on its side, its legs folded, the cow's tongue prodding, only soft, soft, and patient like no human could be. You touch the calf, its warm wet side, its hair sticking together, and that is as close as you can come to the two of them, and it is still far away.

"Leon, what are you thinking? Can you tell us?"

"About in spring. Cows give birth."

"Ah. You lived on a farm, did you?"

"Sometimes."

"Did you have dairy cows on this farm?"

The handkerchief fragments into blossoms. White and thick.

"We had dairy cows."

"But you left the farm. You left the farm to come to Buffalo to shoot the president. Why did you do that, Leon?"

"I don't know."

"You don't know?"

"I don't remember why."

"Are you trying to protect someone, Leon?"

"No."

"Are you trying to protect Emma Goldman?"

"No."

"Do you remember hearing her speak in Cleveland?"

"Yes."

"What can you recall about that time?"

"Nothing."

"Do you enjoy playing with us like this, Leon?"

"No."

"Do you know, your head isn't enlarged in any way, Leon. If it were, that would be a sign of insanity. We don't believe you're insane but that you enjoy this attention from us. What do you think?"

"I think you can think what you want."

On the farm in Michigan, you could have blossoms and snow at the same time and fog lifting off the snow and filling the woods like smoke. The ground smells good, after the nothing of winter, and you stand there smelling it because it is like that.

"Well, good day, Leon," one of them says. "We may not be back. We have all we need, I think."

"Thank you, boy," the other one says.

For what do they thank? What have I done for it?

Kill?

Yes. I have killed someone.

And then I know something. I know now that hell is not flames, but knowing, a knowing in every direction, so this must be it already, hell, the beginning, at the edge of death, inside the dying that is long, not quick like with a rabbit, which you do quick to spare them.

EAMON

He's sleeping good. They want me to leave but can't figure out how to dislodge me without carrying me out, hands and feet tied, because the Major said, *Stay, son.* But inside me I am hearing words I do not want to hear. *Sir, Mr. Cortelyou thinks it's not a good idea for you and your wife to travel to Buffalo.* I told the Major this in Canton when he came to have a look at Jupiter's foreleg and was happy to find it cooled down. And the Major says, *Oh? And why is that, Eamon?* And I can't tell the Major because Cortelyou got me to swear I would not. So I stand there, not knowing what to say, and the Major says, smiling like he does, *You better not go into politics, Eamon, and that's for certain.* I don't take his full meaning, but no matter. It seems a joke, and I like when the Major makes a joke, for he enjoys them. But still, I stand there thinking how else can I say what needs to be said. I am thinking I could say how Mrs. McKinley isn't well enough, and maybe that will take it all in a different direction, away from Buffalo, like in her crocheting when she makes the loops turn. Cortelyou did not want the Major to know he told me about that telegram so he swore me to silence. *Your wife will live another year—until about next February or March—but be careful of yourself. You will be shot or stabbed during the month of June, or else in September.* These words were from the boy astrologer of Hoboken, which is somewhere to the east. I asked Cortelyou what *astrologer* means, and he told me it means a person who looks at the stars and learns things about the future, or so it's said. How do you do that? I asked. He didn't know. Stars don't have any kind of words, do they? I asked. Cortelyou said heavens no, and laughed. He said it was all quackery and devilment and that the Major would say the same thing, but best not to tell the Major any of it. He has enough to be thinking about.

So I did not tell him about the boy astrologer in Hoboken. I just said, *And I don't think it is a good idea, either, sir. Mrs. McKinley will be too tired.*

It was May when the Major came to see Jupiter's foreleg. A fine day. Then June came and went. In July I felt something just under the skin. Just like now, so I want to stay right here with the Major, because it seems like more of the bad will happen if I don't.

IDA

"**N**o."

"But, ma'am—"

"No, Dr. Rixey. I want to be clearheaded, not addled."

"Still, ma'am, I think it's best if you take your medication before seeing the Major. It would be unfortunate if you become upset and then—"

"Do you understand the meaning of the word *no*?"

"Yes, ma'am, I do, but a lower dose might suffice."

"I suppose you are right, Dr. Rixey, but I don't want everything to be vague right now. I want to be able to *see* my husband. Do you understand?"

"I do, ma'am. Yes."

Sometimes I think Dr. Rixey *wants* me half-asleep all the time to spare him the bother of me. But now I believe that if I remain upright and focused and strong, my Dearest will live. So I must be more than I am so that he will live. Before, I needed the haze. Now I am able to walk, on Dr. Rixey's arm, to the room where they have my Dearest, and I can clearly see it all. The room is made up to be a hospital room. Dr. Mann is there—a gynecologist! This still incenses me.

"Dr. Mann," I say. "Where is Dr. Park, the *gunshot* expert?"

He takes my meaning and looks most uncomfortable. "Ma'am, Dr. Park has gone on to another case."

"Oh? And is it a *gunshot* case?"

"Yes, Mrs. McKinley, it is."

"And why should that gunshot case take precedence over *this* gunshot case, doctor?"

"Well, ma'am, I thought we explained it all previously. Dr. Park excused himself because, well, because I am considered to be the attending physician on this case. This means that I am the one in charge."

"Explain it again, Dr. Mann. I was not myself, earlier."

"Ma'am, Dr. Park arrived late. We had already begun. He has deferred to me, ma'am. It is the protocol."

"Protocol? Do you mean rules?"

"Yes, ma'am. It is how things are done, in our profession."

"Or as Mr. Emerson might have written, 'Rules are in the saddle and ride mankind'? So even though you are a gynecologist, you must be in charge here."

"Ida," my Dearest says. "Dr. Mann is an excellent doctor. He's treating me very well, I assure you. Come, sit down and tell me what you've been doing. Have you been in the garden? Is it a fine day out there?"

Of course I haven't been outside in the garden, having just awakened from my potions, but I tell my Dearest that I have and that it is indeed a fine day. I sit alongside his bed, and he takes my hand and smiles. It's astonishing— the power of a word or two.

"Hear that, Eamon?" he says in a weak version of his old heartiness. "Mrs. McKinley has already been in the garden and it's still only morning!"

I look at Eamon and shake my head the slightest degree. It is hardly morning. It must be nearly four in the afternoon.

How strange to see the young man so clearly. Usually, he is a mere shape. He is young—younger than I'd thought. Thick bright hair. Imagine, so much hair. Once I— Tremors begin. I grip my cane harder with my right hand and raise my chin. Eamon, an illiterate young man, and my Dearest doting on him. *Our* children should be here. Our girls. He should be doting on *them* instead.

Chills bang my teeth together.

I must not.

"Dr. Rixey," my Dearest says. "Mrs. McKinley appears unwell."

I focus on the curtain's lace and then follow one strand in the design as it curves around to form a flower. When I reach the starting point, I am no longer shaking.

"I want to stay here with you a while longer."

The sun emblazons a stripe on the bed. Holding my Dearest's hand while he naps, I watch the stripe slowly traverse the white bed linen, pulling the faint shadows of flowers with it. Dr. Rixey sits in another chair somewhere behind me. And Eamon, too, remains where he'd been sitting at the foot of the bed, watching my Dearest. Beyond Eamon are three male nurses in their own chairs. As for Dr. Mann, I believe he has gone downstairs, perhaps to avail himself of an early supper.

It is five o'clock, by the round clock in its oak frame on the wall. Beyond the window, a cardinal whistles. Every now and then my Dearest laughs—in his sleep! Normal, Dr. Rixey assures me. I needn't worry.

Needn't worry. Well, Roosevelt surely isn't, chasing off to his Adirondacks again. Right this minute aiming his rifle, probably, at a deer or a bobcat, his spectacles aglint. That moment before death, an odor he probably savors.

I don't want to think about Theodore Roosevelt or the odor of death. There is no odor in this room! There is no death. I will believe this just as I believe our girls are in heaven. I've created a scene, like a picture to hang on the wall. My namesake, Ida, still an infant, outside in a white basket with a gauzy white covering. Her nurse sits nearby. Everything is June green—grass and trees and shrubbery. A garden blooms with peonies and iris. Ten-year-old Katie sits nearby with a white kitten in her lap. Her frock is blue.

God is not savage. God is not disinterested.

Mr. McKinley will live.

But how, if my brain cannot work properly, can I know this? A specialist in New York explained that the whole nexus of my brain has been jarred by some event, perhaps fever, perhaps grief, and so the apparatus of the mind cannot function properly.

Therefore, *faith* must circumvent the brain's faulty machinery.

Therefore, *believe.*

Am I thinking clearly enough?

I don't know.

THE MAJOR

$\mathbb{J}$udge Glidden is saying, "Take this case, Will. I don't have the time for it."

"But I've never tried a case before, sir!"

"If you don't take it, it won't get tried, and the good doctor'll lose his fine reputation."

"All right, then, sir, but I pity the doctor."

"Oh now, you'll do well by him, I assure you. Besides, a person has to start somewhere. The doc was once in your shoes himself."

In court it occurs to me to ask the plaintiff to show his *other* leg, not the bowed one the doctor supposedly made that way, setting the bone wrong. "Show the court your good leg, sir!" So the plaintiff raises his pant leg on the good leg, and it's bowed too! Bowed as a barrel stave! Bowed even *worse* than the one the doctor set.

"Well, look at that," I say. "The doctor seems to have done better by this man than nature itself! I move that the suit be dismissed, and I recommend that the plaintiff now have his *right* leg broken and set by the defendant."

Laughter whooshes us all right out of that courtroom. It's in me and gusting forth, a geyser of laughing, oh, that was a good day, a *good* day, and Judge Glidden handing me twenty-five dollars, *twenty-five!*—for trying that case. Imagine! I got it right here. See?"

"I see it, Major," Eamon hollers. "Right there in your hand, sir. A grand sum of money!"

I can't stop. The whooshing coming right up and through me, that bowed white leg, bowed as a bow! Should have his *other* . . . bowed even *worse* . . . oh my . . . it comes and comes and there's no stopping it.

LEON

The cell floor is made of large blocks of granite set in tight. The walls, the same, with bars of iron in front of them. The door is steel, with a small slot near the bottom. It is dark. The only light comes from the slot. I walk four paces in one direction and stop. Then I walk three paces in the other direction and come to the cot, which hangs from a wall. Nearby is a bucket for waste. The iron bars and the metal bucket are wet to the touch. So is the stone between the bars. When you contemplate killing a man, you do not think of wet iron bars. You do not think of darkness, waste bucket, and three paces. You do not think of the time that can fill such a place or how you must sit there, listening, even though you do not want to. Listening for the step of a guard. Listening for the tray to bump against the slot. Listening to these thoughts. You wait to feel hunger and then you feel it. You wait for tiredness and then sleep. You think how small it all is now, after the largeness before. You wish they had shot you, but no. Now they don't tell you how it is, if he is still alive or not. They throw you across a room or down on the floor, but they tell you nothing. Maybe they don't kill you because he is not dead yet. Maybe they are waiting, too. Sometimes, I wish I did not do it. Sometimes I can't think why he was supposed to die. I see myself there in line, and he is coming closer, so large, there on the chair, on the platform, and then all I see is the white shirt and vest before me. The line slows but starts again and I am beyond the white, safe, in the morning. But it is not morning, I don't know what it is, and there is the clawing feeling in my chest, like something scraping there, like dogs when they want to cover some stench.

EMMA

If he should die— If he did die—

"Guard. You there! Tell me. Did McKinley die? Or is he still alive?"

"Ain't supposed to say."

"And why is that?"

"Don't know."

"Will the words cut these bars? Blow out that stone?"

"I believe they would not."

"Then why don't you tell me?"

"I have orders."

"Does the chief think my knowing one way or another will pose a grave threat to society?"

"I can't answer that."

"Or make me overjoyed?"

"That I couldn't say. Will it?"

"No. Where's my mail? Surely some letters must have arrived for me."

"I don't know if there are 'r not. They don't tell me about letters."

"All right. I believe you. Can you get me a pen and some ink? They broke mine when they arrested me."

"It ain't allowed."

"I merely wish to make notations in my book."

"I could try an' get you a pencil, but if you go and—"

"Don't worry. I won't attempt suicide with a pencil."

"If you do, I'll lose my job for sure."

These words cause a rush of laughter. "Is it such a great thing, this job of yours? Guarding people who may be innocent?"

"'Tis indeed. Been here thirty-seven years. Have a few more to go to get my pension. But if they set me out now, I get nothing. And who'll hire me?"

"Surely someone will."

"No, ma'am. I'm fifty-eight years of age. I need to watch the path closely."

"Ah, yes. The *path!*"

"You may mock me, ma'am, but you're a lass yet. When you get old, it'll be different. You'll see."

"So! Does that mean he's still alive, and you'll be releasing me soon, so I can grow old and watch the path?"

"It was just a manner of speaking."

"What's your name?"

"Nicholas Boland, ma'am."

"Mr. Boland, I'll thank you for that pencil, and I give you my word that I won't do myself any harm with it."

"You seem like a lady. Not like they're saying upstairs. You remind me of them others. They was polite, too. I was surprised by those boys."

"Which boys?"

"Them Haymarket boys. We had 'em here a while before they took 'em over to Cook County and hanged half of 'em. I believe it was Parsons, Albert Parsons, they had in your cell. Studying his books all the time, just like you. A person would never think they could be vicious and cold-blooded."

"Maybe they weren't, Mr. Boland."

"That's true, too. Ma'am? I just thought of something. I can't be bringing you any pencil to stab one of us with."

"But you just said that I seemed like a lady."

"Ladies can go stabbing people, too."

"Well, I see your point, Mr. Boland."

He doesn't smile.

If I did possess a pencil right this minute, I would most definitely underscore the passage where Nina tells Trepleff in *The Seagull* that in acting and writing fame doesn't really matter, finally, or glory. What matters is endurance, bearing one's cross, and having faith. *I have faith and it all doesn't hurt me so much, and when I think of my calling I'm not afraid of life.*

These words make Trepleff sad, for he sees that she is finding her way whereas he himself has no faith and has lost direction in his life.

I, too, used to be so sure, so certain—like Nina. The past tense of this thought frightens me. To escape it, I turn to Chekhov's drama again, but Mr. Boland interrupts, saying there's a visitor. He unlocks the cell door, and he and the jail's matron escort me to a room beyond the corridor of cells. I'm wondering why this privilege has been extended but fully understand when I recognize, waiting there, the famous Nellie Bly.

"Hello, Miss Goldman. We've met before, you may remember."

"Of course I remember. Hello, Nellie."

The Tombs, 1893. And with the remembering comes some warmth as well as tears I successfully restrain. The intensity of that time, the fervor and faith but also crushing defeat! Sasha and Frick and the Homestead debacle, men and women out of work and children starving throughout the Lower East Side, and I shouting myself hoarse, day after day—*if you are starving,* take *the bread, then!* Words bringing about my arrest, and I first taken to the Tombs and then sentenced to Blackwell's Island even though there'd been no riots. No plundering of bakery shops. Nellie's lengthy interview had appeared in the *World*, a fully sympathetic article about "the little anarchist, the modern Joan of Arc." So there's a great deal between us, despite our philosophical differences. I curb an impulse to embrace her.

"Youse sisters?" the matron asks. Her arms are folded and her forehead is bunched into wrinkles. She is watching us like some overly vigilant schoolmistress.

I shake my head.

"Well, youse two look it."

"Thank you," Nellie says, ever the diplomat.

Nellie is in midnight blue, her nicely tailored suit in the plainer style I myself favor. Her hair is short and thick with curls, like mine, and like mine, too, honey brown. Her full mouth and strong chin also resemble mine. I'm surprised I haven't noticed this before.

"How have you been, Nellie? But I can see for myself. Quite well, judging by appearances."

The matron tells us, in her furry English, that we may sit. It amuses me to see how carefully Nellie wraps her skirt about her knees so that the least part of it will touch the settee's balding horsehair. I take the chair opposite— the same balding hide—and sit well back into it. It's far more comfortable than the wood cot in my cell.

"You must have influence," I say. "No other journalist has been allowed in."

Her skin glows pink. She is a personage now. I've never much admired her literary style—there's something too breathless and ingénue about it, but despite her limitations of ability and intellect, her attempt, eight years ago, to fairly characterize Hannes Most and Justus Schwab, as well as myself, won her a number of followers among the comrades. But I remember how she began her career by writing fiction published in the kind of magazines lying ripped and dog-eared on the table before us. Stories about sixteen-year-old heroines, poor but virtuous. After a dozen installments depicting harrowing misfortunes, the still virtuous young lady, now seventeen and at the height of her loveliness, marries the richest fellow in sight, and those who had befriended her inherit estates from distant relatives while the villain always dies by his own hand.

Needless to say, Nellie's stories—and Nellie herself—became wildly popular.

Does this sting, Emma?

Yes, it does.

But then, exhausting every variation on her theme of virtue triumphant, she turned to journalism. Feigned madness to get herself into Blackwell's Asylum—floated around the world in a hot-air balloon, beating Jules Verne's time—lunatics, tenement dwellers, stunts, and anarchists, too, all became her new gold mine. Curious, how mediocrity rises, its yeast the populace.

(William Jennings Bryan!)

This isn't a new thought, but always a hard one. The warmth has left me, and I feel chilled. My fingernails are blue; my hands quite cold. Nellie is using a costly, green-marbled fountain pen which draws my attention. Her notebook is not a flimsy pad but thick stock bound within fine calfskin.

Curious how mediocrity must costume itself. Well, this I know, too, from having been a seamstress.

"Emma, you appear to be deep in thought, but then, I guess, you always are, aren't you?"

"Not always, no. Is he dead?"

"Is he— Oh! No. He may recover. All the reports are favorable—which leads me to ask you about Buffalo, Emma—may I call you Emma?"

"Of course, but I can't tell you any more than I've already told the chief, here. I had nothing to do with the assassination attempt at Buffalo."

"Who is your lawyer?"

"I don't have one—yet."

"You may still need one. I'd get one, quickly. The assailant is saying— Here, I'll quote him. *Her words went right through me and when I left the lecture I made up my mind that I would have to do something heroic for the cause I loved.*"

I laugh—impossible to hold it back. "Sounds like it's from one of your works of fiction, Nellie!"

Her color deepens. She does not smile in the least.

"And when did the man supposedly attend my lecture?"

"According to one special report in the *World*, three weeks ago."

"I gave no lectures three weeks ago."

"Sometimes there are small inaccuracies."

"Small? I did lecture three months ago."

"Was he there, Czolgosz?"

"Yes. He was there. He told me his name was Nieman."

"So you spoke with him?"

"He asked for reading material."

"And what did you recommend?"

"Several pamphlets. *The Chicago Martyrs— Altgeld's Pardon—* He might have chosen other pamphlets from the rack."

"Something about exterminating rulers?"

"You know, Nellie, you'd make a better interrogator than another I've had the misfortune to meet. But philosophical anarchism doesn't advocate the extermination of anyone—we talked about this eight years ago, remember? Nor would any pamphlet in our racks do so. Nor would I advocate any such thing in a speech."

"Yet philosophical anarchism does assume that the current system of government must be changed."

"It does, yes."

"So one might go on to conclude—"

"But I'm not responsible for the way another person thinks."

"Philosophical anarchism doesn't advocate killing anyone, you say, yet you've also said that assassins act out of sensitive natures and that you can sympathize with them. Is that not true?"

"Yes, I've said that on a number of occasions."

"Well, those are fairly powerful words, don't you think? And not that distant in meaning from *exonerate?* That's why the country is set against you now."

"This country isn't used to nuance."

She looks up from her words at the anger in my voice. "I'm only trying to help. Play devil's advocate, as in 1893."

"I know you are."

"But you need a lawyer, not a mere journalist."

"I had one in 1893, you may recall. It did no good, and the charge was only inciting to riot. This time is different. Are there any . . . petitions being circulated? On my behalf?"

She glances at the much-handled magazines. "None that I know of."

"Well, if you can understand it, Nellie, your readers may be able to as well. Can one not sympathize with someone yet still consider that person's *actions* wrong? Can one not say that your heart is with the person despite what he does? Life is not melodrama. People who act out of sensitive natures . . . act out of a profound regard for others and shouldn't be condemned."

"*Shouldn't?* Even if they kill?"

"Even if they kill."

"And if a son avenges a father's death by killing his father's murderer, is he acting out of a sensitive nature?"

"Some actions are more impersonal than others."

"Do you think Czolgosz's was?"

"Yes, I do. It was aimed at a tyrant. An enemy of the people."

"McKinley? A *tyrant?*"

"He was ruthless in breaking strikes when he was governor. He's on the side of the wealthy and cares nothing about the working man."

"Nothing? Excuse me, Emma, but is it not you who are being melodramatic now? Failing to see the nuances? The shadings?"

"I am seeing the truth."

Nellie looks up eventually and folds her hands over her journal. "Emma, I interviewed McKinley once. Well— Not exactly. I was covering a reception at the executive mansion in honor of the Pan-American Conference delegates a few years ago. At that time he was chairman of the House Ways and Means Committee, and I tried to ask him a few questions about trade matters. He apologized, saying he couldn't really answer them fully that evening. Could I come around to his office the following afternoon? So we set a time and that was that. For the rest of the evening I wandered about, noticing how women of all ages put themselves in his path. Remarkable! He was pleasant to all but lingered with none. The next day I went to his office, but he wasn't there. He had left a note saying that he deeply regretted his absence but needed to be at his wife's sickbed. She was quite ill—again. A few days later he sent me carefully written responses to each of my questions. Nothing about him struck me as tyrannical."

"So he was a Galahad for his wife, but for the working-man?"

Nellie smiles. "I see you're not to be convinced, Emma. Going back to the previous matter, how much weight do you think your sympathy carries? Say I'm a young fellow unable to work because of some illness. I'm also somewhat distant from my family. I have problems that don't show on the surface. And there I am, listening to you say that you're sympathetic with those who commit violent acts for the good of the people. And there you are, a famous figure, and people applaud you and surround you, after your speech. And there I am, off in the shadows, literally and figuratively. I have to wait a long time to exchange a few words with you. How much weight, Emma, do you think your sympathy carries?"

"Did you come here to interview me, Nellie, or are you suddenly taking up a new profession?"

"I came to interview. You know how I always try for the personal. Here's my last question. Some people are speculating that if the president dies, your movement will die as well. That the shot fatal to the president will also prove fatal to the anarchist movement, at least here in our country. Do you think this will happen?"

"No. There may be a setback, but it won't die. One day it will be clear that true brotherhood can only come about through the application of anarchist principles that maintain freedom as a necessary condition of life."

"Then there *are* rules. Anarchism is not lawlessness."

"There are ideals. First, education and then power. Not the other way around. First, we educate ourselves, and then cooperatively work toward change. And we respect one another's—"

"Emma, your friend Alexander Berkman—"

"Allow me to finish."

"Yes, of course. I'm sorry."

"We respect one another's rights. And when we can do that, fully do that, cooperatively do that, we won't need government or heads of government tantamount to an aristocracy."

Nellie scribbles it all down with her fine pen, and then regards me again. "Your friend Alexander Berkman attempted suicide shortly before the assassination attempt. The police are saying—"

"Sasha had nothing to do with the assassination attempt! Please don't bring him into it."

"Well, but he already is, in a way."

"It was a coincidence."

The matron resurrects herself from her daydreaming. "Time," she says.

"What can I send you, Emma? What do you need?"

"For you to write the best article you possibly can."

"I will certainly try. But before I go, Emma, I must . . . I need to ask, was Czolgosz in love with you?"

"Of course he wasn't."

"Nor you with him?"

"I won't honor that with a response."

"That can mean anything."

"No, then. *No.*"

I have no illusions. In her article, the first-person pronoun will predominate. There'll be a lengthy description of the dayroom's elegant furnishings, the comely matron, and of my fashionable albeit slept-in skirt and waist. The love angle will figure in. The article will sell hundreds more issues of the *World* than usual. It will not be sympathetic, for an attempted assassination of the president is not the same as hunger strikes and people dying and a young woman exhorting them to take the bread.

In my cell, I imagine the stories *I* would write, with her green pen and fine paper stock.

At Number 65 Forsyth Street, a small door opens onto an enclosed alleyway that ends, a hundred and fifty feet farther, at a row of privies and a pile of scrap wood, rags, and several moldering mattresses. An odor of rotting fish blends with the septic stench from the privies. Boys chase one another through puddles. Other children kneel on hard mud at the base of the tenement, drawing pictures with sticks.

At the far end of the alley, wooden stairs lead to the five floors of the rear tenement. On the fifth, just beneath the roof, is a two-room apartment. In its front room, once kitchen and living room, Magdalena Ogolowicza lies on a few inches of straw. She is covered with half of a sheet. There is no pillow. An oblong of afternoon light wavers on the floor, near her face. Within that oblong, the dark floorboards appear almost golden, if dusty. Magdalena's skin is white, not the sheen-white of blossoms or feathers, but the yellowing, spongy white of old mushrooms. Her thin lips are the blue of a vein. Some permanent ricture draws them up, revealing carious yellow teeth and bleeding gums.

She is not alone in the room. The popes are there, twelve of the church's three hundred and sixty-six. St. Peter is there, and the current pope, Leo XIII, in a colored picture she has cut from a book and brought with the household goods from Galicia. Now the household goods are mostly gone, but this one picture remains. Sometimes she talks to the popes and confesses her sins to them. Or to the small black crucifix on the opposite wall. Sometimes she leans to one side and spits blood into a coffee cup. This is hard for her to do now—leaning over, holding the cup steady. Blood dribbles out over her chin, her fingers. Sometimes a tooth drops out. She has been sick for three months. Her husband, a garment maker, has been out of work for four. Three of the children playing in the alleyway below are hers, including a one-year-old in diapers. Soon her husband will come in to see how she is. He usually comes when the light has reached a certain place on the floor. Then he will tell her about going to Essex and Rivington and standing there with all the others, will tell her who came to hire, who they were hiring, what they were paying. Sometimes bricklayers. Sometimes carpenters. But seldom garment makers. No one, now, is buying cloaks, hats, suits—and the pawnshops full of them. She has forgotten how to appear hopeful. Has forgotten what hope is like, how it can transform something into something else, like a magician. But she tries not to spit when he is there. Why her mouth is bleeding, she doesn't know. Nor does he, but there seems to be no way to stop it, and there is no money for a prescription. All they have now is his everyday suit and shoes and what the children are wearing, which is hardly anything. Their only other coffee cup holds forty-one pawn tickets.

Magdalena prays for a happy death. She prays for her soul to be clean when she takes her last breath. She wishes no one harm. She wishes only that he will find something so the children don't die, too. As for her, she does not expect to live much longer. Sometimes there are angels in the room, singing. And a spicy smell she knows is incense. Candles seem to throw shadows on the walls. She is already in the box but can still see the candle flames tipping back and forth like flowers in a breeze, and she gazes at them as they tell her she is not alone, will never be alone, and then he is there, she not hearing him on the stairs, and he is quiet so that she knows how it is. The same. His leg casts a shadow like a tree, and she is in a pasture, a young girl, sitting under an apple tree and embroidering a border on a tablecloth that will one day be hers.

On his way to the intersection of Rivington and Essex, a young man, Jesse Peters let's say, sees a familiar woman, dressed nicely, which makes her unfamiliar at the same time. He stops and then takes a half-step backward. He is holding his breath. Then he understands. His stomach fights the bread he has swallowed that morning. He crosses the street, walks in the opposite direction, believing that his wife had not seen him, at least. Allen to Broome to Delancy, up to Rivington and Essex, where men wait and he does, too, and for a while it's blotted out, what he saw, but no one is there to hire, so he keeps going—north to Houston, then east again, the day warmer now, and the smell of the river stronger.

He stops at a fish processing plant, but the stench disgusts him, and he imagines what the water there must be like. He walks north a while before turning east again. And then he steps out onto an old wharf, its split boards baking in the sun. At the end, thirty feet out into the East River, he glances back toward shore. There is no one. The water sparkles greenly. He jumps, holding his nose before remembering not to. His hat floats off somewhere. His ballooning jacket floats.

And he does, too, back to shore on oily waves. He gushes up onto a froth of decaying matter and sinks to the shins in muck that does not want to release him so easily. On the fringe of shore, he looks about for a rock or bricks or a corroded pipe or chain or metal of any kind. He finds nothing suitable. In the expansive light of noon he feels foolish and coldly sane. His hat is gone.

Hatless, he goes back wet, stinking and muddy through the dirty streets. Along the way he spies hundreds of things that might have worked, had he been paying attention.

He allows her to feed him a soup made of boiled potatoes. After gathering their four children from somewhere, she spends the evening trying to clean his suit. It won't be dry, she says, until late the next day, if then. She hangs trousers, jacket, shirt, vest, and stockings on a line high over the alleyway, for everyone to see. His shoes she stuffs with paper and sets on the stairs to catch the air. She hopes it won't rain.

His suit of clothes hanging limp in the brassy twilight causes an ache under his breastbone, and shortness of breath. That night he awakens sweaty and grieving, and in his damp underwear he runs, barefoot, up Allen and east on Grand. A sleepy roundsman snaps awake and pursues. The roundsman hauls him into the Grand Street police station and deposits him in a cell, which isn't difficult, Jesse Peters weighing no more than a boy. They give him beef and barley soup and promise to release him in the morning, when he comes to his senses.

On Forsyth Street, Magdalena Ogolowicza turns to spit out a little blood. Mrs. Heyman, on Chrystle Street, dreams she is dusting an intricate gaslight shade. At 108 Orchard, a tailor holds hands against his ears, but still can hear the baby and his wife's futile attempts to feed it. In the Grand Street police station Jesse Peters sleeps on a cot and in a clean nightshirt. And all over lower Manhattan pawn tickets rest undisturbed in cups and drawers, in prayer books and on sills, anchored by small stones.

Ticket 4,847. William Frieder, pawnbroker, 204 East Houston Street, ring, $1.12.

Ticket 19,458. H. Aufses, pawnbroker, 279 Stanton Street, overcoat, $2.12.

Ticket 4,607. C. Kahn, pawnbroker, 2204 East Houston Street, a man's suit, $3.00.

Ticket 29,625. J.D. Fry, pawnbroker, 129 East Houston Street, woman's dress, $1.62.

Ticket 55,786. William Simpson & Company, pawnbrokers, 108 Bowery, two silk handkerchiefs, two rings, $4.00.

Ticket 33,568. J. Aufses, pawnbroker, 279 Stanton Street, shears, 53 cents . . .

And tickets for silver chains, vests, sheets, tablecloths and shawls, trousers and overcoats, cloaks and rings, studs, silk dresses, canes and toys and books and silver watches and earrings and children's clothing—the children's clothing almost always the last to surrender and first to ransom, when possible. All the rest—the fancy chains and vests and walking canes, the plain and fancy watches, the dishes and shoes, the rugs and hats and silver spoons and knives and forks, the glassware and plates, all the rest numbered and confined to the dimness and dust of pawnshops for weeks, for months, for years, for good, much of it, but sometimes an item swims up out of the murk to find its way into a hand knowing how to use it, onto a back, a head, a foot, onto a table, onto a wall, a floor, a bed, fleshing out once again a life.

Released from the Grand Street station and wandering about in a patchwork of clothing given to him by the police, Jesse Peters comes upon a strange sight near the Washington Square Arch. It is a gigantic bronze bell on a wagon drawn by a team of six horses. The Liberty Bell, someone explains. The Columbian Liberty Bell. Men are giving speeches. Others have set up photography apparatus. The bell has been on parade, and the parade will continue—down Broadway to the Cortlandt Street ferry. From there, it is going to Chicago via the Pennsylvania road. Such is the state of Jesse Peters's mind that he wonders what such an object might bring at Frieder's or William Simpson and Company. A good thirty dollars, he thinks. At least.

So, Nellie, what do you think? If the movement dies, might there be a place for me in your world of publishing?

EAMON

The one they say is a woman's doctor grabs my shoulder, presses down upon it as he leans close and says, "You need to leave now, boy."

There is meaning in the tone. I say, "No, sir, begging your pardon."

He looks over his shoulder at some of the others entering the Major's room. A couple of them come up behind me and I try to pull away from them, keeping quiet about it on account of the Major, but I am sliding away, feet dragging on the carpet, and the Major's eyes are closed and he doesn't know what they're up to, or maybe he does, but can't rise out of it far enough to say *Let him stay* as I know he would, otherwise, if not sunk so deep down.

"We have work to do," the woman's doctor says. "That's all," he says, but in the tone and haste of these words, I know them for a lie. I say, inside myself, *Good-bye, Major.*

The two guards at the hall doorway don't allow me to go back into the room when I say I need to tell the Major something more. I neglected to say my thanks for all he has given me, and this not saying rides high in the ribcage, snagged there like a sharp stick. They shake their heads but later open the door for Mrs. McKinley, on Dr. Rixey's arm. She does not see me. I want to ask her permission, but her eyes are fixed on the Major and nothing else and it is not right for me to break through into that, so I wait in the hall and watch more doctors coming from downstairs, and they all look like undertakers now, and I know he will see their faces that way and maybe know, too, and I curse them for those buzzard faces of theirs and try to push in behind them, but the guards are too quick and pull me back, and I am in the broken-up line at Homestead and they are pulling off our jackets and big hats and throwing them into the river, and they are prodding us with table-leg clubs and old weaponry, and I know what is about to happen next, so I run downstairs and into the yard and then the stable and into the pony's stall, but newspaper-men follow me there and holler, asking for news, and I curse their lot too, damning them to the fires, for it is no way for a man to die, surrounded by buzzards.

LEON

In the story of Job, the Lord decides on a test because Satan asks, "Isn't it easy to be a good person when things are going all right for you?" So the Lord says, "Go ahead and do what you can against Job's things. Spare only the man himself." So then the Sabeans steal Job's oxen and asses. A fire from the heavens burns up his flocks. Chaldeans steal his camels and slay his servants. A windstorm kills his ten sons and three daughters.

Still Job praises God.

So Satan comes back to the Lord. "Strike at the man's own skin and then you'll see," he says. And the Lord says, "Behold, he is in your hand, but yet save his life."

What happens to Job after that? Sores cover him all over. He sits on a manure pile and scrapes away pus. His wife makes scraping motions on the air. "Bless God, and die," she says, mad at him.

I asked the priest at church about this story, and he had trouble explaining it. He had been picking raspberries in his garden, and his fingers were red. I looked at these fingers and wished he would offer a dish of raspberries, but no. What he said was that Job complains and then he repents of complaining and then God gives him everything back.

Everything?—his sons and daughters, too? I wondered. Or new ones. And what was he guilty of in the first place? Nothing, right? Afterward—yes. Afterward, he complains a little. Or as the priest said, Chastised the Lord.

The priest does not explain, though. Here is what I think. At first Job was a rich innocent man, but he becomes a poor guilty one because of the test and all his complaints.

But didn't the Lord let Satan do all that in the first place?

Emma Goldman complains all the time in her speeches yet nothing happens to her.

I walk three steps this way. Three steps that. I twirl in a circle. To make some sound, I laugh. The story is too much to think on. I wish they killed me right off. This is no good.

THE MAJOR

My heart works fearfully as I swim in some cold river. There is a house on shore and I manage to get to it, but inside it is a ruin. Strips of wallpaper curl down from damp plaster. Rodent droppings are scattered over the floor and furnishings. Windows are clouded with ancient dust and flies beating against the panes. This room leads to another like it, and another, the odor a stench of dry rot and droppings and decaying small bodies, moldering cloth and clothing and wet straw fallen from upholstery. I turn and walk back, but the rooms, all similar in their disarray, appear to be infinite. My heart hurts, lunging. This isn't my house. I don't recognize this place at all. There was no new portico outside, I'm certain of it.

So where am I?

On a track cart now, the woods on either side swaying with wind and shadow. In the distance ahead, there is some bright open space at the far end of this green tunnel. The train will be there, and I will be on time after all. But my heart is lunging again. Grackles come swooping down onto a field and march across it like troops on the move, all screeching and keening. Big clouds to the north are dark blue, nearly black. Bare trees all around look like fish bones.

I holler but the sound is negligible. My heartbeat is a runaway horse. Then a black shape before me becomes Dr. Mann, who says they are giving me more oxygen and digitalis.

I don't want it. I want the green woods. The wind there, and shade. The waiting train.

"Gentlemen, *please*."

Do they hear me? I believe not. The fearful heartbeat is too loud and about to burst me in two.

Ida grips my hand.

Ida. Ida. My heart bucks like some wild pony.

I hold up my other hand. Do I? Yes. I see it, raised, and see the ring of them around me. They are small and form a dark horseshoe. I am all white, swaddled up. Oddly, my eyes are closed. I haven't felt this light since the Shenandoah, a stick on a horse, nothing but a stick, and the horse so fast, what was his name?

Heart lagging, then racing to catch up, then tiring, then racing again. How do the words go? *Our Father who . . .*

"Gentlemen . . . I think . . . we ought to have prayer. It is useless."

Somewhere then, singing.

I drift down a ways.

Ida. Hanging on to me but not weeping.

The words are hard to say, but I say them. "Good-bye all . . . It's God's—"

At the window, the sea, lapping at the sill like some melting jewel. I—

EMMA

Nicholas Boland has opened my cell door and has a tray in hand. Atop it is a covered platter. The sensuous fragrance of roasted turkey, gravy, and potatoes fills the cell. "If you want, you can have this in the day room," he says.

"Only if you'll join me."

There, seated at a small table with Mr. Boland and the matron on either side of me, I ask if the man who so generously sent in this food is an acquaintance of mine.

"He's a saloonkeeper from around the corner," Mr. Boland says. He gives the man's name and adds, "Thing is, he's a Democrat. We all are, in here."

I don't recognize the name. "Do you mean to say he doesn't—and you as well—care that the president has been shot?"

Mr. Boland looks at the matron, whose name I never learned. I think I should ask her.

"Tell 'er," the matron says.

And then Mr. Boland does.

The actuality of it—when I had been growing somewhat complacent that he might live—stuns me. I sit there, aware of a hundred implications, while the guard and the matron fill their plates.

"Ain't you hungry, Miss Goldman?" the matron asks. I understand by her words, her tone, that she, in fact, is.

"Why is the chief allowing this meal?"

"Don't know, ma'am."

"Both of you, please—eat. Food shouldn't be wasted."

On tin plates, we eat. It occurs to me to wonder if the food has been poisoned. If so, I will have two other deaths on my conscience as well. My guests eat with downcast eyes, the matron preferring the dark meat. Abruptly, she raises her head and says, "You know, I don't care to watch hangings anymore. Does no good to my heart. I have a weak heart, not like Nicky here. They shouldn't let the public in, is what I think."

Mr. Boland regards her, then me, before refilling his plate. "Good turkey," he says.

Is this to be my last meal, then? It is a feverish thought, for there hasn't been any trial yet. My guests continue eating, noisily, happily. I chew slowly and swallow, chew and swallow. It is all tasteless. They are telling stories, now, about the other anarchists once held here, and I imagine that one day I, too, may achieve immortality in their stories. *They had her in here for a while, that Emma Goldman, before they took her over to Cook County and hanged her like the rest. Ate a turkey dinner with her . . . she invited us to, imagine that . . . she didn't seem crazy, but then you never know what goes on in them heads o' theirs . . .*

A brick shatters the barred window and lands near the table, along with broken pieces of glass. There's shouting outside, and gunfire.

"They want you," the matron says, getting up to turn off the room's electric light. Mr. Boland rushes me back to my cell. "I thank you," he says, locking the door, "for that fine meal, Miss Goldman. It's something to remember."

All night it continues, the pulsing of their shouts, death wanting more of itself.

At dawn, several guards come for me, Mr. Boland not among them. The guards' haste says everything their faces do not. They're scared. We exit the back entry in a pack, they with their revolvers drawn. The air is frost cold. Ahead, in the narrow space between two lines of policemen, are two other prisoners, one with his head bandaged. As this man approaches an open patrol wagon, one of the officers swings the butt of his revolver, striking him on the back of his bandaged head. The man drops to his knees and then onto his side and writhes, kicking the air while holding his head. Two other officers heave him into the wagon and throw the second prisoner in after him.

As I pass the officer who struck him with the revolver, I cannot hold back. "You are a man, surely," I say, "for haven't we just witnessed proof of it?"

I turn my head away, but the black butt of his revolver catches the right side of my face just above the jawbone. My mouth fills with blood and broken teeth. When I awake, I am on the floor of the wagon, the front of my waist and skirt bloodied and blood still coming. I must sit up quickly or else choke on it. Someone hands me my eyeglasses and my book. I cannot speak to say thanks.

At the Cook County jail, we all sit in a reception room, waiting, the bandaged one still moaning. Male and female clerks pass back and forth in front of us, holding papers, delivering messages. Not one glances at us. The pain is duller now but still throbbing in a steady rhythm. The front of my waist is red, and wet. My hands are black with blood. My book is stained. I've been spitting out fragments of teeth, and have to wipe several more from my waist. Worse, however, are these indifferent clerks—and my still raging thoughts of that officer.

What would Sasha say?

Well, you know what we believe, Emma. First, education, and then power.

I pick out yet another sharp fragment of tooth.

I don't know, Sasha. I don't know.

IDA

I believe I know why this happened. There was too much gold that day in October, and all those people still coming to hear the Major. Mary wrapped a long gold ribbon, twice, about my head, Grecian fashion, letting the ends hang down over my left shoulder. I took the new gold-headed cane that said *William McKinley* in gold letters down its side. On the upstairs hall table were goldenrod and purple asters in tall vases. Outside in the street, children were trailing gold streamers from their bicycles. Dogs wore gold ribbons. So did horses. And passing carriages fluttered with gold banners. The trees, even, were turning gold. And you couldn't walk into the downstairs parlor because of all the wheels of golden cheese, the replicas of railroad ties and spikes, in gold of course, and yellow roses and gold keys to various cities and a miniature gold railway car and a marble bust of Mr. McKinley, the stone streaked with pale gold color. And then Eamon brought in yet another gift of a live eagle, in a gold cage, for me to name, its terrible hooked beak a deep yellow and its eyes and scaly legs and feet with their talons. This made the third eagle so far! What on earth will we do with them, I thought, but I named this one *Hanna*, for Mr. McKinley's advisor, who deserved to have a namesake, too.

All afternoon Mr. McKinley stood on a kitchen chair out on the porch, giving his campaign speech to hundreds of visitors, the yard and flowers trampled to mud, the porch in danger of succumbing. A band played after each speech, and the people—women especially—seemed almost delirious. Blessings raining down upon us, all those people worshiping the Major, coming from dawn to dark, but, oh, the pride in my heart to see my darling there, arms raised, words issuing forth, so finely phrased and sensible, his voice so mild and pleasing to the ear, and everyone crying out *McKin-ley, McKin-ley,* and I in a gold-colored frock, thinking, nay *praying,* oh let this be. Let this *be*— even though I feared it, too, feared being the First Lady yet again. How could I manage? Surely, impossible, but hadn't we earned the right? Through our suffering? The golden day seemed almost some compensation. *Because* of that, *this. The Lord taketh; the Lord giveth.* And when, after the election, the Audubon people wrote and asked that I not wear egret feathers at the presidential reception, as I had at the first, setting off a craze for them, I donned the feathers with impunity, and my diamonds, for what were those feathers in comparison to our lost children, and hadn't I earned the *right* to don a few mere feathers?

"Dr. Rixey, why did he have to die? He said *God's will.* Was it because of everything we had?"

My physician has been sitting with his hands clasped before him, his head bowed. I believe he was dozing while I myself cannot sleep. He looks up tiredly. "Ma'am?"

"Did we do something to offend God? Did I? Was it all that gold, during the campaign? The gold wasn't our idea! People brought it all because of Mr. McKinley supporting the gold standard, remember? It *wasn't* a sin of pride!"

"No, it wasn't, ma'am. It just . . . happened. And now I believe it's time for you to have—"

"I don't want anything. I want to think. Why did God take him from me? I wish to know the answer, Dr. Rixey."

"It was an anarchist who shot the Major."

"*Why?*"

"Because anarchists don't believe in government or the necessity for heads of state."

"What *do* they believe in?"

"I'm not certain. I think they want everybody to just . . . govern themselves."

"They must be idiots. That would be mayhem. Where is my book?"

"Your . . . prayer book?"

"My *diary*. Clara? Where is it? The one Mr. McKinley gave me."

"Please, ma'am," Clara says, "you're a bit feverish, and Dr. Rixey has your medicine ready."

"I don't want my medicine. I want to die. Why doesn't God take me? I was the one who wanted it all. The feathers, the gold. He should take me and let him live. Where is my book?"

My maid fusses, as usual, with pillows and blanket. Dr. Rixey says, "Ma'am, the Major has . . . passed."

"I know that he has *died*. I know that. But in the Bible there are resurrections, are there not? Christ raising Lazarus and bringing back Jairus's daughter? If one has faith, if one believes, if one's faith is strong enough, then resurrection is possible, no?"

Dr. Rixey nods, trying to placate me as always, but then says words that have the opposite effect. "All that happened in Biblical times, when Christ was alive."

"I believe there were miracles after his death, weren't there? In His name?"

"I don't know if they involved raising people from the dead, though. Besides, all that was long ago. In other times."

"What times are these, then? Is this time so different that miracles are not possible?"

"I don't suppose, well, possibly not, but—"

"Well, then. Clara, bring me my diary."

EAMON

Cortelyou comes and says she's in a bad place, and I need to be there. I tell Cortelyou I don't know what I can do that they can't, but he's pulling me out of the stable and the dream I was having, and it is better in some ways and some ways not, for I know, again, that the Major is gone, and they can't bring him back, the doctors, no one can so how can I help anyone, especially her? "He came to see her," Cortelyou is saying, and I'm thinking *the Major,* but in the next minute I know he means Roosevelt, coming in a plain carriage so as not to be noticed. "She pulled herself together for that," Cortelyou goes on, "but the minute he left, she got to raving again, words hardly making sense, something about gold and feathers." Cortelyou believes she is about to go over the edge again. "Just do like always," he says. "Roll up the yarn, if she wants that, or unroll it, whatever she wants. If she wants to walk a little, help her. Just be there so Clara and the first lady's niece can get a little rest. That poor maid is about to go off the deep end herself."

There are many servants at Milburn's house, and some of the Major's family as well. I could be more useful in the stable, with all the horses coming in, but no. "Dr. Rixey's worried," Cortelyou says. "Dr. Rixey wants you there for her. He wants the ordinary, you know?"

I don't, but I am a little puffed up by this, anyway, and it shames me and shows how easy the weed of pride can take root and how even in sorrow it finds a person.

Chastened by this thought, I change my boots and follow Cortelyou up to her room, and there she is on a settee, balls of wool to one side of her, and a book on the other. But she isn't looking at anything.

"Ma'am?" Cortelyou says. "Eamon's here." Cortelyou looks over at me and I need to say something. I say, "Would you like some milk, Mrs. McKinley?" but she sits there in her trance and I know Dr. Rixey has drugged her, and I think how they should not do that, for what did their drugs and all do for the Major? It is a hard thought and I'm in the midst of some high wind of feelings. Cortelyou pulls a chair over for me and whispers that I'm supposed to just sit there and wait for her to come around, be there when she "wakes." I am afraid of just sitting there, for then there will be too much thought. Clara whispers that she is going to get off her feet for a little while, and I think how she could just sit here and be off her feet, but I don't say it for I know how much she has to do and how it must be to be in it all the time, every day, no quiet like I have with the horses, but all the time worrying about the next thing and having to take orders and not being in her own life. So it is all right that she goes off to her room.

The book there on the settee is not large. It has a dark blue cover with designs on it, fancy gold ones, and Mrs. McKinley's name in gold. The edges of the pages are gold, too. Not long after I sit down, Mrs. McKinley's niece Mary comes in, and we both sit there, watching Mrs. McKinley. It is almost like some wake, and I don't much care for it. But after a while, Mrs. McKinley comes to herself again and looks about. I ask her once more if she might like some warm milk, and she nods. When I come back with it, she is showing Mary her book and asking her to read what is written for Friday the sixth, so Mary takes the book and reads, *Went to visit Niagara Falls this morning. My dearest was receiving in a public hall on our return, when he was shot by a—*

Mary glances my way before saying, "There is no word written there, Aunt Ida. The space is left blank."

"Go on," Mrs. McKinley says, and so Mary reads *I am feeling very badly.*

"I can't remember the word," Mrs. McKinley says. "They told me, but now I cannot remember it. So I left a space. Do you know it?"

Mary says naught. I say, "I don't know which word she means."

"But I want to know it," Mrs. McKinley says. "I don't want the hole there."

"*Anarchist,* Aunt Ida," says Mary. "That is the word. A woman was behind the plot, it's said. Emma Goldman."

Mrs. McKinley sits there a while before saying, "Write it in. No. Don't. Leave the space."

Why? Because no word in the world can make full sense of it all now? Or maybe it's because she can't even bear the word being there.

There's a throbbing around my empty eye socket and wetness on my face.

Now she doesn't want the milk and I just hold it. Maybe she'll want it in a little while, so I keep on holding the teacup, with its pink flowers.

After some time it comes as a thought will. Just there, like the throb and wetness, and I know what I am going to do.

EMMA

In prison, any break from routine is ominous. When the guard opens the cell door and motions for me to get up, I stand, holding my Chekhov. "Be quick," he says, and then he is gripping my arm and leading me past other cells. A transfer, I tell myself. A simple transfer. But the back of my head is throbbing, and so is my jaw. I am not surprised to be taken into the chief's office. He is no doubt going to tell me about my trial. My heart lurches, and tears burn eyelids despite the resolve I muster.

The chief is sitting back from his desk, his legs crossed, his arms crossed. He is an old man but with exceedingly black hair. His eyes remind me of the base of a hot flame, that blue, but they are cold, staring at me. I've felt such hatred before and am determined not to exhibit fear.

Very quietly, and in Irish intonations, he says, "I want you gone from here. Gone from this town and from this state by tomorrow morning. Do you understand me, now?"

Is he saying I am free? He goes on, "If you're anywhere in this city tomorrow—and we'll be lookin', mind, we'll be shipping you off to Buffalo, where they're clamoring for your hide."

"Are you letting me go, then?"

"I know you're a stupid woman, but are you so dense that you don't get my meaning? I want you gone from Chicago and from the state of Illinois. *Never* come back here."

"I have no money for travel, no clothing—your men took it all."

"You'll have it back."

"I want all the letters that came for me."

"We gave them to you."

"*All* of them. You gave me only the despicable ones."

"Too bad, that. There weren't any others."

"You're lying."

"Ah, well. And what can you do about it, an eejit like yourself?"

"You're hateful."

The chief stares a while longer, to flaunt that very quality, and then nods to his minion. In the hall, the matron gives me my suitcase and jacket and handbag. Then I am outside. I don't know the name of this street, but there must be a streetcar somewhere. It is good it is dark, given my bloodied clothing.

I limp away, my bruised jaw aching with each step. It would be folly to return to Rochester. Surely, they'll be looking there. I picture them questioning Helena, maybe even searching her house.

Where, where, where to go?

I am in Chicago but *free*.

The mystery of it! They could have bought evidence, but they apparently didn't. *Why not?*

Thoughts leaving me jangled, exhilarated, incredulous— and walking, now, very fast because I am thinking very fast.

The beach is awash with long rollers. White water flows under the pier as well. The pier seems to be swaying, and my old fear of water returns. I don't know how to swim, and should I fall or be blown off in this wind—*Never mind, Emma. Keep walking. See? They're here, already.*

One of the figures detaches itself from the dark clump at the end of the pier and walks toward me. Suddenly I'm not sure this person is a comrade. I imagine myself pushed off the pier, my clothing tangling in the pilings, and the headlines, *EMMA GOLDMAN TAKES OWN LIFE.*

The man approaching, for it is a man though I cannot yet recognize him, extends his arms, and I stop. Then I exhale. "Abe!" I say. "They released you, too!"

At the end of the pier, under the roof there, we stand with our backs to the wind and talk—Abe, Max, Hippolyte and I. Abe tells me that several police officers have been indicted for perjury and bribery and were now trying to win public support by evoking the city's long-standing fear of anarchists. All the publicity surrounding my imprisonment was somehow working to their advantage. "Get rid of you, Emma, and he can focus on booting out those others."

"Why not just extradite me?"

"Not enough evidence."

"Since when does that matter, Abe?"

"Now. Too many journalists prowling about—who knows?"

"Well, it wasn't out of the goodness of his heart. All right! First, I want to know something and then I have something to propose. In fact, several things! But first— Abe. That notice you put in *Free Society.* I wanted it withdrawn. I asked you to write a retraction, but you didn't. Why not?"

"What bearing does that have now, Emma?"

"If the assassin realized that you were describing him, realized that we considered him a *spy*— Don't you see?"

"No, I don't."

"If he thought we considered him a spy, could it be that he did the deed to prove otherwise? I asked you to take care of him. I assumed you would understand: find him something to do! He was looking for work. He was earnest enough."

"I didn't want to give him any work."

"But why not, Abe!"

‹ 283 ›

"How could we know who he was? He follows you from Cleveland. You pass him off to us, but how can we know who he is, Emma? He told us he had worked in a cheese factory, but when Shilling checked, he found that it wasn't true. So there was one lie. How many more was he telling us? And I think your theory of why he might have acted is far-fetched."

"I don't think so. He seemed most interested in the cause, very sensitive—"

"Come, Emma, admit that you were taken with him, a handsome lad."

"Don't joke, Abe. Also, I would like to know how the detectives came to link me with him. Do you think he did?"

"He must have. They torture him, he will say what they want to hear."

"Somehow I cannot accept that he would do that."

"No? Emma, you're being naïve. And if, as you say, he was put out with us for that notice—"

"There was that reporter—" Hippolyte interrupts.

"Quiet!" Abe says.

"Tell me, Hippolyte."

"He was from the *Daily News*, or so he said. He, too, was sticking close and pretending an interest in the cause. Then, after the shooting, he comes back and wants to know about Czolgosz. Abe—"

"Blame me! I told him only that we met him through Emma. Now I see the mistake. I should not have said anything. So, yes, my fault!"

"Emma," Max says. "This time you must go to Canada. Millie and I will go with you, if you wish. We can return in several months, perhaps."

I turn and look over the heaving lake. Canada. Safety. I turn back to my comrades. "I have a different proposal, my friends. I propose we use this uproar to our own advantage just as those officers were trying to do. It focuses attention upon our cause, which is all to the good. Now we can set matters straight, reach people everywhere in this country, for surely newspapers will carry the story. We will reach thousands, Abe. Educate them concerning our philosophy and how we regard violence, and our ideals and hopes for all. Now is the time for *reason*."

Abe's laughter is bitter. "Emma, Emma. No one cares about reason now. People are no longer capable of reasoning."

"And as part of our campaign," I go on, "I further propose that we help that boy."

"What boy? Not Czolgosz?"

"Yes. He came to us, and we betrayed him."

"Emma! You're exaggerating it all. Yes, he shot the president, but we cannot know for certain that he acted because of us, because of that notice. He may not even have seen it."

"He'll need a decent lawyer or he won't get a fair trial."

"If we publicly align ourselves with him, our cause is doomed."

Max and Hippolyte agree with Abe, but they are wrong. "Listen, friends! When asked why we support him, we can discuss his motives, the conditions that led to this act and—"

"How do we know they aren't wholly psychological, these conditions!" Abe shouts over the wind. "What do we really know about this man?"

"Then we need to find out, quickly. Abe—"

"No. I will do nothing for him. You talk about betrayal, well he betrayed us by giving the police what they wanted to hear."

"We don't know that!"

"We need money for Sasha now, and for repairing presses and homes, Emma, not for throwing to, to . . . these winds!"

"Abe. Max. Hippolyte. Listen, please. He is one of us in spirit. He acted out of his heart for the people. The least we can do is see that he isn't alone now, that he has a decent lawyer and a fair trial. Remember what happened to Sasha, with that interpreter in court reducing Sasha's carefully composed statement to idiotic fragments?"

"He is not Sasha, Emma. And we don't know that he acted alone or for the people or for anyone. How do we know? It will be madness to jump in where we know nothing. How many more presses do you want destroyed? How many more homes ransacked? And you, Emma— Many are just waiting to get you. How can we help *you* if we're all in prison? And really, what good will it do the cause? I ask you, I beg you, Emma, to think now. I will say no more. I am sorry."

It is hard for me to believe that this is Abe speaking. We are all quiet, and there is just the wind, the seething lake below us, and the crash as waves beat themselves against the shore. I feel the pier shaking under us. The irony of it!

Max speaks to break our own awful silence, but I wish he hadn't. "It's possible," he says, "Czolgosz was in someone's pay and did the deed to discredit us. Or else the police told him what to say about you. I agree with Abe. I don't think it would be wise to try to defend him. In fact, it would be madness."

"But Max, even you say that according to the reports, he's being tortured. Why would the police do that if he's in their pay—or someone's pay?"

Then it's Hippolyte, quiet Hippolyte whom I've secretly disliked ever since Paris, he not wanting to return to America with me after Sasha's failed escape. Hippolyte mewling about having left his miserable boardinghouse job in London to come to Paris with me—*America is no place for scholars!* Hippolyte now saying, "It would be foolish to try to defend him when we know so little. And we have no spies there, in that prison. They might even smuggle him out of the country and not execute him at all. Maybe it was all agreed upon beforehand. Really, we must stay away from this."

"Comrades," I say, "how brave we are."

"Caution, Emma," Abe says. "Not cowardice."

"Often they are one and the same, no? Abe, I am going to write an article for your paper, and I want you to print it. Max, I will give a lecture here in Chicago, and I hope you will help me find a hall. Hippolyte, I am not going to Canada with Max—or you."

"Emma!" they all say.

"I am going to stay in this country. We will not fail. We must not and will not."

THE HONORABLE ROBERT C. TITUS

I'll be truthful. I didn't want this case. I was out of the city when the assignment was made. They wired me—and my old colleague Loran Lewis. I suspect that rather than risk the reputations and livelihoods of men still practicing the law, the bar turned to us, both retired justices of the Supreme Court of the State of New York, our reputations long established, our livelihoods secure, in retirement. Two birds with one stone. I don't mean that we are the birds, per se, although that meaning is apt as well. What I'm thinking is that it surely gets *them* out of a tight spot as well.

No, I didn't want it and told them so. It's distasteful in the extreme to have to defend the assassin. What is there to defend? He himself confessed. The alienists have judged him in possession of all his faculties. There are dozens of witnesses for the prosecution. The crime is heinous.

So, no. I told them I'm not your man for this. It goes against the grain. I've spent long years working this field, doing my considerable best to avoid every ethical and moral pitfall and can say that I have safely crossed the finish line and have earned my peace. Find some young fellow who needs the experience, I told him, somebody who might profit from the exposure.

Then they deployed their big guns: duty to the public demands that I accept, duty to our profession, to the court itself. Czolgosz killed the president of the United States. Would it do to have some obscure public defender plead his case? Would it suit the high seriousness of this crime, the largeness of the thing? Above all, would it truly serve justice? And then, too, if it should slip out that two retired justices of the state Supreme Court *declined*—

Careful, boyo, I thought. You're getting mighty close to the edge there.

That was a clever tactic, though. Of course it would slip out and not necessarily with intention. The sniffing hounds of the national press, the international press as well, would surely find *that* bone.

So I'm afraid this is the only road to take, then—as always, the high one: duty to the public, the profession, the court. Justice demands this sacrifice. Justice demands self-abnegation. And if justice demands tarring by the same tarry stick, well then, so be it. For justice is greater than the greatest of us and capable of elevating the least. Let justice—and the Almighty—guide us and all will be well.

So, yes. Though my heart's not in it, I will do my duty before God and country.

LEON

"Don't you even want to talk to us?"

No. The ends of his moustache hang down like the tails of two dead black snakes. Titus, his name. But what is a lawyer except someone who serves the law, and what is the law except something made up by government, and who does government serve except the few even if they say otherwise.

Besides, what good are words now? Done is done.

The other one says, "Then how can we defend you, man, if you persist in your obstinate silence?" His words are like words in a book. People probably believe him because of words like that.

"Czolgosz," the first one—Titus—says. "We can't sit here forever, you know."

Why?—don't you get paid for it?

Behind my eyes there is a banging of blood, and under each eye, pain. *The whole universe is within you,* Mrs. Heuvel said at that lecture so long ago. *Never be discouraged. Never allow discouragement a place in your heart.* For a long time those words were like lamps inside me. But now I see that words are like clothes made to keep you warm. Sometimes, overcoats; sometimes, suits and good shirts. Sometimes these clothes are fancy, and other times a—

"Czolgosz! Has the devil gotten into you again? Why won't you say anything? We're here to help you."

It's the other one now. Lewis. If he was a doctor you'd want to go to him over the other. His face is broader, his goatee white, like his hair, and there are no snaky tails hanging down over it. The goatee is pointed, like a hoe.

"Look," he says. "We understand that you—"

But he doesn't tell me what it is they understand. His eyes are swollen, and the white part yellow. He shoves his papers together and stands. "The hell with him, then."

"The hell with you, too," I say. They leave and I go on twisting the jacket button that is coming loose.

EMMA

I wrote the article and Abe printed it. *Free Society* is, after all, an anarchist paper, and each of us is as free as the editor to express an opinion. Then Max, brave Max, canvassed hall owners throughout the city, but as soon as he gave my name as speaker, each refused. One, though, did change his mind. I was with Max that day, and although the man at first treated me like a leper and ordered me off his property, I prevailed—shamelessly—through flattery and the promise of fame.

So we have a hall! On the scheduled day, Max and I arrive by streetcar. Other comrades are planning to come by different routes. Before we reach our stop, I look about the car, wondering if any of these people are going to the lecture. But women get off and on, with their parcels. Men read newspapers. No one recognizes me. No one appears to be a plainclothesman. Their apparent indifference to anything beyond themselves stuns me and brings to mind what de Tocqueville wrote about political passion having little hold on those intent upon their own well-being: excitement over small things makes people calm about great ones. I decide to use those words, too, in my speech. But what I see in that streetcar isn't merely calm. It seems more like some stupor. If I were an artist, I'd try to paint such a scene. People in a streetcar, closed off from one another and from the outside world. I'd call it *An Ordinary Day,* and I'd make the ordinary seem awful, in its small ways, and indifference and apathy, a kind of disease. So:

blue faces, sickly yellow eyes. Outside, sun and warmth and color, but the eyes of those in the streetcar cannot take in any of it.

Max and I get off the streetcar, causing no stir whatsoever, but then we see police vans parked everywhere along the street and officers busy rerouting pedestrians and conveyances. The hall itself is cordoned off with planks. Police vans block the street at each intersection. We walk farther along the street and pretend to an interest in a bin of squash outside a grocery.

"Let's go," Max says quietly. "If they spot you now—" He pulls my hat farther down and then tries to take off my eyeglasses.

"Don't, Max. *Let* them see me. And hear me, too."

"Words will be useless here today."

"Words are never useless."

"He betrayed us," Max says. "He set a trap. We need to leave fast."

"Max, I *must* give this lecture to the people. Try, anyway! If I don't, I will fail that boy, but above all, our cause.

"There are no *people* here, Emma, just those officers."

"Then I will speak to the officers! They are the people, too, no?"

"Emma, you are mad. First of all, they won't let you. Secondly, you'll be on a train to Buffalo in no time. This was a bad idea. Abe was right, Emma. Be sensible, please! We must leave here."

My jaw has started aching again. As I remove my eyeglasses, the squash blur and appear to recede into some vague gold mound.

"Max," I whisper, "we are *failing.*"

"No, the time just isn't right yet."

"What if it never will be right?

"Here come two officers. Let's go."

He takes my arm, and then we are walking toward a barricaded intersection. Without eyeglasses on, I see only indistinct shapes and colors. Max walks slowly as if in no hurry whatsoever, but I can feel the tremors wracking through his arm. I am shaking too. Leaving here is wrong. This I know in every bone and muscle, but I allow Max to lead me somewhere, neither of us knowing where.

LEON

*A*s-sas-sin! they chant. It sounds like rain on water. *As-sas-sin . . . as-sas-sin . . .* There is loud pounding, the judge smacking his desk as if he's trying to drive in a nail. He has white hair and black eyebrows and looks as a judge should, but he is angry.

Then it is quiet. "How do you plead?" he asks me.

What does he mean, *plead*?

He asks if I understand the charge. I shake my head. Another man repeats this charge. The man is small, with a walrus moustache, and his few strands of brown hair are combed straight back from his long forehead. He tells me that the charge is first-degree murder. Then the judge asks once more how I plead, so this time I say, "Guilty." Again comes the seething sound in the courtroom.

The judge tells me I can't say the word *guilty*. In New York state, there is a law that says I can't. So they put in the words *not guilty* instead and I can sit down at my small table. Behind me at another table are the two old men who wanted to be my lawyers. I wonder if they are.

It seems so because one of them gets up and starts talking to the judge. He is the one with the snake tails—Titus. He holds his arms close to his sides and his body curves forward, like he can't straighten up. He tells everybody that he is sorry to be here, but that he is doing his duty. He says he will watch out that no evidence is brought in that wouldn't be proper when they try lesser criminals.

So he must be saying that I am a criminal. Well, that is true, anyway. I don't listen anymore. I suppose they will just have to say their words and then they can kill me.

Now the other one is talking. He would like the court to finish early each afternoon because he needs to take a train to his summer home. The place has his name. Lewiston. He says his family is there. He says he is not in good health. When he talks, he rubs his gold watch with his thumb and forefinger. The loose button falls from my jacket and I lean to pick it up, but my guard pulls me back. So I finger the threads where the button was.

When it all starts, they say I fired two bullets. I don't remembering firing the gun twice. I know I fired once. But they say twice. One bullet was found in the clothing, and that wound was slight. The other was in the stomach somewhere, and that wound proved fatal. I don't think I wanted to fire at all. I was surprised the line moved so fast, that he was right there so soon. I didn't know what to do, so I fired. It was just there—the doing, and I in it.

When the doctors talk, they sound angry. Now they are telling about the president's intestines. Behind us somewhere, a woman gasps. The doctor stretches his arms out to each side of him to show all the intestines. His face is red. There is noise from the back of the courtroom. I suppose some people are leaving. They don't want to hear about intestines, but to me it is of interest. It is good to know how things work even in death.

Lewis asks why the doctors didn't use a drain. I wonder, too. It seems you should, to drain out the bad. But the one doctor says the gangrene would have happened anyway, drain or no. I don't know what gangrene is, and they don't explain this word. There are other large words, and I know none of them.

Ignorance is no good.

THE HONORABLE LORAN L. LEWIS

Exactly at four thirty in the afternoon I take my usual window seat and unfold my newspaper. There I am, on the first page. *Defense Struggles.*

It is like watching your house burn down, this. A house you have built and over the decades lovingly added refinements and embellishments.

No. This is worse. Houses can be rebuilt.

I worry that someone might take the seat next to me, and I am simultaneously afraid no one will. But I did not want to deviate from my normal routine, nor give any hint of my true state of mind. And so, the empty aisle seat, inviting anyone to join me.

No one does.

So I look out at shorn fields and distant tree lines and think of Marcus Aurelius's advice to do well what you have in hand to do. Let nothing else matter—whether you are tired or wide awake, whether people praise you or speak ill of you— *Do well what you have in hand to do.* Advice I have taken for the greater part of my life.

As I stand in line, waiting to leave the carriage at Lewiston, an acquaintance says quietly, "I think your cross-examination of the doctor who conducted the autopsy was a model of incisiveness."

"Thank you, sir. I do appreciate your words."

It cheers me! It truly does—but only for the briefest moment. On the platform the man makes it clear by his purposeful stride away from me that he's not interested in further conversation.

Bullets, organs, antiseptics. The lawyer in me knows what I was after, with those incisive questions of mine. Did the doctors? The question before me now is whether or not to pursue it to the full. Take Marcus Aurelius's advice—and suffer the consequences.

If only I didn't have to go back to court tomorrow. I walk through the depot, only a few brave ones greeting me, and there is Bill, waiting with the automobile.

"Good afternoon, Bill," I say, as always. "How's everything at home?"

And he, as always, answers, "Fine, sir. Just fine."

The next morning my old-man's joints hurt, and my head feels congested with thought—thought I am having trouble stringing together after the bad night's sleep. Leaning toward the assassin, I forget what I wanted to ask, but the assassin looks away from me and probably would not answer anyway. When I stand to cross-examine the gynecologist, I feel like someone struggling to rise after a fall, pushing with arms, getting legs untangled, and hauling up the rest.

"Why," I finally ask, "were those bulletins so favorable all along?"

The gynecologist gives a small grimace. "We were only reporting things as they appeared at the time. And too, quite a bit of what the press attributed to us was not always correct."

I consider the floorboards a while, the flecks of golden oak there. My heartbeat begins to frighten me. But I say, "Infection, doctor. Can you tell us, please, what causes infection?"

The doctor stares at me as if I were a madman. "Germs, of course!" he says. "Germs cause infection. Bacteria, compounded with the patient's condition of low vitality as well as by the seepage of pancreatic fluid."

"And gangrene? What causes gangrene?"

"Do you wish a short answer or a volume's worth?"

"A short answer, please."

"Very well. Decreased blood flow to the area, the presence of old blood, which can spawn bacteria, which in turn can cause septicemia and tissue necrosis—that is, tissue death, if you will."

"Are there no remedies for this condition?"

"Of course there are remedies but exceedingly difficult to apply, deep down in the tissues, particularly once they get a lodgment there. Then, they are next to impossible to dislodge and kill."

I understand—the crafty man is really speaking about anarchists. I'm certain the jury will catch on. I don't know what to do now, which way to go. I stand there, mute and frowning. It probably gives me an air of profundity, but what I am thinking is that I'll go to my death branded as an anarchist sympathizer, perhaps even as an anarchist if I proceed along this trail much farther. Still, the old lawyer in me creeps forward again, if only to look down into the chasm.

Pressed, the doctor admits that the bullet hadn't actually entered the pancreas.

Then did the bullet kill the president or did germs do it, sir?

The words hover, all but formed.

The doctor waits, as does the court. I myself wait a moment and then abruptly turn away.

The district attorney takes over. "Given what was known as a result of the autopsy and the case history," he says, "could anything have saved the president?"

"No."

At my table I look down at my dry, spotted hands, the one curving protectively around the other.

LEON

In September at the farm in northern Michigan, we always went to the woods to pick blackberries. They hang there like small black lanterns on canes with thorns like claws. You have to go slow or get pricked. Each berry is all bumps, and on each bump is a point of light, on the perfect ones. You might think they are wet, so shiny like that, but no. Turn the berry to one side, tipping it, and it pops from the stem the way it should. Hurry too much and you will have long scratches up and down your arms. In the wagon my mother dips a cloth in our water bucket and holds it against the scratches. *Leon, you were going too fast, you weren't watching.* The cloth warms and she dips it in the cold water again as the wagon moves like a boat through the woods of pine and fern. Long canes of blackberries try to latch on and straighten like fishing poles but then let go and fly back to where they were, with their red berries waiting to ripen. At night the scratches hurt and my arms are hot and she is there, with a cloth and ointment.

So I see these scratches again when they talk about germs getting lodgment deep in the dark of him. The bullet made the path for these germs, so the doctors are not to blame, no, even though Lewis is trying to say that. If there was no hole, there'd be no germs and no gangrene. It is something, though, to hear Lewis saying that, like he is on my side after all. I had no hope until he said that and now the little bit of it there hurts like those scratches, for I know it can't be.

I decide not to listen to the rest—about secret service men and detectives. Let them talk. Let them build what they need to with their words.

When my mother canned the berries, our house smelled like sugary wine. But she did not can them all; she saved some for us to have with milk. After she died, we moved to Ohio and took the jars of blackberries with us, but Father left her fern in the parlor, just left it behind for the next owner, the green fronds that were like the woods, on days when the sun shone through them.

Now he is asking me something, the judge, I don't know what. I want to keep thinking about the berries and how they smell like wine, when they are cooking.

THE HONORABLE LORAN L. LEWIS

I stand and ask that testimony be closed. Well, what choice do I have? He refuses to say anything in his own defense. We have no witnesses to call upon. This is rather embarrassing. I'd hoped he might relent and at least say a few words. Evidently he believes himself to be guilty, so what good are words at this point? What good, for that matter, witnesses? Still, it is somewhat embarrassing, and I admit this to the court and ask permission to make a few points, in summary, if the court allows.

It does.

In summary, then. "This is indeed a terrible calamity. And it has been shown, without any doubt, that the defendant struck down the president. The only question remaining is whether or not the defendant is sane. If sane, he is guilty of murder and must suffer the penalty for murder. If not, he should be acquitted and confined to a lunatic asylum.

"But we must be careful. Anarchy is dangerous but not more so than mob rule."

I go on to tell a lengthy but relevant story about the man who was secretary of state under Abraham Lincoln, William H. Seward—a story that has often served me well. In short, while still a law student, he defended a Negro named Freeman who was accused of killing an entire family. A mob wanted to hang Freeman from the nearest oak. But Seward went out and met that mob face to face and urged moderation. So Freeman went on trial, and the trial lasted three entire months. Jury selection alone took three weeks.

I tell this story to emphasize the beauty and sacredness of the law. After that, I proceed to talk about the goodness of the president who came to Buffalo to promote the city's big exposition. This of course leads to a disquisition on the greatness of the man himself.

"Gentlemen," I say, "death is a specter no one wants to meet! The defendant went into a building and committed an act which, if he is sane, will cause his own death—"

I cannot continue. This is the saddest blow to me in many, many years. I say so and then have to sit down. I am not ashamed of weeping. Most of the gallery also weeps.

Then Titus is echoing my words.

Fifteen minutes after the court's instructions, the jury returns with its verdict.

Guilty

Well, of course.

Officers lead the assassin away, and I thank God for having reached—nearly reached, the end of all this. Now I have only to walk out and catch my train and rest, before tomorrow's sentencing.

But to my astonishment, people stop me on my way out and want to shake my hand! One says my speech should be saved and studied by future generations.

So perhaps a bit of good has come out of this after all, in the mysterious workings of the Almighty.

VICTORIA

"I am eighteen years old and understand English," I say to the policeman asking questions. "Leon taught me and so did my brother Waldeck, a little. Leon said I should learn. He did not want me to work in our father's saloon on Todd Street in Cleveland. He did not think it was safe for me. He did not like the bartender there or trust him. Leon brought me books. So I know a little. Now I help my sister Celia. She is married and I help in her house.

"Father, Waldeck, and I came from Cleveland because there is a trial, but when we get here they say we cannot go to the trial. Now we are here at the jail because we have no money for lodging. They say we cannot see Leon either, tonight. Why? Do you know? It is a hard thing to be here, right where he is, and not be able to see him or talk to him."

In a kindly manner the policeman asks if I will translate some questions into Polish for Father. Waldeck refused because the trial is all done now, and they would not let us be there. Waldeck tells me in Polish that he would rather go to hell than talk to any of them. But I think it might help us see our Leon if I do what the policeman asks.

"Are we Socialist, Father?" I ask in Polish. "The policeman wishes to know."

"No."

"How do you vote? Do you vote Socialist?"

"No, never."

"Do you belong to a group, Father?"

"What do you mean, group? We go to church, tell him. That is the only group."

"Do you know who Leon saw in town and what meetings he went to?"

"Leon kept to himself. He was Socialist a while. I do not remember when."

"Are you anarchist, Father?"

"Tell him I don't know what that is. We vote Democrat ticket."

"Waldeck, they ask if our Leon ever talked about Emma Goldman. Answer, please! It might help us see him tonight."

"He did talk about her after she spoke in Cleveland," Waldeck says in English. "He mentioned the write-up in the paper. He said he liked that kind of talk. She probably told him to do it. You don't have to translate. I know English."

Because Waldeck says this, the man looks at him and asks, "Did he go to hear her?"

I can tell Waldeck would rather fight him than answer, but at last he says, "I don't know. What I think is somebody else made him do this!"

Waldeck has a hot temper. When he drinks, it is worse. When our train arrived in Buffalo, he gave us the slip at the depot and went off. I think he went to drink because this is too hard on him. Now they want him to talk to Leon so Leon will tell them who else. Waldeck says he is no spy and will not do their dirty work. His voice is very loud, and I am afraid it will anger the policeman. Our father sits with one hand on each knee and looks at nothing. There are many men here who are writing down what we say. I think they will put everything in the papers. It is hard to think this. I want to cry but do not because they might put that in the newspaper, too. Now people hate us and call us names, but we are not bad! So I say to the man asking questions that we go to church and pray. "Our stepmother is mean, it is true, but I try to forgive her in my heart. She picked on Leon all the time because he was different than us. He likes books. When he got sick and could not work, she picked on him all the more. One time she burned his books and some letters. They were from his girlfriend Lucy. He met her in Natrona when we lived there. Another time our stepmother cleared out Leon's room and burned all the newspapers and other papers in the cook stove. When Lucy moved away, Leon found out it was to study somewhere. Her aunt and uncle wanted her to keep on working in her uncle's grocery store, but she didn't want to. She was like Leon. She liked books, too. He thought she gave up on him because she never wrote him any letters. Then one day a long time later she came to our farm outside of Cleveland and asked Leon why he never wrote back to her. Leon said it was because he didn't know where to write, he never got any letters from her to tell him. She said she wrote many letters, but he never answered any of them! When she told Leon about the letters, he knew right away that our stepmother burned them because she is like that. After Lucy left, Leon was very unhappy. I said he should go to her in Philadelphia. He said she was too far up in the world now. Lucy makes soap—can you imagine! She told him that she figures out how to make it and then in a factory they make it. They have special names for these soaps. And she must travel to places to find the ingredients, like in cake. He was very proud of this but also sad, when he tells me. He said it is good that it happens for someone even if not for him. But it hurt him, like when they didn't take him for the war or when he lost his work at the wire factory because he couldn't catch his breath. And now everyone says he shot the president. If this is so, I do not think he did it by himself. Someone forced him to do that. We think he had to draw lots and picked the one that said he had to do it. Maybe they would kill him otherwise. He did not like to hunt and kill rabbits at the farm, but he had to because he was not working and our stepmother said he must earn his food. Leon did not like the farm. For a long time he wanted to leave. Finally our father and stepmother let him sell his share in the farm back to them. So he went to look for work someplace else. He wrote me a letter from Fort Wayne, Indiana, and sent it to Celia's house. I do not know where this letter is now. I took it to the farm to show them, and then it disappeared. I think she got ahold of it, our stepmother. I wish I had it now so you can see his handwriting. It is very good. This is everything I know. Will you now allow us to see our brother tonight?"

LEON

The door opens and she steps into my cell. Behind her are Father and Waldeck. It stinks in here, and I am ashamed. Why they would not let me see them elsewhere, I don't know. In the corridor are reporters. They let them in by fives. She is crying and saying something in Polish as she moves toward me. The jailer pulls her back and roars that she must speak English. I want to hit him but cannot. Instead, I sit there like a bump on a log and pull at threads. She stands a little apart, but I cannot help her. It is like when she was a baby, crying so hard in the back bedroom by herself after Mother died. Now I cannot even hold her. Inside that time again, I close my eyes.

"Leon," Waldeck shouts. "Wake up! Talk to us!"

"Father," I say in Polish, "you come all this way."

"English, dammit!" the jailer hollers. "It has to be in English."

"I am sorry, Father," I say in English. I say the Polish word for sorry, and the jailer slaps me. Victoria cries, and the reporters write. I am so tired. My eyes wish to close, but I ask how it is at home because they have come so far to hear something and I must say something.

Waldeck says it is hard now. He shrugs like on the farm—meaning, what matter, snow, mud, wind. You put up with it. But in Polish he asks if they made me draw lots.

"Talk English!" the jailer shouts again. "Or out you go."

Waldeck turns on the jailer. "Polish, English, what the hell's the difference? Just let him talk, damn it."

The jailer warns me to answer in English.

Waldeck says, in Polish, "Tell us! Your family! I will kill them myself. Tell us in Polish, Leon. The hell with them."

"There is no one to kill," I say in English.

The jailer and another guard grab Waldeck and try to drag him out, but Waldeck is strong. "Leon," he says in Polish, while struggling with them, "what do they care about you now, when they got what they wanted. You see how they are? I warned you, brother. Now you know. Don't protect them!"

Victoria is making herself sick, crying, like before in that bedroom when she was a baby and I tried to pick her up and hold her but it was no good because I was not our Mother. The guards have Waldeck in the corridor now and are pulling him away somewhere. I am afraid they might lock him up, too. Another guard brings water for Victoria. She pays no attention but rushes to me, crying, *Tell them! They might let you go!* For a second or two we hold one another. Then she is being pulled away while my father just watches. One of the guards comes and holds my mouth open while another searches inside. Then they take off my jacket, search it, and my shirt. Somewhere Waldeck is shouting, in Polish, that I am a fool. Why did I kill the president?—for *them*?

Father says nothing and does not look back as he and Victoria are led out.

The cell door clanks shut and I listen to Victoria's crying for as long as I can.

THE HONORABLE ROBERT C. TITUS

Let no man ever say that I neglected my duty. Lewis telephoned this morning to inform me that he would not be coming in for the sentencing. He didn't feel well, he said, the strain, his legs, something. "All right," I said. "I'll be there, then." I expect that he didn't want to have to talk to the reporters afterward. Or, possibly, he didn't want to have to look at Czolgosz anymore. God knows I don't.

Now the assassin is answering every question the district attorney puts to him though earlier he refused to place his hand on the Bible and take the oath, refused to speak at all. Now he tells us what schools he attended in northern Michigan and relates that he was a Roman Catholic. His mother died, he says, and his father later remarried. He tells us that he never drank much and never had the habit of getting drunk. Nor was he ever convicted of any crime before this.

When the judge asks if he had any legal cause why sentence should not be pronounced against him, he begins to speak, but then falters. The judge offers some instruction regarding legal causality. But Czolgosz says that he has nothing to say about *that*. So I tell him that he is free to speak now and should do so if he wishes. "Tell them whatever's on your mind."

I don't believe he heard me, for I was seated. So I stand next to him, repulsive as that is to do, and say, "*Tell them* what's on your mind. This is your last chance." Something, I don't know what, makes me touch his arm. He flinches but begins to speak though in a mere whisper. I am able to hear him but I doubt anyone else in the courtroom can. So for the benefit of the court, I must repeat his words.

"My family," he murmurs, and I echo in my usual booming tone, *"My family—"*

"They had—"

"They had—"

"Nothing to do with it."

"Nothing to do with it."

"I was—"

"I was—"

"Alone."

"Alone."

This goes on for a few minutes, an eerie sensation, I don't mind admitting, our voices interwoven like that. He is adamant about making clear that no one, apart from himself, had anything to do with the shooting. Not his family or friends or any acquaintance. Nor had he told anyone what he was going to do. He didn't know himself, he says.

Dutifully I repeat all that while Czolgosz stands alongside me. The gallery is awfully quiet. I expected hissing, but no, nothing, apart from the massive silence. I'm not poetic by nature yet I have the sense of some imminent avalanche and—yes—fear for my life. Everything seems held in some delicate balance that might be tipped by a mere word.

I remain standing while Justice White addresses Czolgosz and states that by taking the life of our beloved president, he has committed a crime which has shocked and outraged the entire civilized world. He confessed his guilt, and a jury of twelve good men, after learning all they could of the case at this time, pronounced his confession true and found him guilty of murder in the first degree. Further, Czolgosz declared that no other person had aided or abetted him in the commission of this terrible act. The penalty for the crime for which he stands convicted is fixed by statute, and so now it is the judge's duty to state: "The sentence of the court is that in the week beginning on October 28, 1901, at the place, in the manner, and by the means prescribed by law, you suffer the punishment of death."

A detective slips iron cuffs over Czolgosz's wrists and that's that. I can leave now. But out of long habit—I can only suppose this is what compels me—I place myself within the assassin's line of vision as best I can for he has gone into his dopey trance again, and extend my hand. "Good-bye, Czolgosz," I say.

The words seem to startle him, and he raises both manacled hands, extends the fingers of his right hand, and says good-bye to me. Our hands briefly touch, and then I am able to leave the courtroom rather quickly, given that all attention is now focused on the district attorney.

Ah, it's good to be out from under this nasty business. Also good knowing that when called upon to serve, I can still summon the moral courage to do so.

LEON

My cell door bangs open, and three guards are there, one of them ordering me to get up. I do so, at once. Then we are walking past other cells I do not look into, for I suppose everyone is awake and staring out at the commotion we make. Upstairs, the jailer handcuffs his left wrist to my right one with yet another manacle. A guard grabs my left arm. One of them pulls my cap down. I have to raise my chin to see anything. We walk along several corridors and through doors, and finally, a door to the outside. Once outside, the guards and jailer begin running, half-dragging me because my legs don't work right. There is a train, and in the next minute we are aboard it and it is moving. So I know that it was waiting for us.

It is night—and here I thought, morning. But no. All the windows in this car have curtains closing them off so no one can see inside—or outside, either. Every seat in this car is taken. There are guards in uniform and men in fine suits. In the seats facing this way, men stare at me, so I look down at my hands, still manacled.

Someone lights a cigar. Someone else drags a hamper from under a seat and passes the jailer a sandwich. This man also opens beer bottles. After a while, the train slows, and the jailer says, "Just switchin', boys. Hookin' up to the Rochester train."

In a while, the car slides forward again. The jailer gives me a cigar, and the man across from me lights it. He is a small man with a baby's pink skin. His eyes are not a baby's. More like a chipmunk's, quick as anything. I don't want the cigar, but I smoke it a little because the jailer was good enough to give it to me. Yet it makes me feel sick.

"You can talk to them, Czolgosz," the jailer says, "if you want to." He unlocks the manacle linking us, but then his arm is still next to mine. The warmth of it reminds me of Emma's arm, so close, that time in Chicago.

"Go on, boy," he says. "No need holding back now. Talk to them. They'll put your words in newspapers."

The man who lighted my cigar says, "Do you think it was a mistake? Are you sorry you did it?"

"I . . . wish people to know—" What? When they ask if you are sorry, I think they want to know if you suffer. If it is like a sickness you feel. But what good is being sorry afterward? The priests ask the same question in the confessional and won't absolve you if you say you're not sorry. But sorrow doesn't let you snip time off in two places, throw away the rotting part, and graft the other two together. Still, I say that I am sorry.

"So then—can I call you Leon?—do you think your philosophy was a mistake?"

"It is wrong to kill. Say that." Through a crack in the curtains, I see red streaks on the night. From what?—crossing signals?

"You said that you were all stirred up. What stirred you up, Leon?"

I tell them I don't know, anymore. But in my head is her name. *Emma. Emma Goldman.*

"Was it what somebody said?" the man next to him says.

"I was alone."

"Not a wise thing, what you did, eh?"

"No."

"Can't you tell us why you did it, Leon? Did anyone in Patterson—"

"I don't know anybody in Patterson."

"What about Count Malatesta? Know him?" Then he says another name, a Frenchwoman's.

"I don't know those people. I was alone. It's hard now. When you kill, you are not the same person anymore."

"How were you before, Leon? Better? Or worse?"

They laugh.

"How about Emma Goldman, Leon? She get to you, did she?"

"No."

"But you said you did it for the people. Where'd you get that idea?"

"I am not a spy."

"Who said you were, Leon?"

"I don't know."

"Think you had a fair trial?"

"The judge couldn't help doing what he did. The jury couldn't. The law made them do it. I don't want to say now that the law is wrong. It seems too late now but I am sorry for her. Mrs. McKinley. I hope she doesn't die."

"Leon—"

"Let him be a while," the jailer says. "Here," he says to me. "Eat. We got a rough road ahead."

At first I am afraid because of the illness I feel, but the hunger is so strong. The small man with pink skin says, "Leon, I wouldn't let them get away with it. They led you on, didn't they? They got you to do it, right?"

At first I think Waldeck is there, in the car with us, but no. I look at the ham sandwich and see Victoria making it, at the saloon. She takes her time and is neat.

"Nobody did," I say.

The train slows, and there is much yelling outside. One of the jailer's deputies goes out and shouts that the assassin hasn't left Buffalo yet. Somebody yells back that that's a damn lie. "Why'd you pull so far ahead?"

"Because of all the damn ruckus you're making!"

The deputy comes in and curses, saying they got every-thing from shovels and mauls to table legs out there. The train moves on, but at the next stop it is the same. This time the train slows without stopping and then picks up speed again. Everyone in this car is quiet now until one of them asks, "How did they know?"

"Word must have got out," the jailer says. "Like it does." He looks at the reporter with chipmunk eyes. They begin asking me more questions, but I just play the dummkopf and let them believe I'm crazy. I must fall sleep, for there is the chair again and the president and the line moving too fast. I am walking toward him. His shirt and vest are white and just there in front of me, a mountain of snow, and I am walking into all that white.

"Wake up, Leon!"

I open my eyes and see that we are again handcuffed together. Outside the train is much yelling again, only this time the train is stopped, and everyone in this car is standing.

"What the hell we gonna do?" a deputy asks the jailer.

"Bull our way. What the hell else? Guards over there can't get here, so we have to get there, damn it."

Cursing guards clump around the jailer and me. "What about us?" asks a reporter.

"Hell, I don't know," the jailer says. "You boys wanted to come along. Just stay on the train if you want."

We jump off the train into the river of them. Then I'm on the ground and dragging the jailer down. He pulls me up. We make a few feet before someone hits him, and he drops to his knees.

I want it for myself but do not want it for him, so I get up and this time drag him with me. A surge from behind knocks us into the gate. Guards on the other side ease it open a few inches and we press inside. Then they lean against it.

There were no shots. Why wouldn't they just want to shoot me?

Maybe a shot is not good enough for them.

Inside, I look up at the top of the stairway and see the president waiting for me. My mouth opens and shuts and opens again and fills with frothy saliva and I scream and try to wrench away, but a blow knocks me to blackness.

EMMA

Hannes's wife, Helen Minkin, opens the door slightly. "What do you want?" she says.

"I wish to see Hannes."

"He is resting."

"Is he asleep? Is he not well?"

She gives me an evil look. "Helen," I say. "It is necessary."

"Who is it?" he calls from within the flat. From the hall-way, I see that it is a small place filled mainly with books and papers, some of which are stacked on the floor. Many others are heaped in one corner.

"It is Emma," she says.

He curses as he comes into view, wearing a robe cinched loosely. "You see what they did?" he asks. He gestures toward the pile of books reaching a window's sill. Only then do I notice many empty shelves. "A wonder," he says, "they did not make a fire in here and burn everything."

Helen steps aside to allow me to enter so that she can close the door again. The two of us stand uncomfortably close, right in front of the closed door. She appears exhausted, her thin hair pinned up but hanging down here and there in faded wisps. Her eyes are sunken in dark pools of flesh. "It was because of you, of course," she says. "And now you dare come here yourself. They probably follow her, no? Hannes, maybe we should leave. They will be back and this time finish the job."

This is not the Helen of old—what has become of that bold young woman? Her courage and enthusiasm, then,

had given her a sheen that had made her plainness beautiful. Helen taking me in, when I'd first come to New York.
How we'd talked!—I telling her about Yakov and my disas-
trous marriage; she telling me about her work in the movement, and I envying her that rich vein. She knew the city,
knew all the comrades, knew the issues, knew Johannes
Most well. But it was me Hannes asked to marry, later—
and I his prodigy!—Hannes actually begging, kneeling on
the floor of my own tiny flat, then, amid the fabric and
thread on the floor.

*Hannes! I can't believe that you, a revolutionary, wishes
to marry, wishes to possess another human being!*

We can still work together, Emma. Side by side, as now.

*Get up, please, Hannes. You have dust and lint all over
you. No one should ever kneel to another.*

It's that Jew bastard, isn't it? You prefer him over me.

Hannes! Are you forgetting that I am a Jew as well?

I'll go to Helen, then. Helen will have me.

"Hannes," I say now. "We need you."

"I have nothing more to give."

"That's not true. Maybe the work will . . . revive you."

"Only a good shit will revive me, and I can't even do
that."

The words remind me of the scatological references
in his earlier speeches, words that drew crowds to him,
to the astounding aura of power as well as passion that
emanated from him whenever he spoke on any stage. That
time and this slide into conjunction, and a profound sad-
ness verging on despair seeps through me. I recall how
much I had loved this man once, loved the fire in him.
And when that fire began to wane, so too my love for him.

Helen is asking if I want to see him in prison yet again.
"He won't be able to survive it this time, Emma."

I turn to his handmaiden and regard her a moment
before saying, "Perhaps that would not be the worst thing,
Helen."

"You know nothing, Emma. Nothing at all."

Hannes has been staring morosely at the carpet, and now Helen goes to him and urges him to sit down. She sits alongside him and, unbidden, I take a chair opposite the two of them and explain my plan. All the while, she holds his hand and remains quiet, not offering any advice, not saying, *Refuse, Hannes!* for that might work to my advantage.

His focus is upon his bony knees, under the dressing gown, as he says, "I cannot."

"We are still straightening the flat," Helen says, as if in explanation.

Before leaving, I part the drapes slightly to check for any plainclothesman out on the street.

Every comrade I manage to speak with says no. Peukert, Fedya, Haske, Esch, Treemer, Heine, the mutualists, the syndicalists, the socialists—all say no. After Czolgosz's death there will be odes and essays, lamentations and criticisms, perhaps, but now it is simply *no*. What matter, now, that the trial was a travesty? What matter, now, that jurors were selected even if they'd said that they had already formed their decisions? What matter, now, that they took only fifteen minutes to deliberate?—if that is even what they did in those few minutes. What matter, now, that the defense attorneys merely defended themselves? That not one witness for the defense had been called?

No, Emma. We cannot. It's madness. It's not wise. Nobody can defend him. He is guilty, he admitted it!

Friends, you like that word no *so much, how about this: No justice then. No justice for anyone—not just us, should it come to that.*

No.

Friends, united we could do something for him.

No.

Friends, we'd be acting not just for Czolgosz, but—
No.

Comrades, what has happened to shrink us so? Why is it that we contract to the smallest of circles, curling up like caterpillars when touched, the smallest of circles, the self? Why is that?

No, Emma. You are not thinking clearly.

I am *thinking.*

There remains Ed.

Whereas Hannes's flat is small and cluttered, Ed's is as I remember it—spacious and everything within arranged with great aesthetic care. There are new porcelain *objets* on the mantle and in cabinets, but the same fine Persian rug in the sitting room. His French, English, and Greek classics are shelved to either side of the fireplace—no one disarranging these, at least not yet. His wife is a demure younger woman, fashionably attired, her hair in elaborate coils. She serves us coffee and slices of chocolate torte.

"Did you make the torte, Ed?" I ask, smiling at both of them.

Curtly, he answers yes. I sense his anger at my daring to come here, jeopardizing him and his family. In our years of living together after Sasha had been imprisoned, Ed had taken great pride in his culinary ability. For him it seemed an acquisition much like his many antique Asian *objets*. He'd also taken pride in his scholarship, begun in an Austrian jail. As I look at him now, so much the older burgher, I recall that night we first met, at a meeting in support of Sasha, after Pittsburgh. He was sitting in the row behind me, not paying much attention to the speakers but instead, lighting matches and staring at them. A man in his forties, playing like a naughty child. I turned and asked that he please stop, it was distracting.

He did stop. Then when it was my turn to go up, I noticed him listening with full attention. Afterward, he waited a long time in order to walk out with me. Much later

I came to understand that ideals and passion can dim over time, yet one may still try to cling to them, possibly out of some need for self-respect or in some vain hope that it all might be rekindled again. And so the man attends a meeting in support of another whose passionate act landed him in prison, and while attending, he stares—wistfully?—at match flames he himself blows out. And I—too young, still, and succumbing to flattery—allow myself to be taken in like yet another *objet*. Flattered and intrigued and drawn mothlike to those short-lived flames. He was older, sensitive, even compassionate, and he came to love me with a passion he could not find in the movement.

The beauty surrounding me, once, in this flat! The tutorials in the classics, in history. The tenderness, love, and generosity—Ed even financing my nursing studies. It's here, all of it, in this room—and his jealousy and possessiveness as well. And now, strangest of all, maybe, I find myself envying this wife of his, particularly when she excuses herself and then returns with a child dressed for bed, a little girl of about two in a starched white nightgown, needing to say good-night to her Papa. It must be only fatigue, but my heart actually hurts as if from some blow.

After she leaves the sitting room with the child, Ed speaks quietly, urgently. "The trial's over, Emma, and people want this behind them. After all, the man confessed."

"Ed, we know about these confessions, the interrogations preceding them, yes? A good lawyer might appeal on the grounds of due process. The defense presented not even one witness. There was *no* expert testimony as to his sanity or insanity."

"I know all that, Emma, but I can't help you this time. We can't."

He is a *we* now, like Hannes. The escape into home and family. It strikes me now that when something becomes terribly difficult to achieve, one course is to give up and find an easier substitute.

"Be careful, Emma," he is saying. "It was foolish of you to come to New York."

Be careful! And spoken in the same nagging tone as during the hunger riots. *Stay home, Emma. Don't go out tonight. You gave your speech yesterday. You're pressing your luck . . . you're not well enough . . . you're overextending and will get sick again, have a relapse . . . eat this now, I made it for you . . .*

But the nagging, as before, isn't enough for Ed. As in the old days, he has to have the last word as well.

"Whatever the tragedy," he says in the vestibule of his flat, "whatever the calamity, you have to place yourself at its center, don't you, Emma? You always have, you know. Do you need it so badly—the attention? The emotion you unloose—and you at the center of the storm?"

"I'm not surprised," I say, "jealousy taking such an ugly turn—again."

He turns out the hall light before I reach the pavement.

Yet walking away, I am surprised at how love can transmute itself into its opposite when denied.

I stop.

Czolgosz. On the El with me in Chicago— It hadn't been a student's earnestness at all, I realize. But love.

EAMON

He says, "How much you got?"

I tell him.

"That'll do," he says.

Then he says "Lower East Side," and I ask of what, *where*, and he says, "You are a dumb one, eh?" And I say that I am but I found my way here all right, and he says, "That you did, lad, can't imagine how." He goes on and tells me New York is where I need to go. Do I know how to take a train there?

I tell him I know about trains.

"Ah well, then," he says, "good for you," and sips from his dirty glass in his dirty room by the Cleveland docks. Then he gives me a look. "You ain't shammin' now, are you, boy? You ain't the police, are you? Or some detective? Because I always charge the police extra an' they know it but it's all right by them, what do they care, it ain't their money now, is it? What you got behind that patch, boy?"

I show him. He stares a while, then tells me he thought I was trying to fool him with some disguise and nobody does that to Chemin Batteau and lives to tell of it, for he can abide the police, they are critters like the rest o' us, though more despicable, but what he cannot abide is anyone falsifying to him, which is treating a man who don't deserve it like the mud of a slough.

He wants to know who done it and so I tell him.

"Then you *are* a pink!" he says. "You're a goddam *pink* an' not tellin' me?" His man comes toward me a ways with his revolver cocked, but there is something about me that makes him stop and look at his boss. He is scared. When you don't care, it does that. It makes them stop. It is only when you are afraid that they don't. So I tell them the story, and the man just says he hates pinks, reds, the whole damn bunch o' stinky flowers, and he hopes I get her, too. I wonder why he don't himself, if he knows her whereabouts, but then I guess why. He is a toad sitting in the dark, waiting for flies and such to come to him. Then his tongue shoots out and there you are, stuck.

What he says is I am working for him now since I know him and come here to buy information from him. I am his man and I need to tell him names, places, whatever I find out wherever I go, and he will pay me so much for each thing. I need to tell him so many things each week or I am a dead man. And they damn well better be true.

I tell him I am dead already so he can just go back to hell where he came from. He says, "We'll see, lad. We'll see about you. You know where New York is? It's a ways east o' here." And they both laugh. It is all right, them laughing. It is the way it must be now.

LEON

I turn my head to see where I am. Another cell. Stone on three sides and the front closed off by a set of bars with another for a crossbar. A man leans against the crossbar in the cell directly opposite mine. His patchy hair is cut short as a monk's. His face is narrow. He wears a black suit. Alongside his cell stands a guard.

"So yer finally awake," this prisoner says. "Y'missed breakfast an' they ain't keepin' it warm for ye, that's for sure."

My hand goes to my hair. It is stiff and dirty to the touch. Then it goes to my left eyelid, which is hot and sore.

"They had to beat you brainless. You was draggin' six of them about like some madman."

My throat, too, is raw. I sit up and arrange my jacket, which is all crooked. But then I soil it by gagging up the remains of that ham sandwich.

"That's just like me when I first come in! The sickness descends an' stays for the first few days. But ye'll soon be yerself, never mind, eatin' along with the rest of us. The belly don't care about death houses, just wants its fill all the same."

Death house?

"They tell you it's in there, boy?"

The prisoner at the crossbar tips his head toward the door at the near end of the corridor. I look.

"They tell you the chair's in there? The electric chair?"

"I thought Sing Sing is where they have it."

"Here, too."

I tell him that in Ohio there is only one place.

"This ain't Ohio, son!"

He laughs until the guard standing near his cell tells him to stop being the idiot.

"As if I'm the only one!"

This he says as if fearless. The guard goes and then comes back with a spade he clangs against the bars, right where the man's face is. The man goes to the back of his cell. The clanging goes on. I hear it long after the guard stops and a new one comes.

The man is back at the crossbar again. "I'm supposed to be next, that's what they tole me, but then you come so now I don' know. You might have the honors before me. Surely hope so, anyhow."

No. There might yet be a chance to see a field, the woods, Victoria.

"You know they do it in the daytime now, don'cha? All that 'lectricity dims the lights, an' when they was doin' it at night, people in town complained. These lights in here do, too, so we always know cause there ain't no windows an' the lights are on all the time. But it ain't so bad. Better knowin' than not, I say. Heard you're one of them anarchists, that right? Never had the pleasure before. You don' look like they're supposed to look, though."

To let this man talk and talk must be part of the punishment. I am falling in and out of sleep and cannot be sure I am not dreaming. The voice is there when I awake— and there when I fall back into somewhere else.

"Me, I killed a man 'cause he was tormentin' me. Which is a reason, right? Self-defense though they wouldn't believe it in court, the bastards, they . . ."

The words go on. How he'd fallen in with someone who wanted to rob a farmer suspected of keeping a fortune in a carpenter's chest in his barn. How they didn't find any money there, after beating the farmer nearly to death with a whiffletree, and then escaped all right until the partner started blackmailing him . . .

Chains of words like froth marbling waves.

A guard yells, "Bailey, enough of yer damn yammering, man. Yer drillin' holes in me ears."

The prisoner across the corridor chews on a fingernail.

I do not sit up, for that might make him start jabbering again. I lie here, pretending to sleep. My hair, my skin stink. I smell like some old baba who wets her pants. I smell like a potato bin where they are rotting, the potatoes. It is possible I am already turning into dirt.

E. G. SMITH
(EMMA)

Fine worsted material in a rich burgundy color slides from under the machine's needle to the carpet. I pause to rest my eyes before leaning down to gather up the cloth, find my place, and reset the needle. Then I am sewing again. It must be midafternoon by now, and the house still quiet. I sew for perhaps two hours longer and am almost finished with the jacket before the house begins to come alive once more with women's voices. There is the sound of running water and the smell of chopped meat frying. Someone knocks on my door.

"Enter, please," I say, knowing it must be Charlotte, inquiring about her suit.

It is. "Is it ready yet, Miss Smith?" she asks.

"I must ask you to try it on for me again, Charlotte. I want to make certain this fits you perfectly at the waist."

Charlotte is a woman nearing thirty who had once lived in the village of Queens. She had a husband and a child, a boy now about eleven years old, but the husband divorced her, remarried, and took the boy to live with him a few years ago. Soon he stopped depositing money in her bank account. She moved to the Lower East Side to live with a sister, but when this sister married an old friend, Charlotte was on her own. The newly married sister apparently didn't want any potential rival in the household. A year or two ago, I treated Charlotte for venereal disease and tubercular symptoms in this same house.

The suit I'm making, to be worn with a silk shirtwaist, will be perfect for her. "You've chosen well, Charlotte," I say. "This is a good color for you, and the style fills you out nicely." I have a sudden thought of her on the street at night, in this clothing. The prostitutes who'd passed me that night on Fourteenth Street were dressed in similarly tasteful outfits.

She smiles somewhat into the mirror. Her hands are large, with blue veins beginning to protrude. The hands emerge from the jacket sleeves like a peasant's.

"You must be animated from within," I tell her. "That's what is ultimately enchanting. So you must believe in yourself. A costume is one thing; a smile, another. Now, show me this light of yours."

Again she smiles like one afraid of what she is seeing, there in the mirror. Then she turns to me. "Miss Smith, I don't think . . . I can keep on here. It's not . . . I'm not . . . I'm too old . . . and I don't know what else I can do now."

Her voice quivers. Tears well up. "No one wants me, and Madame Ristand . . . she says she may have to ask me to leave soon if I cannot pay my way here."

"Have you tried to find other employment, Charlotte? What about clerking?—in one of the department stores?"

"I asked at Lord & Taylor and Devlin's and, oh, many other places, but I have no experience and they seemed to want younger girls. As in here."

She has lost more weight in merely a week. I see I must take in the skirt. "Charlotte, please sit down if you have a moment."

"I have lots of moments!" Her laugh is rueful.

"Good. Then I will tell you a story about my sewing machine."

"Your sewing machine? Why?"

"Oh, stories are always of some use, don't you think?— if only to entertain. I, too, was married once. I was as young as you were when you married." While working on the skirt, I tell her about meeting Yakov, his impotence, gambling, and jealousy, his threatening suicide. I tell her about the sewing class I secretly attended and the practicing at home and how, one day, he found my patterns and forbade me to go to the class. I conclude with my escape from Rochester and arrival in New York, alone, on a hot summer day, sewing machine in one hand, valise in the other.

"But you were young then," she says. "When a person is young there's more courage, I think."

"Well, blind optimism, anyway."

"And you were probably healthy and strong."

"I was young but not entirely healthy. Yet when you're young, your greatest strengths may be your instinct and passion. My passion was, well, let's just say a grand ideal. And my sewing machine—this machine!—was a means of surviving, day to day, supporting myself. I could teach you to sew, Charlotte. I think they acquire souls, these machines, from being with us through so much, and maybe there's a power here that will enter your hands once you begin."

She looks at the machine, its wheels and shiny steel fittings. "How long would it take?"

"Oh, within a year you might be quite good at it."

"A year! And then to work where? In a factory? They probably won't want me, either!"

"Words like that usually defeat us at the outset, I've found."

"But here there's still a chance that . . ."

I understand the direction of her thought. Here, in a brothel, there is the possibility, however slight, that some man will fall in love with her and her life will instantly change. I recall the man who'd wanted me to be his mistress eight years ago. He, too, wanted someone young. Charlotte is wan and scared and becoming gaunt. I am afraid for her.

"It's not beyond your abilities," I say, "and you're probably a fast learner. You could work for yourself as a seamstress, as I'm doing now in return for room and board here. Let me show you how to thread it and then you can try on a piece of cloth." I find a scrap of the worsted and fold it over. "You'll see! It's really not so difficult. I've found that fear often distorts our thinking."

She touches the curved lapels of her suit jacket and the pleats at the waist. "I could never sew this well. Never! And surely not well enough to support myself."

"You build up skill gradually. I wouldn't ask you to make something as complicated as your suit right off. Also, you needn't make outfits at the start; you could simply do alterations."

Her eyes are filling. "It's no use. It's too difficult for me."

Of course she has lost all confidence in herself. Of course she has lost courage. Night after night of sitting in the parlor and not being chosen has done this. And then having to go out into the streets and not being chosen out there, either. Still, I say, "Why not at least consider it, Charlotte? Don't decide right now."

Sullenly, she says nothing. After a while, she takes off the skirt and jacket and puts on her other clothing and leaves.

I go on sewing, the woman's defeatism riding my shoulders like penetrating cold. With it comes to mind Rousseau's idea that man was corrupted the moment he began to value what was best—good, better, best! We do it all the time, I realize, often unconsciously. How is philosophical anarchism ever going to be an equalizing force? How will it help women such as Charlotte? How will it eliminate poverty and the exploitation of those weaker than another? Eliminate disease and alcoholism and slow wits and a stratified, judgmental society?

Fear and doubt fill me. My hands become sweaty, and I have to stop sewing. Because Charlotte is older, because she is not as attractive as the other women here, she is not valued and so does not value herself. Can we ever change that way of thinking, Sasha?

Education, Emma! You are forgetting!

Education? Then perhaps, Sasha, we might begin with the men who frequent this brothel.

There's a knock on the door, and my mood lifts somewhat. Surely it's Charlotte, returning to say she has reconsidered.

But it's Madame Ristand, telling me that police officers are coming any minute to search the house. One of the girls has a client who told her they suspect that Emma Goldman is hiding here. I must leave at once.

Bundling up the unfinished suit, I tell Madame that I'll finish it elsewhere and get it to Charlotte soon.

She gestures, impatient. *Go. Go.*

Quickly I roll the electric cord around the footpad and tuck both under the machine's neck. I place the cover on top and snap its clasps shut.

Outside in the alley, dry snowflakes cover iced-over puddles. The machine pulls at my arm, not wanting this night either. The air is hard with cold, and Charlotte will be out in it tonight, her cloak held close. I'm sorry I wasn't able to finish the suit for her.

EAMON

I see how it will happen and am restless to go about the streets again. I walk up Broadway to the Broadway Theater, the Olympic, Niblo's Garden, and farther north, to Washington Square and Union Square, and then back down again. I walk up Eighth Avenue to where my grandfather lived. There are more saloons here and nickelodeons and music playing and rogues about, eyeing me, but I don't care. Come for me, I say to myself. Come for me and you will see. It is a poem and I say it and say it. *Come for me and you will see.* And they stay back and I just walk and think how he died here, my grandfather O'Keefe. In a horse car. The shot finding him like it wanted to, only it didn't, it was just there, from the rioting nearby, and he died and then my grandmother Agnes, from bad milk, my father said. And my father leaving the place for the west, and the railroad, in Massillon, Ohio. All that makes the bones, maybe, so I am not afraid here and walk like I belong, like I am one of them after all. Up Eighth Avenue I walk and back down to the riddle of streets at the bottom of the island, where she is, somewhere. I know I will find her. It is something I know.

EMMA

My eldest sister Lena and I embrace, but the first thing she says, one hand brushing at her eyes, is that I cannot stay with them. Nowhere in Rochester is safe. The police have been to their house twice already. "They may even be watching the house right now, Emma!" She is whispering.

I had come to the side door and was so relieved when Lena herself answered my quiet knocking—and not her husband who, though an exceedingly kind man, might have panicked, seeing me on his doorstep. Now she turns off the kitchen light, and we sit at the table with only the street light for illumination. She must have baked today. I can smell cinnamon.

"Did you make your good coffee cake today, Lena?" The scent brings back the time when Helena and I first entered our sister Lena's house after our long journey from Russia. The rooms redolent of coffee cake to welcome us to our new life.

She begins to say something, but it becomes a quiet sob. After a while she says she did it for Harry, the baking. Her son and my beloved nephew.

"He has been so . . . distraught over it all."

She gets up and from the icebox removes something, and then I realize she is heating kvass for me, a generous act so forgiving in nature that it shames me.

"He is better, Lena?" I ask, hoping it is so. This, too, haunts me—the boy's love for the president, his belief that the man was completely without self-interest. This past July we'd even argued the matter, in so far as one can argue with a ten-year-old, even a brilliant one such as Harry. "But Tante Emma! President McKinley *saved* the 'Cubansufferers,' and now he's helping the Philippine people. He'll take care of them now! He promises!"

The boy reads newspapers; he knows that his famous—or infamous—aunt is somehow involved. I fear that by now he wishes to disown me.

"Well, he isn't crying as much," Lena says. "But he's very quiet, very subdued."

"What have you told him?"

"That the accusations are false, of course, and that you had nothing to do with it."

"Does he believe you?"

"I don't know, Emma. This has hurt him so much. I can't keep the newspaper from him. I tried, but that somehow made it worse. Also, he can read them for himself, on Main. He seems compelled, now, to read anything having to do with the matter. It's the only thing that holds his attention these days, the only thing he wants. That's why I baked today. I was hoping to . . . oh . . . make everything seem normal again."

The soup boils, but Lena has both hands over her eyes and is sitting like one utterly fatigued. I remove the kettle and find two bowls. The good, sweet and sour soup carries its warmth down through me. "May I talk with him, Lena?"

"With Harry? But he's asleep!"

"Only for a minute. I want to see him, tell him myself—"

"No. I don't think you should, Emma. It's so hard for him when he's awake and . . . seeing you, suddenly like that . . . he may start crying again, or worse. You can't imagine how hysterical he became after the shooting. I never understood his adulation of the president, yet I indulged him, not thinking that it could be other than harmless. But when the president was shot and then those bulletins gave everyone false hope . . ."

She is not accusing me—Lena never would—yet my insides seem to twist themselves together at her words, and glimpses of some terrible causality, some monumental failure, come in flashes. The need to excoriate myself is equally terrible. *The great Emma Goldman!* Of course I cannot stay here!—quite apart from anything having to do with police searches.

It shames me to the depths, but I must say it: "Lena, forgive me, dearest. I will not wake Harry. I will leave in the morning, very early; no one in the house need know I was ever here, but . . . may I ask you for a loan, Lena? Fifty dollars?"

She says nothing at first. Then, "So much, Emma?"

"I must hire a lawyer."

"I thought . . . we read that all charges against you were dropped. Is that not true?"

Now my face, so cold before, feels scalded. "It is not for me, Lena, but for him, the assailant. The trial was a travesty, a miscarriage of justice. A good lawyer might at least get him a new trial. There's a week yet before his execution."

"You must be feverish, Emma. Are you ill again?"

"Lena, no, I'm not! The boy's trial was unjust! His lawyers defended only themselves."

"Boy? Isn't he older? More like, what did it say? Twenty-eight? We read—"

"It was just a manner of speaking, Lena. I have been trying, and failing, to create a defense fund. I came here tonight because, yes, I need a place, but I also see that it will cause you too much trouble, Lena. Then I thought that you, who are so kind and loving, always, must be as shocked as I am at the handling of the case and might want to see him have justice, at least."

In the semidark of the kitchen, Lena doesn't look at me as she says, "He will never agree to it."

"But must you tell him? Can't you say it's for me alone?"

"You are asking me to lie to him, Emma? My husband?"

"Then tell him the truth. He's a good man. He will understand. May I talk to him? Is he in his study?"

After some time, Lena says, "He is asleep, too, by now."

It is possible that she is not lying to me.

That night I sleep in the parlor and leave before anyone awakens. In the kitchen there's a small hamper of food on the table and alongside it, eight dollars. I take my machine, valise, and the hamper of food and leave by the side door. The morning is cold, with frost on the lawns making each blade of grass stiff and gray. There is nowhere to go but the station.

LEON

My throat closes and I cannot speak. My brother-in-law Frank's eye twitches, like a fly is trying to settle there. He smiles as he does even when he doesn't mean to. He can't help it. My right shoulder jerks, every so often, and I can't help that. It began a while ago and wakes me at night and then I cannot sleep. Now I put my left hand over the place to make it stop. Waldeck is looking at it jumping like that. I ask how Celia is, in her new home. Frank smiles. His eyelid twitches. "Good," he says. His face reddens, probably because he said *good.*

"Do you two come alone?" I ask Waldeck. "Is Father not here with you?"

"He is home."

"He didn't want to come?"

Waldeck glances at the warden. "They told him he wasn't wanted here."

"They didn't want him to come?"

"No, you, brother. They said *you* did not want him."

"But no one said anything to me! No one asked me!"

"Then they made it up. That is how it is with them."

"He can still come, Waldeck. I'll petition the superintendent and—"

"It's too late."

"What do you mean?"

"There's no time, dammit! This is the last night."

Frank smiles. "We wait here for three days, Leon. Finally they say we can come see you because it is the last night."

"You were here all that time?"

Waldeck nods. He is picking at a callus on the palm of his right hand. I turn to the warden, for we are in his office, and now I understand why. *The last night.*

"It's true, Czolgosz," the warden says. "This is your last night."

"Can they be there?"

"Where?"

"In that room."

"No. There'll be witnesses, but not your family."

"Why not!" Waldeck shouts.

"We got a rule is why."

"A rule? A goddam *rule?* How the hell do we know what you're going to do to him?"

"Settle down, Mr. Czolgosz, or your visit is over."

Frank pulls at Waldeck's jacket. "For Leon," he says, "be quiet, Waldeck."

Frank says my name the way they do at home. Le-*on.*

But Waldeck wants to fight. "You make us wait three days! You don't let him see his father! What kind of people are you?"

"Sit, brother. You are here. It's to the good. Sit down and we can talk."

I feel far away from Waldeck's anger. I feel very calm. The thing is so large it makes everything else small. I know they have been drinking, and that is how they passed the time. Lodging above a saloon and sitting all day at a table, eating from the food on the bar, the pickled eggs and pigs' feet, the sausages and head cheese and crackers. And now Waldeck is just Waldeck, needing to fight.

"Tell me about Father, at least," I say. "How is he, Waldeck?"

"How he is, I will tell you! They throw mud and stones at him in the street. He can't go to work. She has to clean his jacket all the time and she curses you. He goes out and what?—more mud. Even when he goes to church. One time there was a bunch of them throwing mud, and he fought them and beat one pretty bad. The police came and arrested him, but the judge let him go. The judge said he should have whipped the bunch. So that is how it is now."

"They are living in town again?"

"Ja. You know how it is. He has to move all the time. Better they should stay out at the farm."

"I'm sorry, Waldeck," I say, and he nods, picking at that callus. I ask the warden if they might have some beer. I say I wish to offer my guests a small drink.

"We don't do that here."

My fingers are so white now. White and puffy. "Waldeck," I say, "at the Buffalo police station, they took my valise. Maybe you could go ask for it. There are two pictures inside. One is for you and one for Victoria. Ask them for it. It's yours now, tell them."

"We called the station. They said they had nothing of yours."

"They are lying. They have a valise. Tell them I told you."

"Leon," Frank says, smiling, "you don't have to take this all by yourself. Tell them about the others, the bastards, and how you drew the short straw."

The words mean nothing to me and seem a waste of this time. "Waldeck, tell Father I am sorry I could not see him one last time."

In Polish, Waldeck says, "You have to tell them who you were in with. They shouldn't get off."

My shoulder jumps.

"They don't care about you, brother. Did anybody offer to help you? No! That's how they all are. Oh, I figured it out long ago. Talk and more talk and fancy ideas, but when it comes down to standing up for somebody—no." Waldeck calls them evil names in Polish. The warden tells him to speak English, so he repeats it in English. The warden says he agrees. Then he says Waldeck and Frank have to go.

Why? Will it be tonight? In a short while? But this, too, seems like a small matter.

"Good-bye, brother," I say to Waldeck and then ask the warden if we can shake hands. The warden nods, and we do. And then I shake my brother-in-law's hand. Waldeck walks out of the room first and doesn't look back. By the clock on the wall it is quarter past nine. I thought it must be later and say so.

"That's the time, all right. You want a priest?"

"A Polish one."

"I don't know. It's late."

"Just nine."

"You do some hard thinking, then, you hear me? I'm not going through the trouble of it all for nothing. We want to know who-all you were involved with before the shooting."

I tell him I will think and try to remember it all.

Two guards take me back to the cell. They talk loud, arguing about who has the first shift guarding my cell. This wakes Bailey.

"Had some visitors, hey boy? Y'know what that means, don't ya? Well, I'm gonna miss you, but maybe the next fellow will at least open his yap once in a while."

"You better shut yours," one of the guards says, "or we'll be taking you first, ya bag o' wind."

I pretend to sleep, but at the edge of it pull back, because this is the last night.

They send an Irishman. I don't want the Irish priest and say so.

The warden says the priest comes to see me so I have to talk to him. I say no. "He is not a Polish priest. I want a Polish priest."

"Well you can't have one, Czolgosz, and that's that. You rather rot in hell, that's your choice."

It seems crazy to me, too, but still I want a Polish one and tell the warden so. He says I can't. He says it has to be in English. "Now talk to the father here, dammit."

"No," I say in Polish.

The warden apologizes to the father. The father makes a little Sign of the Cross and leaves with the warden.

Bailey is hanging on his bar. "What's a matter, Czolgosz, you think God's Polish? You know what? You're in for a grand surprise, lad. He ain't nothin' is what."

The reporters in the corridor scribble. They ask each other what the word I said means. It will be in the newspapers, maybe, about the Polish priest.

I wonder where they put the assassins, in Hell.

"They say you're getting lots a telegrams an' letters, boy. Know what they do with 'em? Burn 'em out in the yard. Have a big fire. Every night they make a fire out there. One thing I wanted t'ask. How come you wash yer face and comb yer hair everyday like some dandy? You must be vain, boy, with that head o' hair . . ."

Maybe Victoria. Maybe even Emma. Words fluttering upward, birds on fire.

"Look at 'im. Head in his hands. Natural for us criminals to look regretful, ain't it, boys? But it's for ourselves, is what. He sure is a dandy, though. Pressin' wrinkles outa his pants. Write about that, why don't ya? If I was one of youse, I'd surely write about that. How about a little compensation for the idea, boys? Some tobacco might be just the thing. I might even share it with the dandy over there. . . ."

On the trolley, her arm from elbow to wrist, and mine right there, elbow to wrist, and only three layers of cloth between.

"Sometimes he holds that Bible they let him have. Is he readin' or foolin'? I say foolin' 'cause I don't see no page turnin'. Either that or gettin' loony as they come. They get like that in here when they don't talk. I seen it before. Or maybe he thinks he's too damn good to talk to the likes o' me. Well, I only killed in self-defense. I didn't go killin' no president of the United States because o' some woman an' you can put that in your stories, too, if you want . . ."

She looks just like a girl. I couldn't get over it. Those curls. The pink cheeks and blue eyes. A girl. A young girl. I nearly couldn't believe it. *Emma Goldman.*

"And at least I got the civility to talk t' folks when they address me an' you know what else? He's greedy, to boot. You should see the fellow eat! Hog in a trough. Now there he goes, see that? Gettin' religion again. Czolgosz! You readin' over there or just foolin'? These boys need to know. Tell 'em an' we'll split the t'baccy, I swear . . ."

The commandment to love one another is the most confusing thing in the Bible. *Love one another as the Father loves you. Beloved, let us love one another for love is from God . . . He who does not love does not know God for God is love.*

And how did He show this love?

By making us. By sending His only Son to die for us.

So that sin might be forgiven.

The sin of Adam and Eve.

But why, if sin was forgiven and mankind washed clean, why do we continue to sin? Why do I go and kill someone? And why be unable to forgive one another?

As I could not when my stepmother burned my tablets and studies and the letters from Lucy. The priest in the confessional asked if the heart sent me or the head, and when I could not speak, he said he could not absolve me unless I was truly repentant and desired to make amends for such anger and hatred against a loved one. He asked me if I remembered the words, *Father, forgive them, for they know not what they do.*

I said I did.

And did I remember the words about turning one's cheek?

Ja.

The two greatest commandments? Love God with all your heart and soul and love your neighbor as yourself?

Ja.

I waited for the absolution, but he said, "Others are waiting. Go. Come back later when you can forgive."

I knelt in a pew afterward as if saying my penance, but I was thinking how odd it is, the priest not forgiving me just as I could not forgive my stepmother, yet the priest telling me I must forgive.

"Boy, y'look like a chicken in there, plumped up an' brooding. Ain't healthful for a man, I'm warnin' ye."

And why, if He allowed Abraham's son Isaac to live, did He let His own Son die?

And nobody better, afterward.

Look at him, my stepmother says. The drupe! Mice use his papers for a toilet. Why shouldn't I throw out?

EAMON

Street lad. One foot wrapped in a piece of carpeting, the other in something like a boot. I gave him coins once, now here he is again. Sharp eyes, for a small lad. Comes back like a cat. Says he is fourteen years of age, but that cannot be true. Nine, maybe, or ten. This city is full of his type, creatures of these streets, wily and cruel and moving in packs, but this one not—why? Says he is working for a Frenchman who dyes ostrich feathers and cleans furniture and sells feathers to millinery houses. Once he worked for a grocer, once for a florist, and once for a man who drew letters on windows. Or so he says, anyway. He looks like a milk-glass dish. Bluish, with a glaze over it. Says he lives in back rooms of places where he works. Thinking of him makes me not think of her so much, and it is a relief of sorts. How does he find me, no matter what street I'm on? Does he follow?—and the Frenchman just a story? Do they have homes, these lads, yet blow about the streets like dust? His eyes are green, not clear but muddied. Says his folks are gone. Lost 'em when they first come here, he says. In the immigration hall, one minute she was holding his hand, his mother, the next he's running to a window all light and then she's gone. He supposes someone took him somewhere and sometime later he became Brendan but he thinks that wasn't his name. Believes I'm a copper on the lookout and wants to help. It was shinin', he says. Shinin' an' shinin' an' so bright he just had to run an' see.

Sounds like a bull to me. Words to cover the emptiness.

One day I have a coat for him. He looks at it a long while but can't take it, he says. The lads won't let him alone. T'will be gone within the hour. I tell him to wear it for now, anyway, and that is how it goes. I take the coat when he leaves and give it to him when he comes. It is a good coat of wool, purchased at Devlin Clothiers, on Broadway. It is where my grandfather John Eamon O'Keefe worked as a tailor. I put a few coins in the pocket, each time, and hear the Major saying, *They feeding you well enough in here, son*? It is like he told me what to do about the coat, and to pick that one, the burnt umber one that looks like bushes in the fall. I tell the lad who I am looking for and he says he will keep an eye out, too, and I believe he will, for his eyes are the kind that do.

I buy him a pair of boots. Have to have them made special by a cobbler. The carpet-wrapped foot is four inches shorter than the other, and crooked. When he goes off in his new boots, I take the coat back to my boarding house on Market Street. I shake it out and brush it, like I did for the Major. Then I hang it up and it is ready for the next day.

LEON

"Utek?"

In the shadows he sits. Spotted Calf Utek. Burnt Pan Utek. His names—because of the birthmark across the left side of his face, the edges dark blue, the rest a burnt red.

Ja, Leon. I am here. You know me!

The last night and Utek here. Utek is bad luck, it is said, and no one will hire him for anything except to sit with the dying. *A beetle, Le-on, that is what I am, I watch with you for death. She's not so bad, death. You want words, Le-on? I give you some words. You want quiet? You can have quiet. You want my hand in yours? You can have, if you want, Le-on. Whatever you want now, you can have. I am here! You talk about society—hoo! A great big word, no? If I walk in the street can I see it? No! Just people, Le-on. This one and that one and that one. Look, Le-on, my hand. Here. Take it. Hold on to it. That is all there is. There is no society, no such big fish like that at all. In the end, just this.*

He grasps my hand in his white one, and I am crying without any effort, tears just there, and it is Abraham Isaak's hand in mine. *I'm sorry, Mr. Nieman, we're a poor group. There's little money to fund comrades except those in the greatest need. Alexander Berkman, for one. We are trying to get his sentence commuted.*

You publish a paper. I will help you distribute it if you tell me the addresses.

You don't know the city.

I can learn it.

In any case we use volunteers. Comrade, let me give you something to eat, anyway, before you go.

I do not want food, thank you.

Then Emma is saying, *All beauty is a good, like love. Neither should be hoarded, restricted, or curtailed in any way. Human beings are not commodities, Mr. Nieman!*

Son? I hear, waking. *Son?*

Father. They have allowed him to come here after all.

But the figure seated on a dining room chair in the cell is not my father; it is a priest wearing the purple stole of the confessional. In Polish he tells me his name and then begins the Latin prayers. In Polish I respond. I tell him I have sinned against the Fifth Commandment and I am sorry for that. It did no good for anyone. In another way I have sinned against that same commandment by hating my stepmother and wishing her death. I don't know if I am sorry for that or not. Perhaps now I am. That is all I wish to say except that I am sorry they would not let my father come here now.

He prays in Latin and then makes the Sign of the Cross over me. I hear the Latin word *absolve*. His hand rests on my shoulder a moment. I see that he is an old man, his face creased and gray, the hair unruly as if he'd been lying down before being called here and then he not taking the time to comb it properly. He says in Polish, that he is not giving me a penance to do. Tomorrow's will be enough.

The guard lets him out, and I am sorry that he goes so soon.

In the cell across the corridor, Bailey is snoring. After a while, my own death guard, who is seated alongside the door to Bailey's cell but facing mine, joins him in that happy pursuit. I lie back on my cot but do not wish to sleep again if that is what it was: hearing voices, words, seeing faces, bits of this and that, and feelings as riled as before. I wish I could feel that lightness that sometimes comes after you confess, but maybe cannot, this time, because time is burning away to the end of its wick, and I can't be sure there will be a new start. It is like walking up to a closed door and knowing you have to go through it. Such a small thing my life has been. I wish I could die in a field. In June. Wind blowing through field grasses, and the scent of clover in the air. And birds fussing at each other and chasing away crows. The seed tassels purple, on some of the bending field grasses. Why did I not think of this sooner, with that gun of mine?

But who could pull the trigger on oneself in a field in June?

Then another guard opens the cell door, and I think that maybe my father is here after all. The thought is stronger when I see that he is taking me to the warden's office. But except for the warden and the guard bringing me there, the room is empty.

"Well, you got your priest," the warden says.

"I thank you."

"I want more than that."

I am seated before his desk. He is sitting to one side of it. I am surprised by the time: 2:15. The windows are dark. So. Still night although morning. I will be dead soon; what does it matter what I say.

Tell them, Leon! Make it up. Say anything. Get back at them. They used you.

Waldeck's voice.

"What do you want to tell me?" the warden says.

"Nothing."

"Nothing?"

"I did it. I'm sorry."

"Czolgosz. We had an agreement, remember?"

"You lied to my father."

"Czolgosz, you said you'd reconsider and I believed you, dammit. I never should have let that priest in first. Too damn tired is the problem."

"You lied to my brother. There was a valise. Did the police steal it? Did they give it to the reporters?"

He rolls his chair toward me, slams it into my legs and slaps my face. Then he kicks his chair away, pulls me up out of mine, and heaves me down on the floor. My head hits something.

"If today wasn't the day, I'd beat you raw. You got one hour. If you come to your senses, we'll give you sausage and eggs. Otherwise, you get shit."

The guard pushes me into the cell. I see double. My body shimmers in spasms.

"Morning!" Bailey calls. "So how'd ya sleep?"

There is no breakfast of sausage and eggs. A guard brings me a pair of dark flannel trousers and a pair of brogans. "Put these on," he says.

"Hoo, boy!" Bailey says. "Now you can play the dandy to yer heart's content."

The warden comes down the corridor, and Bailey retreats to the back of his cell.

"I want to make a statement," I tell the warden.

"That's fine, but you're too late for anything to eat."

"Before everyone I want to make it."

"Well, you can't. You can tell me, but that's all."

"Then I'm not going to say it."

"Czolgosz, you're driving me crazy. I'll be so damn glad to see the last of you."

As two guards link arms in mine, I have time to touch the cot, the thin blanket, and then we are walking in a kind of procession—two other guards falling in step behind, and the warden there, too—to the iron door just a few feet away. Someone opens it, and we enter a room, and there is the chair, a wooden chair with a high back, armrests, and leather straps. It will be over in a minute. Light will enter me and perhaps there will be something afterward.

The fires of purgatory, maybe.

I sit down in the chair and immediately two of the guards begin fastening straps around my chest, arms, and legs. There are people seated in the room, but they are quiet, and I don't know who they are. I look out at them, but they are in shadow. My stomach churns, but my shoulder does not jump, which is to the good. Before they fasten the strap around my jaw, I say I did it for the people. I say I am sorry I could not see my father. No one says anything to me. Two men stand close, watching everything, while the guards work. The warden is there, his hands behind his back. No one steps away from me. I find this strange. I expected everyone to be farther away when they did it. The guards work fast, tightening and buckling, and then another man fastens something to my head. It feels cold there. He does the same to my leg. So that is why the pant leg had a slit in it. It is very quiet in the room. No one tells anyone what to do. They just do it. I wonder how many times a day they do it. How many times a week. Maybe in the beginning it bothered them, but now—no. Like in a slaughterhouse. A rubber cap is pulled down over my eyes. I close my eyes in this dark and draw in a long breath.

DAVIS

My job title is state electrician, and I've been at this job since right when they started this method of execution eleven years ago. Well, it was a new field—still is, in a way—and I was a young man back then and curious as anything and just made a point of learning all I could about it. First I heard of these electrical executions was when Thomas Edison took out a patent. He had some of his boys working on the idea, and he came around to the opinion that it would be more humane than hanging. Which I agree with. Hanging can take a couple of minutes, sometimes, this here is fast if you do it right. That's not to say it was always done right. In the first year or two there were all kinds of problems. It's supposed to cause immediate death, but if the electrician don't know what he's doing, you can burn a conscious prisoner to death instead. I saw this happen with animals. There was a time back in the beginning when Brown, one of Edison's boys, went around towns, demonstrating how it all worked. He was using animals, large ones, small ones, cows, goats, horses, dogs, well, it didn't always work right, to say the least, and was a mess to behold. But they finally got it fixed and the protocol set and by that time, I was already working for the state, and they wanted me to run operations here. That was something of an honor because here was the first place in the country to use electrical executions. Well, they're called electrocutions now. So I said all right. I was a young know-it-all in those days, but when you're like that you make mistakes, and I have to say I made a lot. William Kemmler was the first I did here, back in 1890, and the first jolt failed to stop his heart. Problem was, I couldn't do a second jolt right away. Had to gear up the generator first. Then the next 2000 volts just burst his blood vessels and he was bleeding all over. The whole process took eight minutes. I'm not proud of that. George Westinghouse, he was a big rival of Edison's, said we should have used an axe instead. Well, he was right. That was a real mess. So now, each time we fasten the electrodes, and I set the currents, I make damn sure we're getting it right. The murderers don't deserve it, but I have my pride. That's why I always check how the current is working by hooking up the twenty-two incandescent lamps and doing a test first.

So. Here we are again, and this time I have an assassin, no less. Well, a murderer is a murderer, no matter if they kill a prince or a pauper is the way I figure it. Same black heart. The guards get him strapped in, and I have to give the fellow credit. He's calm as hell. They're not always like that. Sometimes they go berserk on you, and it just jeopardizes the whole process. But this Czolgosz fellow, he's sitting there like he's on a train going somewhere. Well, he is. Straight to hell. My assistant affixes the sponges wet in salt water, so the flesh don't burn, and then fixes the electrodes without a problem, and I go back into my room behind the chair. There's no door to it, so I can see Warden Mead, and I keep an eye on him. When he raises his right arm, I push the lever. The first electromotive force is set at 1800 volts, and I hold it there for seven seconds. I don't have to see to know what is happening. The assassin's body will jump up against the restraining straps like it was filled suddenly with a blast of air. Then I reduce the voltage to 300 and hold it for twenty-three seconds. Then it's up to 1800 for four, then 300 for twenty-six, and another 1800 for five. I come out into the death chamber and wait for the two doctors to pronounce him dead—or not. They say he is, and my job is done.

It took just over a minute and went as smoothly as possible. You couldn't ask for anything better.

"Good work," Warden Mead says real quiet. He's relieved, too. A score of reporters are here and the prison superintendent and someone even making a movie of it— Well, they're not going to find one single thing to criticize today, and that's for sure.

E.G. SMITH
(EMMA)

Czolgosz is striding toward me, his right hand outstretched, and I, on a platform, watching him approach nearer and nearer until he is right there before me, his forehead burnt and raw, his eyes hollowed out, empty of any fluid, and yet he is able to walk straight toward me. I can't move or speak. The crowded hall is silent. He extends his blistered right hand toward me. The smell of burnt flesh makes me scream.

"Emma!" I hear. "*Emma!*" Dan's voice finally wakens me. "You were dreaming again. It's only a dream!"

"The same one!"

He sits at the edge of my cot and takes my hand. He's young, too young, and I'm old.

"Yegor has left already?" I say. It's strange, asking such a prosaic question while still in the throes of terror from the dream. Both my brother Yegor and his friend Dan are university students, Yegor in medicine. Seeing one of Yegor's textbooks on our table often causes pinpricks of regret and doubt. Now it's intensified. I am nothing but self-recrimination and pain these days.

"It's Tuesday," Dan says. "He has that early class, remember?"

"You should go, Dan."

"But I don't have one until ten. Come, I have your breakfast ready. A nice smoked fish, coffee, and a warm roll. Eat and you'll feel better, Emma."

"I mean you should leave here. I will fail you, too, one day."

He is a beautiful boy, the clear youthful skin, the earnest steady eyes that hold only foolish love for me. I don't deserve it, of course. I cannot reciprocate, of course, and yet I indulge him—and myself. What can he find in me to love? Beauty?—no, I am thirty-two years of age to his twenty and worn as an old frock. Courage?—that's laughable. *Courage.* How courageous of me not to have attended Czolgosz's trial! How courageous not to have traveled to Auburn to try to speak there against the execution! How courageous to have fled the hall here in New York when people began hissing and shouting *murderess*. And how courageous to be rescued by two university students with whom I now share this flat on Second Avenue. And, oh, how very courageous of me to have purchased, on the installment plan, a square oak table and four chairs for us.

"I can't leave you, Emma. I will never leave you."

The language of dime novels—but spoken so sincerely I don't doubt its veracity, the poor boy. Blinded by the great Emma's greatness.

Acht, Emma. Get up. You must finish that gown for Mrs. Grinnel today. With its full bodice and drooping waistband, it will make her look like a swaybacked old horse. Still, it's what she wants . . . and what she shall have.

But I don't get up because Dan has lain down alongside me. It's moving, such tender concern—and innocence.

And far away.

LUCY

I was not at the trial, no. But I read about it, of course. It was not just. Jurors were chosen for their antagonistic attitudes. The defense attorneys were hardly interested in their client. Leon had been tried earlier by the press and found guilty. By the people and found guilty. Forms observed but the forms empty. I telephoned legislators in Washington, but they told me there was nothing they could do.

I was angry, of course, but anger is sometimes diversionary, particularly when you know that you yourself are not blameless.

Mr. Darwin's thesis may be applicable here. We instinctively veer away from perceived weakness. It's the body reacting as much as the spirit. The organism knowing what is good for its survival, individual and collective.

I did search for Leon after a lapse of twelve or thirteen years. Curiosity? Nostalgia? Loneliness? My advancing age? Or even, possibly, something more. You might think that in my profession there'd be ample opportunity to form some meaningful alliance, and no need to haunt my past. But there it is. I did. And I did find him living on a small farm not far from Cleveland, a shabby-looking place that seemed to be thwarting any human attempts to improve it. The barn roof needed new shingles. The house needed paint and repair. The pasture needed clearing of burdock, the barnyard of manure. When he came into the cold parlor, he smelled of smoke. His eyes seemed somewhat dull. Before, they were lively with wanting to know things, see things. Immediately, I began to pity him in that house.

"Leon," I said, "have you been ill? Is that why you didn't answer my letters?"

The words shocked him. "What letters?" he asked finally.

I explained that I had written to him for well over a year after I'd moved from my aunt and uncle's house. Well, *run away* the more accurate locution. I had wanted money to buy books, but my uncle wasn't willing to pay me for my work. I was family, he said. Did he pay his wife? —no. Nor did he want me to go to school. I was his niece, and they had taken me in like a daughter, so I shouldn't ask for more than my room and my food. Before leaving Natrona, I told Leon that I was making careful preparation for my escape and that I would write to him from Mrs. Heuvel's. I'd been hurt when he hadn't responded. I thought many things. I was not a scientist yet and didn't think carefully enough. My hurt feelings led me to believe that he hadn't wanted to write to me after all. That I was too bookish for him and that he'd found some other young woman more to his liking.

And so, the later need to know for sure what had happened. Had he *died*? Had he *married*?

Then, at that farm, he told me what I had never suspected: that his stepmother must have burned the letters. That's how she was. He said this flatly and with resignation and he apologized. We sat there a while in silence, both of us trying to take it in. Finally, I asked if he was working somewhere besides the farm.

He shook his head and then went into a brief history of his attempts to keep jobs. At the wire factory in Cleveland, he hadn't been being able to breathe well and so he lost that job and began seeking a cure from many doctors, most of them quacks, from his descriptions. And he coughed a lot. I feared tuberculosis. He said he was taking certain powders but was vague about these medications. I suspected that, given his detachment and poor color, that strychnine might be an ingredient. I warned him about going to quacks and said I'd loan him money for a real doctor, but I did not give him the names of good physicians I know in Philadelphia. I urged him to leave that farm, get away, finally, from that stepmother of his. "Try Detroit, Leon. Or Chicago. I'll loan you money."

His expression became more inward.

I was sorry I'd found him. What had I thought? That he'd be the Leon of 1887, and that now I was ready? What kind of scientific thinking is that? And I was sorry for what his life had become, but not sorry enough to entangle myself in it.

When he shot the president, I saw it as the act of a dying man. Horror filled me at my role in the deed. But what is there to be done except go on.

So. Here I am, in Iceland, with my little tools and specimen box. Below this cliff, light scatters over the blue-black sea. Wind holds the scent of snow. As I lean to carefully detach a piece of lichen from fissured basalt, the perfect name for my new soap just comes. *Black Pearl.*

E.G. SMITH
(EMMA)

They cut and measure, sketch, dissect, and weigh, those men of science, and what do they discover about Leon?

. . . the brain normal though heavier than average . . . No hemorrhages, no sclerotic patches, neoplasms, nor lesions . . . the heart eleven ounces . . . lungs: emphysematous, a few bands of pleuritic adhesions . . . stomach nearly empty . . . intestines normal, pancreas and liver dark but normal . . . evidence of healed genital chancres . . . blistered skin . . . desquamation . . . the only divergence from normality found in the hyperemia of all viscera, from the explosion of veins and arteries, but that, too, normal, under the circumstances . . . the man sane. Infected only by the disease, anarchy.

Infected. Disease. I throw the day's issue of the *World* to the floor.

After I had become infected with the tubercle bacillus, I learned that the bacillus is rod-shaped and only a few microns in length, yet a single dry bacillus on a speck of dust breathed in can lodge in the chest. Other cells futilely surround it, ingest it, grow large. The area thickens into a fibrous nodule, the center soon crumbling like old cheese as it becomes necrotic. The bacilli reproduce, nodules grow elsewhere, filled with noxious liquid that often exudes, leaving cavities in the area. *Consumption*, for it eventually consumes one, like worms. An image haunting me for weeks, and I conscious of breathing out these bacilli, conscious of the rim of moisture, from my lips, on a lunchroom coffee cup. Disinfectants and hot water are useless against the bacilli. Sunlight the only thing known to kill them. So I walked in sunlight. Bathed in it. Opened windows to it. The girl Ed had hired to help me hung bed linen in it, underclothing, my waists, skirts, dresses, suits, coats, and stockings, death in the folds and wrinkles, and I wondering how many I may have infected? And will she get it as well, this girl?

Now I am the carrier of anarchy as once I had been of tuberculosis.

I cannot bear these thoughts.

"Dan," I say. "I must walk. I need to go out."

"Emma, wait until it's darker, please."

"But I need air! I need to move!"

EAMON

I follow them. Ludlow to Delancy, then Allen, streets I know well by now. I believe it is her. A small woman on the arm of a young man. She looks like the one at the meeting where they shouted her down and she ran out. Two young men had been with her then. Only one is, now. The woman at the meeting also resembled the one in Worcester who gave me stew and pie, but they could not be the same, could they?

That her? the lad keeps saying. That the one? That yer wife, sir?

I don't say one way or the other and he tags after me, in the umber wool coat.

Allen to Broome.

The coat makes me think of *him* here, seeing this but not wanting it.

Broome to Ludlow.

They are going back. Should I say, "Are you Emma Goldman?" Or, no. Just look at her up close—and then know.

He is saying, "What you going to do, mister? Not shoot her."

"I don't know if it's her or not."

"I don't believe you need to shoot her, sir, no matter what she done. The coppers, you know, they'll get you, sir."

He pulls at my arm. I take out some coins and give them to him, for that is what I believe he is getting at. Losing the golden goose.

"I don't want that, sir. Thank you, but no. Not all this. How'll you live?"

"Don't mean to."

He shoves it back in my pocket.

Ludlow to Stanton.

It is warm for late October. A moon is rising. I pause to look at it, just clearing a building. It is on the orange side of yellow.

Then I need to go faster. They are far ahead now, with others in between. He pulls to slow me down and makes a pretense of limping. "These boots, sir, I ain't used to 'em. Go slower, sir."

I shove him off as you would a boat and begin running. It needs to be now, on the day of the assassin's death. There's a rightness to it that otherwise might not be.

They are nearly to Houston Street and its crowds, but that does not matter for I don't care to escape with my own life.

A small woman. Black shawl wrapped around her head, the points dangling down her back. I reach to grab one in order to spin her around and see her face, but I am yanked back and spun around myself and then am on the sidewalk, pinned there by boys, a slew of boys. They pluck at pockets like birds. One grabs the Iver Johnson and runs. Another hauls off my overcoat, and the biggest boy smacks my face. Others roll me toward a shop front, kicking as they do so though something tells me they could be rougher, meaner, the blows harder, and I remember how, just before I shoved the lad off and started running, he raised an arm and yelled some nonsense. Then he is there, too, throwing himself at the bigger ones, but they shove him down and pull off his wool coat before commencing to kick him as well. The woman hollers, clapping her hands, and they run, and then she is leaning down over me, and in the tunnel her shawl makes I see her face.

It is her.

They prop the two of us in a storefront, and she has her fingers on my wrist. "Your ribs," she says, "where they kicked you . . . are you feeling any sharp pains?"

I am, but the hell with her. I say, "You killed the Major."

"The Major?" she says. The young man grabs her arm and hauls her up, but she is opening her handbag, and there is a dollar bill floating down. I spit at it, but the lad, he grabs for it. Her last words are the name of some doctor nearby. I don't hear the name and don't care neither. Then the two are gone like you see something sinking back into the water—there in the moonlight a minute and then gone so that you do not trust your eyes and believe you have imagined it, and then I am seeing a body, in that water, and I close my eyes for it is mine, needing to slide down into the dark for good, and I think that is how it needs to be now, underwater, and the peace of it, and maybe I'll see him somewhere, too, in the place of the dead, anyway I'll look, that's for sure, and maybe there he'll be, *They feeding you well enough in here, son?* And it'll be like one of his jokes and we'll laugh and it'll be all right.

But the lad don't let go and I can't drift where I want, he yanking at me until I am back. "Why'd you do that?" I say. "Why the hell did you go and do that?" He is shivering bad without his coat. "Had to, sir. You would of gone and shot her, otherwise, and then what?"

In a while I understand what he is talking on about. "But why'd they turn on *you*, then?"

"It don't matter. That's just how they are."

He has me upright and we are shambling somewhere. Where?

"That doctor she said, sir. I know where he is."

"No," I say, and then we are dining on hot beef stew, the potatoes and carrots thick cut, like the meat, and tender, and it seems that this is where I have been heading all the while, this eatery, for I can hear the Major's words again, and I tell him, "Yes, sir," and I know now, for I can feel it in the riled up air, that he is somewhere nearby and not in the place of the dead at all.

E. G. SMITH
(EMMA)

As I predicted, there were odes to Czolgosz and lamentations in various papers, much of it—if not all—posturing, exercises in self-regard, and perhaps attempts at self-exoneration. But Hannes Most repudiated Czolgosz's act; so did Sasha, to my dismay. I can't get over this—Sasha!—nor do I understand his reasoning that it wasn't a true *Tat* at all, but the act of a twisted individual. What has happened to my Sasha in prison?

These thoughts have been preoccupying me for days while I sew, and they are with me again tonight. Czolgosz acted for the people—this I fully believe. I lean back from my machine and close my eyes. They sting with fatigue, and my back and hip are aching. I shouldn't be sewing so late at night, with my poor eyesight, but I must finish this dress by tomorrow; the puffed, princess-fashion sleeves have yet be attached.

It should be possible. I set the foot of the needle upon the fabric and begin again, but suddenly, out in the hallway, someone is shouting in Yiddish. "Emma Goldman! *Help* me, please!"

"The fire escape, Emma," Dan whispers. He pushes his chair back from the table, where he'd been studying, and motions toward the window.

The man at the door is bellowing even louder now. "You must help me! It is my wife! Please! You are here, I know this! I have heard you are here. Open your door to me, please. Do not allow her to die."

"Emma, it's a trick," Dan says. "Let's go, quickly!"

He has opened the window. I am still at my machine. Again comes the forceful beating at the door. Now everyone in the building will know that E. G. Smith is really Emma Goldman, if they don't know it already. I whisper to Dan that detectives are capable of breaking in doors and need not stand outside, begging, and that we must open the door to quiet the man.

"It may not be detectives at all, but somebody wanting to kill you. Remember last night? They were following us. Get your cloak and shawl! Let's go!"

When questioners asked Socrates if he wasn't ashamed of a life that might bring him an untimely death, he said that a man who's worth anything shouldn't always be trying to figure out what will do him in or not but should only consider whether what he's doing is right or wrong. It was Sasha who showed me this passage. I go to our coat rack, hesitate, and then open the door instead. A man stands there, one man, his mouth quivering, his eyes watery and reddened.

"I am not Emma Goldman," I tell him. "Why do you think that?"

"Everybody knows this! You are nurse! You are Emma Goldman, and I beg you to help me. My wife is dying. I have hired a cab. Hurry, please. You must come with me."

Dan's expression, now, is nearly as distraught as the man's. He's shaking his head and mouthing the words *a trap*.

"Stay here," I tell Dan. "Let Yegor know. I'll be all right."

Closing his eyes, he grimaces. "I should go with you."

"No, no, it's better you don't." I ask the man where he lives and learn that it's a few blocks away. "You see?" I say to Dan. "Tell Yegor I'll be at that address."

Dan unhappily gives in, and then the man and I are in the horse cab he has somehow hired, his face bunched and twisted, the smell of whiskey and sweat pungent. His mouth wavers with the need to cry. He is on the verge of some full-blown panic, and so I encourage him to talk, and he does, in a blend of Polish and Yiddish. His wife Michaela is giving birth but cannot. She is suffering. This is their first child. His wife was named after St. Michael who stabbed Satan with a spear. It was a mistake, coming to America. It is a hard country. Nothing good, everything bad, no work, all bad luck, and now she will die, and then he will die, too. Well, and why not? In the Old Country they were chased out of the village because of the marriage, nobody wanting them, everybody giving the evil eye and so, now, this bad luck, this death.

His sobbing verges on hysteria.

"Stop it," I say. "You've been drinking. Everything just seems hopeless."

"It's no use! How will we feed a child if I do not find work? Maybe the Nameless One is against us, too."

"What is your name?"

He turns to stare at me.

"My name? My name! It is Yakov Bukowsky."

Yakov.

On Oliver Street he manages to pay the driver, and at a tenement we climb outer steps off a side yard filled with piles of broken bricks. I am shivering. If it is a trap, I will soon know. An image comes of a small room with several men, revolvers drawn. A shudder runs through me, but could this man, this supposed Yakov, be such a good actor, then? In a third-story hallway, he opens a door. There is no sound from the room. I close my eyes. When I open them, I see a woman lying on a small bed. Strands of wet hair that might be flaxen, but now are darkened with sweat, stick to her forehead, neck and shoulders.

My fear immediately becomes specific and focused—
she has become too weak! I take a small jar of honey and a
clean spoon from my case and immediately feed a spoonful to the woman and then help her sit up and drink some
water. I order Yakov to massage her lower back.

He won't approach the bed but stares at his wife, his
fist pushing against his mouth.

"*Yakov*," I say, "get me a blanket then, clean if possible,
also some cloth, and heat a pan of water to boiling."

He points to the blanket on the bed. I understand. It
must be their only one. The woman, Michaela, weakly gestures toward a steamer trunk. Yakov is sobbing again.

"Yakov," Michaela says in Polish, "I am still here. It is
all right. Do what she tells you. Please!"

He manages to heat a pan of water, and when it is scalding hot, I scrub with soap and the antiseptic I brought
and order more water heated. Contractions have reached
a plateau. I search for the baby's heart, find no heartbeat,
search again—breath held—and then hear some distant,
small bumping. I smile at the woman and nod. With my
hand, I search, reaching the child's downward head. Good!
But how is it positioned? My fingers seek the raised line on
the baby's head, which will orient me. I come to a ridge,
but it leads, I'm sure of it, to the posterior fontanel. Bad
luck. The baby will have to be repositioned, if possible. My
heartbeat accelerates, but I speak as quietly and calmly as
possible to the woman.

When Yakov sees me trying to reposition his wife, he
goes to a wall and begins banging his head against it. "The
trunk, Yakov," Michaela says. "In the trunk is the cloth."

This makes him stop. He opens the trunk and offers
me a white tablecloth, its borders worked with red threads
making a stylized flame pattern. Their Shabbat cloth, I
realize. Yakov is crying again.

An hour later the baby lies positioned face upward in
the birth canal, and the woman is leaning, again, against

propped pillows, her eyes closed, her breath coming in snorts or garbled words in several languages, sometimes bits of prayer, names, even oaths. I feed her honey and water, but she seems somewhere deep inside that birth, or slide into death. Time passes, measured more by the woman's increasing moon paleness and the baby's heart deceleration. I take out a pair of scissors, Yakov wailing now, and at a height of a contraction, I snip. The baby's head appears, mucus rattling at its nose and mouth. I suction and then nod to the woman, yes, yes, all right, and rock from side to side with her, as a tiny wet shoulder emerges, then the other. In a moment, there it is—a girl.

"Yakov, she is perfect! Look!"

"Your name," he shouts. "It will be hers! *Emma!*"

I wrap the infant in the Shabbat cloth and give her to the woman, then wait for the placenta. Finally, I staunch, cleanse, suture, then spend several minutes observing. When I've finished, Yakov tries to give me coins held in both hands.

"Give me only twenty-five cents," I tell him.

He kneels to offer one of the coins.

"Yakov, get up please. Your wife and baby need you now."

In a lunchroom I take my chances that I won't be recognized. My skirt and waist are bloodied, but these are hidden under my cloak, and no one so much as glanced in my direction when I entered. From a young waitress I order coffee and a roll and then sit in a stupor of fatigue, looking out at the morning, still gray and dull. It reminds me of when I was a practicing nurse, sipping coffee all night in some sickroom. For hours, it sometimes seemed, daylight would come on grudgingly, the light beyond the window remaining tenuous for such a long time. I'd look from my patient to the window, and wonder if it would ever come. But of course, finally, there it would be—the full, clear, light of morning.

An apt metaphor, Sasha dear, no?

But metaphors are one thing and this world another.

The young waitress places my order before me and seems to want to linger, but finally doesn't. Fatigue or no, despair or no, I eat the roll quickly. It's fresh, hot, and dripping with butter. The coffee, too, is excellent. Here she is again, my waitress, with more coffee. "Excuse me, ma'am," she whispers, leaning close. "But are you . . . Emma Goldman? You resemble her very much."

"I've been told that quite often."

My mother heard her speak at the big Union Square rally in 1893. She still talks about it."

"And what does she say, your mother?"

"That Emma Goldman kept her from giving up. The way she spoke at that rally. My brother and I were little then, and our mother . . . she was all we had. I've always wanted to meet Emma Goldman and thank her."

Her eyes are welling up; her fair skin flushes with emotion. After a moment I say, "You just have, my dear, and now allow me to thank *you*."

Biting her lower lip, she stares a while before saying, too loudly, "You must have more to eat than just a roll. My brother will make you pancakes. I'll get you some sausages too—and eggs! Wait, please. You must have breakfast!"

A chill of suspicion rushes over me, but then I tell myself, No! If you think that way, it's all over for sure. So I wait, and while waiting, find paper and pencil in my case and jot down some notes about mornings and metaphors. And soon plates of hot food begin arriving, one after another, filling the entire table.

EAMON

The 1:10 from Akron slides to its stop at the Canton depot, and people clamber off in the usual way, as if scared the cars might suddenly fling themselves away again without warning. There is no one here to meet us and no rush, so we wait for the eager ones to pass first. The lad is holding his cloth cap tight as anything. It looks to be a fine day outside, the sky so blue a picture of peacocks comes to mind. I have seen peacocks at a farm once, and am thinking I will take the lad there to see them. Soon we are out on the platform and that blue hangs over us like a sea. Maybe there is too much for the lad. He is shivering like a horse about to bolt so I keep a good grip on his arm. On our trip west I have told him all about the stable and how there will be cats there, not the starved wild creatures of the alleys, but fat shiny things used to strutting between the horses' legs and everyone else's with no by-your-leave-please. I have told him there will be four horses, two for the carriage, one for pleasure riding, and a pony for children who visit. He already knows where the combs and brushes go and the bridles and saddles and harness and water pails. He knows the horses' names and their breeds and colorations. On the journey out, we had a good amount of time for talk. I have told him about the different sounds horses make when they're hungry or lonely or mad about something. And I have told him where the pitchforks go and the shovels and scoops for grain and the sawdust for the stalls. His countrymen are known to be good with horses, I said, and he will be, too. But now even my belly twists and tumbles, no matter how many words I have said before to ease the way.

Soon we are passing through the depot and out to the front where icicles drip, sparkly, from the roof. There are puddles to cross, and we do, the lad's feet staying dry, I hope, in those boots of his. The sound of all that melt is something I have not heard in a long time and my throat crimps on me. When I can, I tell the lad I will show him a stream in a woods and also a peacock. He gives me a crazed look, with that milk-glass face of his, as if I have just spoken some dire thing. I tell him it will be good to see, don't worry, and I give his arm a squeeze, and then he is pointing to the grandest snow piles in the world, this I am sure of. They're almost too white to behold in all this sun. Sensing what he's after, I say, "Go ahead," and release his arm, and he runs to one and climbs it, and then sits up there like a figure atop a grand cake and waves to me and I wave back. He stays perched a long while, looking all around at everything, and then slides down, all somber, and turns to look at the pile. When he looks back at me, I nod, and he races up it again and slides down, this time smiling, and then we walk the short distance to the Canton house and soon are with the horses. I need to hang onto Jupiter's mane a while and breathe in the smell of him because it's almost too much for a man, hearing the Major saying, *Son, I'm glad you're home.* But after a while, I fit a brush to the lad's hand and slowly he touches Jupiter's flank with it. The horse doesn't twitch or otherwise move, and soon the lad is brushing him just as I'd said he'd be, making the dark coat shine, and then I'm brushing him, too, all the while telling the Major, *So am I sir, so am I.*

A JOURNALIST

The midway attractions have packed up and gone. Now winds from the northwest send geese sailing down their ancient flyways in sprawling lines, but workers at the Pan-American Exposition grounds don't hear their barking, the urgency. They are on bulldozers and steam shovels equipped with wrecking balls powdering the air with chalky dust. Into reflecting lakes and canals go statues and fountains, bridges, buildings, and gardens. All the savage salmons and heavenly blues, the symbolisms and symmetries, the entire radiant realm of romance crumpling into atoms, dust, fill—

For a new real estate development.

Rain, then ice and snow fill the cleat tracks. Surveyors appear with their apparatus and plot out streets, lots, and a little boulevard. A few trees have survived the debacle, astonishingly, and the surveyors try to accommodate them; after all, it will save money. They work fast in bitter winds off the big lakes. Each afternoon the sun sets earlier, falling into its own lake of savage reds or civilized pastels, and the earth hardens further, machinery tracks and boot prints and hoof prints preserved as if in basalt. But a few miles to the west, Niagara Falls is still fuming languidly, thunderous and smoky, its emerald lip glassy under waxing moon and waning moon, under pitch of stars and shrouded sun, its Bridal Veil eternally white.

AFTERWORD

While William McKinley's body lay in state at Buffalo's City Hall, thousands of mourners passed by his casket, including Chief Geronimo and several other Native American chiefs and as many as seven hundred braves who'd been taking part in the Pan-American Exposition. A train conveyed McKinley's bier, along with his grieving widow, from Buffalo to Washington, and finally on to Canton, Ohio. For five days, flags throughout the country were at half-staff, and people thronged railway stations along the route, often singing McKinley's favorite hymn, "Nearer, My God, to Thee." The nation observed five minutes of silence and work stoppage when McKinley's casket left the Canton house for its first resting place in nearby West Lawn Cemetery.

Ida McKinley lived on in the Canton house, often visiting her husband's elaborate vault and praying to join him soon. She died in 1906, and in honor of her funeral—President Roosevelt in attendance—Canton shops and stores closed for the day, and school children were let out at noon. She was interred alongside her husband in the West Lawn Cemetery vault, and in 1908, her remains and those of the former president and their two children were reinterred in a white circular mausoleum, the McKinley National Memorial, adjacent to West Lawn Cemetery, in what is now McKinley Memorial Park.

On October 29, 1901, the day of his execution, Leon Czolgosz's body was autopsied, the brain and other organs dissected, and the body parts placed in a black-painted, wooden coffin that was conveyed out of the prison hidden in a goods truck. The truck took a meandering route to a prison lot and there, according to the earliest reports in 1901, a carboy of acid was poured over the body in the coffin, straw was placed in the grave to allow venting, the grave was covered over and left unmarked. Czolgosz's clothing and personal effects were burned. In 1906, the October 6th issue of Emma Goldman's journal *Mother Earth* was dedicated to him.

The former New York State governor and McKinley's vice president, Theodore Roosevelt, a hero of the Spanish-American War, succeeded McKinley as president at age forty-three, and moved his wife Edith and young family into the Executive Mansion, which they renamed the White House. The Roosevelts' six children brought their puppies and ponies and at least one guinea pig. Bedrooms were opened and aired, a large McCaw parrot presided over the conservatory; ponies carrying children trotted back and forth over the White House lawn, and the president often amused himself hiking the Rock Creek area of northwest Washington.

In the aftermath of President William McKinley's assassination, the word *anarchist* was synonymous with *murderer.* Newspapers across the country castigated anarchists and anarchism in vilifying editorials. An editorial in the *Louisville Courier-Journal* stated, *We do not wait to kill a rattlesnake until his deadly fangs have struck; we should not wait to take anarchism by the throat until it has accomplished its openly avowed ends of assassination.* Emma was referred to as "Red Emma, Queen of the Anarchists." Other anarchists were often called by a simpler epithet—*reptiles.* In his first message to congress, Roosevelt stated that McKinley's assassin was "depraved" and that anarchists should be prevented from entering the country. Those already residing in the country should be deported. Newspapers across the country echoed this view. Soon a new law was passed, the New York Criminal Anarchy Law, and police stations formed anarchy squads whose sole purpose was to break up speeches, lectures, and printing presses publishing anarchist tracts. Vigilante leagues also formed, dedicated to eradicating all anarchists.

Yet despite the harassment and danger, Emma Goldman managed to carry on work that was more than work for her—that was, in fact, her very identity. By 1902, she was back to being Emma, fiery and defiant as she lectured against what she saw as a terribly repressive climate in the United States. By 1905, she was working with Russian comrades in the United States to promote the Russian Revolution, while at the same time she translated and helped produce plays by Maxim Gorky, Anton Chekhov, Henrik Ibsen, George Bernard Shaw, and other modern playwrights.

For his assassination attack on Henry Clay Frick, Alexander Berkman served fourteen years in the Western Penitentiary of Pennsylvania and a final year in a work house before he was released in 1906. Emma and Sasha's romantic connection did not survive those fourteen years, but their bond as comrades was as strong as ever. The two devoted their time and energies to promoting the cause of anarchism through writings, speeches, lectures, and work on behalf of comrades suffering miscarriages of justice. While in prison, Berkman had begun writing *Prison Memoirs of an Anarchist*, smuggling out pages when he could. The book was finally published in 1912 by the Mother Earth Publishing Association, which Emma had founded, naming it after her journal *Mother Earth*, founded in 1906. For a time he also managed the Ferrer Center in New York City. The Ferrer movement in the United States was widespread and promoted what today would be called child-centered education, but with additional emphases upon libertarian ideals, social and economic issues, labor issues, working class movements, and the acquisition of practical skills.

As in the 1890s, an economic depression swept the country in 1912 and 1913, and, once again, Emma and Sasha spoke out for the unemployed, the hungry and starving, railing against a capitalistic system that would wreak havoc on working men's and women's lives. There were marches and demonstrations, mass meetings and rallies; at Union Square in New York City people were clubbed and trampled by police on horseback. In Colorado, striking mineworkers were demanding safety regulations, eight-hour days, the right to be paid in money, not scrip, and the right to organize, among other issues. Colorado National Guard troops were deployed in support of the mine owners, the Colorado Fuel and Iron Company, and skirmishing between strikers and guards ultimately led to the tragic Ludlow Massacre on April 20, 1914, reminiscent of the Homestead affair two decades earlier. John D. Rockefeller Jr. owned a controlling interest in the company and, like Frick, vowed never to give in to the workers' demands. On July 4, explosives intended for the Rockefeller mansion in Pocantico Hills, near Tarrytown, New York, blew the top three floors off a tenement building on Lexington Avenue in New York City, killing four people. Sasha was questioned but not held. Bombs were exploding around the city; the two prominent anarchists prudently left New York for lecture tours around the country.

Both Emma and Sasha spoke on the Russian Revolution and were generally allowed to complete their talks as long as they stayed on topic. Their lectures were broken up whenever they broached anything concerning anarchism or issues of social or even judicial injustice in the United States. In San Francisco in 1916, Sasha garnered enough financial backing to found his own journal, which he titled *The Blast*, blatantly incendiary and dedicated to radical issues promoting social revolution, but new postal regulations aimed at anarchist works soon made distribution impossible. Meanwhile, Emma was lecturing and writing on the need for birth control, which brought about another arrest.

In March of 1917, Emma and Sasha rejoiced at the news of the overthrow of the Russian Romanovs and had great hopes for the future of Russia and, by extension, for their own anarchist cause. They began speaking out against militarism and the draft and organized a No-Conscription League. But in June of that year, congress passed the Espionage Act, and Emma and Sasha were arrested once again, this time for interfering with the draft, aiding the enemy, and encouraging disloyalty—all tenets of the act. They were found guilty and sentenced to separate facilities. Their appeals failed; the two went back to their prisons, and in 1919, after deportation hearings in which J. Edgar Hoover represented the government, Emma and Sasha were deported, along with 246 others, as "enemies of the United States."

Lenin received Emma and Sasha with enthusiasm and encouraged their idea to study the Russian Revolution in order to promote a similar revolution in the United States. But when Emma and Sasha began touring Russia to collect data and see the effects of the revolution firsthand, what they witnessed convinced them that the Bolshevik regime was just as authoritarian and repressive as the regime it had displaced. Disillusioned, they left Russia—in a way, it was an escape—for Sweden, then Germany, and finally Paris. Emma wrote *My Disillusionment in Russia* and *Further Disillusionment in Russia,* which were published in 1924. Sasha's *The Bolshevik Myth* appeared in 1925. He also attempted to aid Russian political prisoners, including many anarchists—nearly an impossible task—and published *Letters from Russian Prisons* to document their heartbreaking plight. Emma embarked on lecture tours in Europe to expose the "Bolshevik myth," but these tours were generally unsuccessful. Too many in her audiences, particularly in England, were still under the Bolshevik spell. The United States granted her a three-month visa in 1934, and she toured the country speaking out against the Soviet regime as well as lecturing on modern drama, but after that three-month period, she was never allowed back into the United States, to her great disappointment.

Emma married a British comrade—a marriage of convenience whereby she could obtain a British passport—and so was able to travel throughout Europe and Canada without the impediments Sasha suffered, such as registering with police departments everywhere and constantly fighting expulsion orders. Emma used the opportunity to lecture on libertarianism, feminism, birth control, Russian political prisoners, the Soviet regime, and the growing threat of Nazism, among other topics. From her vantage point in Europe, she'd become well aware of Hitler's menace. Both she and Sasha realized that Nazism could not succeed without a mass movement behind it, but this it *did* have—a painful and ironic realization, given that they had been laboring for well over two decades to inspire such a mass movement for their own cause.

By all accounts, Emma was a powerful orator and Sasha an excellent writer and editor. Emma wrote her two-volume autobiography while living in the then-obscure village of Saint-Tropez; Sasha gave it its title: *Living My Life*. Emma met Alfred Knopf in Paris—where she'd also met Ernest Hemingway and other prominent ex-patriots—and signed a contract with him. *Living My Life* appeared in 1931. Meanwhile, Sasha, living in Saint-Cloud, not far from Saint-Tropez, had been working on translations, including a Eugene O'Neill play for the Moscow Arts Theater, and wrote a primer on anarchism, *Now and After: The ABC of Communist Anarchism,* published in the United States by Vanguard Press in 1929.

With the rise of Nazism, Sasha, always battling depression, became increasingly pessimistic about the prospects of anarchism to bring about a social revolution. His health, compromised by his years in prison, had been further deteriorating; he was also severely dependent on monetary help from friends, particularly his cousin Modest "Modska" Stein/Aronstam—the "Fedya" of Emma's autobiography and Sasha's *Prison Memoirs*. Modest had become a successful commercial and portrait artist and though he professed neither cause nor creed, he remained unfailingly generous to his old friends. Still, Sasha, at sixty-six years old, decided that he could no longer go on. On June 28, 1936, he shot himself with a revolver and after several agonizing hours, finally died and was buried in Nice, in a communal grave, despite his lifelong wish to be interred in Chicago's Waldheim Cemetery, where the Haymarket anarchists had been buried. But a plot there, Emma learned, proved to be too expensive.

Although emotionally devastated, Emma carried on, now working against the fascists in Spain and writing about the Spanish Civil War for such mainstream publications as the *Atlantic Monthly* and the *Nation*. Again she launched out on lecture and fund-raising tours, this time for refugees of the Spanish Civil War. Four years after Sasha's death, Emma suffered a stroke while living with friends in Toronto, a stroke that left her unable to speak or write. Shortly after a second stroke in May of 1940, she died at the age of 71. Although she had never been allowed to reenter the United States after her deportation in 1919, except for that brief three-month lecture tour in 1934, authorities did allow her remains to be interred in Chicago's Waldheim Cemetery, near her beloved Haymarket anarchists.

ACKNOWLEDGMENTS

For information regarding Emma and Sasha after the McKinley assassination, I drew upon *Sasha and Emma: The Anarchist Odyssey of Alexander Berkman and Emma Goldman*, by Paul Avrich and Karen Avrich, published by The Belknap Press of Harvard University Press, Cambridge, Massachusetts, and London, England in 2012.

While researching historical material for *The Anarchist,* I found the following most helpful:

The Buffalo and Erie County Historical Society
The Cayuga County Museum of History and Art in Auburn, New York
The Labadie Collection at the University of Michigan's Hatcher Library, possibly the largest collection of anarchist letters, papers, pamphlets, and anarchist newspapers in the country
The McKinley Museum in Canton, Ohio
The New York Public Library
The Western Reserve Historical Society

BOOKS:
Avrich, Paul. *The Haymarket Tragedy.* Princeton, NJ: Princeton University Press, 1984.
Berkman, Alexander. *Prison Memoirs of an Anarchist.* New York: The New York Review of Books, 1999. First published by Mother Earth Press, 1912.

Briggs, L. Vernon. *The Manner of Man That Kills.* New York: Da Capo Press, 1931.

David, Henry. *A History of the Haymarket Affair.* New York: Farrar & Rinehart, 1936.

Davis, Elizabeth. *Heart and Hands: A Midwife's Guide to Pregnancy and Birth.* Berkeley: Celestial Arts, 1987.

Fallows, Rt. Rev. Samuel, LLD, ed., *Life of William McKinley Our Martyred President.* Chicago: Regan Printing House, 1901.

Goldman, Emma. *Living My Life.* The Dover Edition, first published in 1970, an unabridged republication. New York: Alfred Knopf, Inc., 1931.

Goldman, Emma. *Anarchism and Other Essays.* New York and London: Mother Earth Publishing Association, 1917.

Johns, A. Wesley. *The Man Who Shot McKinley.* South Brunswick, NJ, and New York: A. S. Barnes, 1970.

Leech, Margaret. *In the Days of McKinley.* New York: Harper Brothers, 1959.

Townsend, Col. G. W. *Memorial Life of William McKinley.* Washington, DC: Memorial Publishing Company, 1901.

Trautmann, Frederic. *The Voice of Terror: A Biography of Johann Most.* Westport, CT, and London: Greenwood Press, 1980.

Riis, Jacob. *How the Other Half Lives.* New York: Garrett Press, 1890; reprinted, 1970.

Speeches and Addresses of William McKinley. New York: D. Appleton & Company, 1893.

Wolff, Leon. *Lockout: The Story of the Homestead Strike of 1892; A Study of Violence.* New York: Harper & Row, 1965.

NEWSPAPERS:

The *Auburn Daily Advertiser,* the *Cleveland Plain Dealer,* the *Evening Repository* (Canton, Ohio), the *New York Journal,* the *New York Times,* the *New York Tribune,* the *New York World.*

PAPERS AND PAMPHLETS:
The Congressional Record. H(May 18, 1888).
The People v. Leon F. Czolgosz, courthouse archives. Erie County, Buffalo, New York.
"Czolgosz Papers." Buffalo and Erie County Historical Society Library.
Pan-American Exposition Official Catalogue and Guide.
"The Pan-American Exposition. Yesterday's Tomorrow." (Pamphlet)

In addition, I'm most grateful to the following: curators Malcolm Goodelle, Sally Hemmings, Stephanie Przybylek, and Barbara Chase-Riboud at the Cayuga County Museum of History and Art in Auburn, New York; Ed Weber at the Labadie Collection at the University of Michigan; fellow writers Robert Mooney and John Vernon, who read early drafts of the manuscript and offered a number of valuable suggestions; Martin and Judith Shepard and The Permanent Press for publishing—and championing—writers of fiction for nearly four decades, and to Judith Shepard, special thanks for her editorial skill. Thank you as well to Barbara Anderson for her excellent copyediting. To my husband Jerry, deepest gratitude and love for being a wonderful first reader and for the endless encouragement and support throughout so many years.